GENA SHOWALTER

ECSTASY IN DARKNESS

Pocket STAR Books

New York   London   Toronto   Sydney

Pocket Star Books
A Division of Simon & Schuster, Inc.
1230 Avenue of the Americas
New York, NY 10020

This book is a work of fiction. Names, characters, places, and incidents either are products of the author's imagination or are used fictitiously. Any resemblance to actual events or locales or persons, living or dead, is entirely coincidental.

First Pocket Star Books paperback edition November 2010.

POCKET STAR BOOKS and colophon are registered trademarks of Simon & Schuster, Inc.

For information about special discounts for bulk purchases, please contact Simon & Schuster Special Sales at 1-866-506-1949 or business@simonandschuster.com.

The Simon & Schuster Speakers Bureau can bring authors to your live event. For more information or to book an event contact the Simon & Schuster Speakers Bureau at 1-866-248-3049 or visit our website at www.simonspeakers.com.

Cover design by Lisa Litwack
Illustration by Cliff Nielsen

Manufactured in the United States of America

10 9 8 7 6 5 4 3 2 1

ISBN 978-1-4391-7577-4
ISBN 978-1-4391-7579-8 (ebook)

Turn the page to read praise for Gena Showalter
and her novels of danger and desire . . .

DATE DUE

PRAISE FOR THE ALIEN HUNTRESS SERIES

Seduce the Darkness

"A compelling and entertaining story of lust, deception, intrigue—and, of course, love."

—*Romantic Times*

Savor Me Slowly

"Gena Showalter doesn't pull any punches in this hot, hard-hitting science fiction romance. With *Savor Me Slowly* she shocked me and scared me and turned me on, sometimes all on the same page. I'm so glad she took the characters to their sensual and emotional limits—and beyond!"

—*New York Times* bestselling author Susan Sizemore

"Danger and sensuality are hallmarks of Showalter's style, and they're both here in this latest Alien Huntress novel. . . . An intense new read!"

—*Romantic Times*

Enslave Me Sweetly

"Showalter first demonstrated her skill at blending sizzling romance and nail-biting suspense set in a convincing futuristic society in *Awaken Me Darkly*. She now continues the roller-coaster-like adventure in an equally entertaining tale that will please a wide cross section of readers."

—*Booklist*

"This well-written book will appeal to all readers."

—*Romantic Times*

Awaken Me Darkly

"Mia Snow is perfect as the alien hunter with the secret."

—*Booklist*

Also by Gena Showalter

Awaken Me Darkly
Enslave Me Sweetly
Savor Me Slowly
Seduce the Darkness

Acknowledgments

An added thank you to the freakishly amazing Kresley Cole, who often has to talk me off the ledge.

One

"And I thought *you* were rough. Those girls are . . ." Dallas Gutierrez shuddered. "What's way worse than rough? 'Cause that's what they are."

"What, exactly, are you trying to say?" Mia Snow leaned away from her desk, crossed her arms, and peered at the gorgeous man across from her. Perfectly tanned skin, perfectly symmetrical features—or so he liked to brag—and the perfectly formed body of an underwear model. Lean, yet sculpted with muscle. All that perfection aside, he was an absolute pain in her ass. "And by the way, I'm not rough."

"Perfect" ice blue eyes rolled. "You once kneed me in the balls and asked me how they tasted. Just to say hi. You're rough."

She had, hadn't she? Memories were *fun*. "Why are you complaining? There were no complications during your testicle retrieval operation. So, anyway, what'd *they* do this time?"

They. Best friends. AIR—Alien Investigation and Removal—trainees Ava Sans and Noelle Tremain.

Dallas tangled a hand through that thick, dark mane of his, looking like a lost little puppy rather than the stone-cold killer he was. "Get this. I took all ten of the advanced placement trainees on an assignment last night. Call came in, you see. Was told a predatory otherworlder was picking on humans at a bar. The fine group of boys and girls I took was just supposed to observe as I threw my pimp hand around, bitch slapping as necessary, and calming things down."

Okay. What had happened to the morose, utterly annoying Dallas of the past few months? The one who whined and complained about, well, everything? *There's a smoking-hot alien queen who wants to screw me, but I can't encourage her because her partners always turn into cannibals*, whaa, whaa, whaa. *My best friend Devyn married his vampire lover so I don't have anyone to play with*, whaa, whaa, whaa. *I'm your husband's blood slave*, whaa, whaa, fucking whaa. If she heard that last one more time, she was going to make him taste his balls again.

He was alive, wasn't he? He had cool new powers like mind control and superspeed, didn't he? Kyrin, her too-sexy-for-words husband, had saved Dallas's ass by sharing his Arcadian blood—and was now training Dallas's ass. Dallas should have been this happy all along.

But at least the old, everything-is-a-joke Dallas was making an appearance today, she thought, rather than the new I-want-to-slash-my-wrists Dallas. Courtesy of Ava and Noelle, a two-woman Apocalypse? She'd have to send the girls a fruit basket. Or maybe something they could actually use, like a fire and brimstone basket.

"Continue," Mia said with an imperial wave of her hand.

Dallas nodded, a bit disappointed. Probably because she hadn't complimented his bitch-slapping abilities. Baby. "The otherworlder refused to calm vdown, said the humans told his woman she hadn't just been hit with the ugly stick but the entire tree had fallen on her, and the assholes owed her an apology. The humans, of course, told me they'd only spoken the truth and that I should arrest the bastard alien for harassing them about it."

"Which you didn't." Even though the arrest would have been standard protocol. But Mia was head of AIR now—three cheers for her boss deciding to retire early!—and was in the process of making a few changes. No longer would aliens be arrested for defending themselves or demanding respect for their race.

Secretly part otherworlder herself, she was flat-out done with prejudice. And now that Kyrin's blood flowed through Dallas's veins—again secretly—Dallas thankfully was, too.

"Nope. I didn't," her second-in-command confirmed with the slightest hint of relish. "Anyway, while I was apologizing to the otherworlder for all humans and their idiot tongues, Ava and Noelle went Death Match on the assholes in question. Now, I didn't see who started it, you understand, just heard a commotion and turned around. By that time the humans, who were both big, burly males, were unconscious and bleeding on the ground, and Ava and Noelle were grinning and banging their fists together in a job well done."

Mia cut back a moan. Changes, good. High incident rate, bad. There was going to be hell—and apparently hospital bills—to pay for that Death Match. Not just for the males, but for herself. 'Cause yeah, top brass would rip into her until she begged for mercy. Which meant they would pretty much rip into her until she bled to death, because she never begged for anything. Well, except when Kyrin got her into bed.

Three boos for her boss deciding to retire early. Had he stayed, this would have been his problem.

"So what'd the girls say when you asked about the carnage?"

"Ava said her hand accidentally slipped and made contact with her guy's nose. I said, Repeatedly? And she said, 'Uh, yeah. I'm *really* clumsy.' And Noelle said her guy was trying to escape, so she took him down like we'd trained her. And oh, we shouldn't worry about the gaping wound in his neck because he probably had that before he entered the bar."

First, how was Noelle such a hardass? The girl was Jaxon Tremain's cousin, and Jaxon was one of AIR's staunchest rule followers. Not to mention, both were richer than Kyrin, who was richer than God. Noelle had been raised in a mansion, for all that was holy, her every need attended to by servants. She should be delicate.

Jaxon's wife a bad influence, maybe? After all, Jaxon

was married to the meanest female Mia had ever met. A female who was part robot—literally! Mishka actually had a longer kill list than Mia. And while Mia's list consisted of gunshot and knife wounds, Mishka's featured acid, thumbtacks, and for the people Robot Girl really hated, spoons.

Nah, Mia thought then. The pair hadn't been married that long, and Noelle's first disorderly conduct arrest had happened years ago. Mia knew because she'd studied Tremain's lengthy file before allowing the overindulged delinquent anywhere near the AIR building.

Now, poor but deceptively sweet-looking Ava, Mia understood. The girl had double the arrests, but then, she'd grown up on New Chicago's dirtiest streets. Just like Mia had. There, you were predator or prey, and there was no middle ground.

How had the wealthy girl and the impoverished girl hooked up? Jail? And how the hell had they *remained* friends all these years?

Mia sighed. "So what you're telling me, Dally, is that it's time to promote these two heathens."

Dallas grinned, revealing straight white teeth. He made a production of that grin, reminding her of a curtain rising from a movie screen, an eager crowd desperate for the show to begin. "I don't know how you do it, Mee, but you always reach the moral of the story without any prompting from me."

"Because I'm smarter than you. Anyway, they gotta complete a mission on their own before I can officially offer them a place on my team."

"What do we got on the chopping block? And by the way, *I'm* smarter than *you*. My IQ is off the charts, man."

If the chart only reached fifty, then yeah. No need to tax his poor brain with numbers, though. Silent, she let her head fall against the back of her chair and stared up at the ceiling. They were inside her new office, and she'd had the panels painted blue and white, a replica of the sky, to help with her claustrophobia. This way, she could pretend she was lying on the ground in her spacious backyard with Kyrin resting beside her.

"McKell," she finally said, thinking of the latest case to hit her desk.

"Ouch," Dallas said. "Dousing the girls in gasoline and throwing them straight into the fire."

"I know."

"Poor McKell, though."

Poor girls. McKell was a vampire warrior able to stop time in short bursts, do his damage with no one the wiser, then restart the clock, leaving the raging flames of hell in his wake. His own people had kicked him out of their underground world for being "unstable." The term amused her—the man had slaughtered hundreds of vampires for daring to lock him up for a few days. Unstable? Try psychotic.

AIR wanted to talk to him about his actions. Preferably alive. But no one had been able to bring him in. In fact, Mia had sent three top-of-the-line agents to apprehend him—bastard wasn't even trying to hide—and he'd sent all three back with severe blood loss, missing fingers, and brain damage. Fine. The agents had been brain damaged before encountering McKell, but then, weren't all men?

Exhibit A: Dallas.

Maybe Ava and Noelle would have better luck. Besides, it was a scientific fact that females always outperformed males. And who was she to mess with science?

Sure, Jaxon and thereby Mishka would kick up a fit when they heard Little Miss Cousin would be going after a vampire, but Mia didn't exactly care. *Bring on the spoons, bitch.* But maybe she'd send the couple on a prolonged vacay, just in case. Plus, it wouldn't do for Jaxon to give the girls a helping hand. And he would. He wouldn't be able to help himself, and that would do a lot of damage to their street cred. The girls were moving up the ladder fast, so they had a lot to prove—on their own—or none of the other agents would ever take them seriously.

And if the girls did this, if they brought in the big bad, no one would be able to question Mia's decision to advance them rather than incarcerate them. Even better, Ava and Noelle might just think hunting and capturing a rabid vampire was a *good time.*

"Prep them without telling them why they were chosen or what's at stake, and send them out." That way, they'd work this case the same way they worked the rest of their cases, without putting on a dog-and-pony show trying to impress her, and Mia could discover just how much determination those "rough" girls possessed.

Dallas snickered.

Mia blinked over at him, confused. "What?"

"You said 'stake,' and they're going after a vampire. Get it? Stake . . . a vampire? Like in old books and movies."

She rolled her eyes. "You're such a child."

"And you're a jealous old woman because you didn't think of it yourself. Said with affection, of course."

"I'm a year younger than you, jackass. Said with annoyance."

"Yeah, but you're only younger physically."

Brain. Damaged. She liked the morose Dallas better, she decided. "Have you forgotten that you're wanted by a diseased alien queen, your best friend is busy with his wife, and you're Kyrin's blood slave?"

Dallas flipped her off, but his grin never faded.

Maybe she wasn't on top of her game, because she automatically returned that grin with one of her own.

"You love me, you know you do," he said confidentially.

True.

"Seriously. You're like my mom, and I'm like your favorite son. No matter what I do or say, you'll always think I'm adorable."

Mia stood and leaned over the desk. She crooked her finger at him as if she had a secret to share. He, too, leaned forward, eager to learn that secret—poor, brain-damaged kid—and she punched him in the nose. "There. Now I'm like the mom who keeps her stupid shithead in line with a firm hand."

He laughed as blood trickled down his lips and chin. "See. Rough."

And he thought Ava and Noelle were worse than her? Good. Then by the time those two were done, McKell might just wish he'd decorated himself with bows and walked into AIR headquarters on his own.

Two

*H*e never stopped sharpening his blade.

Ava Sans watched her target from a few feet away and tried not to drool. Key word: tried. He sat on a large rock in the middle of a government-owned forest. A forest he didn't have permission to be in. Clearly, following rules wasn't his thing. *Bless his heart*, as her mother used to say about anyone in need of spiritual guidance. "Anyone," of course, had meant everyone. Which had been ironic, since her mother hadn't been sober a day in her life.

Concentrate. Golden moonlight framed the target's back, and a crackling fire illuminated his front. He had pale skin and a face that proved God had an A game. And why the good Lord would have chosen to deviate from that formula and create other faces, she would never know. If everyone looked like this man—like fevered whispers in the dark, forbidden chocolate, and sin in its most tempting incarnation—crime would have ceased long ago. Or maybe never even started. Everyone would have been too busy staring at themselves in the mirror to fight. Or maybe they'd be too busy bedding themselves to even stare in the mirror.

Seriously. That face was flawless. Everyone always talked about how perfect Dallas Gutierrez was, but this man . . . His forehead wasn't too long or short, his nose was wonderfully straight, his cheekbones delightfully sharp, and his chin magnificently square.

His bottom lip was plumper than his top, but both were pink and utterly nibbleable. Was that even a word? Anyway. Vivid violet eyes were framed by long feathering lashes, and his black-as-night hair boasted the slightest wave. His shoulders were wide and his body thick, built for war. Which just happened to be her favorite body type; muscles equaled delicious.

In seconds, she'd memorized every detail about him. For the job. Of course. But the best thing about him, besides that devastating beauty? He wore a necklace made of bones. Human finger bones, from the looks of them. Which meant the case of the missing AIR agent phalanges was solved, at least.

Why had he taken them?

Whatever the reason, she wanted a necklace like that for herself. Not only because it would go with all of her outfits, but also because it screamed *powerful* and *just a little insane*. One glance at that necklace, and most people would run, too afraid to bother him. They wouldn't tease him mercilessly for his mistakes and laugh about them days later in front of his AIR peers.

Ava's hands curled into fists. Maybe she'd steal the necklace from him after she arrested him. Food for thought.

What she knew about the man, besides the fact that just looking at him could give a girl an orgasm: He needed to feed—aka drink blood—only once a week. His name was Victor, but McKell, what everyone called him, was his classification. And in layman terms, his classification was "bad motherfucker." Apparently, he was a warrior. *The* warrior. Once leader of the entire vampire army and still savage beyond compare. Unless the comparison was with her best friend Noelle. "Savage" was a wee bit mild for Noelle.

Anyway, Ava had walked into McKell's makeshift camp a few minutes ago, yet he hadn't even glanced up from his task. He hadn't asked her to leave and hadn't questioned her about her sudden appearance and obviously nefarious intentions.

He knew she was here, though. She'd watched his nails grow and sharpen, becoming claws. Yet he didn't fear her enough to bother with her. Or Noelle, who stood beside her. A mistake, but he'd learn. Everyone did.

Ava glanced at her friend, fellow (almost) AIR agent, and partner in many (allegedly heinous) crimes, to gauge the girl's reaction to the man. Noelle, too, stared at him, completely fascinated.

Fascination was a good look for her. Hell, everything was a good look for her. Bastard wouldn't stand a chance. Tall, slender, with silky brown hair and velvety gray eyes, Noelle was always the epitome of elegance. Until she opened her mouth. Then she was the epitome of mean. And sarcastic. And rebellious.

The contradiction intrigued anyone with a pulse.

Wait. Did vampires even have pulses? Ava suddenly wondered. Were they the living dead? Maybe. What did she know? Okay, so. Rephrase: the contradiction intrigued . . . anyone. McKell would be no different.

"Dibs," Noelle said in her hoarse, used-to-be-a-smoker voice.

Ava massaged the back of her neck. "The fact that he's a murderous bloodsucker isn't a deal breaker?"

"With those biceps? No."

Her gaze returned to McKell. He was shirtless, his muscles on full display. Those to-die-for biceps—literally to-die-for, since a lot of people had probably watched their lives flash before their eyes while those meaty clubs descended—mouthwatering pectorals, and rope after rope of hard-won abs.

"You're right." Damn. But since Noelle had already called dibs, Ava would never be allowed to run her hands over that deliciously strong body. Was that a . . . tear in her eye? "Just a warning, though. Your name rhymes with his, and I plan to torture you about that *forever*."

"Still not a deal breaker."

Damn her friend's stubbornness. Stubbornness Ava was intimately acquainted with.

They'd met years and years ago, after Noelle had been kicked out of every private school in the state and no boardinghouse would take her. Ava had understood the reason why within five seconds of meeting the girl. Noelle's first day at New Chicago Junior High No. 17, she'd taken one look at dirt-poor Ava and said, "I'm bored and need a project. You'll do."

Ava, of course, had said, "Project this," and busted her two front teeth.

The next day, Noelle had held her down and chopped off her hair. She'd then given Ava a glittery ribbon to style away the damage. And when the principal had arrived a few minutes later, demanding answers, neither had told on the other.

They'd been inseparable ever since.

"Can I at least have a feel of him when you're done?" Five minutes. That's all she needed. She'd touch every inch of him—if anyone asked, she'd just say she'd *frisked* him—and then, the next boyfriend she had . . . hello pretend vampire. Win, win. Not that she'd had a boyfriend in years. Not that she wanted one in the future. Commitment sucked. But hey, so did McKell. She snickered. Anyway, thumbs up for sex. Which she hadn't had in a while, either.

Noelle shrugged. "You can touch him, but only if you do my laundry for a week."

Oh, no. No, no, no. Even the suggestion was cruel. But she said, "I need some think-time." There was a scar on McKell's sternum, stretching to his navel and dipping inside his pants, and the thought of tracing it . . . maybe she could survive the laundry. *That's craziness.*

"I'm kinda pressed for time, so you've got two minutes to decide," Noelle replied. "Starting now."

Finally the vampire stopped running those silver blades together. Had he been listening to their conversation, as they'd hoped? Was he now waiting for her think-time to end to discover her answer?

Two minutes after her two minutes had passed, McKell growled low in his throat. "I'm right here. Stop talking about me as if I'm not."

That voice . . . God hadn't just been on his A game when he created this being. He'd decided to enter a new league. Rough, raspy, and purring, McKell's voice was like hot butterscotch poured over—hmm, butterscotch. The thought of her favorite candy distracted Ava for a moment.

Yep. Should have called dibs yourself.

"We did," Ava said, forcing her mind on the task at hand. "We stopped talking about you. In fact, you had to break the silence. Remember?"

That earned her a snarl. "Just answer the woman and leave. This is my camp. *Mine!*"

Or *not* have called dibs. Selfish much? "I've decided. You can have him," Ava said to Noelle. "He's a little too cranky for me. Besides that, I promised myself I'd take a razor to my wrists before ever doing your laundry again." She hadn't minded the blood and gore on the clothes. Why would she, when the same stuff could be found on her own? The problem had been folding the skanky costumes Noelle supposedly liked to wear in the bedroom—in full view of everyone inside Suds and Bubbles Laundromat. Costumes Ava suspected Noelle had purchased only for her benefit and subsequent humiliation.

"You're such a prude," Noelle muttered.

"Well, you're a pain in my ass."

"Me? *You're* the ass pain!"

McKell flashed his fangs—long, sharp, and oddly beautiful—before Ava could call her best friend a raging bitch. "Be quiet! Seriously. I preferred the silence." Then, contradicting his own demand, he asked, "So what are you doing here, anyway?"

Mmm, butterscotch. The real deal was too expensive for her to have at every meal, as well as between meals, during the middle of the night, and for all snacks. As she would have preferred. Citywide, sugar was in low supply, the price for it rising every week, it seemed, so she only indulged once a month. Which just happened to be her favorite day of the month. Even if she was on her period.

His voice, though . . . *give me a spoonful of* that.

"Mind out of the candy bowl," Noelle said on a sigh. They knew each other too well.

Right. The vampire had asked a question, and she had a job to do. "We were just passing through, saw your fire, and thought we'd stop by and make out with each other."

His jaw dropped.

"Wanna watch?" Noelle added hopefully.

"Or maybe join?" Ava suggested.

"Whatever. We're not picky."

That violet gaze shifted from one to the other, pupils expanding. He licked his lips, tongue pink and wet and, well, pretty. Was everything about the man attractive? *Doesn't matter.* Good news: even vampires were perverts.

She shouldn't have been surprised, even though a part of her still reeled at the knowledge that vampires existed at all. Sure, Ava had known aliens lived here. They'd walked this planet for over eighty years—and as she was only twenty-three years old, that meant they'd lived here her entire life (duh). All different races, sizes, colors, and shapes.

In high school she'd dated a Teran for six whole days, and they were a very catlike species. Lots of rubbing and purring and shedding. *Too much* rubbing and purring and shedding.

Anyway. Vampires had never revealed themselves, even during the human-alien war, and everyone had assumed they were the stuff of myth and legend. Apparently they'd been living underground for thousands of freaking years. They might have remained a secret forever, even, but AIR had a way of ferreting out the truth.

"Do you always wear weapons when you plan to make out?" McKell snapped, dragging Ava from her thoughts. God, she had to stop letting herself become distracted. And funny that his gaze seemed directed at her, and her alone, boring past her clothes and her skin and, somehow, into her soul. "Don't try to tell me you're unarmed. I can smell the weapons on you."

"Uh, hello. This forest is miles from town, and it's the dead of night. Of course we're armed. Plus, my friend is a freak and likes when I rough her up."

Noelle snorted. "No way. You're the one who likes it rough."

"Please! I'm a fragile flower. You know I like to be treated like a lady."

"I'm not foolish," McKell interjected, his voice now flat. And yet, somehow that timbre crackled with fury. "You're both from AIR. You have to be, despite your . . . distractibility. Only agents would be foolish enough to approach me. Again."

Distractibility—a nice way of saying they argued too much? Probably. And wasn't that a shocker? A savage who didn't want to hurt their feelings. She and Noelle would, of course, use that against him.

"We can do this easy, or we can do this hard," he continued in that same flat, yet furious tone. "Leave, and you can return to Agent Snow just as you arrived. Stay, and you can return to Agent Snow in pieces. Although I'll keep your fingers for touching what's mine." As he spoke, he caressed his necklace. "Your choice."

Butterscotch, even while threatening.

Ava didn't reach for her pyre-gun or any of her blades. She kept her arms at her sides, hands empty. She and Noelle had to be careful with this one. He could stop time—for *them*—while moving freely himself. Which meant he could slash their throats, and they wouldn't know until he restarted the clock.

"News flash: we didn't touch anything that belongs to you," she said, to keep him talking.

"You're here, aren't you? So, what's it to be, girls?"

He'd do it, too. Cut off their fingers without a moment's hesitation. He was cold, and he was hard, and not in the good way, that she could tell. There was no line he wouldn't cross to achieve what he wanted. No black and white for him. Only shades of gray.

Why the hell was he suddenly a thousand times sexier? The dibs system sucked worse than commitment, she decided.

"Dude," Noelle said. "You totally stole my line. Ava, did you hear him steal my line? Easy or hard way," she mocked while pouting. "*I* had planned to say that to *him.*"

"I heard, Noelle. At least give him a chance to apologize, though. We do *not* want a repeat of the last time this happened."

A muscle ticked in McKell's jaw. "Did you also hear what I did to the last three agents who came for me? *Ava.*"

Her name on those wicked lips . . . delectable. She shivered.

Noelle splayed her arms, deceptively innocent. "First, eyes on me, cowboy. I called dibs. Second, we heard. You ate them. So can I sign up for the feasting now, or would you rather I wait until later?"

Now those violet eyes widened, confusion swirling in their depths. A common occurrence around the girl.

"And was that a no on watching us make out with each other?" Ava asked. *No mercy.* No matter how badly she wanted to tongue him.

His nostrils flared, even as his gaze—which had never left her—traveled over her, lingering in all the right places. Her suddenly pebbling nipples, the now aching apex of her thighs. Goose bumps broke out over her skin, the cool night air blending with the warmth from the campfire and licking over her. Another shiver rocked her.

"Well?" she prompted, hating the breathlessness of her voice.

"That's a yes," he rasped.

She almost grinned. Typical male. Little did he know, he'd just bought himself a one-way ticket to AIR HQ.

"Excellent choice! I've been dying to put my mouth all over this little morsel for too long. So come here, you sexy piece of sexy goodness, you." Noelle grabbed Ava by the shoulders and tugged her close, lips lowering to plant a big, wet one.

Ava made sure to moan really loudly as her hands slid down . . . down . . . the seeming delicate bumps of Noelle's spine. She cupped Noelle's ass with her right hand, made a mental note to inquire what kind of workout program her friend had been doing, then curled the fingers of her left hand—the one farthest away from the vampire—around a tiny pyre-gun stored beneath Noelle's too-tight jeans.

"Dear God," McKell said now. Had he expected

them to balk at kissing each other, even after offering to do so?

Without pulling her lips from Noelle's, she aimed the gun toward him, keeping the barrel flat against her friend, hidden. Then she released Noelle's ass, let those fingers trace the waist of the jeans, as if desperate to sink down, past her panties and into heat, knowing the vampire's attention followed, all the while allowing the gun a straight shot.

She squeezed the trigger.

A blue beam erupted, lighting up the night, nailing him in the chest, and stunning him in place. Boom. Done. For the next twenty-four hours, he would see and hear everything around him, but be unable to move.

Too. Easy.

The kiss ended, and Noelle grinned down at her, all white teeth and smugness. "Wow. I really felt your passion for me that time."

Ava rolled her eyes as she stuffed the gun back into her friend's pants. "Shut up."

"Seriously. How long have you been walking around with this huge crush on me?"

"Like you could handle me."

"Egomaniac."

"Narcissist."

Noelle glanced at the unmoving McKell and *tsk*ed under her tongue. "What an amateur."

"I know, right? Mia said he'd be a challenge."

"Clearly our idea of a challenge differs."

"Who falls for the lesbian act anymore, anyway?" Ava asked with a disappointed shake of her head.

"Men. Always."

"Yeah, but this one's a vampire."

Noelle patted the top of Ava's head as if she were a child. And stupid. "A vampire with a penis."

"True."

As if the insects surrounding the camp realized the vampire no longer posed a threat, they began to sing and chirp. Amid the chorus, she and Noelle approached McKell. He still sat upon that rock, still held those blades, only now he was immobile. Both of them crouched so that they were eye-to-eye with him.

"He really is beautiful, isn't he?" Noelle observed.

Since Ava wouldn't be enjoying him anytime soon, she saw no reason to praise him. "He's okay, I guess." God, those eyelashes stretched forever. And up close like this, she could see the flecks of emerald mixed with the violet of his irises. What an odd combination. Odd but gorgeous. Even better, there was a rose tint to his cheeks, as if he was flushed with arousal. For her and only her.

Noelle patted his cheek, just as she'd done to the top of Ava's head. "Don't let this destroy your desire for me, McKell. Like I told you, I called dibs, so if you just cooperate with Mia, you and me will be rolling around in bed before you know it. Well, maybe. You were a very naughty boy, and I'll need to tame you first."

What was AIR going to do with him? Ava wondered. Question him, yes. She knew that. Test his blood, she knew that, too, since certain vampire blood was the only thing that could defeat a deadly alien virus that caused cannibalism in humans. But would they torture him for hurting several agents? Keep him locked up for the rest of his life? Eventually kill him?

A shame if they did. *So pretty.* "Let's discard his weapons and drag him to the car," she said, straightening. Better to get back to business than consider circumstances she couldn't hope to change. And shouldn't want to change.

"But he looks so heavy." Noelle straightened as well, towering over her.

Most people towered over Ava. She hated it, but no one had invented a way to artificially lengthen legs, so she'd learned to deal. And by "deal," she meant she beat anyone who teased her into a bloody pulp. "Hence the reason I said drag and not carry."

A groan. "Why not call AIR and have them swoop in to pick him up?"

"Because we'll miss our Victory Walk through headquarters."

Indecision played over her friend's beautiful face. "I do like a good victory walk, but I don't like the thought of sweating. Oh, I know!" Noelle brightened. "If you drag him on your own, you can have him. We'll pretend I never uttered the word *dibs*."

"Hell, no. I already told you he's too cranky for me. He's all yours."

"You need to get laid more than I do. Your last overnight relationship"—she air-quoted the word *relationship*—"was, what? Six months ago?"

"Seven, thank you very much." And five minutes after the guy had fallen asleep, she'd snuck out. As always. But she'd known then, as she knew now, that having sex with him had been a mistake. He was an AIR trainee like her, and now that all their coworkers knew he'd nailed her—he had a big, stupid mouth— the other guys assumed she was easy, and constantly made a play for their turn.

How much worse would the situation be if she slept with a criminal? Even so sexy a criminal?

"Lookit. I'm only thinking about your health," Noelle said. "You've been so tense lately, and—oh, my God! I just had the best idea." Grinning, she clapped and twirled like a toddler who'd just discovered a room of candy-flavored toys. "Let's take pictures with him before you drag him to the car."

Split-second subject changes were a Noelle Tremain trademark. "No way. And you're helping me drag."

Ignoring her, Noelle settled on McKell's lap. "Me first. I plan to tell everyone he's my new boyfriend. Since he is. Someone, and I won't mention your name, Ava, is just being stubborn about a little heavy lifting."

She was the stubborn one? Ha!

But she knew when she was beaten. Noelle wouldn't budge until she had her pictures. Sighing, Ava withdrew her cell and captured a few images while her friend switched poses. Over and over again. If she wasn't mistaken, murderous rage blazed in McKell's eyes the entire time. *Way to poke at the bear.* And yet she never stopped snapping those pictures. And not because of Noelle.

One, McKell was completely edible on film. Something a guy like him had to appreciate. And two, once AIR had him, she probably wouldn't see him again and definitely wouldn't be able to point at him and say, "Guess what? I bagged and tagged him," to other agents.

Now she could say the words, and when those agents replied, "There's no way a shortie like you could have taken down a hulking vampire like McKell," she could bust out the photos. Everyone would be impressed. They'd stop looking at gutter-raised, baby-faced Ava like she needed to be in a kitchen baking cakes—or in bed waiting for a man and charging two hundred an hour.

"All right. We've got enough pictures to fill a scrapbook. Let's do this," she said. "I wanna go home. I'm starved."

"Fine. I'll help carry. But FYI, you're always starved," Noelle muttered, frisking the vampire and tossing his weapons to the ground.

For some reason, the fury in his eyes increased from I-could-explode-and-kill-you-both murderous to I-could-explode-and-take-out-the-entire-world nuclear. As if removing his guns and knives was a far worse crime than capturing lifelong images of his shame spiral.

"Done," Noelle said, unaware of the change. She slid her arms under his right armpit. "He's now clean."

Ava did the same to his left armpit, wholly aware yet unwilling to let it detour her. "What do you mean, I'm always starved? What are you trying to say?"

"Oh, sorry. I thought I made that clear. I was saying you eat too much, and maybe you should have rethought the miniskirt tonight."

They hefted his big, heavy body up, and her biceps immediately began to shake.

"I look fat to you?" All hundred and twenty pounds of her? Most of which was muscle, if she were being (kind of) honest. Damn, that irresistible butterscotch. She ran her tongue over her teeth, even though she knew Noelle was prodding her only to energize her. "Oh, poor thing, I think one of your contacts has slipped. Let me help." With her free hand, she slapped her friend on the back of the head. Hard.

"Ow! I don't wear contacts, and you know it."

"My bad."

"From lover to fighter," Noelle said with a dejected sigh. "Sad, really, that you let our romance die so quickly."

Ava bit her lip to stop herself from laughing. What a great day this had turned out to be, she thought. And really, it was only going to get better.

How could it not?

Three

As the females tugged him through dirt and leaves, occasionally dropping him, tearing his pants, his skin, kicking him once out of spite because he "could stand to lose a few pounds," McKell seethed.

Puny humans. Taunt him, would they? Take pictures of him in this hated state, would they? Take his weapons, would they? He, who didn't share *anything*. Ever! And that wasn't the worst of their crimes. Kiss in front of him and not finish what they'd started, would they?

They would learn the error of their ways. Soon. He would teach them, as they'd just taught him.

He hadn't expected them to follow through with their "desire" to kiss each other. Much as he'd wished otherwise. Neither had smelled of lust, so he'd known the pretend affection was for his benefit. He'd expected them to lean in, then launch themselves at him just before contact. That's what he'd prepared himself for. That's when he would have frozen them in place and drank from them one at a time before sending them back to AIR, defeated and humiliated.

When they *had* kissed, he'd been momentarily

blinded by lust of his own. The dainty hands of the tiny one, roving over the Amazon's body . . . his blood had heated, singeing his veins. He'd suddenly wanted those hands on *him*. Roving over *his* body.

Suddenly? *Liar.* He'd imagined touching her since the first moment he'd spied her. Which had been a shock. Humans were food to him, nothing more, and a man didn't play with his food. Honestly, he shouldn't have wanted her—Ava, that was her name, and it was as soft and delicate as she appeared—in any way. Not even as sustenance.

He'd gorged only an hour before her arrival, and should have been satisfied for the next six days. But the moment she'd entered his camp, he'd smelled her—orchids, sunlight he'd loathed until that moment, and some kind of sugary candy completely unique to her—and his mouth had watered. His shaft had ached. He was absolutely certain he'd smelled something as decadent at some point in his long, long life, though he couldn't recall when or what.

His reaction was explainable, though. He'd been without a vampire lover for months, so his body would have lusted after anything. *So why didn't you want the tall one who called "dibs"?*

What a ridiculous question. He hadn't lusted after the one named Noelle because she reminded him too much of his own kind, and right now he was furious with all vampires and would rather kill a bloodsucker than screw one.

He ignored the flaw between the two rationales.

And what the hell was "dibs," anyway? He'd visited this surface world many times before being kicked from the vampire caves, but he'd never heard the term. Was it some type of ownership? Probably. The females seemed to think he now belonged to Noelle.

Well, he belonged to no one. The only female he would have bound himself to was Maureen, known here as Bride McKells, but she'd chosen to give herself to another. To Devyn, king of the Targons. As if McKell weren't good enough. As if he wasn't a thousand times better than that bastard Targon scum. McKell had slaughtered entire vampire villages in less than an hour. With no aid! He was good enough for *anyone*.

Even Ava, who hadn't wanted to do Noelle's laundry to be with him. Laundry—the washing of clothes, for God's sake—when there were hundreds of vampires who would have been willing to cut out their own hearts to even touch the dirt on his boots. Well, maybe not hundreds. *Thousands* was probably more accurate, he decided in the next instant, refusing to give in to self-deprecation. He was a prize, damn it!

Even still, now he just wanted to be on his own, left alone, with time to come to grips with the horrid topside eternity that awaited him. And in a hundred years or so, he should be able to say, "mission accomplished." Maybe.

All he knew now was that he hated this world. The sun, burning his beautiful skin and ruining part of his day every damn day. The cloying scents of human food and perfume. AIR constantly trying to "chat." Annoying.

"Come on, Noelle. Put your back into it!" Ava said, irritated.

"I am, damn it! But I can't help it if I'm not strong enough to lug around this much dead weight."

"You're a hundred pounds heavier than me. You should be running laps around me."

"A hundred pounds? You bitch! You better watch your back, because I *will* punish you for that whopper."

Clearly, they despised each other. He'd dealt with humans all the many centuries of his life, stealing them from this surface and carting them underground to keep them as food-slaves. Most argued, yes, but only enemies had argued like these two, calling each other hateful names, complaining, kissing—uh, never mind that last one. That devastating kiss had no bearing on the situation. What did: he could use their dislike of each other to his advantage.

"You once pushed me and the weights you'd tied around my waist into oncoming traffic," Ava growled. "You're strong enough for this. You're just lazy!"

Noelle had once tried to kill Ava? That, he didn't like for some reason. But he wouldn't worry about that now. She meant nothing to him. Well, except maybe breakfast.

"Your brain has clearly rotted," Noelle snarled. "I'm as lazy as Mia Snow on steroids, adrenaline injections, and caffeine overload."

"Don't make me kick your ass."

Would they ever kiss again? he wondered, then scowled. No, they wouldn't kiss again, because he was going to murder them both. *If* they didn't kill each other first. Which seemed highly likely. They were predators, both of them, and they'd probably scratch each other to death if they ever got into bed. An arousing thought. An *irritating* thought, since they didn't deserve a single moment of pleasure.

"I swear to God I'm going to stab you in your heartless chest with a butter knife if you don't—oh, good. I see the car," Ava said with relief. "Act like my friend for five more minutes and actually help."

"Have I told you yet that you're a bitch?"

"No. You've been too busy tilting McKell so that I'd have to take the brunt of his weight."

He liked Ava's voice. Smooth, as deceptively sweet as her face. A face that was slightly rounded, with big brown eyes, an up-tilted nose, and heart-shaped lips. A face better suited for angelic paintings, and yet midnight fantasies were what claimed his mind every time he looked at her. And framing all that sweetness was an even sweeter tumble of amber curls. Curls made for fisting, tugging, pinning so that she would be forced to take the hottest flames of his kiss.

Only thing that wasn't sweet about her—besides her demeanor—was her body.

What she lacked in height, she made up for in curves. She had breasts that strained the white tank top she wore, a waist that flared beneath a dangerously short skirt, and sun-kissed legs encased in calf-high boots.

"Moment he comes out of stun," Noelle huffed, "I'm breaking up with him."

"So I *don't* get to sing about Noelle and McKell sitting in a tree?"

"Shut up. Anyway, I can't be with a man who can't find a way out of stun to help me carry him. It's discourteous, you know? And selfish."

Her babbling made no sense. What an odd woman.

"I agree," Ava said.

She understood that nonsense? *Just you wait*, he thought darkly.

When the females pulled him out of the line of trees and into a clearing, he froze them in place with only a thought. Their minds, their bodies. They were stunned, like him, only they had no idea what happened around them.

Inside, he grinned. Everyone assumed he could stop time, and they were right. He could stop the clock for several minutes at a time. But that wasn't all he could do. He could also stop the people around him while time passed without their knowledge. And that's exactly what he did now.

He held his captors in place for one hour . . . two. He should have grown bored, simply staring ahead as he was, but too much relish filled him. Oh, yes, these females would learn. He knew this area, knew the forest itself was gated to keep humans out, and knew no one would stumble upon them.

They were his.

Ava . . . his . . . *Down boy*, he thought with a growl. To think of her in such a possessive way was to undermine his plan for her. And he—

McKell cursed as he noticed a shimmering curtain of air to his right. A doorway. The air had thickened, dust motes glowing in the moonlight, a tangible glitter that somehow looked like welcoming arms. *Not again*. He'd seen such a doorway every time he'd visited this topside world.

In fact, he'd seen one yesterday, and the day before, and the day before that. Once and only once had he been tempted to touch. He'd reached out, but that dappled air had sucked at him, pulling him closer against his will, trying to swallow him up. He'd raced backward, warrior instincts saving him—sometimes you fought, sometimes you retreated, always you returned later and killed—and the suction had ceased. But he'd never forgotten the experience, and never wanted a repeat.

How did you fight a split in the ether? Especially when that split might be sentient.

Deep down, he thought he knew where the doorway, or whatever it was, led, what it wanted. The answers? To eternal darkness and his damnation. Why target him, though, he wasn't sure.

Pay it no heed and it will go away. As always. He released the women from his mental hold.

No longer fettered, Ava and Noelle continued forward, unaware anything had changed and thankfully avoiding the curtain. Though he knew they couldn't see it. Only he could. Over the years, he'd watched humans, otherworlders, and vampires alike walk through them, as if the air were merely that. Air.

When they had passed the curtain and adjusted to the fading darkness, he froze them in place once again. Another hour, then two, passed quickly for him. Thankfully, another doorway never opened.

Again he released them for only a moment, let them continue with their chat, move forward, adjust, before refreezing them.

Another hour. This one eked by. But finally, he let them go for good.

"Holy shit, my arms are burning," Ava rasped. "And shaking, too. I feel like I've held him for days."

"Me, too. And damn, the sun's coming out already. We're slower than I realized."

"Damn it. Hurry."

Obviously exhausted, they hauled him the rest of the way, tripping and cursing, and stashed him inside the waiting vehicle.

"His skin will burn if we leave him like this. Right? Didn't Mia tell us vampires are sensitive to light?" Ava stood in his open doorway, peering down at him and tapping a blunt-tipped finger against her chin.

Not for a moment did he delude himself into thinking she truly cared about keeping him unharmed.

"So what?" Noelle said.

"So. Mia will be pissed if we bring her damaged goods. Let's cover him."

Good thing he hadn't deluded himself. He would have been feeling supremely disappointed just then. Which he wasn't. Not even a little.

Damn her. He was a vampire, far superior to a measly human, and he deserved her admiration and consideration.

"Shame to cover up that face, though." With a sigh, Noelle tossed a blanket over his head. The material draped his bare shoulders and torso, protecting him from the sun's rapidly strengthening rays. "Happy now?"

"Cranky as the vampire now?"

Muttering curses at each other, they settled into the front of the car. He heard one of them push a series of buttons on the dash. A second later, the air conditioner blasted. Before either female could program the car to return to AIR, however, McKell froze them in place. And this time, he didn't bother releasing them every few hours to keep them from suspecting he was manipulating them. He simply allowed the hours to pass, the sun rising, heating, ruining what should have been the best part of the day.

Hour after hour after hour passed, washing him in gold, then orange, then a hazy pink. Finally, blessedly, that hated sun began to wane, dulling even the pink light seeping through the fabric of the blanket. By the time darkness once again surrounded him, the stun had worn off, freeing his muscles from immobility.

Vengeance.

Scowling, McKell tossed the blanket aside. A moment ticked by as his gaze accustomed itself to the open space. He saw that Ava and Noelle were in their seats, Noelle's hand raised to push more buttons, Ava's deep in a bag, as if she'd been digging through the contents.

What had she been searching for?

He couldn't lean forward and check as he wanted. Clear, impenetrable shield-armor divided the front and back of the car. That wouldn't be a problem, but breaking through it would take longer than he was willing to spend. He glanced at the door beside him. No handles.

The car, he knew, would only obey Ava and No- elle's commands. If they said, "Open," the door would pop open automatically, since it was programmed to recognize and obey their voices, but he wasn't about to free either female yet. At the moment, surprise was his best friend. So McKell did the only thing he could—he kicked the door off its hinges and unfolded from the backseat, a move that allowed him to exit just as quickly as if the car had catered to his voice.

Cool night air wafted around him, bringing with it the scents of pine, night birds, and seductive moon- light. He stretched, his abused body protesting every movement, and that intensified his anger.

So angry was he, in fact, that he slashed his claws into Ava's door with more force than necessary, let- ting them embed deeply before ripping the offending block out of the way. The metal soared over his shoul- der, landing with a heavy thud behind him. Then Ava was in front of him, nothing preventing him from ripping her out, as well.

"I warned you," he growled at her, even though he knew she couldn't hear him. "Easy or hard, and you picked hard." Rather than slash her to pieces, however, he crouched beside her and grabbed the bag.

Motions still stiff, he rifled through the contents. Different sized blades. A badge that read "Agent in Training." His eyes widened. In *training*? She was merely in training? AIR had sent a *child* after him? God, the insult. Almost enough to send him racing to their base, destroying every brick, every human inside, just to prove that he could.

Don't lose focus. He could rant about their insolence later.

Teeth grinding, he continued his search of little Ava's bag. Lastly, he found "butterscotch"-flavored lipgloss. Butterscotch. Not something he was familiar with.

He twisted the cap and sniffed the contents, and his mouth instantly watered. *That's* what Ava smelled like. Sugary, warm, and toasted in the sun. All the things he suddenly wanted to be. The desire was foreign, unwelcome, and not to be tolerated. He wasn't some callow youth, so easily swayed by sexual urges. He'd had countless lovers over the centuries, and knew how fleeting those urges could be. How meaningless. He couldn't even recall a face or a name of one of the women who had warmed his bed. Cold of him, perhaps, but for a man with his sense of possession, he had always purposefully maintained distance in that area of his life.

He stuffed Ava's gloss in his pocket—to torment her with its loss, he told himself, and not because he wanted a reminder of her, of her scent, of the hunger she elicited—then tossed the bag and the rest of its contents behind him. Then he focused on Ava.

Her curls fell over her shoulders, shiny and—he pinched several between his fingers—soft as ocher velvet. Moonlight caressed her, turning her flawless skin to liquid gold. He traced the back of his knuckle along the curve of her cheek, far more gently than he'd meant. That, too, was soft. Would be a shame to mar her, he decided, then frowned. She was already marred. There were several scars running the length of her arms, and many crisscrossing her hands.

He lifted each hand, studying. Too many scars for such a young, "in training" agent. Besides, though some of those scars were clearly newer than others, none were pink and fresh. Which meant she'd been fighting most of her obviously short life. McKell wasn't sure if that disturbed him, aroused him, or amused him.

Scowling again, he slid one arm around her lower back and one under her legs. He carried her a short distance from the car and lay her down, careful, so careful not to jostle. He did the same with Noelle, only he dropped her flat on her ass. Why the difference in treatment, he didn't know. Didn't care to ponder. Then he proceeded to rip the vehicle to pieces, just as he'd promised to do to the girls, piling the remains around them, forming a wall. A reminder of their failure with him.

When he finished, he was panting, covered in a sheen of perspiration, his anger somewhat dimmed. Still. He was tracing his tongue over his fangs, some other unnameable emotion humming inside him as he rejoined the humans and removed their clothing. Noelle was first, and he stripped her without pause. Ava, however, he found himself lingering over, every new inch revealing a deeper appreciation of her femininity and his wavering restraint.

White lace bra. Front clasp. *Nice.* Her breasts were lush, with nipples that were the color of honey-dipped apples. Her belly was flat, with a navel that hollowed perfectly. A tongue could lose itself in that navel. White lace underwear. Ribboned on the sides. Only needed a tug to unlace them . . . *Really* nice. Her thighs were firm, the apex guarded by a tiny triangle of amber curls.

When he finished, he realized pure temptation lay before him.

She's human, he reminded himself. Weak, withering. Food.

Still. He couldn't leave her naked, he decided. If she were to stumble upon a male, that male would want her. Obviously. That male would probably try to "hit on her," as the humans said. She would rebuff him. McKell knew this only because the thought of her accepting returned the plumes of rage. And when her tart tongue finished rebuffing, the male would fight her, as pride demanded. The two would roll around on the ground, and the male's penis might accidentally slip inside her. McKell couldn't risk it. Not because he cared who the woman slept with, that wasn't why he raged, he rationalized, but because, again, she didn't deserve pleasure. Not that she'd find pleasure from her attacker.

His teeth gnashed together. Again, he refused to acknowledge the flaw in his reasoning.

He put Ava's bra and panties back on her, then reluctantly did the same for her . . . friend. Enemy. Whatever. That done, he pocketed Ava's phone and again peered down at the curly-haired witch. *Beautiful.*

Shove your tongue back into your mouth, and finish what you started. He forced all thoughts of touching and tasting from his mind, and withdrew the gloss he'd stolen from her. Then, he began writing directly on her body.

When he finished, he was actually trembling from the effort to resist doing more to her.

In a few days, when he'd gotten his desires under control, he would find her again, he decided. He'd use her as she had planned to use him. Because, if *he* liked her scent, connoisseur that he was, other vampires would, too. They would be drawn to her, would want to drink from her. And rather than having to track them down himself, as he'd had to do before AIR had started gunning for him, distracting him, they would come to him.

Now they ran from him, scared of him. But if they were preoccupied with Ava, he would have no trouble grabbing them. Finally he could question them and discover how they lived here. How they survived in that wretched sun.

Yes, he liked this plan.

Ava wouldn't, though, he thought, and he was grinning as he strode away.

"What the hell?" Ava gasped out. One moment she'd been inside the car, searching for her lipgloss, the sun fighting its way into the sky. She hadn't moved, only a second had passed, yet now she was outside, the night thick and dark, an almost suffocating cloak.

And holy hell, the car was in shambles around her, claw marks slashing through the metal.

"We're in our undies!" Noelle squeaked beside her.

Ava jackknifed to her feet, knees almost giving out as she peered down at herself. No top, no skirt, no shoes. Only her bra and matching panties.

Shit. She searched, but there was no sign of her clothes. "That tricky bastard! He did this." And she floundered between admiration, humiliation, and horror. The strength required to destroy a car like that . . . immense. The intelligence required to outwit her . . . equally so. But God, the knowledge that she'd failed, choking.

What else had he done?

Frantically she patted her neck. Thank the Lord.

No puncture wounds. Still. There was no question McKell had defeated her just as surely as he'd defeated the other agents sent after him. She'd been so cocky, so certain of her success. After all, she hadn't lost a fight since Judy Demarko, the world's biggest seventh-grade bully, had slammed her head into a brick wall and hacked off her hair—why did girls always do that to her?—while she was too dazed to move. All because Judy's ex-boyfriend had asked her out. Well, and maybe because Ava had stashed Onadyn, an illegal alien drug, in Judy's bag the day before, getting her kicked out of school, her reign of terror finally over. But that was merely speculation.

"I thought he could only stop time in short bursts," Noelle said. She stood, as well, and tossed up her arms, the picture of exasperated female. "Yet he clearly stopped *us*."

"Which means you thought wrong." Ava, too.

"Thanks for stating the obvious. You're lucky I don't—" Noelle gasped.

"What?" Ava whipped left and right, scanning the forest for any sign of intruders. They were alone, the insects as quiet as they'd been around McKell. The scent of him lingered, though, as if he'd only just left. Warm, intoxicating . . . necessary.

Oh, hell, no. She hadn't just thought that word. Necessary. She wiped it from her vernacular.

The gasp turned to giggles, and Noelle pointed to her chest.

"What?" she demanded again, looking down and

seeing something golden—letters, she realized—
smeared on her skin, just above her bra. She frowned,
sniffed. Butterscotch. Mmm. Her stomach rumbled.
"What does it say?"

Noelle just grinned at her.

She tilted her head, trying to decipher all four of
those letters. When she did, she gnashed her molars
in irritation. And more admiration, damn it, followed
by a stupid wave of giddiness.

McKell had taken her lipgloss and spelled the
word DIBS.

Four

The next morning, the gun range overflowed with agents, and Ava resigned herself to a half-hour wait. At least. But Mia arrived a few minutes later—two minutes early for their meeting, God bless her—and three stalls immediately cleared, the agents scampering away without meeting their commander's eye. Now *that* was power.

Ava envied her.

Mia claimed the middle, and Ava and Noelle the sides.

In unison, they withdrew and loaded crystals into their pyre-guns, checking the chambers for obstructions while techs placed flame-resistant dummies at the end of the stalls.

Apparently, Mia was a multitasker and liked to conduct her chew-outs while at target practice. Only, as they fired golden beams at the dummies, soot forming where they hit, there was only silence.

Was Mia too pissed to speak?

Ava looked at the woman's target. Three shots to the fake man's chest. She looked at Noelle's. Three shots to the face. Then she looked at her own. Three shots to the groin. No, Mia wasn't pissed. Otherwise her dummy would have resembled Noelle's or Ava's. This was just business as usual. And wasn't that a shocker.

Still. Ava knew this meeting would not end well for her. How could it? After last night's failure, Mia would forbid her to approach McKell. To punish him as she craved. To assuage her curiosity and discover what he'd do next. To tamp down her need to peer into those violet eye and . . . what? She didn't know.

She only knew the desire to see him again was strong. So, would she obey an edict to stay away? She didn't know that, either. The man had her cell, and more than anything, she wanted it back. *Liar.*

Okay, okay. Most of all she wanted to get her hands on him and, uh, choke him. Yeah. Choke him. He'd been way too smug about his victory, writing on her chest like that, then leaving her practically naked. What a show-off. He should be ashamed. Poor sportsmanship always earned a penalty, and choking would be his.

"So . . ." she began, aiming at her target. Of course, she once again pictured McKell's beautiful features as she squeezed the trigger. Had he truly been standing at the end of her stall, his stomach would have exploded that time. "We gonna kick this thing off or what?"

Because they were using pyre-guns, background noise wasn't a problem. Pyres were as quiet as little church mice.

"Didn't realize you were a masochist." Mia exchanged her crystal for a bigger one. The bigger the crystal, the hotter the burn. Working off her stress? Looking at her, that seemed implausible. Even with her obviously violent nature, she resembled a ballerina, not a trained assassin. Black hair, blue eyes. A face more delicate than Ava's.

Despite that face, Mia had earned the respect and yeah, fear of her peers. When she spoke, they listened. They trusted her to lead them properly, intelligently. They saw her strength, saw the spirit of the alpha that lurked at her core. Ava wanted that for herself. Craved it like a drug.

"There are probably a lot of things you don't know about my girl Ava," Noelle said to their boss. She'd never been one to back down from anyone. "Like, she enjoys long walks on the beach, cuddling in front of a fireplace, and a new favorite, being written on with butterscotch-flavored lipgloss."

Mia's lips curved slightly, the echoes of winter in her eyes almost melting to summer. "That's inside info that will come in handy, I'm sure. But to be honest, I didn't command you here so you could listen to me bitch. You did better than any of my other agents, engaging the vampire rather than trying to sneak up on him. You made contact. You weren't drained. You kept your fingers. Three points for you."

Wait. Praise? From the iceberg known as Mia Snow? Amazing. But . . . "Contact or not, we failed," Ava said. She wouldn't dress that fact in bows and lace. One, two, three, she nailed pretend McKell in quick succession. Heart, groin again, and inner thigh.

Where it might be nice to kiss him. Argh. Kiss him? *Idiot!*

"Believe me, I know you failed," Mia replied. Four bright golden beams shot from her gun. All hit the same shoulder, deepening what would have been an injury, not a death sentence. "But it could have been worse."

"I'm not sure how." McKell had destroyed their ride and stolen their clothes, so she and Noelle had had to walk to the nearest convenience store, commandeer T-shirts and bandanas—all that had been available—and hitch home. The male driver had leered at their legs the entire way.

Funny thing, though. She'd felt utterly safe. And not just because she knew how to protect herself with a skill and precision, and hell, a determination, not many regular citizens realized. She'd felt something with her, a presence, a dark storm, scaring away the bad, yet never turning on her.

The vampire? Surely not. He'd had his fun, and he'd slipped away in the night.

Mia fired off another shot. "Like I said, you weren't drained and sent back to me useless."

Fine. A kind-of success. But kind-of wasn't good enough for Ava. Especially since she had a feeling McKell had failed to drink their blood because they were women, and he had a weakness—otherwise known as a conscience—rather than their superior agenting skills.

"Plus," Mia continued, and it was apparent she was

trying not to laugh. "We now know McKell can do more than simply stop time. He can stop people. And strip them. And write on them."

Noelle snickered.

Ava flipped off both women.

Mia shrugged, probably used to such a reaction. "Now you're better equipped to deal with him."

Better equipped to— Wait. What? "So you're giving us another chance?"

"Definitely."

"I never doubted you would," Noelle said, which was funny, since she had whined about the "injustice of being fired for one strike-out" the entire drive here.

"Good. Now listen closely." Mia slapped her gun on the counter, then pinned them both with a hard glare. "I need a blood sample from him, and I don't care how you get it. I have questions for him, too, but those can wait. Blood's the most important thing right now. We found another Schön victim."

"Dead?" Ava asked. She knew the Schön disease worked quickly, turning the infected men and women into cannibals while the virus itself ate through *their* bodies. But there hadn't been a new case in weeks. And before that, Bride McKells had used her blood to heal the infected. So they had a cure. Right?

Just the name, Bride McKells, irritated Ava. Bride had married Devyn, king of the Targons, but had once been engaged to Ava's McKell.

Wait. Hold everything. McKell *wasn't* Ava's.

Would never be Ava's. Her hands fisted. He was a case, nothing more. And she wasn't jealous that the vampire had pined for the female for *decades,* waiting for her to return to their underground world and live happily-ever-after.

There was more to the story, there had to be—because really, what kind of woman picked cocky Devyn Targon over brooding Victor McKell?—but that was all Ava had found in the vampire's file. Had he loved Bride? If so, did he love her still?

Ava's nails sliced into skin. *Doesn't matter. Relax.* He was nothing. Not to her.

Mia nodded, cropped black hair dancing over her shoulders. "One vic means there will be other vics. That's the way it works. And yeah, Bride Targon's blood heals the infected, we think, but we've basically tapped her dry, and Devyn's . . . complaining. We want to test McKell now."

As fierce and lethal as Devyn was, Ava would bet that "complaining" involved knives.

"Tell me I can count on you," Mia finished. A demand.

"You'd be stupid not to," Noelle said. A boast.

"Very true," Ava agreed. How she'd get that sample, she didn't yet know. She'd find a way, though. She always did.

Smile returning, Mia patted Ava's ass. "Good. So go get your man, tiger."

*   *   *

McKell's heartbeat sped up the moment Ava stepped past the line of trees and into his camp, stopping in front of the campfire exactly as she had the night before.

She had returned. He hadn't had to chase her down.

The other girl, Noelle, eased up beside her, but his gaze remained on Ava. She wore a skin-tight black shirt and equally tight black pants. Her curls had been tamed, forced into some kind of twist at the base of her beautiful neck.

He wanted to strip her again, find out if she'd washed his claiming away. He wanted to set those curls free, find out if fisting them would give him as much satisfaction as he suspected. But most of all, he wanted to sink his fangs into her vein and taste her blood. Would it taste as sweet as her lipgloss?

He'd long since given up trying to fight the desires.

Last night, he had ensured she returned home safely, following in the shadows, even when she rode in some stranger's car. The stranger in question was alive now only because he'd kept his hands to himself. By the time McKell returned to this forest, distance between him and Ava, his needs had been stronger than ever, and he'd realized he had already lost the battle.

Had she not come to him tonight, as he'd hoped, he would have gone to her tomorrow rather than waiting a few days. He hadn't wanted to seem too eager, but he *was* determined to have her. And not just to use her to lure other vampires.

"No kiss this time?" he asked, hoping he'd managed to mask that hated eagerness.

He sat on the same boulder he'd occupied last night. Difference was, his weapons were now stored in places the girls wouldn't think to look. Since darkness had fallen, he'd been too distracted, watching for Ava, to even pretend to clean them.

"No." She shook her head, causing moonlight and shadows to fight for dominance on her delicate features. "You've been a bad, naughty boy, and don't deserve a reward."

Her voice . . . as close to sex as a man could get without actually removing his clothing. Sure, he'd considered it "sweet" before. After lying in his cave all day, replaying their interaction through his head over and over again, however, he'd realized that *sweet* obviously equaled *dirty* to his body. "I did nothing to you that you didn't deserve. So a bad, naughty boy? Ha! You, though . . . you took my weapons."

"Yeah, but you got them back."

So she wasn't going to apologize for her actions? "No one takes my things, Ava. Ever. They are mine. *Mine*."

She shrugged, his growing rage clearly of no consequence to her. "Whaa, whaa, whaa, and heard it all before. As if that was the worst of my crimes."

His eyes narrowed. "Why are you here? You can't defeat me, and you know it."

"We know no such thing," Noelle replied. She was still here? "But we're here because we want to talk to you."

She did, perhaps, but Ava clearly did not. That female wanted to shoot him. Anger now filled those dark eyes.

McKell couldn't help himself, wanted to stoke the anger into rage. While she watched, he withdrew her lipgloss from his pocket and coated his mouth. He smacked for good measure. But rather than launch herself at him as he'd expected, she smothered a laugh.

Baffling woman. He'd just taunted her about her failure with him, and she'd gifted him with amusement that stroked his ears. Why hadn't her anger intensified?

"That's a good color for you. Now. Before we start chatting, I want my phone back," she said, crossing her arms over her chest. "No one takes *my* things."

"No. It's mine now, and you know I keep what's mine." There were hundreds of pictures stored in that phone, and he hadn't finished scrolling through them. Well, hadn't finished his *third* scroll-through.

It was just, the camera loved her, paying that angel-face nothing but tribute, highlighting the luminous sheen of her skin, the rosy glow in her cheeks, the sparkle in her eyes, turning the brown to melted chocolate and golden glitter. And, well, he'd learned so much about her. Things he'd needed to know since they were at war and he planned to drink from her and use her—not because he was curious about her, the woman. Of course.

She clearly liked posing next to Noelle while Noelle looked her worst and was not happy about being photographed. Which proved she was delightfully vindictive. There were also action shots someone else had taken, since Ava's hands had been occupied punching different sets of teeth. Which proved she was deliciously feral.

He shouldn't have been impressed by those facts. He shouldn't have been aroused. But he was.

"I'll wrestle you for it," she suggested. "No-rules wrestling, at that, where hands are permitted to roam *anywhere*."

Tempting. To have her hands on him, squeezing at him, her body pressed against his . . . To have *his* hands on *her*, not just squeezing but kneading, his body not just pressed against hers but pinning . . .

"No." He couldn't wrestle one girl and freeze the other. Well, he could, but Ava would distract him, so he'd forget to hold Noelle in place, and then the agent (in fucking training) would attack him. He had a feeling his hands would be too full of Ava for his brain to care about protecting his body.

Why did she entice him so intently? She was beautiful, yes, but other women were more so. At least, he was certain someone out there was, though he had yet to meet her. And why did his mouth continue to water for Ava, even though he wasn't legitimately hungry?

"Fine," she said on a sigh. "Forget the phone. We'll just jump right into our chat."

"Now you're acting just like the other agents," he said, disappointed.

That seemed to please her. "Where do you hide during the day?"

Hide, she'd said. As if he were a coward. Rather than tell her where she could stuff the direction of her chat, he found himself growling, "I *rest.*"

"Whatever you need to tell yourself to feel better," Noelle replied, striding forward and plopping to her ass a few feet away from him. She was *still* here?

He needed to keep better track of her.

Ava claimed the spot across from the girl so that he had one on each side. Their ease didn't fool him, and he remained on guard. Though he needed something to do with his hands. They were empty, and now that he'd thought about that wrestling, they ached to be filled with Ava.

Stupid hands. They kept this up, and he would cut them off. They'd regrow in a few months, and hopefully have learned to behave. "Why do you wish to speak with me, anyway? Aren't you afraid I'll hurt you? Again."

Noelle stretched her long leg toward him and rubbed her booted foot against his. "Are you kidding? One, we aren't afraid of anything, and two, you hurt several other AIR agents. That's why we need to speak."

"I hurt no more than five." He frowned and pulled away from the contact. She was a beautiful woman, but she wasn't Ava, and for some reason, he didn't welcome her touch. Was even uncomfortable with it. Because Ava was watching? Seemingly unaffected by Noelle's attempt to seduce him?

He *wanted* her jealous?

Not missing a beat, Ava blinked over at him. "And because you hurt *no more than five*, that makes your actions justifiable? You removed their fingers without cause, McKell."

He liked his name on those lush, red lips. "They were chasing me and touched my things. What better cause is there?"

The two women shared a look before Noelle shrugged. "You have to admit, Av, he makes an excellent point."

"Of course you're on his side," Ava said, exasperated. She lifted a twig from the ground and tossed it into the crackling fire. "You still have dibs."

"Do not."

"Do too."

"God, you're annoying. Here I am, handing you a slice of beefcake on a silver platter, and you're arguing with me."

"I told you before," Ava growled, "but I'll tell you again. I don't want him."

Noelle nodded, as if her point had just been made. "Like I said. *Annoying.*"

Yes, she was, McKell silently agreed, claws digging into the rock.

"Yeah, well, you're a pesky little fly," Ava said conversationally. "And if you aren't careful, I'm going to swat you away. With my knife."

Noelle opened her mouth to reply, but McKell held up one hand. "Not another word from you, pesky little fly." He didn't like the way she argued with Ava, treating her as something beneath her.

A deadly stillness fell over Ava. "What did you call her?"

His brow furrowed. "A pesky little fly. Just as you called her." Had he pronounced one of the words wrong? But that couldn't be the case. He knew the human language as well as his own.

"What did you call her?" she asked again, whispering this time. A dark whisper, rage in the undertone.

"A . . . pesky little fly?" Seriously, what had he done wrong?

"Oh, are you gonna get it," Noelle sang happily.

Before he could blink, Ava was on him, a catapult of pummeling fists, kicking legs, and snapping teeth. He was so stunned, he could only sit there, enduring the abuse. By the time his protective instincts switched on, it was too late.

She'd already withdrawn a blade. Had already sunk that blade into his side. Then she pulled away from him, standing, panting, glaring down at him, his blood dripping from the blade. Noelle had stood, as well, he noticed, and had watched the entire "fight" with a grin.

"You stabbed me," he said, his shock as dark as her rage had been. Scowling, he clutched his stinging side. "You really stabbed me."

"How kind of you to notice, you bastard!"

"How could I not notice? That *hurt!*" he snarled, though he didn't freeze her. Or retaliate. Still too shocked, he thought. Not disappointed. Not confused. Not upset that she hadn't spared him pain as he had done for her.

"Don't ever call my friend a name like that again." Fury sparkled in her eyes.

"But she isn't your friend." He pressed against the wound, grimaced. He would heal, but as deep as she'd twisted that tip, and twist and twist she had, he would suffer for hours. "Not really."

"She's my best friend."

"And don't you forget it," Noelle added with a nod.

So Ava could call the girl names, but no one else could do so? That made no sense.

He pushed to his feet. The girls didn't back down or even step out of striking distance. Should have been a mistake. A fatal mistake. He should have attacked. But he stood there, breathing in and out, his nostrils flaring with the force he used. "If I were you, I would leave this camp. Now." Before he lost his grip on whatever emotion was keeping him in place.

"Fine. You ruined everything, anyway." Ava raised her nose in the air, as if *she* had every reason to be angry with *him*, grabbed her *friend* by the forearm, and tugged her into the woods, moving farther and farther away from him.

Five

After Ava turned in the bloody blade for testing, and endured an eternity of Mia looking at the weapon, then Ava, then the weapon, then Ava again, silent all the while, shock thickening the air, pride and regret battling inside her, she had Noelle drop her off at her apartment for a little "decompression" time.

The one-bedroom efficiency was small but clean, plain but calming. Her furnishings were threadbare but lovingly patched up. For too many years, she'd lived in filth, her mother too wasted to care about the state of their trailer, *God bless her*, the strangers parading in and out, or her only daughter's wellbeing. Then Ava had met Noelle and started crashing at her place; the luxury had amazed her.

But then she'd begun to feel guilty, as if she were taking advantage of her best friend. Hadn't helped when people started saying she was only using Noelle for her money. And it *really* hadn't helped when Noelle started beating the shit out of everyone who said it, getting herself expelled and causing friction with her family. So right after high school, Ava had moved out of there, too, and gotten this apartment. That's when she discovered a pride she hadn't known she could feel. Pride that she had earned this on her own. Pride that she could take care of herself.

The apartment wasn't luxurious by any means, but it hers.

Yawning, she stripped and showered in her dry enzyme stall. A standard issue, with no extras, but she was lucky to have it. A lot of people had to use public stalls. A walk-in, feed-a-few-dollars-into-the-slot, wash-with-your-clothes-on, walk-out operation. What she'd had to use most of her childhood, with money she'd stolen from the people standing in line with her. Nothing wrong with that method, minus the thief, of course, but she preferred to use heated spray rather than room temp, linger for as long as she liked, and not talk to strangers.

The warm mist seeped into her skin, cleaning her inside and out. After watching McKell's blood slowly fade from her hands, and battling a fierce urge to cry about its loss, blaming fatigue all the while, she closed her eyes and let her mind drift—away from McKell, back to McKell, away again, then curse that bastard, back again. Damn vampire! He shouldn't have bad-mouthed Noelle. Only Ava had that right. Everyone else suffered, as McKell could now attest.

When others even looked at Noelle the wrong way, rage consumed Ava. Rage she couldn't control. Always. Maybe because a threat to her friend was a threat to her happiness. Maybe because, even though Noelle was rich, she'd had as emotionally whacked out a childhood as Ava had had. Her parents had been cold, distant, and unconcerned about their daughter until she embarrassed them. Which she had. A lot. And maybe, in the beginning, that was why Noelle had wanted to hang out with Ava. But the more time they'd spent together, the more they'd realized how much they actually needed each other. They loved and they accepted without judgment or conditions.

They also relied on each other for bail.

McKell had probably thought, as so many others before him, that she and Noelle were adversaries. Which was an easy mistake to make, she supposed. They argued and called each other names, but underneath each of their clashes was affection and purpose.

Hopefully, the mistake wasn't debilitating on McKell's part.

Debilitating. She gulped as guilt filled her. Though what she had to feel guilty about, she didn't know. Really. If McKell had kept his stupid mouth closed, she would have gotten a blood sample another, nicer way. But *nooo*. Now he might be incapacitated by blood loss or infection. Or die.

Die. She gulped again as dread filled her—then anger that she even cared. He was nothing, damn it. An assignment.

Scowling, she left the stall, dressed in a tank top and panties and fell onto her bed. *Don't think about him. Relax, rest.* She had a big day tomorrow. Namely, she planned to bask in the accolades of her fellow trainees because *she* had gotten that blood sample. Finally she'd have the respect she deserved. Then, of course, she would research ways to prevent time manipulation.

Would Mia want her to try to capture McKell again?

You're thinking about him again.

Argh! For hours, Ava tossed and turned, her mind constantly returning to the forest. McKell on his rock. McKell gaping in astonishment. McKell bleeding. A crimson river, shirt soaked to his side. Pain a glaze of frost in those violet eyes.

Stupid McKell. He only had himself to blame.

Realizing the futility of trying to sleep, she got up and brewed a pot of coffee. The sun was out and brighter than shit, anyway, which wasn't really conducive to a good, or even halfway decent, rest.

Nothing was, to be honest. Not for her. She'd suffered from insomnia forever, and figured she would suffer with it the rest of forever, as well. As a child, she'd known that one of her mother's "friends" could walk into her bedroom at any time and hurt her, so she'd taught herself to rouse at the slightest noise. Sadly, the skill had come in handy.

Soon, though, she'd stopped sleeping altogether. And even while living in the Tremain compound, as she called it, with the best security money could buy, Noelle in the bed next to her, she hadn't rested properly.

Some habits were too hard to break, she supposed. Which was a very good reason to finally stop thinking about her vampire. She didn't want McKell-pondering to become a habit. Or an obsession. But . . .

Was he okay?

She sank into the cold metal chair in front of her kitchen counter. This time, she didn't try to clear her mind. Contemplating a man's ultimate fate wasn't obsessive; it was considerate. What if she'd killed him?

Oh, God. McKell . . . dead . . . The possibility seemed more likely with every second that passed and he didn't show up to retaliate.

Bile burned her throat as she dropped her head in her upraised hands, elbows propped against the stone counter. *Why do you care?* And she did. She cared. Because he wouldn't be able to answer Mia's questions, and wouldn't be able to donate more of his blood to the Save a Human from the Schön Queen foundation. Surely. But she couldn't deny that those very logical, acceptable reasons meant nothing to her.

McKell could have maimed or killed her, but had written on her instead. McKell could have chosen elegant Noelle, but had chosen tiny Ava instead. He could have left her naked and defenseless, but he'd let her keep her underwear, and part of her still suspected he had followed her home, despite what common sense told her. Just to ensure she arrived safely. And last night, he could have attacked her, but hadn't.

What had she done?

Breathe, you have to breathe.

Even lost to her rage as she'd been, she had managed to avoid all his major organs. *Good, breathing. Calming.* He would be fine. *If* the inside of his vampire body was humanoid. Oh, God. *Bye-bye, calm.*

What if it wasn't? What if she'd damaged him irreparably?

Perhaps she'd overreacted to his slur just a wee bit, she thought now.

Maybe she'd check on him tonight. Mia would want a status report. Right? Would McKell still be in that forest, though? Would he attack Ava this time? He would have every right to do so. She'd have to find a way to protect herself without hurting him further.

Damn him, why hadn't he frozen her after she'd stabbed him? He could have. Right? Except, maybe when injured, his ability to manipulate time—and people—failed him. If so, that meant . . . oh . . . shit. If so, he was in major danger. He wouldn't be able to protect himself. Especially if Mia sent other AIR agents after him. *Real* agents, this time.

Knowing Mia, that was a strong possibility.

The new agents might not be as gentle as Ava had been, and the thought of someone else hurting McKell . . . angered her, she realized as her nails cut into her palms with the same precision they had when she'd thought of him with another woman. Not to the red-haze degree that Noelle-bashing did, but still. Definite anger.

How odd. She'd never cared about anyone else's well-being. On the streets it was survival first, everything else second. Although, when she thought about it, McKell was *her* target, so she had a right to be proprietary toward him.

Okay, so. Game plan. She'd visit him tonight. If

he was still in the forest, she would subdue him as needed, then protect him from any and all threats. Human, animal, it didn't matter. And when he healed, she would take him into AIR as ordered. That way, she could feel proud of a job well done. Not embarrassed by a job done just because the guy was weakened. At least, that's the rational she used.

Except, when he healed, she would face the same problem as last night. No one could make McKell do anything he didn't want to do. Damn him, she thought again. His ability to manipulate time put a serious damper on her ability to force him to do what *she* wanted.

A heavy, insistent knock sounded at her door.

Ava pushed to still shaky legs and threw her mug in the sink. Noelle was coded into the ID pad, and loved to enter at the most awkward times, so Ava knew her friend wasn't the intruder. Mia, maybe? With new orders? Not McKell. He would have kicked the door in.

As another knock sounded, she trudged to her bedroom and tugged on a loose pair of shorts. She didn't like the way her hands shook. By the time a third knock rang out, this one harder, more insistent, she stood at the entrance, gaping. And still shaking.

She'd been wrong. McKell's (not so beautiful anymore) face consumed her ID screen. He was here. He was alive. And acting civilized.

He stood in her building's hallway, fist lifting to once again bang at her door. His other hand was curled into a fist, too—with a long, black whip dangling from both sides. "I know you're there, Ava. I can smell you. Open. Now."

Heart slamming against her ribs, she did just that. She opened the door. He towered over her, scowling, fangs bared, clutching his bleeding side. Worse, his skin was red and blistered, and those blisters were oozing. Obviously he'd battled the sun to get here. Which meant he had a specific purpose for seeking her out. Killing her? With that whip?

Probably. He smiled slowly, but that smile promised she would like the way he ended her.

She wasn't scared, though. She could take care of herself. What she was, was shocked. Big, strong, okay, fine, still gorgeous even with those blisters, McKell was actually, finally here. Intense relief swept through her, followed on the heels of heat ... need ... *Don't go there.*

"Did you come for revenge?" she asked, gaze immediately lowering to the whip. At the moment, they were the only words her reeling brain could form.

"I'm not healing," he said. The smile vanished, and he shook the whip at her. "Why aren't I healing, woman?" He didn't wait for her reply, but stormed inside her apartment.

His body brushed hers, and despite the clothing between them, despite the situation and the consequences, despite the increase of heat, she shivered. "Come in," she said dryly. He. Was. Here. She couldn't get over that fact.

He tossed a feral growl over his shoulder, gait never slowing. "I asked you a question."

She shut and locked the door, then followed the path he had taken. In her living room, she watched as he fell onto the couch. He studied his surroundings with a single sweep—and she would bet he'd memorized every exit, every conceivable weapon—before glaring over at her. What did he think of her home? Did he see how hard she'd worked for every piece of furniture, or did he merely view her as poor?

There was a flicker of admiration in that gaze, she realized. He knew how hard she'd worked. Now her heart skipped a beat. He shouldn't have been more beautiful just because he was surrounded by *her* stuff in *her* place, admiring, but he was. His black hair hung in disarray, his violet eyes gleamed brightly. His skin, already healing. His lips were parted, kissable.

Don't think like that. Swallowing the lump forming in her throat, she rested her hands on her hips. "You asked me a question, yes, and I ignored it. Twice. Take a hint and stop asking. So how'd you know where I lived, anyway?" Was that breathless tone hers?

"I have your ID," he grumbled.

Oh. Duh.

"And I followed you the other night."

A shattering confirmation of her suspicions. She was delighted to her very soul.

Now she experienced fear. Fear that she was allowing attraction to overwhelm her. Time to paint him in a negative light, and put a stop to the craziness.

"Are you here for revenge?" she asked again, squaring her shoulders.

He ran his tongue over his teeth. Those sharp, deadly teeth. "That will come. Later."

The thought of this man, this killer, having revenge *excited* her, she realized, and the fear grew until she had to rub her chest to ward off the ache. She could suddenly imagine tongue-lashings and well-placed nibbling, moaning, groaning, begging. All because of that butterscotch voice.

Oh, yes. Fear. Her attraction was overwhelming, not dulled in the least. *Fight it.*

"What comes now?" she asked. "The whip?" His answer would determine how they proceeded. Sugar and spice, or absolutely nothing nice.

He looked at the coiled length of leather as if he had no idea it was in his hand. "Oh. This. It's my preferred method for restraining females." He tossed the whip aside, the action making him grimace. "As you are unexpectedly cooperating . . ." He let the thought trail off. "I want to know why I'm not healing."

How many females had he restrained over the years?

Another *don't go there* filled her head. She studied him anew, her gaze dropping to his seeping wound, and the guilt she'd experienced earlier roared back to life, draining the fear, defeating her before the battle could even begin. He wore a new shirt—the tag still hung from the neck—but on his left side, the material was soaked with blood. He was as injured as when she'd left him.

After a second more of consideration, she knew that wasn't true. He'd worsened.

Her own side twitched in sympathy. "Do you normally heal fast?"

"Yes. The bleeding should have stopped hours ago. Was your blade tipped with poison?"

"No!" She wasn't a *total* bitch.

Another growl erupted from him. "What did you do to me, then?"

"Me? Nothing!" *Guilt . . . escalating . . .* If she had to choose between feeling guilty and having her hand chopped off, she'd remove the hand, no question. "Don't you remember? You walked into my knife." Though she'd hoped otherwise, the denial didn't ease the guilt.

"I. Was. Sitting."

"Semantics."

He stared at her, unflinching. "I'd argue your use of the term, but at the moment I'm a little too busy bleeding to death. Fix me!"

"God, you're irritable. But fine. I'll fix you." Maybe then the guilt would truly fade. "Quick question. By fix you"—she air-quoted *fix*—"do you mean sew you up like I would a human?"

"Is there any other way?" he snapped.

Irr-it-able. "You'd trust me with a needle?"

"No. But I'll have my teeth ready to rip into you if you try to stab me with it."

"Comforting. With that kind of threat hanging over my head, I'll probably be shaking too badly to do you any good." She was shaking, yes, but fear *still* wasn't the reason. The shock of his presence, the guilt of her actions, of course, were both still a cause, but so was an increase in desire. He was a warrior to his soul.

Violet eyes sizzled. "Fix. Me. And if you cause any more damage, human, note that I'll hurt you in kind."

"So noted." With another sigh, she padded into the bathroom and grabbed her first aid kit. By the time she returned, McKell had removed his shirt. The bloody material rested on her coffee table.

Frowning at him, she kicked the offending shirt to the floor. "If the table is stained, you're buying me a new one."

He merely raised his chin and motioned for her to get started.

She closed the rest of the distance and knelt between his open legs—and tried not to peek at his man business, covered so *demurely* by his pants. If she did, she'd be tempted to study every ridge and discover if she affected him the same way he affected her.

She needed a distraction.

"So. Have you fed today?" she asked, resting the kit on his thigh.

"Many times." There was anger in his tone. Anger she didn't understand.

"So I'm not in danger of blood loss myself?" Alcohol, cloth.

"I didn't say that."

Needle, thread. Her lips curled as she fought to hide her amusement. She considered the wound. Raw, angry skin. Torn, jagged muscle, like puzzle pieces in need of connecting. Ouch. She cleaned him as gently as she could before withdrawing a half-filled syringe.

"No medication," he snapped, gripping her wrist and holding her hand in place.

She looked up, and her gaze connected with his, crackling. "But this will numb you."

"Or kill me."

And the problem? "Either way, you won't feel the stitches."

"No medication," he insisted.

She shrugged. "Your pain, your choice."

He released her, and she jumped back into her work. She expected him to scream with the first pierce of the needle, but no. Not her McKell. He gritted his teeth and silently endured.

"How did you get those scars on your hands?" He'd probably meant to ease back into conversation, but his pain gave him a dangerous vibe.

"Fights, mostly."

"With who?" If he'd sounded dangerous before, he was positively lethal now.

"Lots of people. In school, I kind of had a temper. I would attack at the slightest provocation. Even when I knew I was going to get my ass kicked."

He chuckled, surprising her. "In school. You *kind of* had a temper. And now you're, what? Calm?"

"Definitely. Calling me an angel wouldn't even be a stretch." She finished the last stitch—he'd needed thirty-nine—and said, "All done," then gently bandaged him.

"I don't think so." Now there was a pout in his voice. "You owe me blood."

Ava could feel his gaze on her neck, burning where her pulse hammered wildly. She . . . liked it. Liked the thought of him leaning down, biting, sucking . . . tasting.

"I thought you'd already eaten." Good. Rather than reveal just how ravenous she suddenly was for what he offered, there'd been an air of impassivity to her.

"What does that have to do with anything? You're to be my dessert." A put-down, from his point of view, obviously, since his tone was sneering.

Maybe she could have allowed it, even then. But was he attracted to her? Or did he just like the smell of her blood? Either could explain why he'd picked her over Noelle, despite the fact that Noelle had wanted him. "Had" being the key word. After he'd called dibs on Ava, Noelle had washed her hands of him, no matter what the girl claimed.

Ava wanted his attraction to equal—or be greater than—hers. Nothing else would satisfy her. *If* she was going to allow him to have her, that is. Which she wasn't. "The fact that I stabbed you wasn't a deal breaker?" she asked, hoping to anger him, distract him.

He growled again.

"What? Too soon to joke about it?" She leaned back on her haunches. She should have stood, walked away, but couldn't find the will to do so.

He didn't move, either. "Why did you stab me? I

still don't understand what I did to enrage you. And you *were* enraged. The emotion poured off you."

How to explain? "Do you have a brother or a sister?"

"No."

"A best friend you love but who irritates the hell out of you?"

"No."

"Mother? Father?"

"No. They died decades ago."

Decades. Wow. So he'd been on his own his entire, clearly too-long life? How . . . sad. Everyone needed a friend. Even emotionally distanced vampires. "Well, imagine what it'd be like if you did have someone in your life. Just one person you cared about. Noelle is that one person to me. She's my only friend and family, and I love her more than anything or anyone else in the world."

"And yet you call her names. Hell, she calls you names."

"One, we're comfortable with each other. Two, we're confident enough in our affections to be honest with each other. And three, sometimes people need to be razed to find their inner strength." Ava flattened her hands on his thighs, knocking the kit out of the way. To balance herself while crouching. That was all. Really. God, he was strong. And hot. All those muscles . . . *Concentrate.* "But anyone else who says an unkind word is punished for doing so."

"I still don't understand. Where I'm from, you treat your loved ones with deference."

"Even when they're bugging you?"

Silent now, he popped his jaw.

She'd take that for a yes. That had to be hell, to never be allowed to express your anger at the person you loved. Pent-up resentment, thy name is McKell. No wonder he hadn't attacked Ava after she'd stabbed him. Not that he loved her, but he *did* want something from her. Clearly.

She was not disappointed. "Why are you here, McKell?"

His fingers wrapped around her wrists, once again holding her hands in place. "We will discuss that. After."

"After." How sensually he'd said the word . . . She licked her lips, hating the way her heart sped into an unending hyper-beat. "After the biting?"

He arched a brow. "You would let me bite you?"

Yes. "No."

"Then, no." Grated, halting. "After the bargaining."

"Oh, really?" Would that bargain involve nakedness? Moaning? She wouldn't say yes, of course, but it was flattering that he—

"AIR wishes to speak with me, yes?"

Wasn't after her body. Disappointment rocked her, undeniable this time. "Yeah. So?"

"So. I will finally talk with them."

She ignored the wave of concern suddenly crashing through her. AIR wouldn't go easy on him just because he turned himself in. "And all I have to do in return is. . . ?"

"Help me track other vampires living on the surface."

"Help you track other vampires? Why?"

"Because." His mouth was a stubborn, mulish line. There was only one way to get what you wanted from a man like McKell. Taunt him. "I seriously misjudged your talents. I thought you'd be an excellent hunter and—"

"I can track them no problem," he snapped. "But that used to be one of my jobs. I would come here and track them, and then execute them for leaving our underground world."

Score one for Ava. An answer, freely given. But . . . wait. Would another vampire be coming for McKell to execute him? She opened her mouth to ask, but he said, "Now they run from me or fight me, even though I only wish to question them."

"Is that what you've been doing today? Fighting vampires?"

A stiff nod. "Among other things."

"Well, no wonder your wound wasn't healing. Moron! Injuries require rest."

His grip tightened on her wrists, almost bruising, yet managing to skate the edge of pain. "Yes, but someone made me a target for every vampire in the area. They scented me out, knew I was weakened and they'd never have a better chance to defeat me, and attacked."

Her stomach clenched at the thought of this man being hurt, and she scowled. *She* was the moron. Concern for the enemy? Again? "Did you kill them?"

"Accidentally," he grumbled.

Good. To attack a helpless man—she almost laughed. As if McKell would be helpless, even buried ten feet underground with his hands and feet tied. Still. Those vampires had deserved what they got. "I didn't realize so many bloodsuckers lived up here."

"They've learned to hide their race."

And now he wanted to do so? Was that why he wanted to talk to them? To learn how they did it? "So you want me to question them for you, is that it?"

"No. Just . . . distract them for me."

Not a bad deal. Afterward, she'd bring in McKell, as ordered, and look like a hero. She would also learn the names and locations of the other vampires, just in case Mia wanted to test their blood, as well. That wouldn't be a betrayal to McKell. Okay, it would, but she barely knew him, and he was the enemy. The sexiest, most erotic enemy of her acquaintance, but whatever. Her loyalty was to AIR.

"I agree. I'll help you find and distract other vampires, and in return you'll talk with Mia Snow. So do we need to seal this deal with a kiss or what?" she asked flippantly. Or meant to ask flippantly. The heated catch of her breath gave her away. Longing . . . so much longing . . . since the very first.

For several seconds, he simply stared at her, gaze eating her up, leaving her panting, shaky. She tried to pull away, to end the madness. To destroy the minefield of awareness.

"Yes," he finally said, and hauled her onto his lap.

Six

Holy hell, McKell thought.

As Ava gasped in shock, hands slapping against his chest to find balance, knees straddling his thighs, he thrust his tongue deep into her mouth. Warm, wet, sweet. That's what she was, and she utterly slayed him, not fighting him but embracing him, giving as much as he did.

She'd wanted it; he'd known she had. Had smelled her arousal, as sweet as the woman herself. But there'd still been a question in his mind. She wanted, but would she acquiesce? She was a warrior, after all, and as fierce as he was. Maybe even more so. Not once since he'd entered her home had she truly feared him.

Now, though, he knew beyond any doubt. She'd acquiesced. Amazingly so.

He moaned in pleasure, and tragically the sound jolted his common sense. *Shouldn't be this good.* Nothing *should be this good.*

Still. He didn't stop. Couldn't. Even though he was shaky and needed to remain on guard. *Especially* with this unpredictable woman. He let their tongues continue to play, to duel, to roll and thrust, sipping, feeding, driving them closer and closer to a ledge they might later wish they'd never built. For it was a ledge of their own making, one that promised a torturous fall, a fatal landing. He could have stayed away. She could have refused him. Neither of them had.

He could have left after she'd practically dared him to sample these tantalizing lips.

They were fools. He'd come here to drink her dry. He'd come here to yell at her, shake her, choke her, *something*. And he'd been primed for a fight. He'd had to avoid *two* doorways on the way here. Usually he merely encountered one a day. That was all. But they seemed to be following him now, more determined than ever to suck him inside.

One look at her, though, those amber eyes ablaze, and he'd forgotten the urge to fight and decided to bargain with her and she had agreed. Oh, yes. They were fools.

This kiss would have to suffice as "something."

But he couldn't regret his choice. Not while her nails sank into his shoulders, not to push him away but to urge him closer. Not while her core rubbed against his shaft, insistent, determined. Not while he plumped the sweet mounds of her breasts, her nipples rasping against his palms. *Sweet heaven*.

He'd thought he would have to force his way inside, but again, she had surprised him. Had allowed him to walk right in, teasing him all the while. She'd even doctored him, those delicate-looking hands gentle on his wound.

Why wasn't she trying to hurt him further?

He knew why he was acting as he was. He was weakened from blood loss. He'd tried to feed before coming here. Many times, as he'd told her, but his stomach had rebelled and he'd vomited nearly every drop. He didn't know why—that had never happened to him before—but he knew where to lay the blame.

Punish her as originally planned.

"McKell," she said on a moan.

Forget punishing her. He must have suspected he would go this route. Why else would he have washed his mouth so many times?

"You don't really like to be treated like a lady, right? *Please* tell me you don't." She'd told Noelle she was a fragile flower.

"I don't. Treat me bad. Real bad."

Thank God. He released her breasts and sank his fingers into her scalp, forcing her head to tilt and allowing him deeper contact. As the kiss spun even closer to that dangerous ledge, intensifying, he slid his hands down her back, along the ridges of her spine, and stopped on her ass, dragging her closer . . . closer still . . .

"Ava," he said on a moan. He tightened his grip on her, probably leaving bruises.

"I'm not convinced you're serious about our bargain," she rasped. "Convince me some more."

"More. Yes."

The tips of his fangs sharpened, ready, eager. He couldn't help himself; he scraped them against her tongue. She jerked, unprepared, groaned, but didn't pull away. She edged the rest of the way, connecting fully, only clothing keeping him from penetration. He sucked. A bead of her blood trickled into his mouth, down his throat, dancing in his stomach, and *he* jerked. The decadent flavor . . . like the sugar sweetness of her lipgloss . . .

Good no longer described this kiss. *Exquisite,* maybe. *Perfection,* definitely. *Addicting,* probably.

Addicted? Yes. He was. And he wasn't sorry.

He needed more, as he'd told her. Had to have more. He sucked, and another bead formed. Once again the drugging sweetness astonished him. He savored before swallowing, the warmth instantly traveling through him, strengthening him, easing the sting in his wound. Finally, it began to heal.

More.

Her hands fisted his hair, ripping several strands free, but not to stop him—to urge him on. He knew because her tongue continued that devastating roll, more insistent now, purrs humming from her throat. Her hips moved in sync with her tongue, mimicking sex, rubbing against him, control fading. He needed to open her pants and delve into her panties. He needed to feel how wet she was. Needed to sink one, two, three fingers into that tight little sheath.

"McKell," she gasped out.

"More," was all he could think to say. But any more, and he would pull from the kiss, sink his fangs into her neck, and drain her. He knew he would. Already an intense hunger beat through him, growing, propelling him to act as instinct demanded. As *survival* demanded.

"Yes, please." Unaware of the animal she provoked, she rubbed him faster and faster, reducing him to that creature of sensation. Only sensation.

Instinct . . . food . . .

No. If he drained her, he wouldn't be able to kiss her again. And he desperately needed her kisses. Her touch. His cock ached unbearably, rising past the waist of his pants, seeking every bit of contact, any contact. Damn their clothing. He wanted to penetrate. *Needed* to penetrate with the same intensity he needed the kiss, the blood. And he wanted to—the core of her rubbed against him again, from base to tip, and his thoughts fragmented. He found himself lifting, grinding against her, shoving her harder, their clothing no longer a concern. Just a little more and he would . . . come, he realized with shock. He would come in his pants like an untrained youth.

And when he came, he really would drain her, instinct taking over completely. In his weakened condition, he wouldn't be able to stop himself.

McKell gripped her hips, stilling her this time. He was panting, sweating, shaking. Frantic . . . starving . . . Oh, yes, starving.

Control. He had to gain control.

Didn't help when Ava licked the moisture from her mouth, savoring the taste he'd left behind. "Why'd you stop?" she asked, and she sounded drugged. Her eyes were glassy, like liquid amber, and her lips a well-sated scarlet.

"For the best." Never had his voice echoed with such menace. For himself. He should have been *eager* to drain her. Resisting merely proved the true depths of his foolishness.

"Whose best?" she asked, nuzzling his cheek with her own.

She was going to kill him. And herself. "Yours," he gritted out

"'Cause you just snuck a taste of my blood and are trolling for more?" Slowly she straightened and ran her hands up and down his arms. She grinned a wicked grin. "God, your muscles are huge."

And he'd thought her kiss torture. Her caress . . . like heaven and hell wrapped in silk, sprinkled with velvet, then bespelled with an irresistible mist. He grabbed her wrists as he'd done earlier and squeezed. "If you don't behave yourself, I'll sneak a whole lot more than you're willing to give."

Her gaze met his, all soft and luminous. "So you liked it?" Another purr as she pulled from his grip and toyed with his necklace.

Do not answer that. Don't you dare answer that.

Her grin returned. "*Tsk, tsk*, McKell. You should know it's rude to ignore your host."

Change the subject. Save yourself, her. "It's also rude to stab your host." There. Better. Except, the reminder failed to enrage him. She'd gotten the better of him, which meant she was strong, capable, and that suddenly filled him with . . . pride.

Pride? Why?

All that lovely amusement faded. "Here's another tidbit. It's also rude to remind your host of the time she stabbed you."

Irreverent baggage. And stupid, stupid increased pride. He liked her wit.

"Were you distracting me so that *you* could stab *me*?" she rasped, arching into him. The very idea should have sent her running from him. Yet still she remained completely unconcerned.

Either she was confident in her ability to protect herself or confident in his *in*ability to hurt her. Either way, his sense of pride increased again. The heart of a warrior beat in her chest.

Stupid, stupid, *stupid* of him to crave her.

"Ava." He needed something to do with his hands, and so he once again latched onto her hips. He squeezed so tightly he knew bruises would form, if they hadn't already, but better to mark her that way than the other. "Stop moving on me."

"McKell. Answer my question. Please."

Had he liked her blood? "What if I did?" He wouldn't admit to the helpless need to possess her. The need to have her curves under him—over him. The need to have her touching, tasting, giving, taking. Oh, taking. Taking more than anyone else ever had. "What would you do if I decided to have you?" He hadn't meant the words as a challenge, but that's how they emerged.

She licked her lips. "Stop you, of course." But she didn't sound confident.

He chuckled. Then frowned. *Beyond* stupid, that's what he was. "I think you've changed your mind about me." How many times had she told Noelle she didn't want him? Countless. And usually a human's disregard wouldn't have bothered him. Humans were beneath him, after all, but he couldn't walk away from this one. As evidenced by his actions today.

"What do you mean?" she asked, settling her weight on her haunches. Away from his erection.

"Before, you weren't willing to do a load of laundry to be with me. Now, I think you would."

She arched a brow. "Hurt your feelings when I said that, did I?"

"No!" The denial echoed from the walls, and his cheeks heated at his own vehemence. "No," he stated more calmly. "I have no feelings. I was simply repeating something you said."

She grinned, and the return of her amusement lit her beautiful face. Again, most people ran from him in terror when he displayed the slightest hint of displeasure. Those who didn't soon wished they had. And really, this one had more reason than most to fear him. Yet she remained on his lap, as calm as ever.

Nibbling on her bottom lip, she traced a fingertip down his sternum. "Well, to be fair, I hadn't kissed you then, so I had no idea what I was giving up."

Another hint for him to get back to kissing her? *Slaying . . . him.* "The bargain has been sealed," he said. Before she could tempt her further, he did what he should have done minutes ago: unceremoniously dumped her onto the floor.

Severing the contact failed to calm him, though. His body still ached, and his teeth still throbbed for another taste.

She gasped in surprise and glared up at him, her silky curls in disarray around her shoulders. "And by *had no idea what I was giving up*, I meant kissing you would be awful and wouldn't have changed my mind. And I was right!"

Liar. Her pupils were blown, her lips still red and swollen, and with the distance between them, he was finally able to concentrate on more than the heaven that rested between her legs. He could hear the rush of blood through her veins, swift and needy. Could smell the desire pouring off her, sweet and heady.

That should have increased his hunger. Instead, his instincts switched gears. From wanting to devour to wanting to protect, and this time, they *far* overshadowed his need for blood. Odd. Incomprehensible.

She popped to her feet and dusted off her hands, all while donning a mask of disinterest. "Anyway, the bargain can't be sealed. We haven't set the rules yet."

"The rules are simple," he said, relaxing in his seat and adopting the same disinterested mask. He liked this couch. Its softness, its worn exterior. Every crease meant Ava's body had rubbed there. Repeatedly. "You'll obey me in all things." Hadn't he made that clear already?

"That's not what I meant." She anchored her hands on the flare of her waist. "Who helps who first?"

"You'll help me, since AIR will want to lock me up." Sure, he would escape the second their questions were answered and he'd fulfilled his promise to Ava, but she didn't need to know that.

"Good point. But in return for allowing the male to go before the female—as is proper—you have to swear not to drink from me without permission. Which I won't give. So that means you'll have to drink from other people."

"I swear." Because he could gain her permission with little effort. "I'll drink from others."

Her lips pressed into a thin line, as if his answer had angered her. Surely he was mistaken. He'd pretended to give her what she wanted. Hadn't he? What fault could she find with him?

"So my blood isn't good enough for you?" she snarled. "Is that it?"

Oh, yes. She was angry. "I never said anything about your blood not being—"

"Just forget it," she said, derailing his rant before it could truly begin. "It doesn't matter. And now that that's settled, when do you want to start hunting vampires?"

Settled? Ha! She was still angry, yet didn't want to hear his rebuttal. He might never understand this human. "We'll start tonight." He unfolded his big body from the couch, his stitches pulling. Thankfully, the nearly debilitating sting never returned.

And wasn't that surprising? Just how powerful was

Ava's blood? He'd had only a few drops, yet he was healing as if he'd feasted. The blisters on his skin had even faded, just from the scent of her, and though he was tired, he could function.

His head tilted to the side, his attention on her deepening, as a thought occurred to him. "Why did AIR send *you* to capture me?"

"Why wouldn't they?" she said, the words lashing as sharply as his whip. "I'm the best."

Aw. He'd pricked her pride. "You are indeed good, but you're also in training."

"So?" She splayed her arms, a look-at-me gesture. "That doesn't mean I'm not the best."

"Yes, actually, it does. Or they would have made you an agent already."

She scowled at him.

Had they sent her because they'd somehow known how potent her blood was? Had they known he'd crave it? Had they hoped he would become her slave? He wouldn't put such an action past them. They were devious like that.

He wouldn't worry about her purpose, though. Not now. There were more important matters to attend to. "Where's your bed?"

She blinked over at him, confusion replacing the anger. "Excuse me?"

"Your bed. Where is it?"

"Why?"

He pushed past her and snaked a corner. Kitchen. Small, but clean. Stone counters, stainless steel sink, metal chairs. Her dishes were put away, and there was a faint scent of butterscotch in the air. His mouth watered, and he fisted his hands. Stupid scent. He almost wished he'd never encountered it before, because now the slightest whiff caused his cock to stand at instant attention.

"McKell," Ava called out behind him, footsteps pounding.

She followed.

He nearly grinned. "Ava," he called back. Another corner, and he stood at the entrance of a small bedroom. The bed was so short and thin, his feet would hang off the edge and his arms would fall off the sides. But the curtains were closed over the only window, muted shadows chasing away the brightest light, creating a homey, well-loved atmosphere, so he would make do.

He kicked off his shoes and climbed atop the mattress. The springs squeaked.

"Just what the hell do you think you're doing?" Ava demanded from the doorway.

He burrowed under the covers, and once again the scent of butterscotch wafted to his nose. Shaft . . . twitching . . . "I'm going to sleep." And after a few hours of rest, he would have the strength to ignore these protective instincts and bodily urges, and start acting like the ruthless vampire he was. More importantly, his mind would be alert and he could figure some things out.

"Why?"

"I need to regroup. Now be quiet."

"Wait. Sleeping? Here? With me and my weapons only a few feet away?"

"Yes." Hopefully, resting would obliterate his foolish urge to trust her, too. But he did. Trust her. Some part of him knew she wouldn't betray him while he was at his weakest. "Don't disappoint me and tattle."

"Or you'll rip me to little pieces and send me back to Mia?" Drily uttered, as if she didn't really think he'd do it.

"Something like that," he muttered. Her way of thinking needed a remodel, too.

"But . . . but . . . "

"You're still talking."

There was a tense pause. Then, "If you want peace and quiet in *my* apartment," she snapped, "you'll have to return *my* phone."

"I don't have it with me," he lied. The phone was in his pocket, where it would remain. Perhaps forever.

"Return it later, then."

"Maybe." Another lie, but he doubted she would have liked the truth.

"McKell," she ground out, exasperated. "You can't just—"

"Still. Talking."

She cursed under her breath before slamming the door.

Was the vampire brain damaged? Ava wondered as she paced the length of her living room. Mia liked to say all men were damaged in some way, but Ava hadn't believed her. Until now.

McKell acted as if they were best friends. He acted as if he owned the place. He acted as if he hadn't kissed the breath right out of her and rocked her entire world. He acted as if her blood was subpar.

Bastard.

Sure, they were partners now. In a way. Sure, they were working together. Kind of. So he should treat her better. Definitely. He should treat her as if he valued her opinion. As if her kisses were amazing. As if her blood was the best he'd ever had.

Bastard, she thought again.

When she'd told him he would have to drink from other people, he'd responded quickly, with no hesitation. Clearly, he'd *wanted* to drink from other people. And that pissed her the hell off. Not just because he'd made her feel subpar, which was irrational—she knew it was, but she couldn't help herself—but because she hated the thought of his mouth on anyone else. He should have demanded access to her blood.

Ava stomped into her kitchen and fixed herself a ham sandwich. And as she chewed with more force than necessary, she realized she was shaking. Not from anger, as she would have liked to convince herself, but from arousal.

McKell's kiss had heated her blood, and the fever had yet to cool. Her nipples were still hard, her stomach twisted into a anticipatory knot, and her skin too tight for her bones. And her tongue ached, damn it! He'd scraped the sensitive flesh with his fangs, and rather than hurt her, the action had intensified her desire for him.

She'd wanted her hands all over him. Had wanted to offer him complete access to her neck. Had wanted to tell him to suck every last drop of her blood. Only thoughts of who and what he was had stopped her from doing so. He was a criminal. A vampire who clearly considered himself far superior to humans.

Dessert, he'd said with disdain.

She couldn't forget. Not what he thought, and not what she'd always wanted. Respect. She would not be known as the agent who fucked her targets. No, no, never. Talk about humiliating. Especially since a few of the other trainees already referred to her as trash.

Street trash. Daughter-of-a-druggie trash. Trash, trash, trash. She was so used to the reference, it didn't bother her anymore. But adding to the list? Sleep-with-anything-that-breathes trash? Hell, no.

After draining a glass of water, she picked up her home phone to ring Noelle. The slide of a door caught her attention, and she dropped the phone, grinning. Noelle must have sensed her need and come running, because her friend was already here.

Ava trudged into the living room, and sure enough, Noelle had let herself in. She fell onto the couch, and stared down at the worn fabric. She frowned.

"You were bleeding?" her friend said. "Which means you're injured. Why didn't you tell me you were injured? And who did it? I'll kill him. I swear to God I'll kill him dead! Is he the one who brought the whip?"

Shit. McKell had left stains on the couch? He was paying the cleaning bill or buying her a new one. "I'm fine. The *vampire* was bleeding, not me."

Gray eyes swung to her, shock in their depths. "He was here? And he brought a whip?"

"Was? No. He's *still* here." She jabbed her thumb toward the back of the apartment. "He's sleeping. And yes, he brought it, but no, he's not going to use it," she added before her friend could ask. She might use it, though. Later. The thought of tying him up— *don't you dare go there!*

Now those gray eyes widened. "You banged him already?"

Unlike the others, Noelle wouldn't view such a bedding as trashy. Noelle was a romantic, though she would probably deny that until her dying breath, and would have praised Ava for following her heart. Or panties.

"Nope. No banging." But she would have, and would have hated herself for it. Despite everything, she wouldn't have stopped him. Would have gone all the way. Taken everything he had to give. Between her legs, his cock had been thick and long and ready, and she'd wanted it. Desperately.

Yet he had been of sound enough mind to stop and toss her to the floor. Now *that* was far more humiliating than being referred to as trash, she thought. She'd craved him like a drug, yet he had remained somewhat detached.

She would *not* let that happen again.

"So what's he doing here?" Noelle asked, merely curious.

"He demanded I patch him up, and then decided he needed a nap." Was her resentment showing?

"So you kissed him? 'Cause, baby, your lips are red and swollen."

Ava's cheeks heated. Probably to the same shade of red as her lips. "You should see my tongue." Now why had she admitted to that?

Noelle clapped excitedly. "Your tongue? Did he bite it? He did, didn't he? Show me, show me! I wanna see."

"No way."

Noelle smashed her hands together, as if she were preparing to pray. "Please. Show me. I won't laugh, I swear."

"Fine." Once Noelle started begging, she didn't stop until she got what she wanted. Ava stuck out her tongue.

Noelle laughed. "Oh, my God. You have puncture wounds."

The heat in her cheeks spread to her neck, her collarbone. "You said you wouldn't laugh, Tremain."

"I lied. You know I'm a liar, so you can't hold me responsible. And he clearly likes to nibble. God, you're so lucky! And to think, I gave him to you. Just gave him away, without sampling the goods myself." She shook her head in disbelief. "I'm usually not such a dumbass."

Ava had never been jealous of Noelle before. Had

never wanted to hide a man from her friend. Noelle had given her so much over the years, she would have happily handed over her probably-traumatized liver if her friend asked. But just then, she wanted to wash all thoughts of McKell from Noelle's mind. She wanted to place a blanket over the vampire's head and never let anyone see him ever again. Except her.

All this jealousy, because of one kiss the vampire hadn't really cared for?

Something was seriously wrong with her. As she'd already decided, she wasn't going to let him kiss her again. Or drink her blood. After all, the reason she had demanded he refrain from drinking from her still applied. If he even glanced at her like he was thirsty, she might strip and beg him for more. Just as she'd begged while he had kissed her.

This way, he wouldn't make a play for her vein. Which meant she would be able to keep her desires and hormones under control. She hoped.

"So . . . your kiss was so hot, he wasn't afraid you'd phone AIR and have them swoop in for a pickup while he napped?" Noelle asked. "Good going, Sans. I'm impressed."

"Thanks." Though she wasn't sure she could take credit. He simply wasn't scared of Ava, AIR, or anything they could throw his way.

Except . . . he trusted her to keep her end of their bargain. So, yeah, Noelle was kind of right. In a way, he believed in her. Baffling. Why would he believe in her? She'd stabbed him, for God's sake.

"Want me to kick him out?" Noelle asked.

Ava fell into the chair across from her friend. "No." Maybe she was just as brain-damaged as McKell, but she liked the thought of him here. Especially in her bed. Later, after she kicked him out herself, she could lie down and pretend to sleep, wrapped in his lingering heat.

"Gonna say anything to Mia?"

"Not yet." She explained her deal with McKell, her vampire-hunting aid in exchange for his willingness to speak with Mia, and Noelle grinned the entire time.

"Ava Sans. Are you in love? Because I have never—"

"No!" she screeched. She gulped and lowered her voice. "No, I'm not in love." She liked to think she was open to the possibly of *one day* falling in love, but she couldn't even spend an entire night with a guy. She always ran at the first sign of commitment. Hell, she ran *before* the first sign.

She'd never found anyone worth the, well, work that always came with coupledom. Work that would ultimately lead to failure.

Someone always walked away. That's just how people were. Kids left their parents, husbands left their wives, and wives left their husbands. Boyfriends and girlfriends realized they weren't right for each other, saw someone prettier, sluttier, smarter, wealthier—pick your poison—and cut their losses. No one stayed together until the bitter end. And who would want to? Bitter ends sucked. So why not get what you needed while the getting was good, and then say good-bye before a single bad memory took root?

"But you've never bargained with a bad guy before, either," Noelle said, dragging her from those dark, hopeless musings.

"He's not a bad guy." Wait. What? "I mean, he's a bad guy, he's just—"

"Nope. No take-backs. You think he's *special*." Noelle's grin widened. "And let's be honest. Only a girl in love would say that a guy like McKell is as pure and warm as the sun outside."

"Will you shut up? I never said anything about the sun. And why are you here, anyway?"

Noelle allowed the subject change without comment. "Two reasons. A few agents are meeting for beers in a little while, and I wanted you to go with me. But you're busy, so I'm not even going to ask." She stood and pointed to an overstuffed bag beside Ava's chair. "Second reason. I brought you my laundry. You got McKell, after all. Oh, and please remember. Light on the starch. And do yourself a favor and look everything over before you head to Suds and Bubbles. I hid a prezzie for you in between the costumes." With that, she let herself out of the apartment, leaving Ava alone.

With the laundry. And the vampire.

Dismissed again. By her best friend, no less. "He came to me, so I don't have to wash a goddamn thing," she called, knowing Noelle was long gone.

"Still talking," McKell shouted from the bedroom.

"Still annoying me," she shouted back.

Seven

*D*allas Gutierrez tipped back his beer and surveyed the bar. It was dim, crowded with humans and otherworlders, a veritable rainbow of differences, and on every wall was a holoscreen showcasing some kind of sporting event. There were three pool tables, and only seven scantily clad waitress taking care of everyone's needs. He wasn't positive, but he was pretty sure he'd nailed every one of those waitresses at some point in the last few months.

He was positive his friend Devyn had, before marrying his Bride, of course. The alien king—who had once collected women of every species, color, size, and occupation—had gone through a "service industry" phase. Not to mention the thousands of other phases. Then he'd hitched himself to Bride a few weeks ago and while Dallas liked the powerful vampire well enough, he wished to God she'd stayed home tonight.

Seriously. All his friends were pussies, pairing off and shit, forgetting they had male friends and needed to do guy stuff. Which was no biggie, really. He didn't care. Except for the fact that he fucking cared! He'd assumed Devyn would resist commitment forever. Like him. But *nooo*. Bride had to come along and ruin everything. Now Dallas was on his own. Every damn night. No one to talk to, no one to share his problems with.

God. *He* was the pussy now. Was he really jonesing to share his feelings?

It was just, sleeping around wasn't fun anymore. He was tired of not knowing his partners' names, of not *caring* enough to know their names. He was tired of everyone around him having someone they loved enough to spend eternity with, ditching him completely.

Eternity. Yep, that's what Devyn and Bride had to look forward to. Which was why Dallas had asked his friend for one night. Just one damn night for the two of them to hang out like they used to. He specifically remembered telling Devyn to "leave the ball and chain at home." So, of course, the bastard had interpreted that to mean his little wifey-poo needed to tag along and their sex toys, aka balls and chains, needed to remain in their bedroom.

Now the couple sat across from him. Cuddling. And a more sickening sight he'd never beheld.

Good thing he'd issued a few other invitations. Hope for the best, but plan for the worst, had always been his motto. He'd called two Rakans, two trainees, Mia Snow and Hector Dean. All had accepted. No, not true. He'd also called Jaxon Tremain, but the guy was currently on vacation with *his* wifey-poo. And that was probably for the best. Heads would have rolled otherwise, what with Noelle, Jaxon's cousin, chasing that damn rabid vampire. She'd almost defeated the bloodsucking bastard, too, and that was a major turn-on.

No *probably* about it. Jaxon was gone, and that was for the best. Dallas's libido would have been a harder blow than Noelle's job. Shitty pun intended.

Dallas's gaze shifted down the rest of the table. The Rakans were new hires, golden-skinned warriors with the ability to spirit-walk. Meaning, they could push their conscious minds out of their bodies, and watch and listen to all kinds of things without anyone the wiser.

Hector was bald, muscled, and had an arm sleeved with tattoos. He was friendly to guys, but ice-cold to women. Not in a gay way, but in an I'm-too-violent-for-the-weaker-sex kind of way.

Dallas liked him. Only one thing kept him from recruiting the agent as his new best friend, but he wasn't going to think about that now. He'd punch someone. Namely Hector.

The trainees were—shit, Dallas had forgotten their names. They were brothers, and both in their early twenties. One was blond (supposedly), handsome, and cocky as shit, and the other was blond, ugly, and mean as shit. They were—

Uh-oh. His problem with Hector had just walked into the bar. Looked like he'd be thinking about her, after all. Again.

Dallas Junior twitched.

Down, boy.

Noelle Tremain sauntered up to their table, tall, elegant, and pure rebellion. She wore a pair of skin-tight jeans, boots that hit her knees, and a top made from what could only be dental floss. Brown hair hung to her shoulders, straight as a pin, in a chic cut that looked tousled rather than subdued and had probably cost her a fortune. Her gray eyes were bright yet guarded. Playful yet unwelcoming. She picked her friends with care.

Rich as she was, she probably had to. Lots of people would have loved to use her. His body was one of them. *Don't think like that.*

"I know I wasn't officially invited," she said in her smoker's voice, earning another twitch, "but I was positive no one would mind if I joined."

She nudged a place for herself between the Devyn-Bride tangle of limbs and one of the in-training brothers before anyone could tell her to get lost. Not that anyone would have dared to do so. Girl was un-predictable in her tempers. And violent. God, was she violent. The thing he liked about her, though, was that a man never had to wonder where he stood with her. You pissed her off, she'd tell you. Hard. Usually with her knee. There was no making you guess, and no crying—on her part, at least.

"Where's Sans?" the handsome brother asked with a leering grin. "At home in bed?"

The ugly one punched him in the back of the head.

Noelle offered the speaker a deadly grin. "One day, Dear John, you're gonna wake up, and your penis is gonna be resting on the pillow next to you. Not that you'll notice its absence, small as it is."

Dallas laughed, and yep, there was another twitch.

Now he remembered, though. The guy's name was Johnny Deschanel. He'd slept with Ava at the beginning of training, and had bragged every day since. What a moron. Every man with sense knew you didn't tell your coworkers when you dipped your wick in the company ink. Then you never got to dip again.

Why had Dallas invited him tonight? Stupid.

Noelle propped her elbows on the tabletop and peered expectantly at Bride. "So what do you know about Victor McKell?"

Bride flicked the length of her black hair over one shoulder, hitting Devyn in the face. At least the conversation forced the couple to stop the embarrassing PDA. "I'll answer when my shock wears off. This is the first time a strange female has ever sat down and spoken to me rather than my boyfriend."

"Husband. I'm your husband. And darling, we had the exact same reaction," the Targon replied in his silky smooth voice. Everything about him was smooth, really. Dark hair, inhumanly ocher eyes. Pale, glittery skin that carried the sheen of crushed diamonds. "Only, I was silent from agony. Does she not recognize my brilliant beauty?"

"I recognized," Noelle said dryly. "I just thought your wife was prettier."

Every man at the table sat up straighter, suddenly straining to hear the rest of the conversation. Girl-on-girl action—hot. Too bad she didn't mean it. Dallas knew Noelle was into men. Oh, did he know.

Sometimes he could predict the future. Images would flash through his mind, some changeable, but most set in stone. And a few weeks ago, he'd seen himself in bed with Noelle. Naked, sweaty. Sated.

That vision had been of the unchangeable variety.

On one hand, go team Dallas. On the other, a man should have a choice about who he slept with.

Yeah, Noelle was gorgeous, and yeah, she turned him on. Stupid twitching cock. But damn it, she was his friend's cousin, and Dallas didn't do his friends' family members. Ever. That was the only rule he lived by. The only standard he'd set for his bed partners. And yeah, that meant he was easy.

But the worst part? The other reason he didn't want to sleep with Noelle? He'd also had a vision of her in bed with Hector Dean. Not at the same time as him, just to be clear. But if both of them slept with her, they would hate each other. He knew that, too.

Dallas could share, no problem. He didn't want to be tied down, and never had. But female-avoiding Hector? Sharing when he finally let his guard down? Laughable.

No question, Noelle was going to end their friendship.

Sad, really, since Hector was the last single man standing. The last friend Dallas had. Losing him was going to hurt like a son of a bitch.

His hands fisted on his chair arm as he studied

Hector. The agent was watching Noelle, expression blank. No hint of attraction was evident. Still. Dallas sighed. If only that were true. The fact that Hector was looking at her at all said more than any emotion could have. ·

"So anyway," Noelle continued. She curled her fingers around Bride's beer and drained the contents. "You were telling me about McKell."

A few masculine groans blended in a chorus of disappointment.

"I don't know why I was doing that," Bride said dryly. "I don't know anything about him."

Noelle arched a dark brow. "You were engaged to him."

"Yeah, as a child. Then my memory was wiped clean, and I was sent to live here. We've chatted a few times, but I promise you, I know nothing about him."

"And what she does know, she isn't impressed by," Devyn added firmly.

Bride just lifted her empty beer bottle and waved it under Devyn's nose. "Be a good boy and fetch me another drink."

She only drank red wine and blood, but Dallas knew she liked to blend in, so she was pretending to throw back a few cold ones.

Devyn's mouth dipped into a pout. "Darling, I can't. You know how jealous you get when every woman in the room watches my ass as I walk away from you. So, really, by refusing to help you, I'm doing you a favor."

Bride rolled her eyes, clearly trying not to smile, and signaled a waitress.

Devyn placed his hand over his heart and met Dallas's gaze. "No need to say it. I'm too good to her, I know."

Like Bride, Dallas found himself trying not to grin. How did the bastard get away with the ego and the laziness? If Dallas had said something like that to one of his dates, he would have been slapped.

A new beer was promptly delivered. Bride didn't drink it, of course, but Devyn did, aiding her illusion. They were both enablers.

"So . . . tell me about vampire weaknesses, then," Noelle said. She reached over, grabbed a few cashews from the bowl in the center of the table, and tossed them into her mouth. "Real ones, not shit from myths."

Bride shrugged, leaning back against her man. "I'm not the best source of information for that. I, well, I don't have any weaknesses."

"True story," Devyn said with pride.

"And I only recently learned there were other vampires out there," Bride continued. "I haven't spent a lot of time with them. They weren't exactly welcoming when I visited them underground."

Noelle scrubbed a hand down her pretty face. "You're *so* not helping."

Dallas risked another glance at Hector. Man was still watching Noelle, expression still blank. He'd wanted so badly to be wrong, but he'd been battling these types of visions for over a year now, and not a single one had failed to come to pass. He was going to sleep with Noelle, even knowing the outcome, and then Hector was going to sleep with Noelle.

"Do you think we failed to talk to Bride while filling out McKell's file?" Mia, too, propped her elbows on the table. She sat across from Noelle, allowing her to glare straight into the trainee's face. "I assure you, everything Bride knows, which amounts to shit, is in his file."

"Hey," Bride said at the same time an unimpressed Noelle said, "never hurts to return to a source with follow-up questions."

Mia shrugged. "Work the rest of the night, then. But me? I'm relaxing for once." Her chair skidded behind her as she stood. "The rest of you can go to hell." With that, she stomped to the bar.

Dallas was positive he heard every person at the table utter a quick prayer for the safe and speedy return of Mia's husband. She always morphed into Cranky McBitch when Kyrin was out of town. And as he'd only departed for a meeting with his people, the Arcadians, this morning, and planned to be gone for seven days, the next seven days were going to be long and torturous.

Bride regarded Noelle intently. "McKell giving you trouble or something?"

"Not me." She waved her fingers. "See, I still have these. He's messing with *Ava*. No one messes with my Ava."

The Rakans, who'd been without female companionship for two years before settling here on Earth, watched her with utter adoration. *Her* Ava? She had to know what kind of reaction that kind of statement would get, but she blithely continued munching on those cashews.

"Really?" Bride furrowed her brow, the picture of confusion and disappointment. "He cut off her fingers?"

"No, no, nothing like that." Noelle licked the salt from her nails, and Dallas moaned, deciding he and Hector were technically only acquaintances. "But he's got to be screwing with her mind, you know? He's not pissed at her for stabbing him. And he wants to work with her, even bargained with her."

Bride tapped her fingertips against her chin. "Hmm. That *is* odd. Usually he erupts with the slightest provocation."

Yeah. A real conundrum. "He wants to sleep with her," Dallas said. They acted as if they'd never met a man with a penis.

Johnny, he noticed, leaned forward to listen to the rest of the conversation, gaze sharp.

Bride asked for details about the bargain, but Noelle refused to give them. She loved her friend, and wouldn't betray her confidence, even for answers of her own. Great. Something else to like about her. Exactly what he hadn't needed.

"Is it true that vampires can't go out during the day?" Noelle asked.

"Not necessarily." Green eyes hardened, and it was clear Bride didn't like discussing her people. But she did it. Anything for her precious Devyn, who sometimes worked for AIR. What would it be like to have someone care that much? Dallas wondered. "We burn easily, so we like to avoid the sunlight, but we don't burst into flame or anything like that."

"And you heal quickly? Faster than humans?"

"Yes."

Noelle's head tilted to the side. "So what does it mean if you *don't* heal quickly?"

"That there's not enough AB negative in my diet."

"That's it? The only problem?"

"Yep."

Now it was Noelle's eyes that hardened, turning the gray to steel. "And when you're hungry, you'll eat anything?"

Dallas cast another glance to Hector, expecting to see more of the same. A blank mask. Only, his friend had his beer poised at his lips, his gaze gobbling up Noelle with massive amounts of heat. Had thoughts of biting and sucking pushed him over the edge?

Didn't matter, really. Here it was, unadulterated proof that Hector wanted Noelle.

I'll fight her appeal, Dallas thought, determined. No matter what the vision promised, he could control his body. He could say no. Even if Noelle stripped and straddled him while he was tied to a chair, slipping and sliding, begging—and shit. *None of that, you gutter-loving bastard.*

"I can't, no," Bride said. "Once I met Devyn, I couldn't drink from anyone but him. If I tried, I vomited."

"And can you blame her?" Devyn grinned like a man who had just experienced the best orgasm of his life. "My blood is the best."

Wasn't bragging when you spoke the truth. Dallas had no designs on the guy, but if either one of them had been a woman, Dallas would have tapped that. Confidence really flipped his lid.

"Mated vampires can't drink from anyone else," Bride added. "Whether the blood's good. Or bad."

Devyn clutched his heart as if he'd been stabbed.

"I wonder if there's a way to *force* the mating . . ." Noelle said, mind obviously drifting.

Johnny tried to gain her attention, but failed. Did he want to know more about Ava and McKell? Probably. Moron, Dallas thought again. Like there was *any* way the asshole would get a chance with those goods again. Ava wasn't stupid. Plus, the few times Dallas had seen her with Johnny, her disgust had been palpable.

Johnny would have better luck with a nice girl from church. Really, McKell was a stone-cold killer, and Dallas wasn't even sure *he* could handle Ava. Girl was a man-eater. And man-eaters were dangerous. *Real* dangerous. Junior twitched again.

Maybe *Dallas* should make a play for—he jumped to his feet with a curse. Everyone's attention swung to him, but he didn't care. The Schön queen had just materialized behind Johnny and was now tracing her fingertip along his shoulder. The trainee didn't seem to notice, was still snapping his fingers for Noelle's attention.

The queen's navy gaze locked on Dallas.

For a seemingly endless moment, he was paralyzed. Never had there been a more beautiful woman. She was petite in every way, almost delicate, like a china doll, with long, pale hair and utterly flawless skin. While looking at her, all a man wanted to do was protect her. After screwing her senseless, of course.

Breathe, damn it. Protecting and screwing her should be the last things on his mind. She had destroyed planets. Ruined countless civilizations. All without a single shred of remorse. And she did it through sex, by hitting men where they couldn't resist. Whoever she screwed became infected with her disease. And if the infected male didn't constantly infect others, in turn, he died.

It was a vicious, never-ending cycle.

Dallas had met her once before, on the day she'd come to this planet. He'd tried to kill her, failed, nearly allowed her to seduce him, despite everything he knew about her, and had battled midnight fantasies ever since. Fantasies that left him hard and aching and moaning for one little kiss of her lips.

God, she was gorgeous. And looked so soft. Smelled like fresh, dewy roses. And would probably taste like—

Fuck. *She's evil incarnate. Don't forget.*

"I've finally returned for you," she said in a smoky voice that rivaled Noelle's. She glided forward, closing the distance between them, tracing her fingers along Hector's scalp as she passed him. Like Johnny, he seemed oblivious.

"Get your fucking hands off him," Dallas snarled. He didn't mind the threat to himself. But to his friends? Hell, no. He wanted to race to her, choke her, watch her eyes close and her body flop uselessly, but he remained where he was.

With anyone else, he could have moved faster than the speed of light and attacked. He could have gotten into her head and forced her to do anything he wished. Sadly, with her, he was as human as he'd been before Mia's husband had healed him, changed him. His "powers" simply didn't work.

How? How did she render him so . . . ineffective?

He'd once cursed his abilities, hadn't wanted them, had thought they made him alien. Now, when he could have used them to save the goddamn world, he cursed the fact that he didn't have them.

"Uh, Dallas," Bride said, standing and waving her hand in front of his face. "Who are you talking to?"

"Who am I talking to?" His eyes nearly bugged out of his head. "Who do you think I'm talking—" He pressed his lips together as understanding dawned. The boys hadn't felt the queen. That had to mean they couldn't see her, either.

No reason to alarm anyone. And no reason to anger the queen—what was her name?—by mentioning her presence and possibly sending her fleeing. Not before he'd had a chance to kill her.

This time, he wouldn't fail.

Grinning, the queen wiggled her fingers at him. "Come, Dallas. Let's go outside. Chat."

He nodded. "I need some air," he told his friends. When Hector made to stand, as if to join him, Dallas shook his head. "Alone," he added. Then he stalked off without any more explanation, following the object of his hatred.

She reached the bar's front door, but didn't stop to open it. She merely walked through it, like a ghost. His stomach clenched. Maybe she *was* a ghost. A ghost who could take corporeal form for sex. And wasn't that just an utterly peachy thought? One, the pyre-gun at his back would be useless. And two, killing her would only be possible while sentencing himself to death.

He stomped outside. The sun was setting, the sky a hazy pink and purple, the air warm. Wonderland, the bar, sat in the middle of a strip club and a Taco Bell, so there was plenty of traffic coming and going through the parking lot.

The queen didn't stop until they stood between two of the metal buildings, hidden in the shadows. Dallas expected several of her soldiers to jump out and grab him—bitch always had her soldiers nearby—but all remained calm. That he could see.

He met her gaze, her beautiful, mesmerizing gaze, and felt himself melting, edging closer to—no, no, no. Grunting, he settled his weight on his heels. *She's the enemy*. He'd remind himself as many times as necessary. "Why are you here?"

Her white dress billowed in the breeze, caressing her. "I'm here for you," she said, matter-of-factly. Just then, her voice was almost childlike. Innocent, full of wonder.

Enemy. "And what do you want with me?"

"My name is Trinity," she said, ignoring him. She frowned, again almost childlike, only this time in a way that reminded him of a kid who hadn't gotten the lollipop she wanted. "Not that you asked."

"Or cared," he lied. Trinity. Merely a name, like his, or was there a deeper meaning to it? Any other name, and he wouldn't have wondered, but the literal translation of trinity was three. There was the woman, the disease, and . . . what? Something else? Something worse? His stomach did that clenching thing again. "Your soldiers are infecting my people. I want you gone." Forever.

How to do it, though? He withdrew his gun, and she might disappear before a single shot was fired off. Not that he even knew if that shot would burn her or mist through her like she'd done the door. Only one way to find out . . .

He had to touch her.

One step, two, he slowly moved toward her.

One step, two, she slowly backed away from him. "I'm sorry about your people, I truly am, but I need my men strong."

Careful. He stilled. "Their strength comes at a very destructive price."

"Yes." She stilled, as well.

"And you're okay with that?" As he tangled his hand through his hair, he stealthily took another step.

This time, she remained in place. "I have to be." Tears filled her eyes, turning them into blue pools of sadness. Startling, against her paling skin.

Should he clap for such a stellar performance now or later? "We found a cure, you know. You won't destroy this planet like you've done to so many others." Another step.

Again she remained in place. "Yes. I know all about your cure." Soft, gentle.

Of course she knew. Everyone she infected, and everyone *they* infected, became linked to her. She knew what they knew. Since AIR had captured one of her closest advisers—Nolan—and later healed him with Bride's blood, she'd known before they had that the guy was on the mend.

Another step toward her, another and another. Almost . . . there . . . "Aren't you worried?" He reached out, so close . . .

In the blink of an eye, she was farther down the alley, increasing the distance between them. Dallas almost shouted, "To hell with it," and grabbed his gun. Only the need for more answers kept him quiet and still.

Damn her. There had to be a way to overpower her, here, now. *Steady.*

"Am I worried that the cure will kill me, since I'm the source of the infection?" She laughed, a tinkling sound. "No. But are you sure the cure works? Are you sure the disease isn't hiding, pretending to be eradicated? Waiting for a chance to strike?"

Junior, the idiot, twitched. That laugh . . . *Enemy, enemy, enemy.* The hair-trigger arousal had to end. And what had happened to her tears? Her eyes were now dry, color blooming prettily in her cheeks.

"Yeah," he said, determined to try again. One step, two. "I'm sure." She wouldn't bait him into believing otherwise.

All of Nolan's symptoms had vanished. The desire to eat human flesh, the oozing sores that had covered his body, the gray, flaking skin and total loss of hair. And since the disease was a living, mindless being, with a never-ending hunger, constantly growing until it had outgrown its host and required the excess to be drained into *another* vessel, there was no way it could "pretend" to be gone.

He mentioned none of that, however. Let her think she'd convinced him. "What do you want from me, Trinity?" he asked again, even as he continued to move toward her.

"I wish to speak to your leader."

Oh, really. "She's inside the bar." He stopped, held out his hand, expectant. "Come on. I'll take you to her right now."

Trinity shook her head, blond hair dancing over her arms. "You will be my ambassador," she said. "I will speak through you."

His arm fell heavily to his side. Dread washed

through him, chilling his blood. "And just how will you speak through me?"

"I'll infect you." A return of the sadness, as if she cared, hurt for him.

She meant to control him through the mental link, he realized. Now he backed away from her. No distance would be great enough. "Not just no, but hell, no." If she turned on the charm, if she sent her guard to hold him down, he would . . . what? Fuck! No answers. He had no answers.

Her eyelids slitted, dark lashes fusing together. "You will cave in this matter, Dallas." Hard, determined.

"No," he grated. "I won't."

"Let's test your resolve, then, shall we? For every week that you deny me, I will personally infect one of your friends. Beginning tonight . . ." Without another word, she disappeared.

Leaving him alone with her threat. A threat he had no doubt she would see through.

Eight

The hunger woke him.

Terrible pains clawed through McKell's body, first tearing out of his stomach, then ripping his ribs apart, then entering his bloodstream and turning every cell he possessed into a dagger. He hurt, ached, throbbed. Too . . . much . . . His fangs were sharpened, ready, his lips bleeding. He must have gnashed them in his sleep, trying to feed from *himself*.

He'd woken up hungry before, but never like this. As if he could die at any moment. Why had he now?

He forced his focus past the pain and took stock, gaze cataloging his surroundings. Small bedroom. Moonlight seeped past the slatted window. Pictures of Ava and Noelle hung on the wall. In them, the two were smiling, flipping off the camera, or standing over unconscious people they'd obviously beaten to pulp.

Mmm, pulp. The pain broke free, once again agonizing him.

Concentrate. Clearly, he was still in Ava's home. He recalled coming here, insisting she doctor him, and then deciding to "nap" in her bed. Partially to piss her off, and partially because he hadn't wanted to brave the sunlight again. He'd never meant to actually fall asleep. Had thought to put distance between them, yet keep her close, while his body healed and his mind centered.

The moment he'd climbed into this bed and realized that her butterscotch scent infused the sheets, his shaft had hardened, plaguing him, demanding he stomp out of the bedroom, find her, and finally have her. All of her. Body, blood. Devotion. He'd resisted, assuming the lust alone would keep him awake.

Lust he still didn't understand.

Well, right now he did. Not only was Ava beneath him—mmm, beneath him—she was over him, beside him, surrounding him. Damned covers! His cock hardened once more, desire sparking back to dazzling life and chasing away some of the pain. But why her? he wondered for the thousandth time since meeting her. She was contrary, argumentative, violent, and determined to lock him away.

Because she had agreed to help him? Not that he fully trusted her in that matter. But no, that made no sense. He'd wanted her *before* her agreement. Wanted her for *more* than his master plan.

A plan that still involved using her scent to attract other vampires. No bloodsucker would be able to resist her. They would smell her, flock to her, and he could swoop in, capture them, and demand the answers he sought. No more hunting them down, only to have them run and hide in this world he hadn't yet learned how to navigate.

"McKell," Ava suddenly shouted.

Danger! She was in danger.

He was off the bed and rushing into the kitchen a moment later. He expected to find her injured or battling an intruder. Instead, she sat at the kitchen table, calmly sipping sweetened coffee.

"What?" he snarled, panting, hurting again, desperate to destroy whatever had scared her. His mouth watered, and his claws sprang out. He would rip into—

"You're lazy. You slept all damn day."

"So you are unharmed?"

"Yes. What made you think I would be harmed?"

"You shouted."

"Like I said, you're lazy. I took exception."

Deep breath in, deep breath out. He swallowed the excess moisture and retracted his claws. Another deep breath, and he was calm enough to claim the chair across from her. "I was healing." And he wasn't yet at full strength. Besides the overwhelming hunger, there was still a twinge in his side where she'd stabbed him.

"That's a lame excuse. Admit it. You're lazy."

Though he wanted to shake her for maligning his character, he merely studied her. She'd pulled her curls into a twist, exposing the elegant length of her neck. At the base, her pulse fluttered exquisitely. Mouth . . . watering . . . again . . . She wore a black T-shirt, faded jeans, and tennis shoes. Average clothing on a far from average body. Those curves were sinful.

"I'm hungry," he said, voice raw, coarse. Too easily

did he recall how delicious she'd tasted. How strong she'd made him feel from just those sips. How much stronger would she make him if he drained her? "Feed me."

"No." Another swallow of that coffee, her throat moving sensually. "And don't forget our bargain. You don't drink from me unless I say it's okay. And I haven't. Said it's okay, that is."

Stupidest bargain he'd ever made. But then, he hadn't realized he would wake up in this pathetic state. And even if he had, food shouldn't have a choice. Humans didn't ask vegetables if they felt like being consumed, did they?

"Then we'll have to go out," he said. Now. Before he forgot himself.

Still calm, she blew into her mug. "You'll have to dress first." She sipped, then settled the cup on the counter.

He glanced down at himself. Shirtless, necklace bloodstained, stitches on display, bandage long gone. Pants ripped and dirty. "Fine. I'll shower, and you order a pizza." That would save him time and effort.

She blinked over at him, confused. "I'm not hungry."

"I know, but I am."

Another few blinks. "I shouldn't have to remind you of this, but you don't eat food."

"But I do eat the delivery boys and girls." Something he'd never attempted before, but Maureen—damn it, Bride Targon—during one of his brief conversations with her, had assured him delivery people were "tasty." He only wished he could rely on Bride for the rest of his needs. Not for information, but for blood and sex.

Except, his hunger and desire actually *waned* at the thought of drinking from and sleeping with her. Ava, however . . . hello, renewed desire. He frowned. Anyway. He couldn't rely on Bride for *anything*. Though she'd lived on the surface most of her life, she had never tried to blend with humans during daylight hours, so she couldn't help *him* do so. Plus, her husband was an ass who wanted McKell's heart on a platter, and rarely allowed them to interact.

"I—you—*argh*!" Ava pounded her fist against the tabletop, rattling her coffee and sending creamy liquid over the rim of the cup. Her dark eyes were blazing, and he realized she'd never been as calm as she'd wanted him to believe. She was angry. Why? Because he wanted to eat someone else?

No, he thought next. This anger was far too strong, too deeply rooted, for that. But he wouldn't concern himself with pondering the answer; it didn't matter. They were using each other. Nothing more. Learning about her wasn't on the agenda.

"Just make the call," he said, standing.

"Hell, no. One, I'm not springing for a pizza I won't eat, and two, no one will ever deliver here again."

"No one will ever know what happened."

A muscle ticked below her eye. "How will you make them forget?"

"I'll command them to do so."

"And that'll work?"

He nodded.

"Prove it."

The Voice came easily to most vampires. McKell, not so much. He'd struggled his entire life. He could use it, but he had to concentrate. He didn't know why.

Rather than argue and use up what remained of his strength, he peered deeply into Ava's eyes, those dark, fathomless eyes, and held out his hand. He focused, drew on his resolve, his will, let it rise up and spill from his lips. "Take my hand," he commanded, his voice low, a hum of power in the undercurrent.

A gasp left her as her arm lifted, shaking, halting every few inches, as if she fought each movement. Finally, her fingers made contact with his, and another gasp left her. And hell, he gasped, too. Such warm, soft skin she had. Where they touched, he sizzled.

His hunger intensified. *Do not grab her. Do not bite her.* He forced his arm to fall to his side, severing contact. *Do not groan.* "Proven. Now make the damn call." He turned away. One step, two.

"Why didn't you command Noelle and me to leave the woods that first night?" she said, stopping him.

"I wanted to see what you would do." Besides, he'd had no intention of showing all his weapons during the first battle.

With that thought, he realized he'd always meant

to see her again. What the hell was wrong with him? She. Was. Food.

At last, he stalked away from her and into the bathroom. Distance, that's what he needed. And time to think. *Like that helped before.* Scowling, he programmed the enzyme shower, something he'd learned to use on the streets of New Chicago, and stepped inside. In seconds, the dry spray cleaned his skin, his wound, and even his pants.

When he emerged and entered the bedroom, Ava sat at the edge of the mattress, the bed now made, not a wrinkle in the comforter. She was glaring at him.

"When will the pizza arrive?" He hadn't meant to snap at her, but damn it, he was on edge. And those few minutes apart hadn't really cooled his desire for her. Still. Seeing her, being near her, eased him somewhat. Not the hunger, never that, but the pain.

Stubborn, always stubborn, she crossed her arms over her chest. "I didn't call."

He stopped in front of her, forcing her to look up . . . up . . . up. "Is this a power play, Ava? Because I assure you, you won't win." As he spoke, his own sense of anger rose. White-hot, blistering. "Do you think to keep me weak? Expecting AIR to bust in and cart me away?"

"No!"

Could he believe her? Yes or no, that brought up another question. "Why *didn't* you call AIR?" Noelle had asked the same—his sensitive hearing had tuned into their entire conversation—but Ava had never really answered.

"Are we sharing excerpts from our diaries now? Do you want to tell me why you picked me, the girl who stabbed you? And don't give me that bullshit about my owing you." She was breathing heavily, blood rushing through her veins.

She was like a lick of flame, and he was the kindling. *Touch her again . . . kiss her . . . taste her . . .* He leaned down, needing her, desperate, lost—

"McKell," she rasped. "Answer."

He straightened with a jerk, then stepped away. They hadn't so much as brushed against each other, but his skin was sizzling again. All over. If he wasn't careful, he would be on her.

"No, we are not going to share our diary excerpts now. We're going to leave."

"What?"

"You heard me. Let's go."

Ava followed McKell through the winding hallways of her building, painfully aware of the plain gray walls, the scratches in the metal and brick, the dirt staining the concrete floors, and then outside, into the cooling night air. Garbage bags lined the sidewalks. Pickup was tomorrow. The scents of rotting food wafted, among other indelicate things, and her cheeks heated. *Doesn't matter.* This was home. He could deal.

Where the hell was he going, anyway? He was still

shirtless, that bone necklace clanging with his every step, and people were staring. Male, female, didn't matter. The males recognized a threat, and the females spotted possible prey. Unable to stop herself, Ava hissed at them all.

Finally, in front of a nearby alley, he settled and crooked his finger at a woman across the street. The woman was alone, carrying two grocery bags, but that didn't dissuade her from crossing the street as if in a trance. Maybe she was. The bastard had powers Ava hadn't known about. He'd told her to place her hand in his, and she hadn't been able to prevent herself from doing so.

If he had told her to stab herself, she would have done that, too.

He was far more dangerous than she'd realized. Far sexier, too.

When he'd told her—so superiorly—that he was hungry, she'd wanted to jump up on the table and become his buffet. All you can eat. To have all that power at her fingertips . . . demanding everything . . . Oh, yes. *Far* more dangerous.

Power was an aphrodisiac to Ava. And the thought of people seeing them together, thinking she had been the one female to tame him, to gentle him, God, it was tempting. The pride she would feel . . . the respect she would gain, she might never know it's equal.

The shame, too. She wouldn't have tamed him, gentled him. No one would *ever* be able to do so. And he was a criminal, she reminded herself. A target of

AIR. If she needed the reminder a thousand times, she'd issue the reminder a thousand and one. She didn't need her coworkers laughing at her, telling her how easy she was. Even though the females would be jealous. No question.

Joking with Noelle about nailing him, fine. But forever being labeled the agent who slept with her targets? No, thank you. She'd told herself that before, but the possibility hadn't been as . . . imminent then. He'd stood in front of her, the bed behind her, desire heating her up, and she'd again fought the urge to offer herself to him. However he wanted her.

Only thing that had stopped her then was the thought that he would reduce her to a meal. A walking cup of joe. Nothing more, nothing less. The way he'd sneered about the pizza delivery boy . . . his disdain for "food" had never been clearer, and it had been pretty clear before. Her hands fisted.

"You better not kill her," Ava gritted out.

"Believe me. She'll love what I do."

"Braggart." Bastard. And if the bitch tried for anything more than a one-way transfusion, she'd lose her tongue. Tongue necklaces were probably a lot prettier than finger necklaces.

"I spoke only the truth."

Shouldn't he demand that *Ava* feed him? she wondered again.

I thought you wanted to be more than a food source.

She did. That didn't mean he shouldn't fight for her capitulation. Not that she'd give it. But if anyone was going to love something McKell did, it should be Ava. He owned her room and board. Well, maybe not board. Now, though, she couldn't protest what he was about to do. She'd seem weak; he'd realize how close she was—no, had been—to giving in. She was stronger now. Really.

The woman reached him, and he tugged her deep into the alley, his gaze detached. Ava followed, studying. The woman was taller than her by several inches, though dressed just as plainly in jeans and a white T-shirt. She had blond hair, cut to frame her pointed chin. Sharp cheekbones, a blade of a nose. Pretty, in an aristocratic kind of way.

Did McKell favor that kind of look?

"You shouldn't come when a man summons you," Ava snapped at her. Just to be helpful, as she often was. It had nothing to do with raging jealousy. "That kind of makes you a dog."

The woman paid her no attention. "Hi," she said to McKell, her voice sultry and inviting. "It's nice to meet you."

McKell backed her up against the brick wall, and Ava's jaw clenched. "Bags," he said.

The woman placed her bags at her feet and straightened. McKell gripped her shoulders and swung her around, so that he faced Ava. His fangs were so long they gapped over his bottom lip. They were so white they practically glittered. Ava gulped as her belly quivered.

"I'm going to drink from you, and you're going to

let me," he said. His gaze never left Ava. "Afterward, you'll leave me without looking back and never recall what was done."

There was that powerful voice, washing over her, causing goose bumps to form on her skin. Her needy, sensitive, aching skin. And somehow, she knew that rubbing all over him was the only way to assuage that ache.

"Yes," the woman said on a happy sigh. Her head tilted to the side. "Yes."

Still McKell's gaze remained on Ava as he descended, as those teeth sank deep, as his lips moved, as he sucked and sucked and sucked. She expected his hands—those big, gorgeous hands—to caress the woman, but his grip on her shoulders never even loosened.

Did the female taste better than Ava? Was McKell enjoying himself? She crossed her arms over her chest, and tapped her foot.

"Sometime today," she muttered.

He growled like a caged animal.

Moonlight caressed him, and his violet eyes began to glow. So purple, so beautiful. So hypnotic, dragging her down, drowning her in waves of that neediness. The emerald swirled there, too, and became her lifeline, reminding her of where she was, who she was, who *he* was, and their purpose. Feeding him.

Me, me, me. My turn. He really was too beautiful for his own good, she thought, disgusted with herself. Most likely, no woman had ever resisted him. But all that superiority, all that disdain . . . no way. Good. Another reminder. Ava couldn't even make things work with guys who worshipped her. There was no way she'd be able to make things work with McKell. Not that she wanted to make things work with him.

Having him inside her apartment all the time, messing things up, expecting her to call and check in. No, no, and no. Which was why she was happy as a commitment-phobe.

Despite her admiration for male power, she liked to be in control of her own life, liked her things where she left them, liked having no one to answer to, and there was nothing wrong with that.

But what about McKell? What did he like? How many girlfriends had he had? Had he ever been in love with a vampire? A human?

Finally, he released the woman.

She stumbled backward, eyes glazed, hand fluttering to her neck. "Oh, my," she said with a laugh. "Thank you." Then she gathered her bags and sauntered off, as if nothing had happened. As ordered, she never once looked back.

McKell, too, stumbled back, though the brick wall stopped him from going too far. He stood there a minute, panting, eyes closing, skin . . . paling?

Ava frowned. "Are you okay?"

"Her blood must have been poisoned. The first few sips were good, but after that . . . and now my stomach hurts."

"Wait. Poisoned how?"

"I don't know." Without any more warning, he hunched over and vomited.

Ava spun, giving him as much privacy as she could. Over and over he retched. Maybe she was as cruel and wicked as her mother had always said, because a part of her was glad that woman's blood wouldn't be flowing through his veins all night.

"This ever happened before?" she asked.

"A few times," he said, spitting. "Lately."

Great. Maybe he was sick, rather than poisoned. But just how did one find out? Human doctors, even otherworlder doctors, had never dealt with vampires.

First things first. "Better?"

"Yes, but still hungry."

Nothing she could do about that just yet. She didn't want him vomiting her blood, too. "Just . . . stay here, okay."

He protested, but was too weak to follow as she raced to the pharmacy two blocks away. There she bought him an "Our Meds Are Best" T-shirt and a bottle of mouthwash. She was huffing and sweating by the time she returned, but he was exactly where she'd left him.

"By the way, you owe me twenty-seven forty-eight," she told him, handing him both items.

"And you owe me a meal." He tugged on the shirt. The material was tight, straining against his biceps. He should have looked ridiculous, but just looked sweeter, as if he didn't take himself too seriously.

She tucked his necklace under the collar, and he

used the mouthwash, rising several times for several minutes. While he couldn't speak, she said, "I *owe* you? Really? I came with you to find someone. I stood by silent and patient while you ate. So how is your lack of sustenance my fault?"

He spit the final mouthful onto the already filthy concrete and glared down at her. "I don't know. It just is."

Irrational shit. "You sound like Noelle."

"Then we're now best friends?" he asked drily. "Finally, I can die a happy man."

At least his warped sense of humor had returned. "Let's be honest. We're hardly friends at all. I mean, I can barely stand you." Okay, that was harsh, even for her. There was no time to apologize, though. Fine. There was time; she simply opted not to use it. She could still picture his teeth inside that woman's vein.

His eyes narrowed, but not enough to hide the challenge suddenly banked there. "You like me. I know it."

She tried not to shiver. "What makes you so sure?"

"I'm strong, courageous, and handsome. What's not to like?"

I like. "You just described about a thousand people I know."

He chomped his teeth at her. "Yes, but none are vampires."

And were therefore unworthy? Hello, renewed superiority. "Fangs do not make the man, you know."

Before he could reply, before she could start shivering again, she added, "So where are we going to round up those other vampires?" The sooner their association ended, the sooner the madness ended.

"I can't round anyone up until I eat."

"What if the next human is . . . poisoned?" What she really wanted to say: what if you're too sick to keep *anyone* down?

He scrubbed a hand down his face. "I don't know."

"Look. Just tell me where to go and what to do. You can return to my apartment, rest, rejuvenate, whatever, and I'll bag and tag you a vampire." Boom. Done.

"No!" As his denial echoed between them, his violet irises once again glowed. "Promise me you will never chase a vampire without me."

Great. They weren't even in a relationship, and he was already issuing orders. "Why?"

He splayed his arms, as if he were the last sane man and dealing with a roomful of senseless women. "Because I said."

"Oh, well, in that case . . . fuck you. Find me when you grow a brain." She gave him a pinkie wave and a smile and turned away, then strode out of the shadows and onto the moonlit sidewalk. Like his meal, she never glanced back.

Thankfully, he followed, and was soon keeping pace at her side. "Do you not realize the fire you play with, human? I'm your superior."

"I knew you felt that way!" No longer was he content to merely hint about it, either.

"Of course you did. I made no secret of the truth. How could I, when it's so obvious?"

Red suddenly dotted her vision, and she had trouble drawing in a breath. Well, a breath that wasn't laced with "fire." She forgot their bargain, forgot that the man had just vomited his guts and might be dying from some horrible vampire sickness. "I'm gonna teach you just how inferior you are, you bastard!"

"Good luck."

Oh, he would pay for that.

Ava removed the mini-taser she had stored in her back pocket and jammed it into his neck. His body vibrated, he struggled to speak, gurgled, and then, when she removed her thumb from the "fry" button, he fell to the ground, twitching.

Ava kept walking.

Nine

She had a temper. He knew that. His fault for forgetting.

Volts of electricity continued to pass through McKell, even though Ava had removed the weapon. His muscles convulsed, locking onto bones, and he could only sit there, immobile, as humans avoided him and Ava increased the distance between them.

If she thought she could escape him, she would soon learn the impossibility of such a task. She would *never* be able to escape him. He would always be able to find her. He knew her scent, her taste, the essence of her branded into his every cell.

But that wasn't the only reason he would forever be able to find her. His teeth gnashed together as he contemplated the truth. He'd thrown up a meal. Again. And even while drinking from the strange human female, he'd been hungry for Ava. Had almost tossed the woman aside and leapt at her, just to have that curvy body near him, his hands all over her, his teeth—or any part of him—inside her. His possession evident to her, to the world.

He'd suspected the worst before, but had refused to ponder or worry. Now he knew, and there was no stopping the worry. She belonged to him. She was his. His woman, his mate. Unless he did something about it, he would never again be able to successfully drink from any one but her.

That was the way of the vampires. When they encountered their mate, the person whose body chemistry best fit their own, they craved that mate and only that mate. No one else could sustain them.

They could have sex with other people, yes. Not that he wanted anyone but Ava. But food? No. It was Ava's blood for him, and only Ava's.

That wasn't a problem for human Ava, of course. She could eat anything she wished. But for McKell? That was a serious fucking problem! His woman was refusing to feed him.

Unfair, and one of the reasons vampires prayed they never mated with a human. Those prayers were usually answered. To his knowledge only one vampire had ever been paired with a human. Still. He'd deal with the food issue later. The biggest problem right now was the sex thing. He and Ava were a couple, yet *Ava* was resisting him and could sleep with someone else.

And she just might. Clearly she didn't care about McKell. She'd allowed him to drink another woman's blood, without protest. She'd actually aided him. Why hadn't she raged? Attacked? Tried to kill the woman for daring to accept *her* man?

Damn, damn, damn. Why him? Why a human? A lowly human? He deserved better, damn it!

He wasn't the first vampire to despise his mate. Not that he hated Ava, but he didn't want to live with the stubborn baggage forever. He just wanted to sip from her for a few years. And keep her naked and in his bed for a few decades.

God, he was so confused about that woman.

Thankfully, when he tired of her, he had two methods of bond-breaking to choose from. The first—a potion. He had only to drink it, and his body would forget it had ever smelled Ava, ever touched her or tasted her. But afterward, he would never again be allowed to see her. Never again be allowed near her. The moment he encountered her, his body would remember, rendering the potion useless, and he would be back where he started.

The second method—death. Not his. Hers. He could kill her, and his body would return to normal. Forever.

Yet neither method currently appealed to him. He needed her help. Yes, he could have found the other topside vampires on his own. Yes, he could have continued on with his life without her, no problem. But if she was with him, helping him, AIR would leave him alone. At least for a little while.

Even when they were sending agents into the forest to arrest you, you were entertained, not bothered. He ignored that line of thought. He wanted to be left alone. Of course. Who wouldn't?

So. He would continue his association with Ava. As long as *she* never drank *his* blood, they would not be officially married, and he could more easily leave her—and find someone else, someone more appropriate—when the time came.

"Need some help, gorgeous?" a female asked him, returning his thoughts to the present.

He blinked up at her. She'd stopped in front of him, and held out a hand to hoist him up. She was in her mid-thirties, with dark hair, freckles, glasses, and a cute button nose. Innocent, kind, and just begging to be ripped into pieces.

Humans needed to be more careful about who they attempted to aid. And since he was now living here, it was up to him to instruct them. He hissed at her, revealing the sharpness of his fangs. She yelped, paled, and scampered away.

"You're welcome," he called as he lumbered to his feet.

He stood there a moment, dizzy, stars winking over his vision, stomach twisting, lungs trying to inflate. *So hungry* . . . But, damn it, the complication hadn't gone away.

He'd promised Ava he wouldn't drink from her without permission. Why had he done such a stupid thing? he wondered again. Until he consumed the vampire potion, she would be the only person he *could* drink from. He wouldn't tell her that, of course. She would realize the power she held over him. Knowing her, and he was beginning to think he did, she would exploit that power.

Therefore, he would have to seduce her and *make* her willing. McKell sighed, ignoring the anticipation working through him and concentrating on the dread. Dirty work, but a vampire had to do what a vampire had to do.

Ava held her new cell to her ear. Noelle had given her the small black phone to replace her old one. It was the "prezzie" she'd hidden between the naughty cop and curious kitty costumes, and a relief to find, rather than some kind of vibrator with fangs, which Ava wouldn't have put past her friend. She vowed to be careful with this one. But as her friend spoke, her fingers clenched so tightly the plastic cracked.

"You want me to *what*?" Ava demanded, even as she loosened her grip.

At her outburst, the people walking in front of her glanced back. She frowned at them and motioned for them to turn around and continue along the sidewalk, before snaking a corner to escape their notice.

"You heard me. Bring McKell to the bar," Noelle repeated.

And place him directly in the line of fire? "No. No way." She twisted to the side to avoid colliding with a group of teens headed in the opposite direction.

She'd entered a newer neighborhood than her own, one of shops rather than apartments, and the streets were far more crowded. Plus, Friday night, everyone was looking for a good time.

"Why not?" Noelle asked.

"Uh, why not?" Bright lights pulsed on her right,

a twinkling kaleidoscope of pinks, blues, and greens, blurring together as she raked her brain for an excuse. Lost in thought as she was, she tripped over her own feet. *Enough.* Scowling, she righted herself and stomped to the nearest building, then leaned against the cold stone. Her heart pounded against her ribs, like a jackhammer against concrete. "Just . . . because."

There was a crackle of silence. Then, "You afraid the other agents will whack him?"

Yes! "No, of course not. One, he can take care of himself, and two, I don't care if he lives or dies." Even saying the words hurt. Die. McKell. He'd been sick, but still she'd tasered him. What kind of person was she? Worse, she'd left him to fend for himself in his weakened condition.

"Liar. You want to protect him. You *lurve* him."

One of her ribs finally cracked. "I hurt him, Noelle." Was he okay? He should have recovered by now. Should have tracked her down and screamed at her. Maybe demanded she kiss him all better. But there was no sign of him. Not left, not right, not straight ahead.

Noelle laughed. "Please. Whatever you did was foreplay."

"Our definition of foreplay differs greatly."

"Whatever you need to think to make yourself feel better about your love of the rough stuff. So lookit," her friend added before she could reply. "The Schön queen was here, and we could really use McKell's help."

"What?" Another sighting? *Now?*

"What's with your ears tonight? Are you really going to make me repeat everything?"

"Continue or die!"

Another laugh, wine-rich, like smoke wafting over the line. "Here's the scoop. That diseased bitch talked to Dallas. Apparently, he was the only one who could see and hear her. Anyway, he's now put the bar on lockdown, and he and the other agents are interrogating everyone here, finding out what they saw, heard, testing the place, that kind of thing."

Ava gulped. Okay. That wasn't so bad. "And we need McKell because. . . ?"

"Duh. Because he can stop time."

"So? The queen is long gone by now. What will stopping time help?" Not that it mattered. There was nothing Noelle could say to convince her to escort McKell into a roomful of angry agents. Someone would try to stun him, guaranteed. That would piss off McKell. A hungry, possibly sick McKell.

A bloodbath would ensue.

She couldn't let that happen. She had a bargain to uphold, and she took her bargains very seriously. Even though she had often double-crossed people in the past, never actually fulfilling her end of their bargains. Sometimes you had to cheat to win, and she'd never minded cheating. Winning was *important*. Never more so than now, but for some reason, she couldn't talk herself into double-crossing McKell.

Maybe because she felt guilty for all the harm she'd

caused him. Maybe because she hoped to prove that humans weren't inferior to vampires. In any way. She didn't know. All she knew was that she wanted him safe.

Tasering him had been a small . . . complication on the road to his safety, but one she would (maybe) apologize for. After he apologized for his attitude.

Where the hell was he?

"Are you listening to me?" Noelle asked on a sigh.

Ava blinked back to focus, and realized she been silent for several minutes. "No. Sorry. But listen, McKell's sick. He can't keep anything down, and—"

"Wait. What? Sick how?"

"He just threw up his dinner."

"You?"

"No. Someone else."

"Interesting. Hang on for a sec, K?"

"Why? What are you—"

Static filled the line. One minute passed, two, allowing Ava's imagination to take flight through poisoned clouds and an acid storm. What. The. Hell? Noelle wouldn't tell the other agents about McKell's condition. She wouldn't. Unless she thought she needed to protect Ava. Then nothing would stop her.

Trembling now, Ava watched for McKell. Still no sign of him, and her heart began pounding for an entirely different reason. What if she'd injured him more than she'd meant? What if someone was even now picking his pockets or stabbing him, and he was unable to defend himself?

She kicked into gear, heading in the direction she'd left him, the phone still clutched to her ear.

"I know something you don't know," Noelle suddenly said in a happy, singsong voice. "And it's about vampires."

"Tell me!"

"I thought we'd have to force this issue, but looks like your overwhelming appeal took over."

"What do you mean? Explain, or I swear to God I'll burn your mansion down." She snaked the corner and increased her speed.

"With my mother in it?" Noelle asked hopefully.

"No."

"Oh. Too bad. Now I have the need to take this secret to my grave."

"Just tell me!"

"I love when you beg."

"Noelle."

"Fine. I think I know why McKell wants to hang out with you so badly."

Because she was smart, talented, and capable? "Why?"

"Because you're his woman."

Way better than her answer, she thought, steps faltering. "I don't understand."

"Remember when you told me he vomits after drinking blood?"

"Since I told you a few minutes ago, yeah, I think I recall a little bit of that conversation."

"*Such* a pain," Noelle *tsk*ed. "*Anyway*. Earlier, you

also mentioned that he'd had a little of your blood and was able to keep it down. You know, when he sucked on your tongue."

"Yeah. So."

"So. Hold your applause until the end of my speech. Like I said, you're his woman. He won't be able to drink from anyone but you without . . . what? Vomiting." An expectant pause. "You may clap now."

Was it bad that she wanted to? "His woman? No way." And yet, the words pleased her on an elemental, primal level. The thought of McKell only being able to sink those teeth into her . . . the thought of McKell needing her . . . the thought of McKell enjoying her and only her . . . yes, yes and yes. But . . .

The plastic phone cracked a little more. *No, no, and no*, she thought next, panic suddenly infusing her bloodstream. If that were the case, he would never leave her alone. He would be around all the damn time. He would expect her to obey him, the superior bastard.

Vampires are better than humans, she inwardly mocked. As if! She was just as good as any vampire. She was worthy, damn it.

Besides, she'd already decided not to become romantically entangled with McKell. Well, part of her had. If he were to drink from her every damn day, she wouldn't be able to keep her hands from roaming over that delicious-looking body. And if she couldn't keep her hands off his body, they would end up in bed.

She couldn't let that happen. No matter how much she wanted it.

Thank God he was such an ass. Every time he opened his beautiful mouth, resisting him physically got a little easier. Right? She couldn't remember. Just then, all she could recall was the intense desire she'd experienced when he'd kissed her and the powerful jealousy she'd experienced when he'd bitten that other woman.

"So why do you need McKell's time-stopping skills at the bar?" she asked, returning to a less upsetting topic.

"If he can stop time, maybe he can reverse time. And if he can reverse time, we can pounce while the queen is here, distracted and talking to Dallas."

"But if he reverses time, won't that affect you? I mean, you still wouldn't know the queen was there." And how would it affect Ava? Would a time reversal wipe away the memory of McKell's kiss?

"Well, stopping time doesn't affect McKell. Maybe reversing it won't affect him, either."

"Nice deflection, but you didn't answer my question. What if the reversal affects *you*?"

"I don't know," Noelle replied on a sigh. "Maybe it won't. Maybe he can reverse time for select individuals, allowing those of his choosing to remain unaffected like him."

"That's a lot of maybes."

"Actually, that's two maybes. Just ask him if he can do it, will ya?"

"I'll ask, but he'll refuse to help." Hopefully. Ava's step faltered a second time. She *wanted* McKell to refuse her? Just to retain the memory of his lips pressed against hers? How selfish was she? "He's not happy with me at the moment."

Noelle moaned. "What'd you do this time?"

"What makes you think I did something? I'm—"

"Earlier you said you hurt him. What'd you do, Ava?"

She had to say it, didn't she? "I, uh, kind of tasered him."

Another moan sounded, then a sigh. "Okay. This isn't completely hopeless. While he's writhing in agony, go buy him a sappy card. That always lets people know you're almost sorry."

"There you are," McKell's butterscotch voice said.

Ava yelped in surprise and nearly dropped the phone. She must have lost focus—again—because she realized he was now keeping pace beside her, as if nothing bad had transpired between them. He appeared fine. Pale, but fine.

Thank God. Relief speared her, stronger than any other emotion she'd experienced that day.

"I'll be there," she told Noelle, "no matter what. As for him, he's not writhing, so there's no need for the card. But he may or may not be with me." She severed the connection before her friend could reply and pocketed the phone.

"Be where?" McKell asked.

"A bar." She grabbed his wrist. Electric currents

must have still raced underneath his skin, because the sizzle seeped into *her*. She turned him, so that they were heading in the other direction. His violet gaze remained locked on her, his lids at half-mast, his lips soft and . . . ready?

Heat bloomed in her cheeks. Was he thinking about drinking from her? She waited for him to try, breathless. Even waited for him to try and take a swing at her for bringing him down like a mangy animal. He did neither. Unfortunately.

Damn it. What was wrong with her, wanting him to make a play for her like that? *Any* play.

"Him who?" he demanded as they meandered down the street.

"You," she answered honestly.

The tension in his shoulders eased. Tension she hadn't noticed before. "So you weren't wanting the aid of another man?"

"No." She could barely handle McKell.

"Then I won't spank you."

McKell . . . spanking her . . . *Someone get this man a paddle.* "Gee. Thanks." Good. There'd been no intrigue in her tone.

"You're welcome. So where are we going? A bar, you said?"

"Not yet." She pointed to a building across the street, even as she raced to the other side. He never fell behind, but he did grab her just before she hit the curb, jerking her to the right.

"What?" she demanded, surprised.

His expression was as tense as his body had been. "I didn't want you walking into . . . nothing. Just be more careful."

Walking into what? She glanced around, saw nothing out of the ordinary. Weird vampire.

"So we're going to Starbucks?" he asked, giving her a little push forward. "How will a coffee help me?"

"You're not the only one who gets thirsty." She entered the building, and immediately cursed under her breath. Despite the late hour, there was a crowd. Was everyone in need of a pick-me-up?

She found a place at the end of the line, noting the way every female there watched McKell. Some stealthily, some with outright awe. Ava couldn't blame them, but she did resent them. *He's mine*, she wanted to shout. Which was absurd.

Had to be Noelle's proclamation. *You're his woman.* To his credit, he seemed completely oblivious to the sudden surge of estrogen and pheromones wafting his way.

"So. This bar," he said.

Ripples of feminine pleasure accompanied his low, purring timbre.

"Right. The bar," she replied. "I'm sorry, but hunting you-know-whats has to be put on hold."

His eyebrows furrowed together, a slash of black against the creamy expanse of his skin. "Because I was a naughty boy?"

McKell . . . naughty . . . She gulped, her blood heating dangerously. He'd said that on purpose, the diabolical bastard. Now all she could think about was naked bodies straining together. *As if you can blame* him. *You were thinking about that, anyway.*

"No. Because I'm an agent, and I have a job to do."

"Oh, well. I'll go with you and help."

Exactly what Noelle had wanted. Exactly what Ava had told her friend wouldn't happen. Yet he'd offered easily, without being asked, without whining.

"You're sick." As she spoke, she watched him closely, gauging his reaction. His expression never changed. No fear, no upset. "You should be resting."

"I'll never be too sick to protect you." Seductively uttered, as if they were discussing favorite sexual positions. Oh, yes. He was doing it on purpose, and she had *every* right to blame him. And punish him. With a severe tongue-lashing.

She tried to mask her shiver with a cough. "I think I've proven that I can take care of myself."

"True. But even the best soldiers need backup upon occasion."

Even the best soldiers, he'd said. Did he consider her a "best soldier?" Did he respect her skill? The pleasure she took from that was immeasurable. "You'd be willing to take a pyre-ray for me?" she asked, serious. "Because I'm heading into a den of vipers. Well, vipers to you. To me, they're colleagues. They might shoot you first and ask questions later."

"Vipers smipers. And yes, I would absolutely take a pyre-ray for you." He was as serious as she had been, with no hint of sarcasm.

"Liar." He had to be. But the pleasure she'd considered immeasurable? Just exploded into thousands of tiny stars, the intense glow of them probably seeping out of her skin.

"About your safety?" He shook his head, a dark lock of hair falling over his brow. "No."

Her eyes widened, even as she reached up and smoothed the hair back into place. Still the connection sizzled between them. "But . . . why?"

Before he could answer, they reached the front of the line, and she ordered. Her mouth watered as her butterscotch mocha was prepared. And when the steaming cup was finally placed in her hands, she sipped, moaned. This was a rare treat, but she'd earned it. She hadn't slept with McKell.

They walked outside, the cool, clean air once again enveloping them, and McKell sniffed, face slowly turning in her direction. "That coffee smells like you," he muttered huskily. "Delicious."

His voice was like a caress, hot and insistent, and her blood heated yet another degree. "I just tasered you. Why are you being so nice to me?" The moment she asked the question, the answer slapped her in the face. He'd realized she was his, too. He wanted, *needed* her blood and would do anything, even treat her like a cherished princess, to get it.

What a bastard.

"Perhaps I realized the error of my ways," he said with a shrug.

She nearly snorted. There was no reason to let

him know she knew about the vampire mating business, and a thousand reasons not to. Namely, power and manipulation. Still. She wanted to ask how things worked. Like, what would happen to him if she died? Like, could he sleep with anyone else, or would he want to rely on Ava for that, as well? Like, what would happen to him if she refused to feed him?

Would he . . . die?

She pursed her lips, not liking that thought any more than she had earlier. And what if they were wrong? What if she wasn't his?

She'd give him another taste, she decided, and test his reaction. If they were right, if she *was* his, she would keep him addicted and craving what only she could give him—which in turn would keep him strong and (hopefully) malleable. And that was the one and only reason she was about to offer her vein.

Protesting too much?

Oh, shut up.

You're talking to yourself, you know.

Yes, and I believe I told you to shut up. She stepped into the next dark alley she encountered, since she knew he liked those, stopped, finished her mocha, licked the cup clean, cursed that there was no more, then held out her arm. "You may have a sip," she told him regally. "But only a sip. Okay, maybe a few gulps. But that's it. Any more than that, and you'll have to say good-bye to your balls."

He looked at her wrist, where her pulse thumped

wildly, and then her eyes. "Why are you offering?" he asked, clearly suspicious.

Time to lie her ass off. Except, the words emerged on a surprising sigh of truth. "We're headed into a nest of AIR agents, like I told you, and I need you at your best. You seemed to handle my blood earlier, so I figured you could keep a little more down. Plus, you were being nice and that deserves a reward."

Positive reinforcement. If she pretended to reward him for being nice, he would continue to be nice. And as an added benefit, the bite would hurt and she would stop craving it. Stop wanting to tear other women away from him.

His fingers wrapped around her wrist, gentle and warm, still sizzling. Finally, he was touching her again. She licked her lips; she just couldn't help herself. But he didn't swoop down and bite. Not yet. He stood there for several heartbeats of time, the wait making her ache. Eager.

"Why are we going into a nest of AIR vipers?" he asked.

"Scared? I understand." Negative reinforcement would work, too, she supposed, then frowned. What? Did she now *want* him to go with her? *You'll protect him. Take a pyre-ray for him just as he claimed he'd do for you.* Better that than splitting up. No telling when he'd return.

His nostrils flared as he inhaled sharply. "I'm scared of nothing. I'm merely curious."

She tried not to smile. So easily manipulated, her

vampire. She'd just assured he would go with her, no matter what. Now, he had to prove himself.

His gaze cut at her, the violet hard as an amethyst. "You suddenly smell of smugness. Which means you were baiting me, you tricky hussy." His thumb traced a figure eight over her wrist, even while he pulled her closer, the jewel-rigidity in his eyes softening. His warm, minty breath trekked over her face. "But I don't mind. I like it. Now. Why are we going into a nest of AIR vipers? You have yet to explain."

Resistance faded. Fighting would have accomplished nothing, the ache inside her too strong. Once again she forgot everything but the vampire in front of her. What they could be doing, what they would soon do.

"Ava," he entreated.

Focus, think. He'd asked a question. "There's an alien queen who wants to destroy Earth," she said. "She appeared in a bar a few blocks from here, and now all the patrons are being interrogated and I'm gonna help with that."

"All right, then." Finally, he lifted her wrist. His tongue emerged and licked over her skin, leaving a sheen of wet and more of that heat. "I'll help, too. After." Still he didn't bite. Just hovered, waiting.

Every second that passed was more excruciating than the last, intensifying the ache. "Just do it." She'd meant to snap at him—anything was better than this torturous anticipation—but the words were breathless, all her need shining through.

"You'll learn, female, that it's best not to rush this." Slowly, so agonizingly slow, his fangs sank into her skin.

Oh, sweet heaven. Not once did she feel pain. His teeth must have produced a numbing drug, because all she felt was the erotic glide of his tongue, the intoxicating suction of his mouth. And now that he'd bitten her, the ache should have vanished. Only, the ache spread, becoming a far worse traitor to her common sense.

She'd wanted this, demanded it even. A mistake. A mistake she would pay for for the rest of her life.

Her knees weakened, and her bones liquefied, sending her deeper and deeper into his body until she was using him as her sole means of support. He allowed the connection, but didn't take advantage. She wanted him to take advantage. Her nipples pearled and moisture wet her panties, both reducing her to a creature of sensation. A creature whose only purpose was achieving climax. She was shameless, willing to do anything.

If only he would nibble a path to her neck. If only he would spread her legs with his knee, rub his erection against her core, then spin her, press her against the brick, rub her harder, faster, creating a dizzying friction, then strip her, penetrate her, *claim* her.

She would force him if necessary. Yes. Yes. She would trace her hand along his chest, feel the bump of his scar, wonder how he'd gotten it, run her fingers along the waist of his pants, feel the tip of his erection, the bead of pre-come, and—

With a groan, he disengaged from her, severing all contact and moving out of touching range.

Her arm fell heavily to her side as she panted, fighting past the haze of longing to concentrate on him. "Wh—what's wrong?" What she really wanted to say: *Give me more.*

"Had a . . . few gulps . . . already." At least he was panting, too. That meant he was equally affected. Right? "Promised. No more."

Anger sparked. Why hadn't he ignored her demand? Why hadn't he tried something sexual? Had he not liked her taste? Had he—

No, no, no. Ava cut through those thick threads of anger, snapping them apart, allowing other, saner emotions a path to travel. She couldn't think like that. She'd wanted him, yes. More than she should have. But there'd been a purpose to this experiment, one she couldn't forget.

"How do you feel?" she asked, having to utilize every cell in her body for strength. Only problem was, those cells still craved McKell and urged her to lean toward him.

"Fine. I feel fine." In that moment, utter hostility radiated from him.

Why, she didn't know. Her gaze raked him. His color was high, his lips puffy and stained red. A bead of blood trickled from the corner of his mouth, and he quickly licked it away, closed his eyes, savored. The sight of his tongue . . . *get yourself under control.* He wasn't shaking, but his muscles were clearly knotted, stiff.

She waited. He didn't hunch over, and he didn't vomit. That could only mean one thing. According to vampire lore, she *was* his. Truly his. Any lingering disappointment and anger drained from her completely.

She was his, she thought with a grin, and there was nothing he could do about it.

Ten

*A*va was his, McKell thought with a frown, and there was nothing he could do about it. Yet. There was no denying it now, either, not in any way. Not while the proof settled so sweetly in his stomach, strengthening him, burning him so magnificently, reshaping him into something far more lethal than he'd been. Her protector.

Damn, damn, damn. Because pairings were all about body chemistries and hormones, he could blame no one but himself. Well, and Ava. But why would his own body pair him with a human? He was offended, insulted, and . . . sated.

The first mouthful of Ava's delightful blood had been heaven. The second, hell. He'd wanted more, all, every drop. Wanted her in every way imaginable. Stopping had been painful, but that need to protect . . . Ingrained.

His strength had improved with every swallow. His senses, too. His gaze could now cut through the dark as if sunlight followed him; every inhalation cataloged the scents around him, his brain instantly sorting them out and revealing exactly where—and who—they came from. The perfume of Ava's skin—

the orchids he'd discovered their first night together, a coconut milk he hadn't, and that hint of sugar. Dirt, paint—new and old—coffee, syrup, even aged, unwashed urine at the side of the building. He could feel his body healing completely, flesh weaving back together, stitches popping out.

All wonderful, except now, without pain and weakness and hunger clouding his reactions, his shaft was hard as a rock. He wanted to strip his woman, throw her down, and sink deep inside her, thrusting, consuming, branding. And she wanted it, too. Need still pulsed from her.

He imagined those soft fingertips gliding over the slit in his penis, spreading moisture, gripping him, sliding up and down, wringing an orgasm from his very soul.

You were only supposed to seduce her into sharing her blood—not allow her to seduce you.

"Well," she said, slapping her hands together in a job well done. "Now that we've taken care of *that* . . . let's roll."

How unaffected she suddenly sounded. He fought a wave of anger. Earlier, he'd saved her from walking into one of those glimmering doorways. Did she know? Did she thank him? No. Now he'd saved her from being ravished by a vampire in public. Still no thanks was forthcoming.

"You don't wish to discuss your feelings for me first?" he demanded.

Her eyes narrowed, the thickness of her lashes

shielding the brilliant amber of her irises. "My feelings?"

"Yes. I just drank your blood, and you enjoyed it. Were even aroused by it." He sniffed the air, the delicious air that enveloped her, savoring the lingering scent of her desire. "Surely you wish to tell me how you—"

Scowling, she whipped out the small taser and held it out for his view. "We do not discuss feelings. Ever. Not even the ones you obviously have for me. Understand?"

He wasn't within her reach, but he jumped backward, anyway. Too well did he recall how those volts had incapacitated him. "Fine," he snapped. What was wrong with her? Females loved discussing their feelings, analyzing everything, and discovering how much of his time he planned to give them.

He might have been waiting for Bride all these decades, but he hadn't waited alone. He'd taken lovers. Many lovers. Nothing serious, nothing long-term, and certainly no one human. Each of his partners had had one thing in common. That silly urge to discuss *everything*. From what he was feeling at the moment to what he expected himself to feel in a few years.

Why didn't Ava?

She holstered the weapon and walked away, saying, "Follow or not. Get hit by a bus or not. Whatever. I don't care."

As if she truly meant what she said, she continued down the sidewalk without ever looking back. Why, that little . . . that . . . female! McKell gritted his teeth and chased after her, shouldering humans out of the way. No one dared confront him about his bulldozing tactics. Perhaps they realized how close to the edge of lethal he was.

"You must not realize the great favor I've bestowed upon you," he said when he reached her side. Once there, he watched for one of those doorways, certain another wouldn't appear tonight but unwilling to lower his guard. "You are my food-slave." She was much more than that, but he would never admit it aloud. "Yet I treat you as an equal."

Her gaze flicked up to him, amber fury glowing within. "The favor *you* have bestowed upon *me*? And did you just call me a food-slave?"

"Yes to both. Time and time again, you have hurt me, yet I have never retaliated. I only give you pleasure."

She didn't face him again, just increased the speed of her stride. "Pleasure? Ha! You are such an egomaniac."

"And you're deluded."

"Expectant bastard."

"Ungrateful harpy."

"Pig."

Silence.

The names they'd shouted at each other echoed through his mind, and he blinked in shock. He'd just slighted his woman. Twice. And he wasn't sorry. He actually felt . . . better. Calmer. How odd. A vampire female would have broken down and cried, had he said those things, and he would have wallowed in guilt. Perhaps even have been executed by the king for the disturbance to their world. Ava merely hurtled another insult at him. And yet not once had there been hate woven into her tone.

Yesterday, hell, an hour ago, he hadn't understood how Ava and Noelle could call each other names yet still claim to love one another. Now, though, the truth was so clear. They had simply been expressing their discontent. And it was nice. To never have to hold back for fear of hurting someone's feelings, something he'd always had to do with his vampire lovers. . . . It was freeing.

Because vampires lived in a small, underground world, escape rarely an option, peace was essential. Hurting feelings could lead to discord, discord to war, war to total elimination of the people. Therefore, his every word had been measured. Speaking his mind, the truth, had never been an option. When execution had been the most likely result, burying his emotions had seemed prudent. He simply hadn't realized the weight that kind of existence had pressed upon his shoulders.

"Thank you," he told Ava, unable to mask his awe.

Her steps slowed, and he received another flick of her gaze, minus the anger *"Thank you?* Is this a trick?" She frowned, slowed even more. "Wait. Don't answer that. Just . . . put your game face on."

Game face?

They stopped in front of a red brick building with

two guards posted at the entrance. Both were men, and both were holding pyre-guns. AIR agents, no question.

Ah. The bar. Now he understood.

He could smell every weapon in the vicinity. The soot on the barrel of the guns, the metallic twang of blades, the bloodstains on the tips of throwing stars, a piece of sharpened wood, poison, the sour motes emitted by grenades. For a moment, he wondered if this was some sort of trap to imprison him so that Mia Snow could finally speak with him. Kill him.

Ava was tricky enough to plan something like that, but why would she need to? he wondered next. He'd fallen asleep in her home. She could have cornered him then. Could have removed his heart, even, and he would have been defenseless.

He schooled his features, revealing no hint of his emotions. Not that he knew what he was feeling at the moment. "Game face on," he said.

Ava pointed a finger into his chest, her brown eyes suddenly unreadable. Or . . . dare he hope he saw concern in those sensual depths? "Behave."

"I will if you will."

She squared her shoulders and faced the guards, flashing her trainee badge. "I was called in," she said, "and he's with me."

They moved aside, allowing her to pass. McKell followed her, the men watching him through narrowed eyes. Did they know who he was? Probably. They reeked of anger and hints of fear.

Just to be on the safe side, he stopped time for them, not releasing them until he stepped through a set of double doors. The bar was small but well lit, with a concrete floor painted to look like grass and gravel, and walls painted to look like a haunted forest. The many tables and chairs littering the area looked as if they were comprised of real wood, but they smelled like metal.

Civilians had been ushered into the far corner, guards watching their every move and ensuring they remained docile. In contrast, agents bustled in every direction, taking samples from the pool tables, running tiny, beeping machines over the walls. He recognized a few of those agents, and made sure to stroke his necklace when they glanced his way. A pointed reminder of the consequences of messing with him.

Each had the same reaction. The bleaching of skin, the increase in heart rate, and the profusion of sweat. Excellent. Finally, reactions he expected.

Someone he didn't recognize muttered, "Vampire," and then the word spread like wildfire, echoing all around him. Soon, those who possessed all ten of their fingers stopped what they were doing and stared over at him, unaware of the danger they courted. A few even withdrew their guns.

Just as he geared up to stop time, and perhaps slap them around while no one could see him, Ava stepped in front of him and spread her arms, acting as his shield. "He's come in peace," she announced.

At first, the thought that she wished to protect him

delighted him, even though he should be offended that she doubted his ability, his skill. She might not want to discuss her feelings, but this proved she did have them. Why else would she place herself in danger to keep him safe?

But then, the thought that she had placed herself in danger had him wishing for a hacksaw. *No one* placed his woman in danger. Even the woman herself.

McKell pushed her behind him, blocking her from view.

"We need him for the investigation," she finished, moving to his side.

With those words, any lingering delight evaporated like mist. She hadn't shielded him because of her feelings, as he'd supposed, hoped, but for her precious investigation. Yes, a hacksaw would be nice. Still. He tried to push her behind him again. She resisted.

"I don't want to brag," Noelle said, disrupting the terse quiet. She had been hidden in the shadows of a far corner, and now strode to the bar, lifted one of the overflowing shot glasses resting on a tray, and tossed back the contents. "But my friend just did what no one else could. She brought in the wicked vampire of the far south."

The wicked vampire. He liked that.

"I could have done it, too," someone muttered.

Ava stiffened.

"Who said that?" he snapped. How dare *anyone* question her skill!

No one stepped forward.

Ava relaxed, so McKell tried to force himself to do the same. The urge to kill continued to simmer, unwilling to be bottled. As he well knew, there was one thing guaranteed to put him in a better mood. "You should kiss your friend hello," he whispered to Ava. "It's the polite thing to do."

"We only kissed to distract you," she whispered back.

"Never, ever say that again. You enjoyed it. I know you did, and I'll not be convinced otherwise."

Her lips twitched.

And there it was. The one thing guaranteed to calm him. Her amusement. Helped that those lips were lush and pink, and if he leaned down just a bit, he could lick them.

Now isn't the time. He hadn't forgiven her for her casual disregard, he reminded himself.

A dark-haired woman stepped from the crowd of agents, her expression no-nonsense, her eyes a cold metallic blue. She was short, slim, young, and had the delicate face of a dancer. Mia Snow. At long last. He'd caught a glimpse of her once before, when her team raided the underground vampire caves and McKell escaped captivity, along with Devyn Targon.

Captivity. How he loathed the reminder, especially in a roomful of his enemy, for memories suddenly swamped him, holding him as surely as the iron bars had. He could hear the drip of water, slow, insistent, smell the dew on the crystals knifing from the ceiling, and feel the walls closing in on him. He hadn't been fed, so hunger had gnawed at him, weakness eating at him.

Years ago, he'd been ordered to kill Bride. As powerful as she was, the royal family had feared her. And they'd had every right. Every vampire possessed a supernatural ability, but Bride, well, she possessed *all* abilities. There was nothing she couldn't do. Which was why her kind were considered dangerous; which was why her kind, the *nefreti*, were slaughtered the moment they were identified. Always. But he'd loved her, or thought he had, and so, rather than remove her head, he'd sent her to this surface world. Anything to save her.

He'd had her memory erased, then branded his name into her wrist, meaning to find her one day, return her to their world, and finally wed her. He would have given her a new identity, of course, and no one would have known what she was, who she'd been. Only, his plan had failed. He'd returned her to the underground world, and the vampire king at last learned of his treachery, sentencing him to eternity in the dungeons.

He should have thanked Mia for aiding his escape, but at the time, he'd been pissed at her refusal to let him near Bride. Because, like Bride, she had sided with Devyn, and McKell had wanted only to punish them. So he'd ignored Mia and every single one of her summonses. Now, he felt no animosity toward her. *Shocking*.

"I ask you to come see me, and you snub me." A glaring Mia stopped a few inches away from him. She smelled of the ice that was crystallized in her eyes. "I send a few people to escort you, and you hurt them. Maim then. Now you have the nerve to show up at a crime scene and—"

McKell held up one hand, silencing her. "Shall I leave, then?"

She popped her jaw. "Sans, escort McKell to headquarters. Now."

"But he might be able to help us," Ava said, and then launched into a speech about the merits of reversing time. "I thought Noelle told you about this."

"Actually . . . " Noelle joined their circle, hands stuffed in her jean pockets. "I thought Ava and I could break the idea to you together. You know, in a calm, this-is-for-the-best discussion."

Ava moaned. Mia cursed.

While they continued their "discussion," McKell inhaled deeply, looking for a distraction from the memories still shrouding him. He tensed. There was something familiar spicing the air . . . something he'd once adored. He finished his survey of the bar, and could only shake his head against another onslaught of shock.

Think of the devil, and she would appear. Sitting on one of the pool tables were Bride and her husband, Devyn. They were focused on each other, and talking about—McKell's ears perked—Bride's desire for a bubble bath.

He waited for his chest to tighten as it always did when he saw them together, but . . . it never did. Actually, he didn't react at all.

He recalled the day he'd raised his sword to take her head, as ordered. Recalled the way those emerald eyes had looked up at him, filled with trust and love. Recalled how he'd placed her well-being before his own.

If his plan had worked, they would be wedded now, with a child to spoil.

Would he still have craved Ava if he'd been wedded to Bride? Vampire spouses drank from each other, and—as he had proven today—sickened when they drank from someone else. Even someone human. At the moment, he couldn't imagine not wanting Ava, even with a devoted Bride at his side.

Bride's scent didn't heat his blood. Her body didn't make his hands itch for contact. The thought of her with Devyn didn't send him into a killing rage. And what the hell was that strange man in the corner doing, eye-fucking Ava with an intensity that staggered?

McKell flashed his fangs, but the man didn't notice. He was too focused on Ava, mentally stripping her. Kill, McKell would kill him.

"What the hell do you think you're doing?" Ava suddenly demanded.

At first, McKell didn't realize she'd spoken to him. Then she grabbed his arms and shook him, clueing him in. "That man." He pointed, flashed his fangs again. "Who is he?"

Ava followed the line of his finger and blushed. *Blushed.* Why? If she returned the eye-fuck . . . "Uh, that's Johnny Deschanel. Just ignore him. Please."

"Who is he to you?" McKell snarled.

"No one."

He didn't believe her, and his claws were elongating, sharpening.

"I'm going to allow you to help us, McKell," Mia said before he could storm over, slash, slice, destroy. Ava had never blushed before, and her denial had been too rushed. "The Schön are dangerous and unpredictable, and I need every man I can get. Especially someone with an ability like yours."

Hack. Saw. "How magnanimous of you," he muttered, gaze remaining on Johnny. He wouldn't doubt if this was what Mia had planned all along. Pretend to want to incarcerate him, then offer him his freedom in exchange for his aid.

"Afterward," Mia continued, "I'll expect you to go to AIR headquarters and answer a few questions for me."

He shook his head. What would pain this Johnny the most? Limb removal? Or watching his own guts spill from his stomach? "I will do so, but only after Ava helps me with something."

"What?" Mia's red-hot astonishment lashed him.

Had she never been denied? "I apologize if I gave you the impression that the answer was any of your business." *See me, Johnny. Fear me.*

Ava and Mia gasped in unison. Noelle chuckled.

"What?" He'd apologized, hadn't he?

Johnny straightened and smoothed the wrinkles from his shirt. McKell once again stepped forward, but Ava tightened her grip on his arm. Would have taken only a single tug to free himself, but that would dissuade her from touching him again, and he didn't want to dissuade her.

If you won't see me, see this, he projected at the man as he wound his arm around Ava's waist. *She. Is. Mine.*

Mia recovered quickly. "Fine. Don't tell me what you have planned. Ava and I can discuss it later. Meanwhile, if you hurt one agent, just one, I won't hesitate to slice your throat."

"What happens if I hurt two?" Another man approached Johnny, slapped him on the shoulder, and then he, too, focused on Ava as if he had every right. So. Two would die this night.

"Don't fucking hurt *anyone*," Mia shouted.

Temper, temper. Seriously. He'd been nothing but polite. "Very well," he said. "But I should warn you, I'm not an easy person to slice. People tend to lose fingers when they try." See. Polite. He hadn't threatened her as she'd done to him. He'd merely stated a fact. "Now, if you want to save your agents from my wrath, tell those two to mentally zip their fucking pants."

Johnny finally noticed him. McKell flicked his tongue over his fangs. A warning. A promise. The agent paled.

"McKell," Ava said, exasperated. And, if he wasn't

mistaken, just a little happy. She hadn't once protested about his arm being around her, either. Sweet
progress

You can concentrate on your woman now. He looked
down. A mistake. Ava stepped away from him, and he
mourned the loss of her heat.

"Will you please pay attention," she muttered.
"You're causing a scene."

"Yes, he is." Mia glared at her. "He's your responsi-
bility, you know."

She sighed as if the weight of the world had been
placed on her shoulders. "Yeah. I do know."

A grin. "I always knew you were a smart one, Sans,
so I probably don't even need to say this next part, but
good job," Mia said with an approving nod. "You did
the impossible. I'm impressed."

Ava's chin lifted, pride filling her eyes. "Thank—"

"Hey, dumbass! I didn't give you permission to test
anyone's blood," Mia shouted to another agent, already pounding toward the dumbass in question, Ava
forgotten. That didn't lessen Ava's reaction. So much
pride . . . still growing . . .

So. She responded well to praise. He made a mental note to praise her. Often. Only until he was done
with her, of course, and he had everything he wanted
from her. But oh, he liked that look on her. And anyway, she had deserved the praise. She was the most
resilient person in the bar. She backed down from
nothing, even her boss.

Noelle propped her hands on her hips and regarded Ava intently. "Did you ask him about the time-reversal thing?"

"Not yet." Ava massaged the back of her neck. "He's in a bad mood."

He loved when they discussed him as if he weren't in the room; he really did. "You expected me to reverse time? Sorry, but I've never had the ability." He'd tried. Many times. Always he'd failed. "Now, Noelle. I have a question for you. Ava, you are not to answer for her."

"Wait. You can't reverse time?" Noelle asked with a pout. "Not even a little?"

"No. Now. Who is that man to Ava?" He pointed to Johnny, who was wiping the lint from his shirt-sleeve.

"There goes my genius plan," Noelle said, disappointed, but she followed the line of his finger and scowled. "Oh, him. He's a bad memory."

Ava groaned. "Don't you dare—"

"She slept with him."

"What?" He hadn't meant to shout, but the volume of his voice had been uncontrollable in the light of Noelle's confession. "When?"

"A few months ago," Ava whispered, another blush in full bloom. "It was a mistake."

Death and pain weren't good enough for the bastard. Only total ruination would suffice. McKell would ensure the man suffered eternally. No one touched Ava, *his* woman, without his permission. Ever. Even months ago. When he hadn't even known her. Irrational, but his sense of possession was so great, time offered no kind of barrier. And if Ava protested his logic, well, he would give her permission to ruin the life of every woman *he* had ever slept with.

Johnny must have realized they were discussing him in a negative way, because he glanced up, scowled. Then he made another fatal mistake. He clapped his hands, demanding attention, and said, "Look, everyone. Ava brought in the big, bad vampire. I wonder how she convinced him to . . . come."

Several agents snickered.

No, total ruination wasn't good enough.

"McKell," Ava began, suspecting his intensions. "Don't."

"Must." With only a thought, McKell stopped the clock. As everyone froze around him, unaware of what he was doing, he stomped to the puny human, punched him in the face, heard cartilage snap, and returned to Ava's side. He wished he could freeze time for a longer period of time and inflict more damage, but he couldn't. When he tried, he only weakened himself. A bar filed with AIR agents was not the place to weaken himself.

Soon, though, he'd get Johnny alone. *Nothing* would stop his wrath then.

The clock restarted, and he watched as Johnny grimaced and rubbed his now bleeding nose, having no idea what had caused the break. And were those . . . tears in the agent's eyes? McKell sharpened his study, grinned. They were.

He nearly beat his chest in satisfaction. *I caused that.*

Why had Ava willingly stripped for such a bastard? Why had she allowed him to tease and taste her?

A growl rose from McKell's stomach and churned in his throat. He stopped the clock again, closed the distance, punched the man again, cracking jawbone this time, and once again returned to an unsuspecting Ava. And this time, when he restarted the clock, the bastard dropped to his knees, moaning in pain.

"McKell," Ava muttered.

"What?" he asked innocently.

Her lips twitched, surprising him, before she turned her attention to Noelle. "So what have you learned so far?"

"No one remembers seeing the Schön queen, but that man—" She pointed to a very pale human male, who was hunched over in his chair and clutching his middle. Three guards pointed guns at his head. "He's already exhibiting signs of the disease."

"Why hasn't he been quarantined, then?"

"He's not stunnable, and everyone who approaches him, he tries to bite. And as you know, biohazard suits don't stop the disease from spreading, so our clothing certainly won't."

Ava was in danger, McKell realized, and that he wouldn't tolerate. "Allow me to take care of him."

"McKell, wait—"

For the third time that evening, he manipulated time. He approached the diseased man and slammed his head into the tabletop in front of him. When McKell restarted the clock, the man remained unconscious, slumped over the metal surface. "Now you can cart him wherever you want."

Ava spun, clearly confused by his seemingly instant change in location. "You have to stop doing that! And don't you dare touch him," she said, rushing to his side to tug him away. "He might be bleeding."

McKell performed a quick scan of the tabletop. "No droplets."

"Thank God." She shuddered with the force of her relief. "Contact with infected bodily secretions is what spreads the disease."

"Between humans, perhaps." Human illnesses never affected him. Still. He allowed her to usher him the rest of the way without protest. "You aren't to go near him again. No matter what. Understand?"

Ignoring him, she instructed the guards to carry the man out of the building and into a cell at AIR headquarters. She proceeded to ignore McKell for the next hour, in fact, helping Mia, talking to the other humans. When one of the females—one who reeked of guilt—refused to answer her questions, Ava glanced around to ensure no one watched her, before pressing a blade to the woman's thigh.

The woman began babbling, spilling details about stealing money from the register. Not helpful, but that explained the guilt. Guilt Ava had sensed, even with her inferior human senses.

She was a competent soldier, he thought. If she

couldn't get what she wanted the conventional way, she found another way. He liked that. He liked *her*.

Do not soften. Any more than he already had. If he did, she would constantly lead him around by his ever-randy swim team, as he'd heard Devyn Targon say once.

A few times, lucky-to-be-alive Johnny Deschanel tried to edge to Ava's side. McKell always stopped time, punched him, then pushed him to the other side of the bar. Finally, the guy caught on and gave up. Soon after that, Mia Snow called it a night and told the agents to go home. They'd sort through the acquired evidence tomorrow.

Ava approached McKell rather than Noelle, and he found that he liked that, too.

She looked him up and down. "You good?" Still concerned for his health?

"Yes. You?"

"Yeah. Tired, though."

Tired meant bedtime. Once again he wrapped his arm around her waist, ready to usher her from the building. "Learn anything?" he asked, scanning the area, ensuring no one would be following them.

"Only that—"

"Tell me later," he interrupted. "I have to go." Johnny had just exited with that other agent. Tragically, bedtime would have to wait. First, he had a reckoning to ensure.

"You have to go?" Ava called. "Where?"

"Later." McKell raced after his prey.

Eleven

Thanks to Ava's delicious, life-altering blood—mmm, Ava's blood. McKell almost turned around, almost returned to her. *Vengeance first.* Determined, he continued following Johnny. And thanks to Ava's blood—mmm—he had no trouble tracking the agent through the darkness.

He would drain the bastard. Cut off his fingers, one at a time, then his toes, one at a time. He would peel flesh from bone, slice into muscle, remove limbs, organs. Death would always remain a short distance away.

And Ava, who is responsible for you, will pay.

His steps faltered. If Johnny was hurt in any way, everyone would know McKell was responsible. Ava might lose her beloved job. And if she lost her job, she would hate him. He didn't want her hate.

He needed her devotion.

In a blink, the reckoning morphed into a recon mission. He would learn everything he could about Johnny. Then, tomorrow, he would prove how much better *he* was. Simple. Easy.

Disappointing.

For Ava, he would persevere.

Currently, Johnny was with the other agent who liked to stare at Ava. Jeremy was his name, and his scent was similar to Johnny's. Perhaps they were brothers. They kept pace beside each other, unaware of the vampire stalking their every move and listening to their every word.

"You gotta leave that girl alone," Jeremy said.

Ah. He was the smart one.

"You're my twin, bro. Not my probation officer. I don't have to do anything."

Yes. Brothers.

"Maybe you didn't notice the rabid vampire eyeing you like man-corn all night."

"I noticed," was the grumbled reply. Johnny rubbed his nose, his swollen jaw. "I think he sucker-punched me, like, ten times."

They snaked a corner, the sidewalk free. Not many people were out now. Most were at home, snuggled in their beds. As McKell would soon be. With Ava. His delicious Ava.

"No way. I never saw him go near you," Jeremy said.

"He can control time or some shit like that. Believe me, he approached."

"Well, you shouldn't have watched Ava like that."

Smart? Jeremy was a genius.

"She wants me," Johnny said with enough fire to torch an entire village. "She's just playing hard-to-get."

Once again McKell's nails elongated, sharpened. Surely Ava wouldn't be blamed for a little scratch on the man's trachea.

"Are you fucking kidding me? She slept with you, then ignored you afterward. That isn't playing hard-to-get. That's playing he's-bad-in-bed-and-I-want-nothing-to-do-with-him."

I'm amazing in bed, McKell thought smugly, nails retracting a bit. Once she sampled him, Ava would never want to leave him.

"Fuck you, Jeremy. You can't even *pay* a girl to get in bed with you."

There was no hate or malice to the claim; Johnny spoke as if he were simply stating a fact both men knew and accepted. McKell pictured the agent in question. Unlike Johnny, Jeremy had thick black brows and a too-long nose. His eyes were black, like bottomless pits. Those eyes weren't evil, though. They were kind, concerned, yet hardened by life.

Still. Not an attractive face, but he was bigger than Johnny. Taller, more muscled. Jeremy would have been the better choice for any female. So why hadn't Ava chosen *him*? Because she appreciated beauty?

McKell didn't like the thought, even though he himself was beautiful. The boast wasn't egotistical of him. Like Johnny, he was simply stating a fact. A fact he'd been told his entire life. Still, he thought again. He would have preferred Ava to look beyond the surface. Beauty faded. Not his, of course, because he didn't age, but hers would. She would age.

He frowned. He didn't like the thought of her withering, then dying, either.

You're going to tire of her eventually.

Would he, though? His desire for her seemed to grow with every moment that passed.

"You're an asshole," Jeremy said, "but I don't relish the thought of finding pieces of you all over New Chicago. So do me a favor and stay away from her. Okay?"

"You're acting like I have no skill. I could take him."

McKell barely managed to silence his snort. And just how did the human plan to "take him"? With his puny pyre-gun? He should ask the other AIR agents how that had worked out for them.

"Just . . . watch your mouth, too," Jeremy said. "Okay? Please. You keep badmouthing Ava, and you won't have to worry about the vampire. She'll end you herself."

"Whatever, dude. I'll see you tomorrow."

The two men branched apart, heading in opposite directions. McKell continued to follow Johnny. The agent plowed ahead, lighting a cigarette along the way. Cigarettes had been outlawed years ago.

Dark smoke plumed around him, and the few citizens who were out and about frowned and waved their hands in front of their faces. One even dialed the police to lodge a complaint.

Maybe I can help with that. If Johnny were to light himself on fire with one of his cigarettes . . . well, there would be no puncture wounds or claw marks to incriminate McKell.

He smiled for the first time since leaving the bar.

A woman stepped in front of Johnny, and the agent

ground to a quick halt. "Out of my . . . way," he said, tone changing midway. From angry to intrigued.

McKell stopped, too, and studied her from the shadows. She wore all white, a dress that flowed around her like water, had short black hair and a sweet, humanoid face most men probably drooled over. But she wasn't human. She couldn't be. The smell of rot wafted from her, strong enough to cause bile to rise in his throat.

Exactly what she was, he couldn't tell. The clothes fit the description Dallas had given of the Schön queen, but the hair didn't. Supposedly, the queen had long blond hair. Could she change her appearance, perhaps? He wouldn't have thought so, but that smell . . . more than rot, it was undiluted disease. Disease in its purest form. Grotesque. Yet she appeared healthy, completely unaffected. Another characteristic of the queen.

"Hello," she said in a voice that was more song than anything, humming against his eardrums.

Dallas had mentioned nothing about her voice. Not that McKell had overheard, anyway.

"Hey," Johnny replied in what he probably considered a sexy purr.

There were three men behind the woman, and they were cloaked by shadows of their own. McKell could see them, though. They wore all black, were as tall and muscled as he was, and watched the woman with impassive expressions. They were armed. He sniffed. With pyre-guns set to blazing. Protecting her?

Johnny didn't seem to notice them. He remained relaxed, on the prowl. "You shouldn't be out this late. The streets are dangerous. Especially for stunners like you."

"I'm lost," she said, twirling a strand of her hair.

A lie. McKell could smell that, too.

Beside her, a doorway of air opened. Bright, those dust motes like outstretching arms. *Come,* McKell thought he heard inside his head, the voice male, soft, and directed at him. As every time before, no one else seemed to notice. Not even the woman, with her deceptively shrewd gaze. *Please.*

Silently McKell backed up a step. He'd always suspected, but now he knew. The doorway *was* sentient. And clearly chasing him.

Dangerous, that voice said. *Be careful. Please be careful.*

Here to protect him? Or to at last trick him, sweeping him to his damnation?

A similar doorway had brought the vampires from their home to this one, thousands of years ago. Though it hadn't spoken. He'd even heard gossip that a similar doorway had opened for his mother, had stolen her, then returned her months later. She'd never spoken of what had happened during her absence, but she had cried herself to sleep for a long time afterward. So, he could guess. *She'd* been damned.

Go, he mentally shouted at the door.

The air shimmered, wavering, then faded. He hadn't expected obedience.

"Where're you headed?" Johnny asked. "Maybe I can help you find your way."

With one threat thankfully gone, McKell focused on the other. How charming the soon-to-be agent was. Was *that* how he'd won Ava? McKell could be charming, too. When he wanted to be.

"Well . . . to be honest, I don't actually have any place to go," the woman said with a sweet smile, her charm far greater than Johnny's, but no less fake.

"I could take you to my apartment, I guess. If you wanted. You could . . . call someone?"

"Yes. I would like that."

Before they could wander off, McKell stopped time. Approached. He removed the weapons from the men, tossed them in the Dumpster behind them, and memorized their faces in case he ever ran into them again. He also patted down the woman. She didn't have a weapon, but this close, he could see past her . . . skin? Perhaps. It was as if she'd cloaked herself in a beautiful, radiant mask, shielding the world from the hideous monster that lurked beneath. Pitted flesh, oozing sores, missing teeth, hair frizzed and matted. Inhuman.

The queen. Had to be.

From what he'd heard, she was treacherous, destructive, vile in a way only the soulless could be. AIR was desperate to stop her, but Johnny deserved what she would do to him. What McKell *couldn't* do to him. What McKell wanted to do to him.

But as cold and unfeeling as McKell was, probably as soulless as the bitch in front of him, he couldn't allow it to happen. Because of Ava. Letting her co-worker suffer this way could very well bring the disease to her doorstep.

So. The lucky bastard had been saved. Again. Scowling, McKell returned to the shadows and freed the group from his time-stop, unable to hold them any longer.

They kicked back into gear, unaware of what had happened. The guards wouldn't even suspect they'd encountered a foe until they reached for their guns. He didn't follow, allowing the distance to grow between them. Only when they were out of hearing range did he withdraw Ava's phone, scroll through the address book, and find Mia's number.

The head of AIR answered on the second ring, barking a command for him to speak. He did, telling her what he'd discovered, what he thought, and where the group was headed. She cursed as if she were being tortured, told him to return to Ava and stay put, then hung up on him.

He pocketed the phone, certain he deserved some type of reward for his actions this night. He'd saved an enemy, after all. For Ava.

His lips curled into a smile. Since he'd done the saving for Ava, *she* would have to supply the reward. McKell knew exactly what he wanted . . .

Where the hell had McKell gone?

Ava remained in the bar, drinking with Noelle despite her fatigue and sulking about his disappearing act for half an hour before asking her friend to drive her home. She didn't have a car of her own—they were too expensive—and she didn't want to walk.

Noelle was far more intoxicated than Ava, but the good news was, there was no such thing as drunk driving. Not anymore. Cars drove themselves. All humans, otherworlders, and bastard vampires had to do was punch in the address of the destination, and bingo. Done. All that remained was the time spent on the road.

"Two things I gotta tell ya," Noelle said as the brand-new vehicle wound through the streets. Rich as she was, she'd had the bright red sports car delivered the day after McKell destroyed her sedan. And yes, her words were slurred.

"Tell me." Ava's were, too, for that matter.

"First, I'm sorry I called you fat the other day." Noelle was the world's nicest drunk. After a few shots, she always regretted everything she'd done and said for the past—however long had passed since her last drink. "You looked gorgeous, but I was feeling bitchy because I'd called dibs on McKell but he only had eyes for you."

She tried not to grin, she really did. "He did?"

"Yeah. And it was fucking depressing. I'm pretty, aren't I?"

"The prettiest."

Noelle fluffed her hair. "That's true."

"What's the second thing you wanted to tell me?"

"First, you gotta tell me how you do it."

The car hit a bump, and her stomach lurched. She leaned against her seat and peered up at the open ceiling panel. Stars winked in the sky, blurred together, danced, and caught her mind up in the twirl. "Do what?"

"Get men to follow you around like little puppies."

"I don't." Proof: Where the hell was McKell?

"Do. Johnny Deschanel still wants you. Jeremy Deschanel would like a go at you, too. And McKell would follow you into hell—and did!—but nobody wants me." Pouting now.

Ava closed her eyes and turned her head in Noelle's direction. Only when the spinning stopped did she allow her lids to open. "Everyone wants you. Well, not McKell. You're right about him." *He's mine!* "But did you see how fast he flew out of the bar? He couldn't get away from me fast enough." Now *she* was pouting.

"Oh, that. I know what happened." Noelle waved a dismissive hand through the air, then frowned as she wiggled her fingers. "He— Oh, no. No, no, no. I have seven fingers. How did I get two extra?"

"You can get them surgically removed." God, she was smart. "Now, what were you saying about McKell?"

"I don't remember." Noelle tapped a nail against her chin, brightened. "Oh, yeah. He followed Johnny. Probably to kill him."

"Really?" She couldn't help it. She grinned again.

She'd imagined three likely scenarios for his departure. One, meeting a food-slave-slash-lover. Two, needing space. From *Ava*. And three, meeting a food-slave-slash-lover.

She frowned. Her math might be a little off. Oh, well. "A man defending my honor. How cool is that?"

"Five bucks says McKell cuts off Johnny's penis."

"Ten says he'll remove the man's heart." A girl could hope, anyway.

Sleeping with Johnny was one of the stupidest things she'd ever done. But she'd been feeling lonely, had drunk just a little too much, and well, she'd thought she was crawling into bed with his brother, Jeremy. He was stacked, just like she preferred. Just like McKell.

McKell. Her McKell.

Yeah, muscles were still her weakness.

"I'm never drinking again," she said, then lifted the bottle of Jack she'd brought with her and drained the rest of the contents.

"Me, either." Noelle confiscated the bottle, realized there was nothing left, and licked the rim. "Dallas was looking pretty hot, huh?"

"I guess." To be honest, Ava had only been able to see McKell. That dark hair, those violet eyes. The way he kept stopping time to punch Johnny in the nose. What a hero.

"So was Hector. Looking hot, I mean. But he's pretty much a bastard, so I'm not sure I'll go for it."

Hector was muscled, and before McKell, Ava had actually sized him up and called dibs. Not that she'd ever done anything about it. "He's yours, if you want him."

"Concentrating on McKell?"

"No. He's *not* a potential lover." *Except that he is.*

"Why? He's off the must-kill list. I mean, Mia wouldn't have let him stay in the bar if he was still on it. So he's no longer your enemy. He's your helpmate."

"Helpmate? Do you hear how ridiculous you sound? But think about it. If I sleep with him, I'll no longer be regarded as a competent agent. I'll just be the girl who has to sleep with men to get them to cooperate. You heard Johnny, right? 'How'd she get the vampire to *come*?'" she mocked.

The car stopped at an intersection. Built-in sensors also knew when to slow down, when to speed up, and when to halt abruptly if something unexpected flew in the way.

Noelle pressed a few buttons, forcing the car to move forward despite the red light. That option was *not* something all cars possessed. "Alls I'm saying is that you're too worried about what other people think of you. You always have been. McKell likes you, and you like him. Go for it. Everyone else can go nuck themselves. Wait. Is that the right word?"

She couldn't refute Noelle's claim. She *was* worried about what other people thought; she hated herself for it, but couldn't change how she felt. Too many years of being called "trash" had left her raw and scarred inside. Even though she often professed to be unaffected. Even to herself.

Alcohol brought out the honesty in her, she supposed.

"And Ava? News flash. The vampire slept at your place and came with you to a job. People already think you're sleeping with him."

She scrubbed both hands down her face. Without her arms holding her steady against the seat, she banged into the window when the car turned. "Ouch." Frowning, she rubbed her now-stinging temple. "No one knows he slept at my place but you."

"Like I can keep a juicy bit of gossip like that to myself."

Ava rolled her eyes, then moaned. Mistake! Another wave of dizziness slammed her, caused her stomach to do the lurching thing. "You'd never tell. You love me too much."

"Oh! That brings me to the second thing I wanted to discuss with you."

The car slowed and angled toward the curb on their right. Ava saw her building. Run-down, with peeling paint and soot-stained glass for windows, rather than the shield-armor higher-end apartments used.

"Tell me before I go upstairs and puke my guts out," she said.

"My mom's decided to host a"—Noelle gagged—"cocktail party. You have to come."

Ava was shaking her head—and moaning again—before the last word had left her friend's mouth. "No. Your mom hates me, and I hate her."

"Please. I can't do it without you, and I have to do it."

Please. The plea singed her ears. As if she could say no now. Noelle never begged. "Fine. But you'll owe me."

"Anything!"

"You can start by doing your own laundry."

"Hell, no." Noelle shook her head, then moaned louder than Ava had. "Anything but that."

Someone tall and wonderfully roped with sinew and muscle unfolded from the shadows of the building, stepping into the light seeping from the streetlamps, revealing black hair and glowing purple eyes, and snagging Ava's undivided attention. McKell, she realized, heart suddenly careening.

He was here.

He scowled and crossed his arms over his chest.

Darling caveman. "I'm afraid the laundry is non-negotiable. Oh, and we'll discuss the rest of your new duties tomorrow." If she remembered this conversation. "Open," she said to the door, and the block instantly obeyed.

"Duties? As in more than one?" Noelle screeched.

Ava emerged. "Close," she said to the car, ignoring her friend. The door clicked shut, muffling any reply Noelle might have made. Gaze drilling into an obviously fuming McKell, she approached. And only fell once. Okay, twice.

When she reached him, he didn't kiss her hello as was proper. He sniffed the air, deepened his scowl, and hefted her over his shoulder fireman-style to carry her inside.

Twelve

"Where'd you go so fast earlier that you couldn't even kiss a girl good-bye?" Ava asked McKell when he finally set her on her feet. Took a moment, but her head finally cleared, and she looked around without losing her dinner—that entire bottle of Jack.

She was at her front door, she realized. Why that was a surprise, she didn't know. She'd been outside her building just a few minutes ago, and McKell had carried her through the doors, up the elevator, and down the hall. Maybe. The night's events were beginning to blur together.

What she did know? The vampire owed her a kiss.

Kiss, kiss, kiss. Her mind kept snagging on that one word. That must mean she needed one. Desperately. Therefore, once she and McKell reached the privacy of her living room, she'd take one.

Decided, she placed her hand on the ID box. Blue lights scanned her prints, and a few seconds later, her door unlocked, opened.

"Before I answer your question," McKell said, catching her by the waist and holding her in place, "you're going to program my ID into that thing, so that I can come and go as I please."

What an excellent idea. Then he could kiss her anytime she wanted.

She lifted his free hand—no reason to disturb the warm, insistent arm still wrapped around her—and pressed his fingers into the pad. After she entered the code, another blue light erupted, this one memorizing. A few seconds, that was all that was needed.

Eager to collect her prize, she turned to face him. "Now . . ."

"That's it?" he asked, scowling as he lowered his arm.

"Mmm-hmm."

McKell released her and barreled past her. *Without* kissing her. "Where did you go after I took off?" he demanded.

Her disappointment finally managed to rally her common sense, reminding her of three things. She wasn't a slave to her hormones, he'd promised her an answer but hadn't delivered, and he should not have waited outside for her, as if they were a couple and he had every right to do so.

Time to instruct him. She spun on her heel and followed him inside. "I stayed at the bar." Oops. She hadn't meant to answer him.

"Drinking," he snarled, sprawling on her couch. And he was holding the whip he'd brought the first time he'd come here, running the length through his fingers.

"You say that like it's a bad thing." She fell into the chair across from him and moaned. World . . . spinning again . . . And the stupid spinning caused her stomach to do that stupid churning thing.

"Too much alcohol can kill humans, you know."

"I haven't had too much."

"How can you tell?"

"I've had a lot more on many occasions and—this next part might come as a shock, so brace yourself—I'm still alive." Maybe.

He was far from amused. "You should see how green you are. In fact, you're probably dying right now. And if you die, you will sorely upset my plans for you."

"Plans that involve kissing me?" At the thought, her stomach settled. She licked her lips, eager to finally begin.

His nostrils flared and his pupils dilated, signs of arousal, surely, but all he said was, "You won't be able to hunt vampires."

Oh. *You aren't disappointed. Because you aren't a slave to your hormones, remember?* She closed her eyes and rubbed her temples. "Is that why you're so pissy?"

"I am *not* pissy," he gritted out. "Only females are pissy. But yes, we will soon kiss."

How superior he sounded. Something that had always irritated her in the past. And yet, it was delight whisking through her now, softening her. They woiuld soon kiss! "So where did you go earlier? You promised to answer me if I programmed your ID into my box, and I did." Tomorrow, she might regret doing that. Tonight, she only wanted to celebrate.

McKell propped his head against the back of the

couch and peered up at the ceiling. "If you must know, I followed Agent Deschanel. Johnny, you probably like to call him. Or John. Or Love Bunny."

Noelle had been right. "Three things, vampire. He's still in training, so he isn't technically an agent yet." There was no way she would let anyone, especially McKell, grant Johnny Deschanel a title he didn't yet deserve. "Next, he isn't my Love Bunny. And finally, did you follow him because you were jealous of his association with me?" Please, please, please.

McKell snorted. "Hardly. I followed him because he was a suspicious character."

Finally they were getting somewhere. She gripped the edge of the chair and leaned forward. "Suspicious of wanting to get my clothes off?"

"Of foul play."

"Foul play with my body?"

Now *he* leaned forward, blazing gaze locked on her. "I wasn't jealous, damn you."

Liar. "So did you cut off his penis or cut out his heart?" Fingers crossed he said heart. Noelle would owe her ten whole dollars, and she already knew what she would buy. Butterscotch-flavored lipgloss to replace the one McKell had stolen.

"What?" He shook his head in astonishment. "Neither."

"Oh." Her shoulders sagged. So close to victory, yet so far away.

"You are . . . disappointed by this? Because I can return to him and remove his penis, no problem."

At "return to him," hope had sprouted wings. At "penis," those wings had withered. Foiled again. Her shoulders sagged a little more. "So you would have gone for the penis? Because a man loves with his heart, and isn't loving a woman worse than boinking her?"

Another shake of his head. "Yes, the penis, and no, loving isn't worse. Boinking is. But again, you sound disappointed."

McKell had just said "boinking." She snickered. Then she remembered that she'd just lost her bet with Noelle and wouldn't be getting that lipgloss. "I am," she said on a sigh. "There goes ten hard-earned dollars." Sure, he hadn't actually performed a cock removal, but intent was just the same. "And now that we've got that settled, let's backtrack a bit. Do you want to hurt him because you were jealous of him?"

"I told you. I wasn't—I'm *not* jealous. Of anyone!" Pause, grumbling. "But I called dibs on you. Which means you belong to me. And he was looking at you. At *my* property."

Fight the urge to cheer. "Jealous, jealous, jealous," she *tsk*ed.

"Am not!" He snapped the middle of the whip taut, his knuckles white over the leather.

Maybe fight the urge to taunt him, too. "I was with Johnny before I met you, so the dibs system doesn't really apply."

More grumbling, but she couldn't make out the words, only the frustration behind them. "Why were you with him, anyway? He's a sad excuse for a man. Even a human man."

"If you must know, I thought I was with his brother Jeremy." She ignored the "even a human" part, too busy trying to eradicate the growing heat in her cheeks.

First, renewed astonishment fell over McKell's face. Then, relief. Then, anger. She did a double take, certain she was misreading him. But, no. The anger was real.

"Why did you want to be with *him*?" he demanded. "I mean, I thought it would be better if you were uncaring about appearances. But damn it, this is worse."

Worse, how? "Hello. Did you see his muscles?"

"Well, mine are bigger." He gave another snap of that whip.

He spoke only the truth. His muscles *were* bigger, which meant, so was his sex appeal. And not just to Ava, strength aficionado. One glance from those wicked violet eyes, and a woman knew what she would be getting from him: pleasure in its purest form.

Hands, kneading. Legs, twining. Shaft, pumping. Nothing taboo. No inhibitions.

Raw need curled through her.

Why hadn't he kissed her yet? He'd promised to do so, right?

"I can't talk about this anymore," he said, tossing the whip aside and rubbing at his eyes. "I'm too close to storming out of here and decapitating both brothers."

Her desire faded. "So you think less of me?" Like, say, *trash*. "For sleeping with someone before you?"

"Of course not." The sudden sincerity in his tone relaxed her. "You're a woman with needs, and believe me, I'm grateful for those needs. I simply cannot tolerate the thought of another man touching . . ." His jaw clenched. In and out he breathed, the air rasping, harsh. "We have to change the subject. Now."

She understood. He didn't begrudge her past, just as she didn't begrudge his. But the thought of him with someone else, even before he'd met her, was far from pleasant.

Which was odd, now that she thought about it. They hadn't slept together, and she'd told herself— several times—that she wouldn't venture down that path with him. Yet she couldn't deny that every bone in her body screamed *mine*.

He was right. They needed to change the subject.

"What do you want to talk about?" she asked.

A moment passed. He shrugged, the action like a neon sign pointing to the wide width of his shoulders. "I think I ran into the Schön queen."

So casually offered, with just a hint of expectation. She could only stare at him and try to process. "Okay. Wait, wait, wait. What did you just say?"

"She had dark hair, but this woman was definitely diseased." He waited now, as if he expected something from her.

Yet again, his tone was so casual he could have been discussing the weather, rather than the case that could change the fate of the world. "Tell me everything."

He did, from the way the brunette had appeared out of nowhere, to her proposition to Johnny, to the exquisite mask she'd worn, to the guards standing silently behind her the entire time.

"Why didn't you apprehend her?"

"And risk carrying the disease to your door? No."

Argh! Ava dug out her cell phone and dialed Mia. The conversation was short but not very sweet, McKell leaning forward, watching her expression the entire time. His expectation had swelled. Maybe because Mia quickly informed her that McKell had already called and that she was taking care of things.

"You should have incapacitated her in some way," Ava growled as she dropped her phone on the table beside her. He was strong enough, wily enough. And damn it, his concern for Ava was panty-melting. "AIR would have forgiven you for everything and stopped harassing you."

"They aren't harassing me now."

"Fine. *I* would have stopped harassing you."

His eyelids dipped to half-mast, and what remained of his emotions drained: anger, expectation, everything. Except desire. Desire that heated the entire room, crackling and charging. "I don't want you to stop."

The hello and good-bye kisses she'd so badly wanted, well, she was finally in danger of receiving them. She gulped, swallowing the lump trying to block her airway. "Then I would have harassed you nonstop," she whispered.

His gaze moved to her lips. "Would you have allowed me to feed from you? Whenever I wished?"

No. "Yes." Maybe.

In a blink, he was on his feet. The desire drained, as well, and determination took its place. "I'll hunt her down and apprehend her now."

Ava's desire vanished just as swiftly. So. He hadn't craved *her*. He'd craved a never-ending happy meal. She should have known. Suspected, at the very least. "You're staying here," she said, standing, swaying. "Mia told me her orders. We're not to interfere."

"Mia isn't my boss." He moved toward the door.

Scowling, Ava jumped in his path. "She's mine."

He halted just before contact and glared down at her. "Out of my way, Ava."

As if he couldn't move her. "You had your chance. You blew it. So, like I said, you're staying here." *Do not tremble. Do not show a single weakness.*

Down, down he leaned, until his nose was level with hers. Still he didn't touch her. "Just how are you going to stop me?"

God, he smelled good. Her living, breathing butterscotch buffet. *Focus.* "We're partners, right?"

He offered a reluctant nod, one that finally brushed skin against skin. There was no preventing her shiver then. The heat, the sizzle . . . consuming.

"Well, partners have to trust each other, and right now, neither of us trusts the other. Right?"

Another nod, another brushing of their noses.

Another shiver from her. "Rather than getting me in trouble, we're going to spend the next few hours learning to trust."

"How?" One word, but like his whip nonetheless. Where was that thing, anyway? *She* could tie *him* down with it.

"Well, there's an exercise I've seen people do." Good thinking. "You stand behind me, and I fall back. You catch me, and boom, I learn to rely on you and trust you to always protect me."

He arched a brow, clearly doubtful. "Learning to trust is that easy?"

"Yes." A lie. She wouldn't trust him, not fully, no matter what—he saw her as food, damn it!—but the exercise seemed like a really good idea just then. Not just because they would be wasting time, distracting him, but because he would have to put his hands on her to catch her. And she really wanted his hands on her. Not for pleasure, but for inoculation.

She *had* to overcome this craving for him.

"And while we're doing this," she said, squaring her shoulders, "you can tell me all about vampires. Everything I need to know to capture one." Tomorrow, she would fulfill her end of their bargain.

Several minutes ticked by in silence. He watched her every torturous second of those minutes, gaze hooded, yet still managing to wreck havoc on her nerve endings. They felt razored, sensitized.

"All right," he finally said, voice as devoid of emotion as his eyes. Eyes that fell to the hammering pulse at the base of her neck.

Thinking of drinking from her, even now? she wondered as she gave him her back. Dangerous on her part, perhaps, but she wasn't too worried about him swooping in for a taste of her. At the moment, he was too interested in gaining rights to her blood, and if he took a sip without permission, he'd never gain those rights.

"Are you just going to stand there?" he asked, whisper-soft.

That whisper traveled the length of her spine, and she had to steel herself against another decadent shiver. "Tell me something about vampires first." While she prepared herself for what was to come.

Another pause. Then, "Each vampires has a different ability."

Do it. Just do it. She allowed herself to fall backward. "Yours is manipulating time."

"Yes." He caught her just before she hit and held her there, suspended in the air.

She gazed up at him, his face upside down yet still beautiful, and licked her lips. His hands were as warm and strong as she'd imagined. "What are some other abilities?"

"Teleporting." His voice was strained as he eased her to her feet. "Mind control. Camouflage. Vampires like Bride can do everything, though."

She prayed the strain wasn't from her weight. "Bride." The name echoed through her mind, and then she remembered. Bride, his former fiancée. A spark of jealousy ignited. Did he still yearn for the lovely, dark-haired vampire? "She can do everything?"

"Yes. Everything," he replied, unaware of her sudden shift from nervous anticipation to fury. "Well, except manipulate time. Now, is it your turn to catch me?"

"No. Still mine. I'm stuck on the word *everything*." Ice crystallized the words, making them as hard as diamonds. Again she fell back.

Again he caught her—still warm, still strong, but even more so—and held her suspended. The violet of his eyes snared her. "Anything you can think of, she can do." The strain in his voice was even worse. "What's hard to understand?"

I am. I'm heavy. Unlike lithe little Bride, who couldn't weigh more than a hundred and ten soaking wet and weighed down with rocks. "Just shut up."

And wow. Bride was not only beautiful and sensually lean, she was beyond powerful. No wonder McKell had waited so long to marry her and no other.

Hello again, inferiority complex, Ava thought hotly.

McKell set her back on her feet. His fingers remained splayed over her ribs, hard but not bruising. "My turn now?"

"No. I'll tell you when. Until then, keep catching me." Each word ripped from her throat, leaving a raw, venom-burned wound. Why was he so eager for his turn, anyway? She was going to drop his ass flat. Like he deserved. "Were you upset when Bride married Devyn?"

"Yes."

Bastard! "Why didn't you kill him?"

"Because killing him would have made her hate me."

And he wanted—still wanted?—Bride to love him? Depression replaced her anger. "I don't like this game," she said. Really, she didn't like *Bride*. All-powerful Bride, she inwardly mocked. Possessive McKell had let someone he considered his go, rather than fight and cause hatred.

He flattened his hands on her shoulders and forced her to turn. Then he pressed, forcing her to stay. She peered up at him. Despite everything, she liked the sear of his palms, the tickle of his fingertips, and wanted them to dip, to explore.

"Any more questions? Or may I have my turn now? A turn you *will* give me."

She definitely had another question. "Vampires feed on humans, right? And yet, once they're married, they can only feed on their spouse. So what happens when two *vampires* marry?"

There was a sharp intake of his breath, a narrowing of his eyes. "So you know about vampire mating habits, do you?"

Oops. She hadn't meant to alert him to that fact.

His gaze explored her face, searching for the answer she refused to give. He must have seen the truth, because he flicked his tongue over one of his fangs. "Vampire spouses only feed on each other."

Now that he knew that she knew, there was no reason to hold back. "Then why don't all vampires feed on other vampires and leave humans alone?" Uh-oh. Was her resentment showing?

His grip tightened. "Because feeding on each other will wed them, and most vampires do not wish to be wed. Ever."

"Why?"

"Because eternity is a long time to be together."

Eternity. A blessing and a curse, she supposed. A forever of pleasure, as well as pain. "You guys don't die?"

"By natural causes? Rarely."

"Then isn't your underground word getting crowded?"

"No. It's difficult for vampires to procreate. More than that, I was a good exterminator."

Ava imagined a vampire kid running around her place and wasn't completely repulsed. Interesting. Usually she hated kids. They were too . . . needy. And messy. And clingy. No way did she want to be responsible for the way someone else turned out, blamed for their failures and mistakes. But a little McKell with black hair and violet eyes . . . was a shockingly sweet image.

"You've had my blood," she said, head tilting to the side as she tried to work a few things out. "And if I was to have yours, we'd be married?"

He gave a stiff nod. "If you're thinking about drinking from me without permission, be warned that I will remove your teeth with pliers and seal your mouth shut, so that you never have the opportunity to—"

"Let me stop you there." Ava reached up and closed his mouth for him. "I won't be drinking from you. *Ever.*"

At first, he gave no reaction. Then he wrapped his finger around her wrist and squeezed, a fire suddenly smoldering in his eyes. "My blood tastes delicious."

"Don't care. Your blood could be liquid gold, and I wouldn't want it. I'm not getting married. Not to you, not to anyone." Drunk or sober, she was confident in that.

"But I'm a prize."

"So am I."

"Yes, but I'm a vampire."

"Like that helps your case," she said dryly. "Vampires suck."

"I know." He released her and stepped back, increasing the distance between them, the fire sparking white-hot. "Would you want to wed a human?"

"By definition, not marrying anyone means I wouldn't marry *anyone*, no matter their origins."

"So you wish to remain alone?"

Hadn't she just said that? "Yes."

Now the fire spread to his cheeks, painting twin pink circles there. "We'll see about that. And now, little human, it's my turn to fall. You had better catch me, or I *will* punish you." He spun, giving her his back.

"McKell, I can't—"

Down . . . down . . . he tumbled, ignoring her protest. She reached out, to catch him or slap him, she wasn't sure. But she never made contact. One second she was standing up, floundering, the next she was flat on her back and McKell was looming over her, pinning her and grinning wickedly.

"You didn't catch me," he said. "I get to punish you."

Her mind reeled at the change, but her body didn't care about the impossibility, simply reacting. Nipples beading, back arching, legs spreading. "You stopped time and moved me, didn't you?"

"Prove it," he said, and then kissed her.

Thirteen

Ava meant to fight him. Perhaps knee him in the balls, slug him, even stab him again. Only, he was feeding her kiss after delicious kiss, hello and good-bye wrapped in one drugging interlude, his tongue thrusting into her mouth, as warm and strong as his hands and far more insistent, and her resistance melted. Had she ever really possessed any?

She wound her arms around him, one hand sinking into his silky hair, the other cupping the back of his neck, holding him hostage, taking, giving. Demanding more. He was so big, so heavy, he should have crushed her, *did* crush her, but she found she didn't need air. She just needed him. His weight, his heat, *his* breath.

He'd reduced her to a live wire. A wire that couldn't spark without contact. Her legs spread farther, and his lower body moved, resting between them, poised. The thick length of his shaft pressed against her core, teasing. He didn't move again, though. Didn't rub, even a little, creating friction, such delicious friction, and that was probably for the best.

Probably? Ha! But she was as grateful as she was disappointed and confused. Had he rubbed against her, she would have been tugging at his clothes, demanding fuller contact, desperate for climax. He had to know that. So why wasn't he moving? Why was he maintaining such a lingering pace?

Did he not plan to take this to the next level? Did he simply wish to put her in her place? Remind her that he was in control, that she was merely a human who craved a man out of her league? That she was good for food, and nothing more? Earlier, his concern had been for her blood, not her passion.

The spark dulled. Chilled. Left her cold. She pulled from the kiss. "Don't do that again," she rasped.

"What?" He kissed his way to her neck.

Despite herself, she angled her head for better contact. She wasn't sure if she wanted him to kiss her there or bite her. All she knew was that, if he *did* bite her, she would have to kill him. Sad but true. She couldn't allow him to break his word without consequences—even if she would enjoy the breaking.

"Ava. Answer."

Oh, yeah. He'd asked a question. What did she not want him to do? "Stop time and . . . position me."

"But you like how I positioned you." He licked.

She shivered. "Yeah, but I don't like being forced." *Force me.* Wait. What?

Rather than sink his teeth into her neck, he moved lower. Kissed her sternum as if she weren't wearing a T-shirt. "I'm not forcing you."

What was he planning to do? "Are you purposely frustrating me, then?"

"No. I'm trying to *relieve* your frustration, and collect my reward." Lower still. He stopped and rested his chin on her pubic bone, looking up at her without any emotion. "You do want to reward me for helping AIR, yes?"

"Yes." She gulped. "Just . . . promise me that you won't stop time for me again."

He snorted. "I'll make no such promise. You use what weapons you have at your disposal, and I use what weapons I have."

Irrefutable.

A few minutes passed, yet he never moved from his new position. Finally, she forced her gaze away from his beautiful face. His blank expression had never wavered, and she feared what *her* expression revealed. Longing. Need. More of that confusion.

She peered up at her ceiling, flat, white, but every second that ticked by caused her anticipation to intensify. When would he move? When he did move, what would he do? And why was she giving him this time? She should find the strength to stand and walk away. If he felt nothing, she didn't want to feel anything either.

"Why aren't you running away from me?" he asked, breaking the silence. "I could do anything I wanted to you, and you wouldn't be able to stop me."

Promises, promises. "I'm not afraid of you."

"Others are."

"Well, why aren't you running from *me*?"

"I'm not afraid of you."

"Others are," she parroted.

He kissed the flare of her hip, soft, sweet. "Your nipples are hard."

Way to change the subject, she thought, shivering. "I know." No reason to deny the obvious.

"I've seen them, you know." His voice was drugging desire, melted and poured over her.

Do not moan. Do not arch. "When?"

"When I stripped you. The first night I met you."

Do not cup your breasts. "You left me in my bra and panties."

"Actually, I stripped you naked, then decided to return your undergarments to protect your modesty when you traveled home."

Do not ask him to demonstrate exactly how he stripped you. "So . . . did you cop a feel?" She nibbled on her bottom lip, gaze returning to him unbidden. Mistake. Or not.

No longer did he appear unaffected. The color had reignited in his cheeks, his eyes an inferno of the desire she'd heard in his voice. This was more than hunger on his part. This was need. Why had he tried to hide it? The answer didn't matter, really. She reacted. Moan, yes. Arch, definitely. There was no stopping her now.

"Cop a feel?" He blew on her belly, warm breath seeping past her shirt. "Are you asking if I touched you?"

A fever spread through her, pulling her skin taut. "Yes, that's exactly what I'm asking." *And begging for.*

"No. I didn't." Another breath wafted over her. "But I wanted to," he added on a moan of his own.

Pulling . . . tauter and tauter . . . "So you liked what you saw?" Whispers, echoes of her need.

"Oh, yes."

"Even though I'm a lowly human?"

A minute passed, then another. He never replied, and she was glad. She hadn't meant to voice the fear, or even acknowledge it, but it was there, buried deep, yet somehow never far from the surface. Right now, though, she didn't care. Couldn't. The here and now was for pleasure, only pleasure. Pleasure he wanted, too, no matter the other things that had passed between them.

He smoothed her T-shirt away from the waist of her jeans, revealing a patch of needy skin. His tongue dipped inside her navel, swirling, and the fever spread again, causing her veins to expand.

Another moan slipped from her.

"Say the word, and I'll open your jeans and move lower."

Anything. "What word?"

"Yes."

And have his tongue dip into her core, licking, sucking, tasting? Her body arcing into him, demanding more? Satisfaction leaving her utterly sated? Until the fever returned—and it would return.

"No." A tiny voice of reason in the face of unequivocal temptation. Still. *Stupid, stupid girl.* But she couldn't regret her decision. Much. A kiss on the mouth could be written off. Heavy petting, too. But a kiss between the legs? No. That was sex.

He stiffened, lifted slightly. "Why not?"

She almost grabbed his head, almost pressed him back against her stomach. She had an excuse for her resistance, she knew she did, she just had to remember what it was. An eternity ago, she'd even told Noelle—oh, yeah. It came to her in a rush. "I just can't sleep with an AIR target."

"I'm helping AIR."

"So." An uncaring statement meant for her, not him.

"And besides, we wouldn't be sleeping." He darted back up, covering her body with his own. "We would be pleasuring." His weight shot the air from her lungs, and as she opened her mouth to breathe, he descended. No more hesitation. No more lingering.

His tongue plundered deep, destroying her reason. Their teeth scraped, and his hands slid underneath her, lifting her up, pressing her into his erection. Finally, rubbing. Hard. Perfect.

Another moan emerged. So good. Stupid clothes. She despised them. Wanted to rip them off. Almost ripped *his* off, as her fingers kneaded his back, traced the length of his spine.

The rasp of their exhalations crackled in the air. They continued to grind against each other, propelling her need to new, vehement heights. Soon she was groaning, gasping, biting at *him*. No blood, she thought. No blood. There was a reason, but again, she had to remember what it was.

He didn't seem to care what she did. He just fed her kiss after electrifying kiss, panting, sweating, groping. Unrelenting.

This was what she'd wanted, what she'd needed. And as always with this man, being with him was heaven and hell. She knew she should stop, but couldn't. Consequences were for tomorrow, pleasure for today. Right?

He lifted one of his hands and massaged her breast, fingers rolling against her hardened nipple. How she ached. How she craved. More, more, more.

You already told him no more, she thought, that small kernel of reason returning.

Stupid.

"McKell," she gasped out.

His grip tightened, as if he knew where she was headed and hoped to misdirect her. The ache increased—and so did the pleasure. It had been a long time for her, but she wasn't sure she'd ever wanted a man this desperately. As if she couldn't survive another moment without his cock inside her. Maybe because he tasted like butterscotch. Maybe because he felt like the final piece to the puzzle she'd been trying to finish for years.

All from a kiss.

That . . . scared her.

Think. She had to think about this, rather than plunge headfirst into an abyss of complications.

Again, she pulled from the kiss. "What do you hope to accomplish, kissing me?" she managed to say. Hopefully, he would stop before they reached the point of no return. Because she still couldn't stop him. Physically she could have, maybe, but not mentally. Not emotionally. She had to have this.

He lifted his head, and she wanted to scream. His lips were swollen, pink, and wet. "I told you. Pleasure. For us both."

"We can get that anywhere." Liar! She wanted him, and only him. Loved what she'd done to his lips. Loved that he looked well-kissed, aroused beyond measure, his features tense, desperate.

Fury flashed through those violet eyes, angels and demons dancing in the midst of the flames. "You will not touch another man, Ava."

Loved that he'd said that. "And if I do?"

"I'll kill him." Simply stated, proving the unbendable oath behind the words.

"Do you plan to touch another woman?" What was she doing? Why was she pushing him like this? And in this direction?

"No."

That was why. She'd needed his assurance, and the relief that accompanied it. "Not even a precious vampire female?" Ah. The deeper reason. So clear now. The question of his superiority and her inferiority had never truly left the surface.

He ran his tongue over his too-sharp teeth. "Not even."

He didn't sound convinced *or* convincing, and that pissed her the hell off, wiping away her relief in one fatal sweep. So she was supposed to abstain, but he could do as he pleased? She raised her knee between their bodies and planted her foot on his stomach. One forceful kick, and he was flying backward.

He hit her couch with a grunt, but he didn't freeze time or launch at her, merely settled comfortably against the furniture and glared over at her.

Panting, she sat up, shoving the hair from her face.

"What was that for?" he demanded.

"For your being an ass."

"How so?"

Her lips pressed together in a mutinous line. As if she would say it aloud. Again. "You were telling me about vampires. Why don't you finish telling me so we can get to work?"

McKell peered over at Ava, confused by her, yet still so highly aroused he could have torn her home apart. She'd tasted unbelievably sweet. Had been soft beneath his hands. Soft and curved and perfect. His hands itched to return to her. To learn more about her, to memorize her.

His back stung from where she'd dug in her nails, beseeching him for more. More—which was exactly what he wanted to give. He'd almost ripped her jeans from her body and licked into her feminine core, even though she hadn't asked as he'd instructed.

Had he done so, he might have died from the pleasure. Pleasure he'd meant to give her, taking nothing in return, addicting her to his touch, his tongue, before convincing her to giving him total access to her vein.

Only, along the way, her blood had ceased to matter. Only her passion had concerned him. Then she'd pushed him away. Why?

What had they discussed before her passion had faded? Her being with another man, he quickly recalled. His teeth gnashed together. The thought of her with someone else nearly sent him into a killing rage. Whether he liked it or not—whether *she* liked it or not—she belonged to him just then.

She'd demanded assurance that he wouldn't stray, and he hoped that meant she wanted him all to herself. So he'd given her that assurance—even though he knew he would one day purge her from his system. He would have to, if he hoped to wed someone of his own race, as was proper. Someone who wouldn't wither and die, leaving him alone and suffering.

That assurance was more than he'd ever given another. And he'd meant it. While they were together, he wouldn't be with any one else. Which wasn't a requirement, damn it! He couldn't drink from anyone else, but as he'd already considered, he could damn sure fuck a thousand others. But would he? The answer was still a solid no. Did she appreciate that, though? Again, one big, solid, fucking no.

"Ignoring me?" she said, her calmness scraping his already raw nerves.

"Nothing else to tell," he replied darkly. "You'll lure them to me, and I'll take over from there."

"And if they attack me?"

The thought of that angered him far more than the thought of her with another man. Something that made absolutely no sense. He would prefer her with someone else, rather than drained of blood? If so, that would mean . . . no, no, hell, no. He wasn't going there.

"McKell," she snapped. "An answer, please."

"If they attack you, kill them or I'll do it for you. It's that simple." His rage wouldn't be, though. If anyone attacked her, even his own kind, he would lose control of his sanity and allow his rage to consume him. He knew it, felt it. The world would *suffer*.

"But if they're dead, they can't teach you how to live here."

"If they try to hurt you, I won't want to learn from them." Would only want their blood to flow in a crimson river, soaking the concrete.

Some of the tension left her features. "What's the best way to lure a vampire, then?"

All she would have to do was walk into a room, he thought. Any bloodsucker who could resist that sweet scent was stronger than him—and no one was stronger than him. "We'll dress you in plain clothes, make you look weak and shy."

"*That's* attractive?"

No. "Yes." He didn't want her in the scanty clothing his kind preferred humans to wear, making them more easily accessible. "They'll think you're easy pickings." Plus, as small and delicate as she appeared, no one would suspect her of lethal strength and violent urges.

His cock ached. All that strength, all those urges ... he'd had them underneath him.

"Okay," she said with a nod, drifting that sweet scent his way and managing to intensify the ache. "I can do that. But how will I recognize a vampire? I mean, unless your fangs are extended, you look human to me."

"Anyone who tries to lure you away, you will bring to me."

"And if they aren't vampire?"

Then they would still deserve the beating he gave them for daring to try to lure his woman. *Temporary* woman. "I'll know the moment I smell them, and will send them on their way." Broken and bloody.

"Sounds tedious and boring, and not to mention like shooting an enemy in the dark. Which means, if you need that translated, we'll be relying on luck."

He shrugged. "I can think of no other way. If they scent me first, and they will if I'm by your side, they'll leave. Whether they want to drink from you or not."

"Well, maybe you should walk into wherever you think they'll be, and I'll wait at the back door and grab the runners."

Smart, but such a plan placed her in too much danger. "You won't be able to stop a fleeing vampire on your own, Ava. Besides that, we couldn't be sure what exit they would take."

The corner of her lip curled. "I stopped you, didn't I?"

Ache . . . intensifying again . . . "And I stopped you back. Only my caring nature saved you. Something the others might not possess."

She snorted. "Caring nature. Please. By your own admission, you just wanted to strip me."

"That's not the only thing I wanted to do," he muttered. Then, more clearly, "You won't know what the vampires are capable of, so you won't know what to fight against. You won't be able to stop more than one, either."

"Two pyre-guns can stop two vampires."

"And if there are three?"

Her eyes narrowed. "I'll freeze two, then fire at the third. And if that doesn't work, I'll fistfight him."

The woman had an answer for everything. "And the fourth? Fifth? No, don't reply. We'll do things my way or not at all."

"Oh, well, in that case, I pick not at all."

And he'd found her smugness attractive? His teeth gnashed as they often did in her presence. "Then I won't help AIR. With anything. Not with vampires. Not with the Schön disease. Not with the Schön queen. I won't answer Agent Snow's questions, either."

After only the slightest hesitation, she said, "Fine. Your way."

Smiling, he eased to his feet. "Thank you. We shall begin tomorrow. As for tonight, get some rest. You'll need it." He strode to the front door, and it opened automatically, allowing him a straight shot into the hallway.

"Hey. Where are you going?" she called.

"Until tomorrow," he replied as the door closed. Tonight, he needed to have a serious heart-to-heart with himself, and allow his anger with her to fester. Falling for this woman wasn't acceptable. Being charmed by her every word—despite his irritation with her—was not acceptable, either.

Surely there was someone out there who was prettier, wittier, and nicer. Someone better suited to him and his needs. Someone with fangs. Tonight, during his heart-to-heart, he would search. Find a starting place for his and Ava's hunt.

Because, what she didn't know and what he would never tell her, what he'd realized a short while ago, was that if he could find and question bloodsuckers who had learned to live in the daylight, he could also find her replacement.

Fourteen

*A*nother sleepless night. Of course. Ava expected no different despite McKell's command to rest and her body's desire to obey him. She'd wanted to call him about . . . oh, a thousand times, and ask where he'd gone, and what he was doing.

By nine the next morning, when she suspected he would be sleeping himself, Ava gave up trying to rest and finally caved to the impulse. He had her cell phone, and what better way to punish him for stealing it?

After three rings, he actually picked up. "What?" he barked.

He was alive, at least. Ignoring her raging headache, she relaxed into the mattress, the covers plumping around her. "How dare you answer my phone, you thieving bastard." The hangover added spice to her tone. "Have you been answering *all* my calls?"

Static sounded, and she imagined him rubbing the fatigue from his face. Such a human thing to do, so slumber sweet. The pain in her temples migrated to her chest. "Ava?"

"Who else would be calling?"

"Your friend Noelle. She called all night long," he

grumbled. "And she never talks about anything of importance. I now know about her favorite shoes, what foods agree with her and what foods do not. That wasn't pleasant to hear about, by the way. Oh, yes. And I know she's considering chopping off her hair, and can't decide if she wants to sleep with Dallas or Hector."

I love that girl. "Who'd you vote for?"

"You. I offered to be there, and give instruction as needed. You're very difficult to please, you know."

A chuckle and a moan mixed in her throat, emerging as a cough. One part of her wanted to continue down that path with him, knowing very well where it would end. Heavy breathing, dirty talk, wandering hands, and climax. The other part of her wasn't brain-damaged.

She rolled from bed, phone propped against her shoulder and bones creaking in protest. "Anyone left any messages for me?" she asked as she padded into the kitchen. Yawning, she filled the coffeepot with synthetic coffee beans and water. Most food was synthetic, most meat was from cloned animals, and even fruit was somehow a copy of the real deal.

Apparently, after the human-alien war, supplies had dwindled, and unapproved scientific methods had been the only chance for survival. Suddenly those methods had met with approval.

"People left messages, yes," he said, but offered no more.

"Well, what are they?" Thankfully, the scent of caffeine soon filled the air, chasing away the last remnants of exhaustion and alcoholic excess.

"I don't know. They were for you, so I ignored them. You're welcome."

Bastard. The pot finished its nearly instant percolation, and she poured herself a cup of coffee, then added the last of her butterscotch creamer. Wait. The last? She held the dispenser to the light and shook. Sure enough. Not a single drop remained. Shit. She needed a moment of silence to mourn its loss.

"Ava?"

"Just a sec." *I'll miss you, sweet creamer.* She sighed. "Okay, I'm back. So, if you won't tell me about my messages, tell me what you did last night."

"No. I won't."

The sudden edge of menace in his voice increased her curiosity. "Tell me."

"No. I'll tell you what I plan to do for the rest of the day, though." The menace faded, gentling to . . . desire? "I'll be sleeping and thinking about you. What about you?"

Thinking of her. She almost melted. Almost. Sadly, it was lesson time. And today's moral? Keep secrets and suffer. "Better question: *Who* will I be doing today? But the answer's the same. You'll never know," she said, and severed the connection. Let him stew on that.

She drained her coffee, showered, and dressed in the standard AIR attire. White button-up top, black slacks, and faux leather boots. She anchored her hair in a lumpy ponytail. With her curls, no style would ever be smooth.

Noelle picked her up fifteen minutes late. As usual. "We look ridiculous, wearing the same outfit like this," was the first thing her friend said as Ava slid into the passenger side of the vehicle.

"Ridiculous, but cute."

"True."

The sun was already too bright and too warm, the streets crowded with humans and aliens driving to work. Most were harried, almost spastic, while a few were calm, concentrating. Ava hoped she appeared calm, even though she felt harried. Fact was, she couldn't stand being late for anything.

No matter how late they were, though, Noelle *never* looked harried. Today, she was as beautiful and elegant as always, even in that white button-up. And, to be honest, they should have looked like they were wearing matching outfits, but they didn't. Noelle's shirt was clearly made of expensive cotton—*real* cotton—and appeared so soft Ava was tempted to strip and rub all over it.

"Oh, and to apologize for my tardiness, I brought you a butterscotch latte." Noelle held out a plastic mug.

Salvation. Even though she'd already had her morning coffee, she drank greedily.

As the car meandered to AIR headquarters, Noelle said, "McKell go back to your place last night? I know he left again because I called him. Repeatedly."

"I know, and thank you for that. But nope," she grumbled. "He didn't return."

"Is he playing hard-to-get?"

"Nah. He's playing Irritate Ava." Why hadn't he told her what he'd done after leaving her apartment? Had he slept with some random female, turned on as he'd been, and didn't want her to know because he suspected Ava would never allow him to drink from her again? Well, she didn't care who he slept with. She'd told him no. Had left him primed. But damn it to hell. He'd promised not to see anyone else. Hadn't he?

Only thing she truly remembered about last night was the fact that he'd kissed her and left her.

"Irritate Ava is my favorite game," Noelle said. "You're so cute when you're mad."

If he *had* slept with someone else, she'd slap him on the back in a job well done. Just like she'd do for any male friend she had. Not that she had any male friends. Not that she wanted any male friends. Men were stupid, stupid, stupid, and controlled by their stupid dicks, and that bastard McKell was going to be *stabbed* in the back if he'd slept with someone else. Ava would rip him into ribbons and tie those ribbons on every bedpost she could find. A symbolic gesture McKell wouldn't understand because he was stupid!

"Uh, Ava?"

"What?" she shouted.

"I didn't mean it. You are *so* not cute when you're mad. Your cheeks are bright red, you're panting and sweating and ripping my brand-new, pristine interior apart."

"What?" The haze of red faded from her gaze—until that moment, she hadn't even realized the red had appeared—and she looked around. She was still inside Noelle's car, her nails were scraping over the leather seat, and she was gritting her teeth so forcefully, her jaw ached. "Sorry. I'm sorry."

"No worries. Swear."

One by one she picked her nails out of the seat.

A few minutes later, they reached AIR's main gate, a simple iron bar that stretched from one guard post to another. A few yards beyond, the landscape was flat and bare, boasting no trees or flowers that would allow anyone to hide. There, in the center, sat AIR.

On the outside, the building appeared to be nothing more than a two-story warehouse comprised of metal and dark red brick. In actuality, three other stories were hidden underground. Three that she knew of; there could have been more. There were cameras and weapons everywhere, camouflaged between the bricks.

Security was taken seriously here. Protestors—alien advocates—had once raided the old building, allowing a dangerous prisoner to escape.

After two ID scans, she and Noelle were allowed to park in the underground lot. Took another ID scan to be allowed to walk out of the lot and into the building, and then several fingerprint scans, even a retinal scan, and three badge verifications to hit the elevator.

"I wonder what's on today's agenda," Noelle muttered as they strode down the long, plain hallway toward Mia's office.

"Don't know." No matter what, Ava wouldn't allow herself to think about McKell for the rest of the day. He would consume her, and that was dangerous.

They stopped in front of Mia's door, and a grinning Noelle pressed the speaker button. "Noelle Tramain and Ava Sans reporting for duty, sir."

"Funny," Mia's raspy voice said from the speaker. There was a pause, then a click, then the door slid open.

Mia sat behind her desk, paperwork strewn around her. Her lips were compressed into a mulish line, and bruises formed half moons under her eyes. Most likely, her night had been as sleepless as Ava's.

Dallas occupied a chair across from the desk, his expression as grim and tense as Mia's. Unlike Mia, however, he radiated guilt. Why?

Ava and a now somber Noelle stepped inside, and the door closed behind them automatically. Ava suddenly felt . . . caged.

"We found Johnny," Mia said, jumping headfirst into business. "He's infected."

Ava's jaw dropped as a denial surged up her throat. "With the Schön disease?"

"What else?" Dallas asked grimly. His gaze skimmed over Noelle, lingering a bit longer than necessary, before skidding away. For some reason, his guilt seemed to intensify.

"Fuck," Noelle breathed.

"Yeah. That's exactly what he did. Fucked the queen." Mia pushed out a breath. "Not one of her servants or lackeys or whatever they are, but the queen herself. So his infection has spread quickly, more quickly than any of the other victims. We gave him the last remaining supply of Bride's blood, and that slowed things down, though we don't think it's healed him completely."

Bile joined denial, but she swallowed them both. Now was not the time to allow either to overtake her. She had to stay strong, and she had to keep her wits. Poor Johnny. She harbored no ill feelings for him, well, no death wish, even though he was a tool for kissing and telling.

"No one here has been able to get any details out of him," Mia continued. "But you, Ava, once slept with him, so we thought—"

"Accidentally," Noelle interrupted.

Dallas's brow furrowed. "Excuse me?"

"I, uh, accidentally slept with him," Ava explained, cheeks heating as they always did when this subject arose.

A delicate hand punched through the air. "I don't care if you fell from a ladder and somehow landed on his dick. He has feelings for you, so you're going to talk to him."

Not for a second did she think about refusing. If there was anything she could to do help, anything at all, she was going to do it. "What should I ask him?"

"I want details. What did she say to him? How did she fuck him? What position? Did they do anything afterward?"

"Also, ask him if he's noticed any changes in his body, besides a hunger for human flesh," Dallas added.

Mia propped her elbows on her desk, pinning Ava with her ice-blue stare. "If you're scared, we can find someone else. Just say the—"

"I'm not scared," she growled. A lie. The thought of being in the same room as a person with a highly contagious disease terrified her. What if Johnny spit on her? What if he leapt at her and bit? Would she be infected, too? Would that stop her, though? No. "I'll do it. Just tell me where is he, and it's done."

Dallas nodded in satisfaction, gaze returning to Noelle before again skidding away, as if he didn't trust himself to prolong even so small a contact. "I'll lead the way."

"I'll come. For moral support," Noelle said.

A muscle ticked below his eye, but he unfolded from the chair, tall and leanly muscled. A dark avenger. As he strode past Ava and Noelle—both of them had to step to the side to provide a space for him to exit— the door opened. Without missing a beat, he hit the hallway. Reminded her of McKell, when he'd left her apartment. On a mission, determined.

But she wasn't going to think about him. Or that. Not even to distract herself from the dangerous pool she was about to jump into.

She and Noelle followed Dallas, silent. Along the

way, Noelle twined their fingers and squeezed in reassurance, offering comfort.

Thank you, she mouthed.

Noelle nodded, and looked away from Ava as quickly as Dallas had looked away from her. To hide her fear, Ava knew. She gave a squeeze of her own, letting her friend know all would be well. She kept the *I hope* to herself.

A few twists and turns, agents striding in the opposite direction, and they finally entered the interrogation wing of the building. So soon? she thought, panic suddenly beating hard fists in her lungs.

You can do this. You will do this.

Dallas stopped in front of an unmarked door, then motioned to the entrance next to it with a tilt of his chin. "This one's ours. That one's yours." He opened his own and once again motioned with his chin, to Noelle this time. "Hustle, Tremain."

Noelle didn't budge. "Shouldn't she be wearing protective gear or something?"

"You know that won't help."

Comforting.

His eyes, as icy a blue as Mia's, but somehow warm despite that, met Ava's. "He's restrained. You can touch him, even lick him, and you'll be fine. Just don't blow him or screw him. That's when problems arise. So if you don't think you can resist doing those things . . ."

"I can resist. Swear to God, I can resist." Finally, the panic faded.

He nodded his approval. "Tremain. What about that hustle?"

"Good luck. Not that you'll need it." Noelle gave her a quick hug before striding past Dallas and into the room.

He followed and shut the door in Ava's face.

After a deep breath, she pivoted on her heel and approached the second door. Her hand shook as she reached out and flattened her palm on the ID box. Blue lights sparked at her fingers, then traveled to her wrist. Entire process took less than two seconds, but those seconds lasted forever—and yet not long enough.

The door slid open, and she was suddenly peering into a white room that boasted only one frivolity. A mirror. A mirror Dallas and Noelle stood behind. Johnny had been restrained, as promised, his hands cuffed to the arms of his metal chair and his ankles cuffed to its legs. He wouldn't be able to leap at her, she thought with relief, but he could still spit on her. Bye-bye relief. At least the cold wash of panic remained at bay.

She raised her chin and marched all the way inside. He watched her, silent. She claimed the chair across from him, a table stretching between them, and studied him. Dark half-circles had formed under his eyes, like Mia's, only bigger, and raw. Lines of tension branched from his mouth, and his skin possessed a sickly yellow tint. His lips were dry and cracked.

"Nothing to say to me?" Even his voice was different. Lower, harder. Frayed at the edges.

Just like that, even her hesitation evaporated. This was Johnny. Eager, if clueless, Johnny. She could handle him. "I've got plenty to say, actually. We'll start with how stupid you were."

Something thumped against the back of the mirror. Ava imagined Dallas pounding against the shield-armor, wanting to bust his way past the obstruction and slap her for kicking things off with criticism, and Noelle latching onto his forearms and refusing to let go. Dallas probably didn't conduct his interviews this way, but Ava didn't care. She had a plan. She was going to irritate Johnny so much he would be willing to answer *anything* to get rid of her.

She just prayed it worked.

"How could you sleep with her?" she demanded.

His eyes, glassy and blown, narrowed. "Jealous?"

As she'd learned the day after crawling out of his bed, when he cornered her at her desk and told her that he was willing to give her another chance with him, everything began and ended with Johnny's ego. "Do you want the truth or a lie?"

Another thump against the glass.

Johnny popped his jaw. "She was hot."

Typical, but truthful. Good. "And that made who and what she was okay?"

"I didn't know, damn it! She looked human."

"And smelled human?" McKell had mentioned a putrid scent.

"Yes, damn it."

So only McKell could smell the rot radiating

off her? Interesting. That put him in a position of power.

"Why'd they send you, anyway?" Johnny demanded. "Everyone knows I had you, and now I'm done with you."

"That's what everyone knows, is it?" She didn't try to mask her sarcasm.

His eyes narrowed a little more, becoming slits, his lashes shielding the emotion in his eyes. "Just ask your questions and get out, Ava."

Gold star for her. The plan was a success. Only, it wasn't pride that accompanied the victory. How sad that a once-future agent had been reduced to this. *Just get it over with.* "After you left the bar, she appeared to you on the street." A statement, not a question.

He answered, anyway. "Yes."

"Where'd you guys go?"

"Straight to my apartment."

"Did you talk along the way?"

"Yes."

"About what?"

A lift of his shoulders, followed by a grimace, as if even so small a movement was torture. "About how much she liked me."

Ava allowed her doubt to show. "You're telling the truth? Not exaggerating?"

"No, I'm not exaggerating." Those lashes parted, and he pinned her with a dark stare. "Some women find me attractive, you know."

"I know," she told him softly. She simply wasn't

one of them. "So tell me exactly what she said, what she liked."

Another shrug, limited because of the restraints and clearly just as painful. " 'Oh, Johnny, you're so strong. You're so beautiful.' " The falsetto was mocking, dripping with self-deprecation. " 'I'd love to see your bedroom. I'd love to touch you.' "

Didn't take much to piece together what had happened next. "You cared only about having sex, not about what kind of person she might be." Of course.

He nodded, a stiff jerky motion.

"What happened once you got to your bedroom?"

"The talking stopped."

"Be specific."

Fury flashed through his expression, and for one second, one priceless second, he resembled the agent she knew and not the sick, dying victim he'd become. "She stripped me, stripped herself, then crawled into bed with me."

"Did you kiss her?"

Another nod.

"What'd she taste like?"

He laughed, but it was a bitter song, acrid and hate-filled. "What does that matter?"

"We're trying to figure this woman out. Trying to find ways to identify her, to destroy her. To prevent her from doing this to other people. To save you." As she spoke, Johnny's fury and bitterness dulled, softening his features. "Help us. Please."

Silence. Such heavy silence.

"What if she goes after Jeremy next?" Ava hated herself for playing on what had to be one of his deepest fears, but they were discussing life and death. Victory and defeat. What if the queen went after Noelle? McKell?

Johnny hung his head, staring down at his lap. Another bout of silence stretched between them, and Ava suspected she had failed. She didn't know what else to say, but she leaned forward and rested her arms on the table, sliding her hands closer and closer to his side.

"Johnny. Please. Why won't you tell me?"

"I know where you're headed with this, and it's humiliating," he snapped, trying to jerk from her coming touch. His chair moved not an inch.

With a sigh, she settled back in her seat and hooked fallen tendrils of hair behind her ears. "Would you talk to someone else? A man?"

More silence. Heavier. Then, "She tasted like . . . roses," he admitted, surprising her. "That's the only thing I can think to compare it to even though I don't actually know the taste of roses."

"And you liked it?"

"Yes."

"Did you . . . did you taste between her legs?"

"See! I knew you were going there."

Ava didn't back down. "Did you?"

"Yes," he lashed out. "I did."

Now they were getting somewhere. "What did she taste like there?"

"The same. Roses."

O-kay. What was so humiliating about that? "Did she come?"

A growl pushed from his lips. "What the hell does that matter?"

Ah. Finally. The reason for his humiliation. No, the queen hadn't come that way, and Johnny had taken it personally, as if he were lacking. "Thank you for your honesty. Now, afterward, you. . . ?"

"Fucked her. Yes."

"And did you use a condom?"

"Yes, damn it. I'm not stupid."

So. Either the disease was stronger than latex, or Johnny had contracted it through unsuccessful oral sex. Or maybe both. Maybe he'd been doomed either way. Hell, maybe kissing her on the mouth had sealed his fate. "Did she say anything while you guys were having sex?"

"No. She was a moaner, not a talker." The fury was returning to his tone, laced with annoyance and sprinkled with something else. Something she couldn't name.

"Did you see anyone else in your apartment?"

"No. I was kind of busy concentrating. You remember how devoted I was to your body, right? Now, are we done here? Because I'm fucking tired!"

"No, we're not done. And let's keep me out of this." Any moment now, he would kick her out. That much was clear. How many more questions could she get him to answer before that happened? She gentled her tone. "So you guys had sex. Did you notice anything different about her?"

"Like what? Like did she have two vaginas?"

"Did she?"

"No," he snarled. "She seemed human the entire time."

One down. Only a thousand more to go. "So when did you realize you were infected?"

"When Mia and Dallas busted down my door last night. I woke up . . . hungry." His gaze fell to her chest, where her heart pounded, and he licked his lips. "Yeah. Hungry."

Ava shifted uncomfortably in her seat, caught herself, and stilled. "Is that hunger the only change you noticed?"

A stiff shake of his head. "I could hear her voice in my head. *Can* hear her voice." Another lick of his lips.

She ignored the urge to shift again, pulling herself from his gaze, however briefly. "*Now?* You can hear her now?"

"Yes," he whispered.

That kind of bond required strength. Just how powerful was this woman? "What's she saying?"

"I don't know. Most times she speaks in a language I don't understand."

"Repeat something." Maybe Noelle or Dallas would be able to translate. Not Ava, though. That much she knew. New languages had always been difficult for her. In fact, she was lucky she didn't—always—butcher her own native tongue.

He opened his mouth, said a word she didn't understand, no longer whispering, then grimaced. "I—I can't tell you anymore. Hurts too much."

"Hurts how?"

"How do you think? Bad."

Was the queen somehow cognizant of what her victims said? Could she control them? Make them feel pain when they displeased her? "Okay, let's backtrack a moment. Was the Schön queen gone when the agents burst into your home?"

"Yeah." He once again spoke in that whisper, barely audible. Why? "She left right after the sex."

"So what happened after the sex, *before* Mia and Dallas arrived?"

"She dressed and left, and I fell asleep."

"That's all?"

Color flooded his cheeks. "Yeah." The creepy, whispering tone had thankfully been absent that time.

Liar. Had nothing else happened, he wouldn't have blushed. "You might as well tell me," she said. "I won't leave until you do."

"Oh, really? You want to know that badly?" Again, he licked his lips. Again, he started whispering. "Come over here and ask me nicely. I'll tell you anything, everything."

Oh, no, no, no. There would be none of that. "I'm not going near you, Johnny."

Slowly he grinned, and damn if his teeth weren't longer and sharper than she remembered. She almost flinched, but managed to remain in her seat, still and seemingly calm.

"Who said my name was Johnny?" Whispering, yet humming with power. The glassiness left his eyes, leaving clarity—and a fathomless knowledge he'd never exhibited before.

Goose bumps covered Ava from head to foot, and not the good kind, as possibilities whizzed through her mind. A split personality? Insanity? Or something far more sinister? Like—

"My name is Trinity, and I'm the queen you seek."

Like that. Ava gulped.

"After sex, and before the agents arrived, I told Johnny that I would know all his thoughts, all his actions. I told him I would control him. I told him he would not be my last victim. I told him, or rather, I promised him your precious vampire would be next."

Fifteen

Drip. Drip.

McKell lay in the heart of his cave, peering up at the rocky ceiling. It was so low, he wasn't able to stand without scraping his skull and he had to crawl in and out. The side walls hugged him close, keeping him in a tight embrace. Almost like the coffins humans used to theorize about. As if he would actually sleep in a coffin. He wasn't dead. He was very much alive. More so than ever before.

Drip. Drip.

Darkness surrounded him, the sun's rays kept completely at bay. He always knew when the sun set, however. Or rather, his body knew. A burst of strength would overtake him. Nowadays, so would a burst of hunger. For one person, and one person only . . .

He'd lived in these caverns his entire life, knew which ones were used by other vampires—and therefore ruled by Manus, king of the vampires—and which were not. This one was not, had only one entry, and therefore only one exit, and did not descend deep enough to reach the city.

Situated a few hours from the human town as it was, in a wasteland with thick, stinging air, topside visitors were discouraged, as well. Actually, he'd never encountered another living being here. And as he could control people and time, traveling back and forth wasn't a problem.

Here, he could relax, knowing the doorways wouldn't find him. Or talk to him. He could sleep without worry. He could dream about digging into the vampire city directly below him—sometimes he thought he could hear the murmur of their voices— defeating Manus, and claiming the throne. Vampires respected might, after all. And if anyone could take down the powerful, mindreading Manus, it was McKell, the man who had led the army for centuries.

Would he, though? No. His men deserved peace. A lifetime with their families. Too many would die if war erupted, families torn apart. But oh, how he missed his men. Most days, he could ignore the sensation. The hollowness. But every time he came here, he was reminded. They'd fought beside each other, bled for each other, and some had even died for their fellow soldiers. That kind of loyalty didn't fade just because a king proclaimed McKell a traitor.

Traitor. As if. He hadn't killed Bride when he had been ordered. She'd looked up at him with those green, green eyes, so trusting, and he'd spared her. Where was the crime in that?

Truly, that wasn't the act of a traitor. Yes, she was what the vampires called *nefreti*. All-powerful, as he'd told Ava. What he hadn't mentioned to her was that the *nefreti* were utterly unstoppable when riled, their natural inclination for survival overriding even the smallest hint of compassion. And yes, a *nefreti* had killed Manus's brother, so the royal family had every right to fear them. That didn't mean all *nefreti* deserved to die.

And though he'd saved Bride and cast her to the surface world with every intention of finding her later and tricking the king into thinking she was someone else, though she had then chosen to live with another man, McKell still couldn't regret his actions. Not in any way. Not when they'd led him to Ava.

Ava.

During the night, he'd trailed vampire scents as planned. He'd discovered a large group at a dance club, of all places. Mostly males, but a few females. He hadn't entered, had merely watched from the shadows outside, next to human garbage cans, hoping to mask his own scent. He hadn't attempted to question a single one, knowing the rest would run and he'd have no one to observe.

None had seemed to notice him as they left. Even the times he'd been "talking" to Noelle on the phone. Chattering baggage. As he'd studied the vampire females, there had been . . . nothing, no reaction on his part, and he had reeled.

The thought of getting to know them on any level had even blackened his mood. The thought of exchanging blood with them had sickened him. The thought of kissing them had left a terrible taste in his mouth.

He couldn't replace Ava. *Wouldn't* replace her. To

always hold his tongue, never speak his mind—hell, no. He wasn't doing that again. So, Ava stayed. Forever. He would still interrogate as many vampires as possible and learn how to live in this crazy human world. He would still insist Ava help him. The more time he could spend with her, the better. But later dismiss her to mate with a female vampire? Again, no.

Once he'd made that decision, his entire outlook had changed. From brooding and murderous to happy and eager. He should have known from the beginning. Just thinking about Ava caused him to grin.

She'd meant to anger him earlier, when she'd mentioned "doing" someone else. He knew she wouldn't, though. The way she had kissed him . . .

She had lost herself to the passion. She had moaned for more, clutching at him and rubbing against him. She wanted *him*. No one else would do for her, just as no one else would do for him. They might not like feeling that way, but they were helpless to change those feelings.

Thank God.

She simply enjoyed torturing him. Which was a good thing, he thought with a surge of satisfaction. A point in his favor. She enjoyed torturing Noelle, as well. And as she professed to love Noelle . . . did that mean she loved him?

Better question: Did he *want* her to love him?

He planned to stay with her, yes, but love was a

huge burden to carry. Mainly because women became so clingy. He had to admit, though, that he liked the thought of Ava clinging to him.

And if she loved him, she would probably stop resisting his sexual advances. She might even allow him to drink from her anytime he wished. He could move into her home—after he made some improvements, of course—and sleep in her bed, with her in it, every day.

Yes, he wanted her to love him, he decided. Not just desire him. Not just enjoy him. He wanted her love. So. Rather than simply seduce her, he needed to romance her, as well.

Simple, easy, he thought. Yeah. Right.

Ava paced her living room, from the couch to the recliner and back again, her phone pressed to her ear. Finally the ringing ceased, and Mia answered.

"Snow."

"Have you gotten the test results for McKell's blood?" she asked, bypassing pleasantries. The sun had set a few minutes ago, so she knew McKell was on his way here. Tonight the vampire hunting truly began.

"Yeah," was the dead-end reply.

O-kay. She'd known that already. After she'd left Johnny's cell, she, Noelle, and Dallas had returned to Mia's office. Her panic at Johnny's—the queen's—threat hadn't yet faded. *Still* hadn't faded. Might never fade, actually. McKell assumed he would remain un-affected by the virus, or at least he had when he'd en-countered the infected human, but his contact had been minimal. A threat hadn't wrapped itself around his neck like a noose, tightening, drawing him ever closer to the end.

Mia had already watched the interrogation feed, and had smacked Ava on the shoulder in a job well done. Then Mia had said, "Two great discoveries in one day. You're becoming invaluable, Sans. Keep it up."

"Two great discoveries?" Ava had asked. "Johnny was the first, yes, so what was the second?"

Mia had paled, smacked her on the shoulder again, and told her to go home and rest. Rest. As if that would be possible now, in the middle of a crisis, when it never had been before.

Ava had spent the last few hours thinking about ways to destroy the queen (nothing had come to her), how to protect McKell from further notice (nothing had come to her), and that second discovery of Mia's. Finally, one answer had slid into place: McKell's test results had arrived. Now, she wanted answers.

"And?" she demanded. If God loved her, even a little, Mia would tell her that McKell was immune, there was a cure, and the world was now safe.

"And I decided not to share them with you. You're too close to him."

She peered up at her ceiling. *Why do you hate me so much?*

No reply. She massaged the back of her neck. For once, she didn't deny her relationship with a man. She *liked* the thought of being close to McKell. "I can get you more of his blood if you need it." Maybe. Since that "McKell is next" announcement, she'd been feeling oddly protective of the jerk, wanting—fine, needing—him in top shape.

Why hadn't he arrived yet?

"Then get me more." Mia's command promised retribution if she failed.

She stopped in the center of her living room, wishing she were at AIR and Mia were close enough to slap. "Not unless you share the results. That's how this works." Again, maybe. But this was a negotiation. She would say anything necessary to get what she craved.

"Actually, that's not how this works at all. I'm your boss." Such a hard, unflinching tone had probably never met with resistance. "You do what I tell you."

She should back down before her ass was fired, but backing down had never been her nature. If it had, she would be stuck in the gutter, addicted to drugs and alcohol like her mother had been, bless her heart, occasionally whoring herself out as the need for a fix overrode any sense of degradation. Or as loser boyfriends requested bail money.

"*Actually,* Agent Snow, I don't care who you are. You want the vampire's blood, you give me the details I want." On this, she would not waver.

There was a pause, tense and heavy, then a sigh. "You'll make an excellent agent one day, Sans."

Astonishing. She'd just refused to play nice, yet Mia had praised her. "Thank you."

"But don't think I'll let you run over me every time you have a new case," Mia continued as if she hadn't spoken. "I like your determination, so I'll give you a pass. *This* time. And just so you know, I've never given anyone a second pass."

"Noted."

Another sigh crackled. "Okay. Here it is. My official finding is . . . his blood is weird."

Ava surged back into motion, but had lost track of where she was and plowed into her recliner, her toe instantly throbbing where she'd stubbed it. Cursing under her breath, she twisted, landed on the cushions, and balanced the phone between her cheek and her shoulder as she rubbed her toe.

"Weird? I don't understand."

"As you know, we can't take a sample of Schön infected blood because the virus is alive and won't leave the victim's body if there's not a living being nearby. So filling a vial is impossible. To test, we have to feed the vampire blood to an already diseased individual."

"And were you able to do that?" The only living victim—besides Johnny—was the human from the bar. That she knew of, that is.

"No, but let me backtrack a little. We were able to test McKell's blood on its own to determine if it was like Bride's. And in some ways, it is. Much more so than the other vampires we've tested."

She'd had no idea other vampires had submitted—

willingly or not—to AIR testing. So what the hell else didn't she know? "That's good, right?"

"Yes and no."

More non-answers. Wonderful. Ava fell against the back of the chair, and the stupid thing flattened like a cot. She barely cut off her yelp of surprise. "Could you please give me straight facts?" she asked, shoving her tumbling curls from her face.

"Bride's blood healed human disease, but left the blood . . . untainted, for lack of a better word. Still human. McKell's rejuvenates human blood, as well, only his . . . takes over. It's so strong, so potent, that the blood it's mixed with becomes vampire, as well."

If she'd been standing, she would have fallen. "So anyone who drinks his blood will become a vampire?" She rubbed her throat, mind racing. Had she had a sip? A single drop?

"Yes. Human, animal, doesn't matter. Whoever ingests his blood becomes vampiric. Just like in those old movies. I'd compare him to a human man with too much testosterone. What makes him vampire practically seeps from his pores."

Panic bloomed, and it felt as if thousands of little needles were poking at her. If she'd had a single drop . . . No, no. She thought back. He'd sucked hers, but she'd never tasted his. More than that, she was still human, normal.

Slowly she relaxed. Good. Okay. Fine. But she would be *very* careful in the future, never forgetting what could happen if a kiss spun out of control. She didn't want to become a vampire. Ever. To only be allowed to venture out at night? Even McKell hated that. Sure, he was looking for a way to live successfully in the sunlight, but what if he never found it?

And to only ever be able to drink blood? McKell's blood, at that, since they were supposedly mates. There'd be no more butterscotch for her. Not without sickening. No, no, and no!

On the plus side, her always aching body added, McKell might finally view her as good enough for him. Ava frowned. She didn't want to be considered good enough simply because she had grown fangs. She wanted to be good enough for who she was and what she'd made of herself. On her own.

Not that she was thinking about dating McKell. Or sleeping with him. Well, she might be thinking about sleeping with him—stupid fantasies of writhing together, naked and moaning, never left her head—but that didn't mean she'd ever follow through. Last time they'd ventured down that road, she'd found only disaster. He'd stopped abruptly, left, and now she had no idea where he was or what he was doing.

"Still there, Sans?"

"Yes. Was just thinking, sorry. So, are you going to feed McKell's blood to Johnny?"

"We're still debating. I think I told you that Johnny's already had some of Bride's blood, but another thing we've discovered is that vampire blood doesn't always mix well with other vampire blood."

What exactly did "doesn't always mix well" mean?

The recipient exploded? And did it have to do with vampire mating habits?

Before she could ask, Mia added, "Another problem with McKell's sample is that, what if his blood *doesn't* destroy the Schön disease? Then we'll have a Schön-infected vampire who's stronger than ever and in need of drinking blood *as well as* infecting others to stay strong."

Good point. "So what would happen if *McKell* was infected by the Schön?"

"Don't know. And I'm afraid to find out."

A knock sounded at Ava's door. She popped to her feet, heart suddenly pounding against her ribs. McKell? Surely not. Like Noelle, he could now let himself in. That didn't stop hope from sprouting wings and flying through her.

God, she had to get herself under control where that man was concerned.

"Thanks for the information, Agent Snow."

"Welcome. I'll expect a new sample ASAP."

"You'll get it." Again, maybe.

They severed the connection. Ava placed the phone on a side table she'd spent months saving for and padded to the door. McKell's strong, beautiful image filled the ID screen, a relieving déjà vu of the last time he'd visited. He was here, and he was fine. And as always when she spotted him, her skin tingled.

She pressed a few buttons, fingers trembling, and the door slid open. Suddenly, only air separated them.

And such sweet air it was. He smelled of the earth, like rain and crisp leaves, yet there was just a hint of butterscotch. On purpose? He wore a fresh black T-shirt, a pair of black slacks, and both fit him perfectly.

His dark hair shagged around his face, but it wasn't tangled. The strands were brushed to a blue-black shine. Clearly he'd just come from an enzyme shower. Whose? she thought, hands fisting.

"Why didn't you just walk in?" she asked. She wouldn't throw accusations around. She'd ask nicely. She'd taunted him with her phone call, made it seem like she was going back on her word to mess around with him and only him. Sure, it had seemed like a good idea at the time, a way to show him two could stray. Now . . . she would just have to deal with the consequences.

"I'm being polite," he replied.

So he was polite now? That was new. "We have a few things to discuss," she said, happy that she sounded calm, assured.

"Then we will discuss them." He strode inside, a bag slung over his shoulder. That bag, big and bulky, banged into her chest and knocked her backward. No apology was issued.

Frowning, she followed him into her bedroom. The frown faded as she became enthralled by a vision of McKell stripping, crawling into bed, cocking a finger at her, silently commanding her to join him. Enthralled, yeah, but she panicked, too, because she was already edging down that road again, the one where she forgot the rest of the world and thought only of sex and blood.

He tossed the bag on the floor and faced her. Questions about his blood could wait. Questions about the shower had to wait, too.

"*What* is that?" She jabbed a finger at the bag.

He squared his shoulders, as if preparing for a fight. "My things."

Duh. "Why did you bring your things here?" *Don't say you'll be staying. Don't you dare say you'll be staying.*

"I'll be staying for a while." His chin lifted, his violet eyes blazed. Just then he was total determination. "You know, moving in."

She shook her head, the panic rising in a tide of bile and ice. She'd never allowed a man to move in with her, not even for a single night, and she never would. Not even this one. *Especially* not this one. Resisting him was already a losing battle. If they were together every minute of every day, and every sultry night, she wouldn't just lose; she would end up in flames, a pile of ash.

"I live alone," she squeaked. "Always."

He crossed his arms over his chest a familiar action that caused his shirt to strain against his biceps. Those perfectly defined, sinewy biceps. She licked her lips, and his still blazing gaze tracked every millimeter of movement. *He's killing me . . .*

"I'm tired of racing from my place to yours, then yours to mine."

First, he'd done that once, maybe twice. Second, "You have a place?"

He nodded stiffly.

"And that's where you showered?" The question slipped out before she could stop it. Nicely, as planned.

"No." His face scrunched with disgust. "I used one of those public places, since I didn't want to arrive here dirty. Thankfully, though, I'll never have to use one again. Now that I live with you."

Even her relief that he hadn't used some other girl's shower didn't stop her from yelling, "No, no, no."

"Yes, yes, yes."

"No!" She stomped her foot.

A mix of anger and confusion flashed over his features before his expression smoothed, and he regarded her with adoring patience. "Be reasonable, Ava, darling. We're working together. Helping each other. Every minute we spend together is for the greater good."

Darling, he'd called her, nearly melting her. He was up to something. She knew it, but that adoration . . . that patience . . . as if he was willing to do anything to spend a single moment in her presence . . .

Stay strong. "Greater good, huh? How?"

"What did you learn about Johnny?" An answer in the form of a question.

He couldn't know that. Yet. "Johnny's sick." And Ava *did* need to guard McKell. Oh, God. She was caving, trying to talk herself into saying yes to cohabitating.

"So that *was* the queen I encountered?"

"Yes." Might as well tell him the rest. "And now she wants *you*."

"Me?" He blinked but otherwise remained unconcerned. "Why would she—wait. How do you know she wants me?"

Now was not the time for *that* discussion. How would he react if he knew she'd spoken to her diseased ex? And, really, having him here, for a little while and only a little while, might not be so bad. Guarding him *was* important. She could protect him from the Schön queen. Be there, ready to strike, to save the day.

Talk about earning respect.

"I'll let you stay," she said with difficulty. "On one condition."

He grinned as if he'd just discovered a human blood farm. "I've noticed that with you, there is always a condition."

Hey! "What does that mean?"

"Exactly what I said." He reached out and smoothed a lock of hair behind her ear, patient and adoring again. "Now, tell me about this condition."

A tremor slid the length of her spine. How was she supposed to resist him when he did things like that? "I, well, need another sample of your blood."

"Why?" he asked, arm falling back to his side.

"For AIR."

"Again, why?"

"They're looking for a cure for the Schön disease."

"And they think my blood will help?"

Did he know how powerful his blood was? Did he know how easily he could turn others into vampires? Probably not. Otherwise, he might have turned Ava already. Despite the fact that feeding her that blood would wed them permanently.

Actually, no. That didn't fit his personality. He wasn't the type to sneak around to get what he wanted. He stated plainly, issued demands, expected those around him to obey, and that was one of the things she liked most about him.

"They won't know until they do a few more tests. Which means they need a new sample."

"It's *my* blood. Mine."

"I know. I need it, though. For the greater good."

A flicker of frustration, quickly masked. "Fine. You may have another sampling. You don't need to stab me for it, do you?" As he spoke, his voice tightened, and understanding crystalized in his eyes, lightening the violet to a rich lavender. "That's why you stabbed me before, isn't it?"

Uh-oh. Caught. "Let's leave the past in the past, shall we?"

"I will if you will," he said pointedly.

Meaning what? She had to forget the inferiority complex he'd given her? "Very well." Maybe. He was as new to this mate business as she was, and commitment *was* the scariest thing on the planet. Not that they were committed, she added before any part of her could latch onto the thought of permanence. So, of course they had taken jabs at each other. Forgiveness should be easy. *Should be.*

"Thank you." The grin he rewarded her with could have melted a frozen bar of chocolate. "I must admit, I expected more of a fight from you."

"Welcome. And I'm not unreasonable, McKell."

Melted chocolate? No, that grin widened and turned him into a living, breathing butterscotch sundae. "Shall we seal this deal with a kiss?"

The mere suggestion shot lava-hot bolts of lightning through her. "Not yet." *Yes, yes, yes.* "First, a few ground rules about Chez Sans."

Good-bye, grin. "I've already agreed to your condition."

"Yes, and now you need to agree to the rules." If she didn't voice them now, she never would. And was she truly talking with such speed? Trying to get to that kiss? "One, no leaving your shit around. Two, no walking around naked. Three, no guests. Four, you sleep on the couch. Five, no making calls and jacking up my phone bill. Six, don't ask me to add anyone else to my security ID. It's not gonna happen. Seven, don't leave crumbs of any kind *anywhere*. Eight, you have to pay rent. Nine, my stuff is my stuff. Leave it alone. Ten, no killing anyone or even drinking from anyone—like, say, delivery boys—on the premises."

He listened while tapping his foot. "Is that all?"

She thought about it, a snap of time that seemed to last forever, then nodded. "Yes." *Now how about that kiss . . .*

"Then I have a few rules of my own."

Oh, no. They weren't going there. "You can't make any rules. This is my home. And now that that's settled . . ."

"If we're sharing, it's my home, too."

Frustrating man. "Absolutely not. The only reason you're staying is because of my generous nature."

"Rule one," he said, ignoring her. "I will leave my— shit, is that what you called my precious weapons and clothes?—around if I like. But you may pick them up and store them somewhere of your choosing if they bother you. Two, you may walk around naked anytime you wish. Three, guests are allowed if I approve of them. Four, I'll sleep in your bed. You may sleep on the couch if that bothers you, but I hope you'll rethink that. Five, I have your cell phone, so I have no need of your home phone. Six, if I need someone added to the ID, I'll add them myself. No worries. Seven, I have no problem with this rule. No crumbs. Eight, as I currently have no money, I'm happy to pay rent with my body. Nine, thank you for sharing your stuff. Ten, I promise to only invite delivery *girls*."

Oh, really? "You can't drink from anyone but me, moron." And she'd never been more pleased by that.

"Then we can both strike rule ten from our list of demands." How satisfied he appeared, as if he'd backed her into a corner.

Clearly, he considered himself a clever little boy. Well, she would show him. She closed the rest of the distance between them, his body stiffening a little more with every inch of ground she gained. Rather than hurt him, or jump him, the sexy bastard, she bent down and grabbed his bag. Then she marched to the only window, opened it, allowing moonlight to seep inside, and—

Blinked.

The bag was no longer in her hand. Was nowhere to be seen, actually. Worse, she was once again in front of McKell, and he was smiling that siren's smile.

"Rule eleven," she gritted out. "No manipulating me with your ability."

"You manipulate me all the time." Was that a . . . pout?

She gasped with affront. "I do not."

He arched a brow. "Don't you? You have only to look at me, and I'm putty in your hands."

The confession went straight to her head. This was the first time he'd complimented her, *truly* complimented her, as if she were his equal—or perhaps even his superior. And she'd thought him irresistible before . . .

"Fine. Manipulate time. Can we seal the deal now?" She leaned into him, rising on her tiptoes, flattening her palms on his chest, ready to enjoy the kiss he'd promised her.

"First. My rule eleven," he said just before contact. "No other men, Ava. I'm the only one for you, because you . . . you belong to me."

She froze, popped her jaw, then fell back on her heels, ready to nail his ass to the wall. "Actually, I don't." He had reduced her to property, like a house or a car. Or a slave.

"You do."

His insistence was both frustrating and flattering. She focused on the first and ignored the other. "So, are we hunting vampires tonight or not?"

He nodded. "We are."

"Let's go, then."

"No kiss to seal the deal?"

"Fuck you."

He gave her another butterscotch grin, and motioned to the door. "After you, darling."

Sixteen

Apparently, vampires preferred inebriated humans. They were easier to lure, and no one took them seriously when they shouted about being bitten and partially drained. That was why, after a wardrobe change—the white button-up and dark slacks Ava had been wearing hadn't been mission-compatible, in McKell's opinion—she found herself leaning against a metal counter in a fetish bar.

Bubbles floated through the air on clouds of thick, dark smoke. Pounding music created a dizzying rhythm, and gyrating bodies littered the dance floor. Cages hung from the ceiling, and scantily clad alien females ranging in color from the brightest gold to the darkest silver writhed inside, as if they were captured in the throes of ecstasy.

How she envied them.

Pleasure was not on her agenda. "Buttered Toast," she said when the six-armed, blue-skinned bartender finally approached her. BT, the only alcoholic drink that tasted like her favorite candy. A consolation prize.

He nodded, reaching for bottles, pouring, while fixing someone else a tequila shooter and someone else a rum punch.

When she had her drink in hand, Ava sipped and turned, surveying the crowd. Lots of faux black leather, face paint, whips and chains. How . . . cliché, she thought. She supposed the vampires could be themselves here, without worrying about fear and recrimination. They could blend.

Was this the fate that awaited McKell? What if vampires *couldn't* live in the daylight? Would he be disappointed? Try and return underground? Or would he embrace this way of life?

She didn't like the thought of him clubbing every night, all kinds of skanky girls trying to rub up against him, but she didn't like the thought of him leaving the surface, either.

Just find a vampire and get this over with. Even though she doubted vampires they found at night could teach him how to live during the day, but a promise was a promise.

A few guys were watching her, waiting for her body language to morph from Stay Away to Mating Season. Who to encourage, who to encourage? All of them appeared human to her, but then, as she'd told McKell, so did he.

So, just how was she supposed to tell the difference?

She wasn't, she recalled, as she continued to sip her drink. Okay, she drained it and signaled for another. She was just supposed to lead as many people as possible to the alley outside, where McKell waited. She was supposed to lead them one at a time to minimize the chance of placing herself in harm's way. Ugh. One at a time would take *forever*. And how would it look if she kept going in and out of the club with a different person? Everyone would realize she was up to something. Or think she was a whore.

She didn't mind the latter—that could actually work to her advantage—but McKell had told her to act shy, demure, and weak. And really, the clothes he'd chosen for her reflected that image. Clothes that had come from Noelle's bag of laundry. Bitch hadn't yet picked it up. Anyway, he'd liked the Naughty Librarian ensemble—white shirt, tie, barely-there plaid skirt. With added scarves and leggings, of course, so not an inch of her body was truly revealed, her skin somewhat protected. Ava felt ridiculous. Her curls were knotted on top of her head, and she wore a pair of cat-eye–shaped glasses.

At least she (kind of) fit in. There was a flaw in McKell's logic, though. A shy, demure girl would not dress up. A shy, demure girl would not be here, soliciting attention.

She downed the rest of her second drink, then pretended to stumble forward, planning a quick recon mission around the dance floor. Only, three steps in, someone finally approached her.

"Hey," he said.

"Hey," she replied.

For several agonizing minutes, she flirted with him. All the while, his gaze flittered between her lips and her breasts. Fangs never sprouted, but what did she know? Finally, she said, "Let's go somewhere private."

He readily agreed, and she led him to the back of the building, past the door. Cool air caressed her, and so did the guy, his fingers skimming the curve of her ass.

She jumped out of his reach. "Don't touch the goods."

"Human," McKell said, stepping from the shadows. His features were taut, his hands fisted.

Great. All that flirting, wasted.

"What's going on?" the guy asked, nervously glancing between them. "You robbing me? Well, the joke's on you. I don't have any cash."

McKell fisted his shirt and propelled him into the wall, then motioned Ava back inside with his free hand.

"Don't hurt him," she said.

"I'll use my voice on him. Swear."

"Okay. I'm trusting you."

"Let me go," the guy begged, perhaps sensing the menace that constantly poured off of the vampire. "Please."

McKell held tight as Ava entered the building. Determined, she wound her way through the crowd, loosening her tie and unfastening several buttons on her shirt, displaying the lacy edges of her bra, but more importantly, displaying the thudding pulse at the base of her neck. That drew attention, all right, but *still* not the right kind. Four more men hit on her and all four were human.

On that fourth trip outside, she noticed a new smattering of blood on the concrete, and realized

McKell was punching the guys before sending them on their way. She didn't scold him. Most likely she would have done the same thing, had the situation been reversed.

Still. This was getting old, she thought, trekking back inside.

Two males stopped her before she reached the bar. Both were handsome, and both were switching their focus between her mouth and her breasts, just like the others. These two were of the faux-leather variety, with spiked collars, and crimson-colored makeup painted to look like blood trickling from their mouths.

Fake vampires, for sure. She almost brushed past them. Almost. They were tall, as muscled as McKell, and danger radiated from them. So did hunger. Maybe . . . maybe the painted "blood" was their version of hiding in plain sight.

"Would you like to retire to the back rooms with us?" one asked, and there was something strange about his formal words and deep voice. Something . . . distracting, whisking through her mind, making her forget . . . what? who?

McKell. His name blasted through her mind, and she recalled that she was here to hunt.

"So . . . would you?" the other asked silkily.

She didn't want to, wanted to take them outside, but . . . no, actually, she *did* want to go to the back room. Her blood was heating, her body humming. Touching these men would be nice.

Ava frowned, shook her head. That wasn't right. The only man she wanted to touch was McKell.

McKell.

Again, his name returned her to her senses. He was the reason she was here. Hunting vampires. "I'd rather go outside," she said. "Out back."

"No. You want to go to one of the back rooms."

Yes. That's what she wanted. Wanted so badly. "Let's go, then."

Both men smiled happily, as if they'd never doubted their appeal. And maybe they hadn't. There was something strange about them, something she should know, and that voice . . . her mind fuzzed, and she lost her train of thought.

They wrapped their arms around her waist and ushered her to the back of the club, where several open doorways loomed. They urged her through the middle one. Why was she allowing them to lead her, again?

Inside, the smoky air thinned, the bubbles cleared, and she saw several black couches. All occupied. Men and women, men and men, women and women. Roaming hands, straining bodies. Moans and groans. Sex scenting the air. No biting, though. Biting, like McKell needed—

Once more, she was jarred back into focus. McKell. Vampire. Hunting.

"Come," one of her companions said, urging her the rest of the way inside.

Hunting smunting. "Yes, I— No." She shook her

head, and pressed her weight into her heels. God, what was wrong with her? She shouldn't be doing this. Didn't want to do this. Only one man tempted her. "I changed my mind. I don't want to do this," she said, pushing her thoughts out of her mouth.

She managed to disengage from their arms and stride away before they could speak. Why had she even *considered* being with them? She was McKell's. Kind of.

Behind her, she heard sputtering, but the men didn't chase after her. Good. She would have had to kill them. Although, she should be escorting them—

Them. She skidded to a halt, frowned. "Them" who? She'd just come from outside, and McKell had just proclaimed her fourth guy human. Right? She looked around. She stood in a hallway, naked bodies painted on the walls. How had she gotten here?

What the hell was going on?

Just find McKell one more person and call it a night. There were rooms behind her, she realized. She changed directions and peeked into all three, finding drug users and various sexual acts being performed, but no vampires. Meaning, no one had tapped into a vein like a beer keg.

But in the middle room, she spotted two men standing near the doorway. They were handsome, as large as McKell, and they watched her intently, hungrily. For some reason, that made her uneasy. The unease intensified when she backtracked into the club and they followed her.

Get away, instinct demanded. Smoke once again enveloped her, hiding her—but in the next instant, she forgot why she wanted to hide. Forgot the men.

Just one more person, she reminded herself, marching onto the dance floor and winding through the writhing bodies. Hands reached for her, hips bumped against her. She allowed the music to sink into her bones and propel her into motion, swaying, grinding. Hopefully luring. All the while her gaze scanned.

A few seconds later, she spotted two faux vampires dancing with a blond female. They seemed familiar somehow, made her heart leap in . . . fear? As if she'd dealt with them before. But that couldn't be right. That . . . she *had* dealt with them, she realized. She'd spoken with them. They'd taken her into that hallway, then somehow made her forget she'd ever met them, and only when she'd thought of McKell had her wits returned.

And now, their attention was off her and on the blond. Was that why she'd suddenly remembered what had happened?

Either way, they were vampires. They had to be.

Her blood chilled, becoming a river of sludge in her veins. They were far more powerful than she'd realized. McKell had warned her, but she hadn't listened. Stupid of her, and a mistake she wouldn't make again. These two could play with human memory, hiding what they didn't like. They could even compel humans to do what they wanted. Look how easily they'd led her to those rooms.

They were snaking themselves around the blonde, who was also human in appearance. She had short, pale hair, her eyes heavy-lidded, her lips parted. She wore a white halter top and a short black skirt. Flaming red high heels revealed black-painted toenails. One man was in front of her, the other behind her, and both licked at her neck.

Ava debated what to do, how best to lure them outside. Before a single solution presented itself, one of the guys clasped the woman's hand, tugging her from the dance floor. She willingly followed, perhaps in a trance as Ava had been. The second one stayed close on her heels.

There was only one thing she *could* do, Ava realized. Stupid or not, she chased after them. Would have been nice if they'd headed toward the back door instead of the front, but no.

They quickened their steps, and she did the same, her heart pounding wildly. When she reached them, she grabbed the one closest to her, stopping him. McKell, McKell, McKell, she thought, as the vampire's gaze whipped to her. Black eyes, so deep, like a pit, only insanity waited at the bottom. Contacts? And why hadn't she noticed before?

He had a beautiful face . . . so beautiful . . . those eyes didn't promise insanity, no, no, how wrong she'd been, they promised—McKell, McKell, McKell. She continued her study. The vampire had high cheekbones, lush lips, like McKell's, but the arm she held lacked sizzle.

"Don't speak," she said. McKell. "Just head outside with me. To the back of the club. I'll make you happier than you've ever been."

The vampire barked something over his shoulder, speaking in a language she didn't understand and had never heard before. Her brain fogged—until she wondered if McKell spoke that language, too. The fog cleared.

The other guy stopped and honed in on her, as well. The moment their eyes locked, she knew she was dinner. He nodded. The blonde had stopped, too, and trailed the new direction of his focus. Her eyes narrowed; she might have hissed.

McKell. Ava offered both vampires a fake, drunken smile. "Let's all be quiet, go outside, and have sex." Too obvious?

"You changed your mind." His voice was cultured, his tone melodious.

McKell. "I did? I don't remember." McKell. "All I can think about is the fact that I want to be with you."

His smile was slow and wicked. "Come, then."

"But what about me?" the girl pouted.

His gaze never strayed from Ava. "Go away. This one was our first choice, you a distant second."

McKell. "Outside?" She pointed to the front door, then shook her head. "Too many people that way. Let's go that way." Now she pointed to the back door. Where McKell waited.

He shook his head, dark hair swaying. "The alley reeks of garbage."

She'd been out there and had noticed a slight smell, but recalled the way McKell had cringed. Just how acute were vampire senses? "And the front reeks of car exhaust."

"That's why we're going to a new location. So, are you in or out, beautiful?" The second vampire, the one closest to her, leaned down and whispered, "I hope you say *in*. The things I'll do to you . . . "

Though the fog remained at bay, she barely restrained herself from leaning into him. McKell was out there, waiting, but if she protested any more, these men would leave her behind.

"All right," she said. "Let's go outside." The moment they cleared the building, and were distanced from possible hostages, she would scream for McKell. He would come running, and hopefully catch them.

Rather than lead her out, both men stiffened, sniffed the air.

"Is there a problem?" she asked.

"McKell," one of them whispered.

McKell was here? Thank you, thank you, thank you. She scanned the crowd . . . searching . . . there. She experienced a starburst of giddy relief. He'd come inside.

He spotted her, as if attuned to her, and scowled. And then, heaven save them all *then*, he stalked toward her, deadly intent in his gaze.

The man she held tried to tug from her grip, but she dug in her nails, holding tight. At the same time, she swung her free hand into his nose, smacking the cartilage with the heel of her palm.

Blood spurted, and he yelped, his knees buckling. The other leapt into a run, leaving his injured friend behind. McKell was too far away to reach him, so Ava sprinted after him, pushing through humans and otherworlders, hearing their curses but paying them no heed.

Except, when she next blinked, she found herself outside—though she'd never reached the double doors. Another blink, and she was in front of her car—AIR issued and a loan from Mia. A scowling McKell was beside her, a vampire hanging from each of his arms.

He was manipulating time, she realized, and relaxed.

"Program my voice into the car," he commanded.

She did, a process that took a minute, maybe two, and in another blink she was inside the car, in the driver's seat. She looked to her right. McKell now sat in the passenger seat, watching her expectantly. And, if she wasn't mistaken, with dread.

Moonlight caressed him, golden and creamy, just as it had in the forest, as if every ray searched until finding him, just to stroke him lovingly. His violet eyes were bright, his lips redder than usual. One of the vampires had punched him, she was sure.

Speaking of, "Where are the vampires?"

He blinked in surprise, the dread a rising deluge, then motioned to the backseat with a tilt of his chin.

Had he expected her to balk about the time manipulation? Probably. She'd tried to make him promise not to do it, after all. As dire as the circumstances had been, she wasn't going to chastise him. She was grateful.

She turned, gasped. Sure enough, both vampires were unconscious and slumped over each other. *Gold star, McKell.* He'd done what she hadn't. Won.

"Thank you for coming to get me," she said, facing him.

"You're . . . welcome?" A question, not a statement. "Is this a trick? I didn't trust in your ability to protect yourself. I caved to worry. I—"

She chuckled, cutting him off. "No trick, I swear. I was dying in there."

"Dying?" A menacing whisper, the intent to cause suffering in the undertone. He leaned toward her, grabbed onto her, gaze raking her, probing for injury. "I will murder—"

"Not *literally* dying," she assured him. "They were walking all over me, making me forget my purpose." *My morals.* She didn't think she would have let the bastards touch her, though. Or that she would have touched them. In the end, she would have snapped to her senses. Surely.

McKell eased off her, and smoothed his T-shirt with practiced strokes. "Understandable. The dark-haired one, the one you were groping, can talk people into anything, even things they don't want to do. Well, humans. And he can do so better than most. The other, his brother, can hypnotize."

The one she was *groping?* "If you consider breaking his nose groping, I feel sorry for you."

"We sent them topside a few years ago, on a hunting raid for food," he continued blithely. "Only they never returned, and I never caught word of their defection, so we assumed they were dead."

Two years. In all that time, they would have found a way to live here, blending in, perhaps venturing out unharmed during the day, *if* there were a way to do so. Exactly the kind of answers McKell had been wanting. So. Her first day on the job? Perfection. Tomorrow, she could take him into AIR.

Ava ignored the twinge of regret in her chest. He'd promised. They'd bargained. She'd helped him capture a few vampires—two equaled "a few"—so all that was left was for him to turn himself into AIR for questioning. Or whatever else they had planned for him.

She no longer feared that Mia would want to kill him. Not with his potent vampire blood, his ability to scent out the Schön queen, and his kinda sorta willingness to help.

"So where do you want to take them?" she asked, thumb jabbing toward their unconscious bounty.

A moment passed while McKell considered their options. Finally, "Our place."

Wait. What? Our place? *Our* place? No, no, no. That was wrong on so many levels—because she actually *liked* the sound of it. "One, we're not taking them anywhere near *my* place." *Calm.* "Two, a little fact about me: I like my stuff without blood spatter. And you do plan to beat the answers out of them, yes?"

"Yes." McKell could have been carved from granite, so hard was his expression. "Fine. Let's take them to Noelle's place."

Ava nodded, breathing in more of that calm. He hadn't fought her about the apartment being hers and only hers. And that was good. Very good. That was not disappointing.

"Noelle's it is." She programmed the car, and the engine roared to life. A few seconds later they were on the road and headed toward the wealthy side of town. She switched the car's phone on and said, "Noelle Tremain." A pause, a crackle of static, and then the number was being dialed.

Noelle answered on the fourth ring. "What?"

"It's Ava?"

A smack of gum. "This your new number?"

"Nah. Just borrowed a car from AIR. Listen, we're on our way to your house. You there?"

"Nope, but I can be there in ten. Who's we?"

"Me and McKell. We'll be there in fifteen, so that works."

"What's on the menu?"

"We found two vampires."

"I found them," he piped in. Or rather, growled. "Ava made out with them."

"I did not make out with them! They mind-raped me, and I didn't know what I was doing."

Noelle laughed. "This is going to be a fun night. I can tell."

"*Anyway.* We need to interrogate them," Ava said. "Broken bones might be involved. Spilled guts, too."

"Awesome. I'll get the torture chamber ready." *Click.*

She wasn't kidding, either. Chez Tremain did indeed have a torture chamber. They'd snuck down there a few times during their high school days, just for funsies and to prove their bravery. Noelle had never told her why the upstanding Tremains had one, but Ava had guessed it had something to do with the girl's dad. He was dead now, but she suspected he'd been with the secret service or some shit, because he'd always been traveling, and on the rare times he'd been home, odd characters had been in and out of the compound at all hours of the day and night.

She'd found it very sexy at the time.

Maybe she was still that awed little high school crush-waiting-to-happen at heart, because the thought of McKell in that dungeon, throwing his strength around, probably flexing, maybe doing some cutting . . . sexiest image *evah.*

Shivering, she glanced over at him, intending to give him a good eye-fucking, but saw that he was glaring at her. Why?

No way she'd ask him. Too needy.

"Let's stargaze," she suggested as a distraction. Without waiting for his reply, she opened the solar panel on the roof, leaned her seat back as far as the shield-armor separating the front and back of the car allowed, then peered up at the night sky. So pretty, the pinpricks of light whizzing past, blurring together.

The perfect romantic backdrop for making out.

Damn it. New distraction. "So," she said, trampling the silence.

"You're determined to irritate me tonight, aren't you?"

Irritation. Good. She could work with that. Maybe. "Don't I do that every night?"

"Tonight you outdid yourself."

"Well, I'm a good agent." In training.

"That wasn't a compliment! But of course you wouldn't realize that. You're clueless. First, you smell too good, but you won't let me have another taste. Second, you touched him. I never told you to touch *anyone*. I told you to lure vampires outside. Outside. Without touching."

Another jealous fit. Soothing, after the other-woman suspicion she'd harbored after their kiss, and then again while she'd waited for him to return to her apartment. She took pity on him, though, because every dark word out of his mouth made her awareness of him electrify.

"Look, he was getting away from me, and touching him was the only way to stop him. There was nothing sexual about it. I'm not going to be with anyone else while we're . . . involved." No gagging on her part. "I agreed to your rule eleven."

"Good. I won't be with anyone else, either," he said, and this time, thank you God, *this time*, he sounded confident. "I only want you." He grabbed her by the forearms and hauled her into his lap, forcing her to straddle him. "And by God I'll have you."

She stared down at him for several heartbeats of time, silent, hands balled on his shoulders, suddenly panting, remembering the way he'd rushed in to save her, how easily he'd done it, the way she'd had to think of him to stay sane, and how easy it had been to think of him at all. How she craved him constantly, how he'd moved in with her, and that wasn't as repugnant as she'd always feared, how he belonged to her and she belonged to him, and they'd just admitted it.

How, just then, she couldn't think of anything she'd rather do than lose herself in his kiss.

"We never sealed our bargain," she rasped.

He cupped her cheeks, his thumbs brushing the corners of her lips. "Then we had best do so."

Their mouths met in the middle.

Seventeen

Dallas knew someone had broken into his apartment before he saw the front door was slightly ajar. Not because of a psychic vision, but because a break-in was the perfect ending to his shit-infested day. Oh, and he smelled roses and gunpowder in the hallway. No one in this wing could afford fresh flowers, and gunpowder was only used by street gangs who managed to get their hands on old weapons.

He knew it wasn't a street gang that had kicked in his door.

Trinity had found him again.

He palmed his newest gun, an experimental weapon he'd commandeered after Trinity's warning at the bar, and punted the door the rest of the way open. Instead of stun or death rays, instead of bullets, this gun ejected darts of poison that broke the blood-brain barrier in an instant, supposedly paralyzing the victim. Or killing. Whatever. Trinity might still be here, might not, and the poison might work on her, might not, but no telling who else had accompanied her.

Immediately he saw two males guards stationed on opposite sides of the entry. Their backs were pressed against the wall, offering him their profiles. They knew he was there—a fucking chimp would have known after that door-busting thing—but they didn't move, didn't twitch.

He fired, anyway, nailing one than the other in quick succession. The red darts whizzed through the air and nailed both males in the neck. They groaned, twitched, and collapsed. Excellent. The paralyzing agent worked. Maybe a little too well. Their chests stopped moving.

Oh, well. They had invaded his home. They deserved what they got.

Best thing about these darts, though, was that they didn't cause bloodshed. The tips were shoved through a pyre-crystal before ejection, and the heat cauterized the ensuing wound before a single bead of blood could form.

"Was that entirely necessary?" a familiar female *tsk*ed.

The queen. Trinity.

She'd stayed.

Dread increased the flow of his blood, which in turn increased the speed of his inhalations. Every lungful of breath infused her scent—roses, stronger now, as if they'd bloomed in a frosted field—with his own, until he wasn't sure if he was Dallas anymore or if he belonged to her.

"Put the weapon away, and I'll reveal myself."

He gritted his teeth. He couldn't see her, but she'd sounded loud enough to be standing right next to him. He wasn't hers, he reminded himself. Would never be hers. Right now, he was Kyrin's, the guy who'd fed him Arcadian blood and saved his life all those months ago. The guy who'd made him what he was. Psychic, able to control people with his mind, and fast beyond measure. Not that any of that helped him with Trinity.

"You made good on your threat," he said, sheathing his gun. He didn't want to, but knew deep down she would stay true to her word. All the while, he stealthily punched in Mia's number on his cell. Hopefully she'd answer, listen, realize something was wrong, then beat feet to get here.

Sure enough, the queen walked around him, from back to front, a second later, fingertip dragging over his shoulder and chest. Only, that finger misted through him, insubstantial. A dart would slide right through her, too, he realized.

The top of her head only reached his chin. Her hair was dark now, he saw, and chopped to her jaw, but everything else was the same. Those soulful eyes, those soft lips. That flawless skin.

He spread his legs, hands remaining behind his back, a classic I'm-not-moving-from-this-spot, you-can-totally-trust-me stance.

"Yes," she said, deceptively sad. "I infected one of your agents."

Are you there, Mia? Did you hear that? Do you know who I'm dealing with? He stored the phone in his pocket. "He wasn't an agent, Trin. You don't mind if I call you

Trin, do you? You're a queen, I know, but I don't think we need the formality. Johnny was only in training."

Trinity whirled full throttle, robe twirling at her feet, eyes glittering. "In training? Well, that's disappointing. But no matter. He'll serve me well." Her gaze skittered to her fallen comrades. "You owe me another guard."

He owed her? *Owed?* Bitch. "I killed two." Were there others here? Others he couldn't see? "But you only want me to replace one? Gee. Thanks for the discount."

"No discount. I've already taken Johnny."

He bristled at this second reminder. "Actually, we have him. Not you."

She laughed, soft, gentle, and just like before, it was like hearing bells. "Not for long."

What did that mean? She'd spring the guy? He'd try and escape? He'd soon die? "So why'd you pick him, hmm?"

"You didn't seem to like him, so I thought I would be doing you a favor." Another whirl, and she was gliding to his couch. Another, and she was easing down, peering over at him with a half-smile.

Good. He'd relaxed her. Time to up his game.

"You're allowed to show your thanks," she said.

He arched a brow, a fuck-you expression she would hopefully interpret as a simple refusal, and strode over—*careful, have to be careful*—then leaned down and tried to pinch a lock of her hair between his fingers. Like mist, cool, whispering.

"I liked the blond better," he said. He let his arm fall to his side—*See, Trin. You can trust me*—praying Mia was even then gathering troops to raid his place. How would they take her down, though, when they couldn't touch her?

She stood, never quite brushing him. Before his eyes, those dark strands lengthened and lightened until they were completely devoid of color. He could only watch, wide-eyed.

To his knowledge, only one other person possessed such an ability. Macy Briggs. An AIR agent who could switch identities with only a thought. Macy could change more than her hair, though. She could change faces, gender, bodies. Everything. They'd always assumed she was harmless. Could she be one of the Schön?

No, he thought next. She had married a Rakan warrior, and the two had most definitely had sex. For several weeks, Dallas had been the guy's shadow and had seen some things he'd never be able to scrub from his memories. Yet Breean had never shown signs of cannibalism or sickness.

"No reaction to my talent?" Trinity asked with a pout.

He shrugged, backed up a step. If she thought he feared her, she would become smug. Maybe make a mistake. Maybe materialize. But he couldn't outright admit to being afraid. She'd know he lied. "I've seen better."

Anger darkened her eyes, but was quickly

masked. "Have you, now? Well, I'm new at camouflage. In a few weeks, I'll be as adept as your Macy
Briggs."

Don't show your surprise. "So you've met Macy?"

She shrugged now, a mimic of his. "We haven't
been properly introduced, no."

So she'd watched the agent, studied her. *Learned*
from her. And Macy had never known, or she would
have said something. Hell, Dallas had never known.
"And you picked up her . . . talent." He snapped his
fingers. "Just like that?"

Trinity turned slowly, offering her profile like a
model on a runway, before looking at him over her
shoulder. "Yes. Just. Like. That." One step, two, she
walked away, not leaving the living room but pacing
circles in the center. Caging him. "That's my way. I
see, I want, I have."

Refusing to be cowed, he followed her. Watched.
She ghosted through his laundry, empty beer bottles,
food wrappers, and video games. Dallas had a little
problem cleaning up after himself. Someone usually
took pity on him and hired a maid (Devyn) or did the
work herself (one of his many bed partners).

"That makes you selfish," he said casually.

"That makes me happy. Others merely wish they
could take. I actually can. Why shouldn't I enjoy?"

"Because those others get hurt."

"Actually, I give them a gift. They become like me.
Able to adapt to anything. Able to *do* anything."

"As long as they continue to infect others."

"Yes. A small price to pay when given so much in return."

The destruction of living beings was "a small price"? "So what happens when everyone in the world is infected?"

"They start killing each other." No remorse. Not even pretend this time.

"But you continue on to another planet?"

"Yes."

"How is that a gift, then?" *Where the hell are you, Mia?* He began to wonder if she'd ever picked up. If he'd simply gotten her voice mail, and she wouldn't hear this conversation until tomorrow, when it would be too late to do anything.

"For the time they live as Schön, they're powerful. Beautiful. Beloved by their lovers; if feared by outsiders. Better to have such things for a short while than to live forever without ever knowing true power."

"But you don't give your victims a chance to pick. You force."

She spun, facing him, eyes blazing, before again giving him her back and pacing those circles. Along the way, she danced a hand through the clothes, looking them over this time and then forgetting them. "Until they experience it, they don't understand the joy I'm offering."

Yeah, *cannibalism* and *slavery*, two words he'd always associated with joy. "Why have you given *me* a choice, then?"

"You are unlike anyone I have ever met. You are

two races, Arcadian and human, something that should be impossible. And . . . I think I like the way you resist me. A novelty, I'm sure, and one that will eventually fade, but your spirit is pleasing for the moment, so I have no desire to damage it."

Had to be a lie. Otherwise, she would have seen the critical flaw in her plan. "If we sleep together, and I'm infected, that spirit you just praised will be damaged." Johnny now lived for her and her alone. Johnny did whatever she wanted and nothing she didn't. Hell, she even talked through the guy, threatening the vampire, McKell. "You won't have what you desire most."

"How like you to think that *you* are what I desire most. Don't get me wrong. I like you, I do. And like I said, I'm intrigued by you. But I'm willing to sacrifice you without any hesitation to get what I truly want."

That shouldn't have irritated him. He didn't *want* to be wanted by her. "So what do you truly want?"

"That isn't for you to know."

She would say no more on the subject. There had been finality in her tone, as well as irritation. If he wasn't careful, she would leave before Mia arrived. *If* Mia arrived. "For the record," he said, changing the subject. "I like all AIR agents. Those in training, those out of training. So don't do me any more favors, okay?"

A raspy chuckle escaped her. "I warned you I would infect someone. You even know my next target."

"Unless I sleep with you."

"Yes."

"So that you can speak through me."

"Yes," she said again.

In the light, her blond hair resembled fallen snow-flakes. Fitting, since she still smelled of rose-covered ice mountains. *Idiot.* "Why not use one of the men you've already infected? Mia wouldn't balk about speaking to one of them."

"Your people do not trust them." She tossed him a grin. Fleeting, but soothing.

God, she was gorgeous. What would it be like to kiss that grin off her face? What would it be like to hold her, *have* her?

Clearly, the more time he spent with her, the more she dominated his thoughts. Much more, and he'd be begging to bed her. He'd give Mia five more minutes. If she failed to arrive, he'd do something to piss off Trinity and make her leave.

"They won't trust me if I'm infected," he said, returning to the conversation.

"They won't care that you're different. They love you. That much is obvious. They'll do anything, even bargain with me, to keep you alive."

"And what do you wish to bargain for? Tell me that much, at least."

Another grin, just as fleeting, but making him crave. "I will leave this planet, cause no more harm, if your Mia will give me that which I desire most."

He experienced a pang of regret. *Get yourself under control, damn it.* "And that is?"

Finally she stopped, faced him. There was no hint of amusement this time. "I'll tell you after you sleep with me. Not before."

He closed the rest of the distance, careful, so careful, and flattened his hands on what should have been her shoulders. Still that mist, that coolness. "Let me feel you," he beseeched softly.

"Why?"

"Because you can. Because you're not afraid."

She didn't stiffen, as he'd expected, but softened against him, leaning into his chest. Slowly, her body warmed, became solid. Her appeal, far greater. The scent of roses mated with his every cell, his mind clouded with more thoughts of kissing, touching, and he had to force himself back on track.

"Did you offer this bargain to the other planets you . . . visited?" Destroyed. He slid his hands down her back, along her spine, and stopped at the curve of her waist.

She nodded, her hair tickling his chin.

Perhaps she didn't realize what she'd just admitted, but he did. Those planets had been unable to deliver, whatever it was. Which meant Mia, and therefore Earth, would most likely be unable to deliver. So he would have sacrificed himself for nothing. No thanks.

Closer he leaned . . . hoping to distract her with his nearness so that she wouldn't notice that he had removed one of his hands from her body, was even then shifting that hand behind his back, reaching for the dart gun. "Maybe I can get it for you," he whispered into her ear. "On my own."

"Can't." Her eyes were luminous blue pools.

"Because I'm a man, and you need a woman?" His fingers curled around the hilt, even as he fought the urge to kiss the shell of her ear.

"No."

"Your one-word answers are annoying." Silkily said. He could ignore temptation no longer. He kissed the shell of her ear, soft, light. Her disease spread through bodily fluid. He could lick every inch of her skin and remain unaffected. A thought he shouldn't have relished, but one he did. This close to her . . . yes, lick.

She sucked in a breath. "Sorry."

"Why?" he insisted, forcing his mind to return to the mission. Not kissing, not licking. He fisted the back of her robe, preparing to strike. "Because I'm not in charge? Well, Mia isn't either. Not really. There are a lot more powerful people out there."

"I know." She pulled from him, danced around him. He spun with her, never giving her a glimpse at what he still held behind his back. Thankfully, she stopped in the same position as before. Facing, close. "But I've been to many, many planets, and one thing is always the same. The military, especially the forces patrolling otherworlders, is revered. Unquestioned. Mia might have bosses, but her troops will obey her. *Not* her bosses."

Again, he didn't think she realized what she'd admitted. What she wanted involved the military, which involved national security. "Hate to break it to you, baby, but AIR is questioned all the damn time. There's even an Alien Pride parade scheduled later this week, to protest the need for us." Had she known what he'd been planning? Was that why she'd danced around him?

Her hands glided over his belt before tracing up his shirt. "Do you want me, Dallas?"

"What do you think?" He kissed the shell of her ear again. His tongue inched out, but just before contact, he lifted his head. *No.* "That's not difficult to figure out, I'm sure." He was hard as a rock, and that rock was pointed directly at her like a heat-seeking missile. He wanted to rub.

She chuckled. "True. You do, you want me. But your erection isn't the reason I know. I'm a mind reader."

He'd wondered. "Are you now?" If that was the case, he was in trouble. She would know that he'd called Mia. That Mia might be on her way. That he was still holding the gun. Yet here Trinity stood, unmoving, unafraid.

"Oh, yes. I am."

Why tell him, then? Why give away the advantage? "Then tell me what I'm thinking."

"That you'll do anything to be with me."

Maybe she *could* mind-read; maybe she couldn't. But the true power, he realized, was that she could make him want whatever she said. She'd spoken, and the words had blasted through him, reshaping him, making him desperate. He would do anything to be with her.

Fight. You have to fight. She was a killer, he reminded himself. Dangerous. Destructive. He tried to force his hand into motion, to shoot her at last, but a heavy lethargy settled in his limb, stopping him. Before he could panic, he thought he heard hinges squeaking behind him.

The cavalry?

He spun Trinity with the arm still on her, the one still working. "You can read my mind? Tell me why I just did that?" Hopefully she would think he'd done it simply to test her ability, never realizing any agent who entered his living room would now have a direct shot at her back.

She gazed up at him, all little-girl innocence and burning sensuality. A sultry combination. How many men had fallen for that act? Countless, he was sure. Because it made his mouth water even though he knew the consequences.

"Don't move me like that again," she said.

"I won't if you swear not to infect anyone else."

Silence.

"Just give me time to think about your offer. Okay? Just a little time." From the corner of his eye, he saw three black-clad agents tiptoe from the hallway, weapons drawn. Oh, yes. The cavalry was here.

Trinity smiled, a little sad now. "I'm sorry, Dallas."

Stall her . . . "Because you won't give me any time?"

"No. For your pain."

They fired. She disappeared, and each of the rays—two stun and one pyre—slammed into his stomach.

Fuck! The burn was massive, consuming. He would have collapsed, would have grasped his stomach to staunch the flames, but the stun rays had frozen him in place.

In unison, the shocked agents ripped off their masks, and he saw Mia in the middle, Devyn at her left and Hector at her right.

Mia was pale as she rushed to him. "Shit! I'm so sorry. Get the medics in here," she yelled over her shoulder. "Now!" Then she grabbed one of the shirts on his couch and pressed it into his wound.

Motherfucker! That pyre-fire was a kill wound, having burned a hole just below his ribs, scorching one side of his intestines. He'd endured this type of wound before. That's when Kyrin had fed him Arcadian blood. He'd healed then, and he would heal now. That didn't lessen the pain, though. He couldn't even curse out loud.

"Fuck! I'm sorry, I'm sorry, I'm sorry," Mia babbled. "We thought she was unaware. We had a clear shot. We took it. I'm sorry, I'm sorry, I'm sorry."

It's all right, he tried to project. He would have done the same thing.

"Dallas, man. I tried to lock her in place with my mind." Devyn could control other people's energy, but more and more, otherworlders were learning to prevent him from doing so. "Thought I had, really, the moment Mia gave the command to fire." He scrubbed a hand down his face. "I don't know how the queen escaped."

Hector, the asshole, seemed to take everything in stride. "Got any beer in the fridge?" he asked.

Mia slapped the agent's shoulder. "For God's sake, show a little sensitivity."

"What?" Hector threw up his arms. "Everyone in this room knows he's going to be fine."

Not many people knew of Dallas's change from human to otherworlder, but Hector was right. The three of them did. Still. Would a little worry have been amiss?

"Plus," Hector continued, unaffected by Mia's hate-filled glare. "Your frantic call dragged me out of bed, and I'm thirsty. So . . . Dallas. Beer? Blink once if the answer's yes."

Stun affected limbs and jaw, not eyelids, not heartbeat, not lungs. He blinked, but prayed Hector could read the fuck-you blazing in his eyes.

Chuckling, Hector patted the top of his head and sauntered off. Prick.

Finally, in sprinted three guys with a gurney. They managed to lift him up and lay him flat. Hurt like a bitch. There was a sharp sting in his forearm, then drugs were pumping through his system, at last dulling the pain and weaving dark over his eyes.

"You die," Mia said, "and I'll kill you real bad."

The perfect lullaby, he thought dryly, and allowed himself to drift away.

Eighteen

McKell flattened Ava against the seat, pinning her with his weight. She didn't seem to mind. No, she reached up, one hand tangling in his hair, nails biting into scalp, the other sliding down his spine, riding the ridges and leaving a path of fire.

Time was his enemy just then. So was his body. He had just meant to kiss her. To soften her. To begin her seduction, their romance, their *life*. Instead, their lips had met, their tongues had thrust together, he'd tasted her candy-sweetness, felt her luscious heat, heard her gasp his name, and he'd become lost. Lost with no hope of being found. Now he only cared about completion.

He felt like he'd been waiting for this moment, this woman, all the centuries of his life. He didn't care that vampires slept in the seat behind them, didn't care that the woman in his arms was human and unworthy.

Actually, *unworthy* did not apply, and he knew it never had. Ava was worthy of him. He was unworthy of her. She had hunted bloodsuckers for him, and even though they had been stronger than her, she'd held her own, punched one and chased the other. Her determination was unparalleled.

"McKell." Another gasp of his name. "Are you day-dreaming? Let's do this!"

He reacted to her eagerness with an insatiable growl of approval. The exotic benediction in her tone . . . if he let her, this woman would be his downfall. He kissed her, hard and deep.

When she arched her back, mashing her breasts, so wonderfully plump, into his chest, he wanted to let her. Falling seemed . . . fun. No one else had ever fit him so perfectly. Or made him ache so desperately. Or controlled his body quite so forcefully. She walked into a room, he grew hard. She spoke, he grew hard. She allowed herself to be tugged into his lap, he grew hard as a steel pipe.

"Spread," he demanded.

She opened her legs farther, allowing him a deeper cradle, and he took it greedily, rubbing against her. Full contact, cock to feminine core. Only thing preventing him from shoving deep inside her was their clothing.

"That's . . . that's . . ." She groaned, eyes squeezing shut, nails still digging, slicing.

He watched her and lost his ability to breathe. Beauty. Such beauty. Not even the vampires could hope to compare. Passion colored her cheeks, the length of her lashes cast shadows, and her lips, red and wet, glistened in the moonlight like a thousand tiny rubies shaped into a heart. Her amber curls were splayed around her delicate face, a wicked frame to a heavenly canvas.

He wanted their clothes gone. He wanted the vampires killed. No one else should ever see Ava like this. No one. He wanted out of the car, where they were trapped between the seat and the dash. Although the lack of space forced them to press as closely together as they could, so her every exhalation caressed his face, her scent enveloping him, the air charging with their arousal.

Her eyelids cracked open, revealing a sliver of those toffee irises and blown pupils. "You stopped kissing. Again. We done?"

He was panting, sweating. "Not even close." He wouldn't just kiss her, he decided. He would touch her. All of her. Despite their surroundings, their potential audience.

McKell just kind of fell on her, then, tongue plundering. She welcomed him with abandon, taking, giving. He, too, took and gave. He kneaded her breasts, her pearled nipples abrading his palms. Her heart slammed with so much force, he felt the beat inside his own body. And her blood rushed through her veins, a determined stream that created a roar in his ears. A delicious roar.

His mouth watered as his fangs sharpened, lengthened. Just being around her, he could barely keep his hunger under control. Kissing her, there was no such thing as control, the fine threads broken completely. There was only need and desire.

Would he ever get enough of her?

Her tongue scraped one of those fangs, and a bead

of her blood slid down his throat. He swallowed with a moan, warmth instantly pouring through him, strength fast on its heels. No. He would never get enough.

"McKell," she rasped, tunneling her fingers under his shirt. Skin to skin . . . heaven, hell. Salvation, damnation. Everything, nothing. Her, just her. "Take more," she pleaded. "Please, take more." Then, for a moment, she froze. "But don't you dare give me *your* blood. Please? Okay."

"I won't." But oh, he wanted to, he realized. Wanted to mate them permanently, forever. Prove to her, to everyone, that she was his. Only his. Finally. He wouldn't marry them, though, because they had a few things to settle first. He doubted her reason was the same, so her absolute refusal to drink from him irked.

"I'll kill you if you do." Even as she spoke, she relaxed, arched, body becoming fluid against his. "I swear."

"Shut up, Ava. More kissing."

"Where?"

His woman wanted his mouth elsewhere. He could oblige. Smile forming, he licked the pulse at the base of her neck. "Everywhere."

She scratched his back, stinging so good, before stiffening again. "Wait. I . . . we . . . maybe we should . . . I don't know, slow down."

If by "slow down" she meant "go faster," he was on board. "Why?" His tongue stroked that still gorgeous pulse, tracing the vein, heating the blood inside, preparing her for total possession.

"You aren't my type?"

She'd probably meant the words as a statement, not a question, and he took offense. He stopped grinding, stopped licking. Only glared. "What kind of man is your type, then?"

"I don't know." As her nails glided forward, scraping his pectorals, she lifted up and nibbled on his bottom lip. "Rich and cute. I'm flexible on the cute part, though."

He closed his eyes, savoring her attentions. She didn't want to slow down, then. Had only uttered the words because she felt they were expected of her. "I can obtain money."

"Honestly?"

He thrummed her nipples, making her gasp. "You said nothing about being rich through honest means."

A shiver moved through her and vibrated into him. "Oh, well, then. Scratch the money part. I want cute."

"I'm cute."

"No, you're dazzling. But no one can know about us until the case is over. Assuming we're still together, then. Okay? That's the only way I can allow this."

"We'll still be together then." Best she know that now, though this reaction was far better than the panic she'd offered when he'd moved in. Still. That she wanted to hide him, as if he were shameful . . . he didn't like it, wouldn't allow it for long, even for the good of the case. For the moment, however, he wanted her and would have given her the moon and stars had she asked. "Besides, if you kiss a man, but no one knows about it, it never really happened. Like the tree that falls in the woods . . ."

A moment passed, their panting breaths the only sound to be heard. Then she smiled slowly, wickedly, arousal blending with satisfaction. "There's a new requirement for my list. A devious mind, and baby, you've got that, too."

"So you want me?" he asked, rewarding her with another heated lick, this one up the column of her delicate neck.

"Yes." A gasp. "But if you're just doing this to soften me, to get on my good side for a blood donation—"

He pressed, his erection playing hide and seek with her sweet spot. "You have a good side?" Raw tone, taunting words.

Her next moan was broken, hoarse. "Ha, ha. I mean, if you're going to prime me up, then demand I give you blood as payment, I'll kill you. I swear to God I will. And yes, you now have two death threats hanging over your beautiful head."

He pressed again, silencing her, his cock practically singing at the contact. "If you meant to prime me up only to demand I finish you off, I'll have no problem with that."

"Smart-ass." She tongued his mouth, hot and clearly as hungry as he was. "But you're so devious, and you know how that revs my engine."

He released one of her breasts to blaze a trail down

the flat plane of her stomach. Her soft, quivering stomach. She had several blades strapped there, and he twisted them aside to dabble at her navel for a moment, unable to help himself. Such delightful skin. By the time they ended this, he would have explored all of her. Every burning inch.

"McKell," she moaned, and never had his title sounded sweeter. "You're priming me."

He'd waited all these centuries for Bride, but now, more than ever, he couldn't regret that he hadn't won her. He would have missed this opportunity. He would not have seen Ava like this, consumed by pleasure, beseeching him for more.

"Just as you're priming me. But Victor, darling. My name is Victor."

"I know. Can I call you Vicki?"

He chuckled softly. Irreverent baggage. Even now, while the pleasure beat so strongly between them. "You can call me whatever you wish." But it wouldn't get her what she needed.

He unfastened her jeans, creating a gap just large enough for his hand. Trembling, he tunneled through and found her panties. They were damp.

She thrashed her hips restlessly. "Do it. Please."

And now his irreverent baggage was a commander. He liked. Not that he would obey.

Remaining on the outside of the fabric, he cupped her. Still he felt the heat, the wetness. His cock, already hard and desperate, filled all the more, making him impossibly harder, and far more desperate.

The car eased around a corner, tilting to the left, and they pressed deeper into the seat. Streetlamps stood closer together, and as they continued to speed down the roads, Ava was illuminated, then cast into shadows. Illuminated, shadows.

My beauty, he thought proudly. He traced the soft skin around the edge of the panties, never quite touching the place she needed him most. Over and over he teased her. Almost caressing her clitoris . . . teasing . . . no, not this time. Light as a feather, letting her know he was there, that he could do more at any second. Nope, not this time, either.

Finally, she had clearly had enough, her desire, her need, propelled to new heights, her hips following his every motion, her skin a fever of sensitized nerves. Yet still he didn't touch her there. Just a little more . . . nope, missed again.

She balled her fists and pounded on his chest. "Do you need a map?"

"No. But I do need confirmation." Not doing what she wanted, what *he* wanted, was putting a strain on his body. Perspiration sheened his skin. His blood was like fire in his veins, scorching him to ash. The ache inside him . . . Each of his muscles was taunt, his skin pulled too tight on his bones.

"Of what?" She went still, a goddess carved from stone. To find relief? Even in so small a way?

He would give her none. "I need confirmation that you know who's here with you. That you know whose hand you crave." The hand in question finally glided over her center. A quick movement, only slightly more satisfying.

A reckless cry parted her lips. "Yours. I know it's yours."

"And who am I?" Another glide, this one lingering. He'd just found the corridor to heaven; he could no longer stay away.

Another cry filled the space between them. "Why do . . . you want . . . to know?"

"I don't want you forgetting later." Direct hit. "I don't want you thinking back and convincing yourself you were with the wrong person. Someone better suited to your list." Direct hit, harder, more forcefully.

"That only happened once!" Her knees squeezed at his waist.

"Ava." A warning. The only one she'd get. Not that he thought he had the strength to leave her like this.

She flashed her teeth at him, pearls in the darkness. "You said you'd finish me off."

"And I will." He was the one to go still this time. Any more contact with her sweet femininity, and he would take her all the way. "Without asking for blood."

"But you already took some. You sucked on my tongue."

And you begged for it. "You didn't have a problem with that."

"Just . . . finish me, damn it!"

"When you tell me what I want to hear." *Please.*

A low growl erupted from her throat. "Fine. You're McKell."

He flashed *his* teeth at *her*, and they were much, much sharper. "Who. Am. I?"

A pause. Then, a snarled, "Victor, okay? You're Victor. Now, will you stop with the he-man act and get to—"

He shoved her panties aside and thrust his finger deep inside her. The cry that next left her was neither reckless nor relieved. The cry that left her was animalistic, her back shooting off the seat. In and out he penetrated her, those silky walls gripping him, greedy for more.

More, he could give. He inserted a second finger, stretching her.

"Yes!"

In. Out. Hard. No mercy. He had none. She wanted none.

"Thank you! Yes, please, more."

He bit through her shirt, her bra, not hard enough to break skin, but just hard enough to suck her nipple into his mouth and flick his tongue against the jeweled peak. What color was this nipple? he wondered. He wanted to see. Wanted her naked. Yes, he'd seen her before, but she'd been unconscious then, not lost to passion. Would that passion flush her skin to a dusty rose?

Through the speakers, he heard one of the vampires in the backseat moan, as if about to waken.

Mine! McKell stopped time only long enough to open the shield-armor separating front and back, punch the bastard in the nose, causing blood to splatter, then command the block to return. He resettled on Ava, fingers probing back inside their new favorite spot, never missing a beat. She gripped his shoulders and continued to slam her hips into his, rocking against him with every ounce of her strength.

His cock loved every motion, every point of contact, swelling, heating, her fever becoming his, his becoming hers. He'd never spilled his seed inside his pants, but he was close to doing so with Ava, his sac drawn tight, every inch of him wanting to crawl inside her—and if he couldn't, punish him for the lack.

"Close," she rasped.

"Closer." He razed his fingertip along that bundle of nerves and pressed.

"McKell!" she shouted, inner walls suddenly clutching him. Her come drenched his hand, and he had to bite the inside of his cheek to stop his own orgasm. Oh, yes. He'd never been this close.

Several minutes passed before she relaxed into the seat. They were both panting, but a resplendant smile lifted the corners of her lips. She stretched, a contented feline who'd just consumed an entire bowl of cream.

"Your turn," she said silkily. "I got caught up and forgot about you. Sorry."

"Don't be. I'm not." Slowly, reluctantly he removed his fingers from her. As she watched, he licked them, one at a time, finally tasting her as he'd longed to do since the first moment he'd met her. Though she had just experienced the ultimate in satisfaction, desire once again heated her eyes.

"Delicious," he said, and meant it. Total femininity, an aphrodisiac. Sweet.

He ran a still-damp finger over the seam of her lips, bent down, and fed her a kiss. To his surprise, she reached between their bodies and fit a hand over his engorged shaft. So sublime was the sensation, he had to reach up and slap his palm against the windowpane. The glass cracked from top to bottom. He didn't care. Either he hit the glass, or punched the seat below her, possibly scaring her.

"Yes!" he cried. "More."

She squeezed, moved that hand up and down, tantalizing his tip, spreading the drop of moisture there, even through his clothes, then descending to his balls and tugging those. Closer still . . .

The car slowed, then stopped as Ava worked his zipper. Sweat heaven, yes! He needed this, had to have it, would die—

There was a knock on the door.

Rage sparked to instant life, and he twisted, meaning to lash out, to kill without mercy, then return to his woman and finally finish this. A smiling Noelle waved at him, unafraid of his murderous intent. She even wiggled her eyebrows suggestively.

"Go the fuck away!" he shouted.

"Not until I've had a little of this," Ava said with a husky chuckle.

Noelle mouthed something, but because of the

glass and the roar in his ears, he couldn't hear. But then, he didn't need to hear to know what she'd said. "Open." The window lowered, and she leaned inside, still grinning.

"Hey, y'all. Whatcha doing?"

"Noelle?" Ava stiffened. A moment later, she was shoving at McKell's chest. "Damn it! I can't believe we're already here."

He lifted, straightened, and righted his clothing while she righted her own, her cheeks bright red. His probably were, too. "Why couldn't you live farther from the club?" he mumbled.

Noelle's grin widened. "So I can enjoy moments like this. Duh."

"Well, you don't have to stare," Ava gritted.

"I know, but I want to," Noelle replied, still completely unabashed.

"You are such a bad friend."

"*You're* a bad friend. I'm still waiting on my laundry."

"You're doing mine now. Remember?"

He listened to the byplay, trying to get his body under control. Impossible. The fire continued to rage, his muscles continued to twitch, and his cock continued to ache. It was going to be a long night. Unless . . . "Go inside. I'll meet you in . . . five minutes." He could take care of himself in that short amount of time.

Both women snorted.

"Hardly," Noelle said. "We've got business."

Yes. A long night.

As Ava scooted passed him, she commanded the door to open. The latch separated from the vehicle and she moved the rest of the way out, practically knocking Noelle to her ass.

"This is your fault, McKell," she snapped over her shoulder.

"My fault?" He scooted out, too, and unfolded to a stand. "How is it *my* fault?"

"Your tree theory sucks!"

"Tree theory?" Noelle switched her attention from Ava to McKell, McKell to Ava. "Color me intrigued."

"Shut up," they shouted in unison.

"Fine." She held up her hands. "Be that way. I'll just get the prisoners."

McKell held out his arm, stopping her from approaching the backseat. "No! Don't touch them."

Far from intimidated, she anchored her hands on her hips. "Why not?"

"Yeah, why not?" Ava demanded.

"They're mine."

Noelle's eyes widened. "You're seriously so possessive you can't even allow someone to touch your *prisoners*?"

He didn't say a word, just crossed his arms over his chest.

"Wow. I'm suddenly unsure why I ever called dibs," Noelle said with a shake of her head. "Thank God I changed my mind and gave him to you."

"You're so lucky to be single," Ava said, and damn if she didn't sound truly envious.

His gaze narrowed on her, but he spoke to the car. "Open." Like the front door, the back expanded. He reached inside and grabbed one of the vampires, anchoring the bastard over his shoulder. Then he bent to grab the other one. Only, the one he held slammed into the top of the car. He straightened, bent again. Same thing happened.

"Ava," he said, pivoting to face her. "I will allow you to get the other one." And he wouldn't mind, he realized with surprise. He'd always had a problem with sharing, though the inability had grown worse over the last few months.

When he'd lived below, in the vampire underworld, he'd rarely allowed anyone inside his personal cave. They would have put their hands on his things, and he wanted to cut off the hands that touched his things. With Ava, he actually *liked* the thought of her hands on the things that belonged to him.

Maybe not the vampires, he decided then. They were male, and she only needed to put those beautiful hands on him. But everything else, yes.

"I mean, I'll allow Noelle to get the other one."

Ava stood beside Noelle, and both women watched him. Ava blew on her nails, then buffed them on her shirt. "I wouldn't dream of touching something that belongs to you. So, yeah. We'll be in the house, waiting. Take that five minutes if you still want it."

With that, both women gave him a pinkie wave and strode past the open iron gate, up the hill, and into the large . . . home. Fortress was a better word.

Large, sprawling, and dark, with manicured lawns and armed guards patrolling the upper walkway.

Grumbling under his breath, McKell tossed the vampire he held onto the ground, then reached in and dragged out the other.

This was definitely going to be a long night.

Nineteen

God, McKell was sexy, lugging two full-size male vampires over his shoulders, stomping up the winding staircase in the Tremain mansion, and dumping the bodies on the floor of the "interrogation" room. All without breaking a sweat or panting. Like he did when he touched her.

He was pissed off, though. That much was clear. His violet eyes were stormy, and his lips were turned down in a fierce scowl. That just made him sexier, Ava thought. And she'd had all that sexiness on top of her. Just a few minutes ago, at that.

He'd kissed her with abandon. He'd tasted of butterscotch, as if he'd sucked on several candies before sucking on her. His hands had moved over her with utter possession, teasing and taunting and demanding a response. Without a doubt, he'd *owned* her. Whatever he'd wanted, she would have done. Would have begged to do.

She shivered, remembering.

His long, thick fingers had sunk inside her, and she'd felt penetrated to her soul. Writhing against him had been her only option. Stopping would have killed her. Had they been anywhere but a car, two guys in the backseat, she would have demanded he fuck her. Hard, possibly forever. *Shocking*.

Forever still wasn't for her. But God, she'd wanted him. Even after he'd given her the most intense orgasm of her life, she'd wanted more of him. Wanted more even though he'd made her work for that orgasm, following his naughty fingers, silently pleading for contact.

She'd hoped to do the same to him. Torment him before finally allowing him release. Only, they'd reached their destination first, and she was still peeved about that. Not embarrassed at having been caught by her friend, as she should have been, but upset that she hadn't gotten to finish him.

Now, McKell—Victor—was probably in pain. Surely cursing her name. He'd shown her paradise, and she'd shown him hell. That was what embarrassed her most. Like she was an incompetent. Like she couldn't pull her sexual weight.

Just then, his gaze lifted, found Ava, darkened—she shivered again, knowing the passion that still lurked inside him, hungry, unsated, waiting—and then swiftly moved away, scanning the entire room in less than a heartbeat.

What did he think of the teardrop chandelier? The tiny angels painted on the walls? The beaded pillows, the precious china locked in intricate hutches?

"I'm to question them *here*?" he demanded.

Noelle frowned. "Apparently the torture chamber has become the new storage closet. This is our fourth dining room, unnecessary, and will have to do. So what's wrong with it, anyway? Looks perfect to me."

He pointed to the plush white carpet. "Blood is red. Soon the rug will be, too."

As if hearing and understanding his meaning, both unconscious vampires moaned.

Fangs peeking out from his top lip, McKell then pointed to the two chairs Noelle had pushed together. "And those . . . those just look comfy."

True. Both had cobalt velvet cushions at the back and rear, and swirling flowers had been carved into the wood. Real wood, with a glossy maple finish. They were gorgeous. What a shame to ruin them. But Noelle had never cared about family heirlooms like those probably were.

"If you don't have the stomach for torturing, just say so and get out," Noelle said. "Don't blame the furniture."

"Not have the stomach for torturing?" His color deepened with fury. "Just watch and learn, little girl." After he threw the vampires into the chairs and tied them down, he slapped them into wakefulness.

They blinked open their eyes, revealing glazed, glassy irises. Ava fell into the couch that had been moved in front of the chairs, and Noelle plopped beside her. Would it have been bad to ring a servant for popcorn?

"What'd they do to deserve this, anyway?" her friend asked. "Kill someone you love? Burn your apartment down?"

"Nah. They just have information about successful vampire living."

"Those bastards! Wait." Noelle's features scrunched in confusion. "What?"

"McKell doesn't know how to live in the sunlight, and they might."

"Suggestion," Noelle said, raising her hand like a schoolgirl. "It's called sunblock, and it's sold at any local grocery."

"The chatter can end anytime," McKell snapped without looking at them.

Noelle rolled her eyes, and Ava drummed her fingers against the armrest. Both vampires had been watching and listening to the byplay, she realized, forgetting McKell entirely. Otherwise they would have been screaming. Still.

"She makes a good point," Ava said.

"Ava."

"Well, have you tried it?"

"Woman." He whipped around and finally faced her. "I didn't interrupt your work at the bar. Please don't interrupt mine."

"Sorry," she muttered. Torturing was his job? Why did that add to his already off-the-charts sex appeal? "I won't say another word." She even pretended to twist a lock over her lips and toss the key aside.

He nodded and returned his attention to the men. Before he even said another word, their expressions became mulish.

"I know who you are," one said, "and I know what you can do. But I'm not telling you shit."

"Me, either," the other agreed.

McKell flicked her an irritated glance, as if their refusal was her fault. Like she'd ruined his street cred or something. She blinked innocently.

"My God," Noelle gasped. "That voice . . . it washes over you, consumes you. Mama wants a taste."

"Concentrate on McKell, not—" What were their names? "Not them." She'd just call them One and Two. "That's what I do." Wait. She didn't like the thought of Noelle relying on McKell. For anything, even this. "Concentrate on me."

"Help us," One began, gaze locked on Noelle. There were flickers of light in that onyx gaze, stars in a silken sky. "You have only to—"

McKell punched him so hard Ava thought she heard the guy's brain rattle against his skull. "I don't want to hurt you, but I will if you force me. Here's rule number one. You will focus on me, and only me. Speak to the women again, and I'll cut out your eyes."

Both vampires trembled, nodded.

"I'm concentrating on you, but I still want to help him," Noelle whispered to her.

Ava squeezed her knee, ready to fight her if she tried to stand.

"Now, then." McKell rubbed his hands together. "I want answers, that's all, and answers are easy enough to give, yes?" They trembled under his scrutiny. "So let's begin. You've been here two years.

Your skin is smooth, unburned, and you seem to have money."

True. They were clean, their clothing unsoiled, a soft leather, and their hair had just the right amount of product. "Maybe they steal," Ava suggested.

"Ava!" This time McKell didn't face her, but his voice still wrapped around her, tightening, becoming a vise grip. "I thought your mouth was sealed."

"Sorry," she muttered, shoulders sagging.

"Maybe we steal," One said mockingly.

Two nodded with a smug grin.

Ava was surprised McKell didn't start hitting again. And wow, she really was undermining him. She'd spoken, and the vampires had lost their fear.

"Do you go out in the daylight?" The words sounded as if they'd been pushed through a meat grinder, rather than McKell's throat.

"No," Two said.

"You're lying," McKell replied.

One lifted his chin. "Prove it."

McKell shrugged. "That, I can do. We can wait until morning, and I can toss you outside, tie you down, let you stay there. For hours. Maybe you'll burn, maybe you won't. Either way, I'll know the truth."

Both vampires paled. At the thought of being burned? Or at the thought of proving beyond a doubt that they'd learned how to endure the sun's rays? She frowned, mind buzzing. Why would they care about the latter?

"You found us in a nightclub. At . . . what? Night."

One's eyes narrowed, though he couldn't quite conceal his defiance. "Anyone with sense would realize we're telling the truth and can't go out in daylight."

Anyone with sense? A spark of anger bloomed in Ava's chest. McKell had been nothing but patient. Kind of. Yet One had the nerve to call *her* man senseless? She pushed to her feet before she realized what she was doing, withdrew a blade from the holster around her waist, and marched over to vampires.

She couldn't help herself. She stabbed One in the leg.

He howled.

McKell looked at her, and she thought she saw a spark of pride in those purple specks. "Thank you," he said, surprising her.

"My pleasure."

Noelle clapped. "I give you an eight-point-nine for form. Had to deduct for faulty finish. You didn't twist the hilt."

"As if you could have done any better," McKell told her without looking away from Ava.

Ava rose on her tiptoes and placed a swift, hard kiss on McKell's lips. He'd defended her skill, the delightful man. Even if she *had* forgotten to twist the hilt like any decent agent would have done. He was grinning as she returned to the couch.

When One's howling finally ceased, tears streaming down his face, McKell said, "So. I'll ask again. Do you have any trouble in the sunlight? And before you answer, you should know that I've heard rumors. Everyone in the underground has. It can be done."

One gulped.

McKell continued, "Do you think I immediately killed every vampire I hunted and found living here? No. I returned them to the caves and . . . chatted with them."

"Time out," Noelle said, hands forming a cross. "If you chatted, why don't you already know the answer?"

Good question. Ava imagined he was very good at *chatting*.

He sighed, as if he'd already resigned himself to more interruptions. "Everything I was told, I've tried. None of it has worked. Which means I was lied to. And it's too late to get the truth from the liars."

Because he'd killed them. *Nice*.

"That might be why I'm especially vengeful when lied to now," he finished, pointed gaze on the vampires.

"We're . . . we're not telling you what we know," Two rushed out, pallid now. "We can't."

"If you think to keep the truth from me because I was once the enforcer of vampire laws, think again. Those laws no longer apply. I'm as much an outlaw as you. Tell me, and live." McKell withdrew the blade from One's leg and thrust it into Two's. More howling ensued. "Don't, and die." He twisted the hilt, and the howling became pleading.

McKell glanced back at Ava. To ensure she watched? She nodded her approval.

"Nine-point-nine," Noelle said.

He frowned. "Why was I deducted?"

"You waited too long to do the twisting."

His frown deepened, but he gave no reply. Ava was surprised, though, that he wasn't chastising Noelle for such an "honest" critique. Most men would have. They would have thought the girl was insensitive or crazy. Yes, she'd heard both descriptions before. Many times. And Ava had put the ones who'd said so in the hospital.

But McKell—for the most part—just went along with them, as if what they did and said was normal. And that . . . delighted her. *Seriously? It* delights *you?* Now she was the one frowning. She wasn't supposed to like him more with every minute that passed. She was supposed to be growing tired of him. Like she had with every other man in her life. Before they could grow tired of her.

McKell faced the vampires. "Stop blubbering. You're an embarrassment to our kind."

"But that . . . that hurts," Two sniffed.

"Which you can blame on yourself. I gave you a choice, didn't I?"

More blubbering, more sniffing, and Ava shook her head. McKell was right. That was embarrassing for all vampirekind.

With a swift jerk, McKell withdrew the knife. As predicted, blood dripped onto the carpet. "Let's try this one more time. How do you—"

There was a knock on the door, distracting him. He glanced at Ava. She shrugged, a don't-look-at-me gesture. She and Noelle had done much worse than a little torturing over the years, so everyone here kind of expected such behavior.

Noelle sat up ramrod-straight and growled. "Just a sec," she called to the intruder. Then, to those in the room, "I told everyone to stay away, but clearly someone didn't listen and needs to be fired."

Another knock.

"What?" Noelle shouted.

No one replied, but the metal door did slide open. Mrs. Tremain, the ironfisted matriarch of the wealthiest family in New Chicago, marched inside on a cloud of expensive perfume. "*What* is going on in here? *Who* is screaming?"

As always, her expression was stern. No telling what kind of treatments she did to her face, but it was unlined despite her fifty-something years. She wore a starched button-up shirt and a pencil skirt. She was thin. Too thin. And when she spied the bleeding vampires, she merely arched a barely-there brow.

Her gaze narrowed on McKell, who still clutched the dripping knife. "*Who* are you?"

"Mother," Noelle said, exasperated. "We're kinda busy here. Come back later."

Mother Tremain straightened her spine as though she'd been slapped. "*What's* going on?" she demanded again. "*Who* is that man? *Are* we being robbed?"

Ava despised the way she annunciated the beginning of each new sentence.

"Help us," One suddenly begged.

"Please," Two pleaded.

Mrs. Tremain's gray eyes glazed over, and she took a step forward. "Yes. Yes, I'll help you."

Nice to know even disapproving matrons weren't immune to vampire wiles. Ava popped to her feet and waved a hand in front of the woman's face. Distraction was the only thing that helped. "Hey, Mrs. Tremain. Nice to see you again. Long time, huh?"

The glaze faded, replaced by disdain, and the old woman's chin lifted. "Ava Sans. I should have known." So much disapproval rested in that tone. "Noelle has always liked bringing home the trash, rather than leaving it at the curb where it belongs."

McKell strode toward her, bless his heart, as if he meant to defend Ava's honor. For the first time in Ava's memory, something managed to intimidate the staunch matron, truly intimidate her, and Mrs. Tremain backed up a step as two hundred and fifty pounds of enraged vampire bore down on her.

"McKell," Ava said, and he instantly stopped, surprising her. "You can't kill her. Or believe me, she'd already be dead."

"Can I hurt her?"

"No," Ava said at the same time Noelle said, "Yes. Mother, I told you what would happen if you ever insulted my friend again. I'd marry a bum right off the street. I swear to God I was telling the truth."

The matriarch kept her attention on McKell. "As if you have the courage to—" She squeaked as he started back up.

"Please don't," Ava added. For McKell's benefit. She didn't want him in trouble with the law.

Again, he stopped. "Very well."

No question, he was getting a reward when they got home. Home. *Their* home. Just for a little while, but still theirs. A bolt of awareness traveled through her, lightning to her nerve endings.

Where had her fight gone? Her resistance?

Noelle hurtled a pillow at the woman who had always considered Ava beneath every member of her family. "Mother, I told you I had important business up here. Now get out before I tie *you* to a chair."

That chin lifted yet another notch. "Fine." She turned to leave, throwing over her shoulder, "But you *will* clean this room when you're done."

"We both know that's not going to happen," Noelle returned. "And tell Cook to fire up the grill. I'm in the mood for a steak."

"And maybe butterscotch cookies," Ava suggested. "Tell her she used too much nutmeg last time, and—"

The door closed with a snap, and there was a moment of charged silence.

"This is the best day of my life," Noelle said with a grin that lit her entire face. "My mother yelped. Did you guys hear it, or was I just dreaming?"

"I heard," One said through his tears. "And I'm only speaking to McKell."

Ava reclaimed her spot on the couch. "Me, too."

McKell used both hands to wipe his face, as if the motion could also wipe away the memory of

Mrs. Tremain's distraction. He returned to the vampires. "You were just telling me how to survive in the sun."

"No, we weren't." One shook his head violently.

"Not even if you stab us again. But please don't stab us again."

McKell lifted his leg and rested his foot on One's injured thigh. "I wouldn't be so sure about that. But, lucky for you, I'm willing to negotiate. Tell me what I want to know, and the women will kiss. Each other."

Both men blinked, looked at each other, looked at Ava and Noelle. One lost his glaze of pain, and Two licked his lips.

"They have to kiss first."

"And then we'll tell you everything we know. Promise."

McKell removed his foot and faced Ava, then motioned with his hand. She just blinked at him.

"Well?" he prompted. "Get started. Kiss."

She planned to reward *him*, not everyone in the room. "First, this is *your* interrogation. We're just here to watch, listen and learn. Remember?"

He pursed his lips. "Ava."

"Second," she continued, "you're caving to their demands? Well, I won't allow it. Either they spill the secret, or there's no kissing. And I won't budge on this."

"Yeah," Noelle said with a nod. "We won't budge on this. No matter how sexy their voices are." She gave the vampires a pinkie wave. "And no matter how bad I want to get my tongue into my little firecracker's mouth."

One nodded in invitation, and Two wiggled his brows.

McKell splayed his arms, as if he were powerless. "You heard the females. Answers first, kiss second."

One and Two faced each other, whispering, debating. "We shouldn't tell him, even for that kiss."

"He'll find out eventually."

"Yeah, but he'll kill us just as soon as we tell him."

"I think he'll kill us if we don't. He said so, remember?"

"But when he knows, he'll make it painful."

"Rumor is, he's been kicked out of the underground. Maybe he won't care. He hates humans, and didn't he say that he no longer enforces vampire law?"

"Has anyone ever told you that you're stupid? He could be lying. The woman he kissed is a human, so he can't hate them too badly."

"You're the stupid one."

Did she and Noelle sound that dumb when they argued? Geez! She'd had enough, was getting upset that McKell wasn't getting what he wanted, and was close to stabbing someone again. "Offer ends in five . . . four . . . three . . ."

"Fine," One rushed out. "I'll tell." Deep breath in, hold . . . hold, slow release. "If you drain a human to death, once every night, you develop a resistance to the sun's deathly rays. But you have to kill every night, because the effects only last twelve hours."

"That's the only way?" McKell asked.

That's all he cared about? The guy had just admit-

ted to murdering someone every night. Stab someone? No, she had a target, and a simple stabbing
wasn't violent enough.

"Yes," was the eager answer. "Now about that
kiss . . ."

"And that's all you have to do?" McKell asked now.
That's *all*?

Another eager, "Yes. So back to the kiss . . ."

Those bastards! All of them. McKell included.

He twirled the blade he still held. "I'm not done
yet. Most other vampires living on the surface world
know this?"

"If they don't, they learn pretty quickly." One's gaze
swung to Ava and Noelle. "Is that all, because—"

"And they willingly do it?" McKell asked.

"Of course." Two's irritation was showing, but he
hurried on. "Humans are merely food, after all. And
I know, I know. Humans are our food, and we've always been forbidden from killing our food because
the supply could run out. But listen, we don't do that.
That's why we were out tonight. We stopped killing.
Trying to blend in during the day was a waste of time.
We thought to get jobs, you know. Real jobs. Be pro-
ductive. But why work when you can simply convince
people to give you what you want?"

"Thank you for being truthful," McKell said.

If he told her to kiss Noelle now, Ava really would
grab another knife and sink it—

"By the way. I lied. There'll be no kiss." With one
fluid slash, he cut One's throat, then Two's. Both

gurgled in pain and shock, bled, color fading, bodies twitching . . . passed out. "Don't worry. They'll recover." He tossed the knife on the floor. "But for their crimes, they are my gift to AIR. Your people may do whatever they like with them."

Ava relaxed against the couch. Bless his sweet little heart. He'd just earned himself another reward.

Twenty

McKell wasn't surprised when Ava and Noelle left him alone with the unconscious vampires. To "ship his property to AIR on his own, as he most likely wanted to do, possessive ass that he was." What *had* surprised him? They'd expected a thank-you for their *consideration*. Aka a back rub, followed by a foot rub, followed by hand-feeding them dinner. Before taking off to "do shit he shouldn't concern himself with," they'd been very vocal about their desires.

Females. He'd let them go only because they'd sworn to remain inside the house.

So, alone in the dining room, McKell surveyed his handiwork. The vampires were unmoving—and messy—and there was no way in hell he was going to spend the next hour patching them up for safe travels to their new home, while the girls did God knew what. Only one way to handle this, then. He delegated their care to the two guards waiting outside the door, ordering the men to bind those slashed necks and drive the vampires straight to AIR headquarters, making no stops along the way.

They nodded and jumped into action—after admitting that Ava had already commanded them to do exactly that.

Females, he thought again. Only this time he was grinning. His woman was clever.

Now he surveyed the room itself. Ruined, as he'd first warned Noelle. But she hadn't seemed to care about the possibility and subsequent reality, so he wouldn't either. Besides, he well knew how possessive some people could be about their things, cough cough, and he didn't want to upset Noelle's harpy of a mother by moping up a single drop of blood and touching what now belonged to her.

So he left the room exactly as it was with a muttered, "You're welcome." See how nice he was? He wasn't even going to demand a thank-you of his own.

He strode down the hall, following Ava's scent, but stopped midway as a thought struck him. Scent. He was following her scent. Her *human* scent.

The vampires' scent . . . He'd never noticed one.

Frowning, McKell backtracked to the bloody room. In the club, he'd recognized their faces, so had known what they were, but had assumed they were scentless because of the many humans that surrounded them. Plus, he'd been worked into a cold, dark frenzy because one of them had practically embraced Ava.

In the car, he'd been too wrapped up in kissing Ava to care or consider. During the interrogation, he'd been too wrapped up in *impressing* Ava to care or consider. But now that she'd left, now that their blood was spilled all over the floor, he realized they still didn't smell like vampires.

They smelled human, and that human scent was stamped inside his nose. A consequence of draining humans to death?

Maybe. But they'd claimed to have stopped. That begged the question: How long ago had they stopped? Yesterday? The day before? A year? And since they smelled human, would they heal like a vampire or die from their wounds?

They deserved the latter, so he still couldn't regret his actions.

Killing their food supply went against every vampire rule in existence. McKell might view the humans as beneath him—well, most of them—but he would never do such a thing. Not even to walk unfettered in the daylight.

No wonder the vampires he'd hunted and tortured for leaving the underground had taken their secrets to the grave. Like these two, they'd known he would have made their deaths ten thousands times more painful if he'd known.

He left the room a second time, certain there had to be another way to impede the sun's harmful rays. Equally certain Ava would help him find it. He had only to uncover her whereabouts, take her home, make love, feed, make love again, and put her immense brainpower to use. He picked up his pace.

Like the rest of her world, this home was too open for his tastes. Too spacious. He needed walls at his sides, closing him in. Like his cave. Perhaps one day he'd take Ava there. Make love to her there.

Again he quickened his steps. Left, right, right, left. Up another staircase. Down one. Through a kitchen. Every servant and guard he'd seen on the way in was now gone. Where was Ava? If she'd left . . . He frowned as a morbid thought occurred to him. Had he frightened her? Had she lied and run from him?

She'd seen him nearly kill two men, yes, but she'd already known he was a killer. A killer who always acted without hesitation. Well, only once had he hesitated, but Bride didn't count, since they'd already been betrothed and he'd considered her to be his exclusive property.

His head tilted to the side as he pondered his willingness to later let Bride leave with Devyn the Targon. A willingness Ava would not receive. The thought of her walking away from him permanently, and for another man at that, filled him with so much rage he could have clawed every piece of furniture to shreds and returned the walls to plaster and dust. But he wouldn't hurt *her*, he thought with conviction. Even then, even lost to the red haze of fury, he would be unable to hurt her. She was . . . precious.

She made him laugh, something no one had ever done before. She understood him, helped him. Drove him to be better. He hadn't killed those vampires, and he hadn't made them beg and suffer for hours. See? An utter improvement.

So, what did she think about him? Now that she'd seen his violent, yet merciful side?

He would ask her, and she would tell him the truth. She always did. No matter how deeply the truth cut. That was something else he liked about her. Her honesty. And after she told him that she still craved him—she hadn't run, she just hadn't—they could return home and, what? Make love. His shaft was still hard, still aching.

Where was she? Where was *anyone*? The servants and guards had probably left with the old crone. Perhaps she'd wanted no witnesses for her daughter's deeds. That implied caring, though, and the crone hadn't seemed to care about anything but hating Ava.

He should have killed her, he thought. He'd wanted to. How dare she look at Ava as beneath her? No one was better than Ava. She could rule this planet if she wished. She was the best of the best.

Where you are, sweetness? Her scent led him to a music room. There was a piano, a harp, drums and several guitars, but no Ava. He sniffed. The crone had been here recently, as well.

His frown deepened. He didn't like the thought of Ava wandering around without his protection. No matter how skilled she was. The hag could have paid a group of men to attack her. If so, heads would roll.

McKell had never been a discriminating killer. Whoever the king had ordered him to kill, he had killed. Male, female, young, old, it hadn't mattered. Rebels and deserters were rebels and deserters, no matter their sex or age. But this time the kills would be personal. He'd enjoy them.

"Ava," he called.

No reply.

A quick stride through the chamber, and he caught Ava's butterscotch scent again. Good. But, no. Impossible. She couldn't have gone through the far wall. Unless . . . He knocked on said wall until he heard the hollow echo of a hidden doorway. Ah. Of course. *Such* a clever girl. And as he'd known, she hadn't run from him.

His fingers brushed gently, searching and finding a telling seam. Naughty vixen, trying to do something in secret. Not that he'd let her get away with it. He straightened and considered his options. With hidden passages, there was always a latch, but discovering that latch would take time. Time required patience. Patience he didn't have.

He clawed an opening in the wall, plaster falling away in chunks, dust plumping around him. When the void was a little wider than his body, he slipped through. Female voices echoed. Finally.

Grinning, McKell descended a well-lit staircase, turned a corner, and found another open doorway that led into . . . another room. With an arsenal. Guns and knives hung from the walls, and there were actual shelves piled high with grenades, throwing stars, and all kinds of other things he couldn't name.

Ava and Noelle were talking and laughing as they suited up, probably adding one hundred pounds of death to their bodies. A . . . what was that? His lips curled in distaste. Was that what humans referred to as a dog? Yes, that sounded correct. Dogs had nearly been wiped out during the human-alien war, and most people had robotic imitations now.

This one appeared real as it perched between the women, eyes darting back and forth between them. It had ratty dark brown fur, a large pink tongue that stuck out with drool dripping from it, and a long tail that wagged. And wagged and wagged and wagged.

"What's going on?" he demanded.

The dog jumped excitedly, then trotted to him and wound around his legs. He grimaced. Neither of the women acted surprised to see him. They just kept checking pyre-crystals.

"Got a text from Mia," Ava said. She'd changed into jeans and a T-shirt. "The Schön queen cornered Dallas again, and now he's in the hospital."

McKell tried to shoo the animal away. "Is he infected?" It remained at his side, fur softer than he'd realized, but still. Annoying.

"Nah," Noelle replied. "Friendly fire."

"And you plan to. . . ?" He glanced between them. The dog used his inattention to its advantage, licking his palm. He couldn't help his yelp of disgust. "Don't do that again, or I'll gut you."

Rather than racing away in terror, the dog gazed up at him with big, brown eyes.

"That's Hellina. Hell for short," Noelle said, motioning to the dog with a tilt of her chin.

The ugly thing was female?

"And we're going out to kill vampires," Ava said, as if it were obvious.

His brow furrowed. He was having trouble connecting the dots. "What does one—Dallas's injury—have to do with the other—vampire hunting?"

"Well," she said, shoving a thick, curved blade in the sheath now hanging at her side. "Both piss me off."

"I see." Was he to be one of her victims? Would she now try to wash her hands of him? Try to kick him out of her apartment? "Are the actions of my people a deal breaker, then?" Translation: Would he have to seduce her into liking him again?

Such a dirty, dirty job.

Noelle laughed, and Ava's cheeks reddened. "No," Ava said. "AIR needs you."

What of you? he almost asked, but didn't. He didn't want an audience for that particular conversation.

Hellina rubbed against him, demanding his attention. Not knowing what else to do, he reached down and scratched behind her ears. She closed her eyes, as if she'd never experienced so expert a touch. Which, of course, she hadn't.

"You're gonna stay here, because, as you've proven, all the vampires run away from you," she continued. "Plus, dawn will arrive soon, and unless you want to drain me completely, you can't survive out there. There are a thousand other reasons but we'll leave them at blah, blah, blah."

"First, you can't handle vampires on your own, Ava."

What would have happened to her at the club if he hadn't saved her? The thought of her facing defeat again, without him, perhaps with stronger vampires than the ones they'd captured, caused his blood to churn into acid, blistering his veins. "Second, like you said, dawn will come all too soon. How will you know where to look for vampires?" He'd given her no pointers, no starting point. "Human clubs will be closed, yes?"

"Yes, but here's the thing." She lifted a bone dagger and pricked her finger on the tip. His mouth watered at the sight of that crimson bead. "The vampires walking around in daylight are the ones I want. As a bonus, I'm sure AIR would love to use them as pincushions to test against the Schön virus. They'll deserve it, too." She rubbed the bead on her jeans.

No argument from him. "But how will you find them?" he asked again. This time, the words were slurred. *Don't let the hunger overtake you. Not yet.* He had to make her understand the trouble she was courting.

"When I'm done, I'm taking you in to see Mia," she said, ignoring his question completely. "I kept my end of our bargain, so now you have to keep yours and talk to her."

So. She didn't mean to try to exterminate him for the actions of his people. Despite his relief, he offered no reply. Not even about her desire to leave him behind. And that's all it was. A desire he wouldn't grant. But he would deal with that in a moment. *After* they'd addressed his consuming disappointment that they wouldn't be having sex tonight as he'd planned.

"Did I ever tell you about your blood?" Ava asked before he could command Noelle to cover her ears. She anchored the bone dagger to her wrist, and sucked on the tip of her finger to force the pinprick to close.

Mine, he thought, jealous that she tasted what he so craved. But all right. This conversation he would allow. Blood was almost as important as sex. He leaned a shoulder against the doorframe, stopped petting the silly dog, and crossed his arms over his chest. "What do you mean?" *His* blood?

Hellina whined. He ignored her.

"Anyone who ingests it will be turned into a vampire."

"Impossible." Despite what her books and movies claimed—which his kind studied, because information was power—vampires couldn't turn humans. They had tried. Still. This explained her absolute refusal to drink from him, and her threat to kill him dead if he snuck her a single drop. She'd feared being turned.

Hellina nudged him, but he again ignored her. Never should have touched her in the first place. Now he smelled like her, like wild animal. Disgusting. "We're born, not created, I promise you."

"Apparently, *you* can create them."

He laughed at how little she apparently knew about his kind. Hellina nudged him yet again, and with a sigh, he renewed his petting. Anything to stop the pawing of his pants. "Such a thing has never been done before."

"How do you know?" she insisted. "Have you ever shared your blood with another person? Someone human?"

"No." That didn't mean . . .

Noelle snorted. "Shocker. McKell, being selfish."

He ignored her, too. "There's one way to prove your claim, Ava. Drink my blood right now." And sweet heaven, did he adore the thought. More than he'd ever thought possible. He still didn't think she'd turn into a vampire—silly girl—but they would finally be mated completely, with her willing cooperation.

She would still age, but he suddenly didn't care. He would have her for the rest of her life. Enjoy her. Share with her. Those few years would be better than an eternity without her.

Ava bent down and shoved a pair of barbed-wire cuffs in her boots. "This may come as a surprise to you, McKell, but I don't want to be a vampire. Ever. I happen to like being human."

"You might like being vampire more," he said, offended. Which was foolish. She simply couldn't be turned. "And what does this have to do with anything, huh?" Trying to distract him from his purpose? He wouldn't put it past her.

"I was thinking." She straightened, amber gaze locked on him. Holding him captive. "If we incarcerate the Schön queen, maybe you could give her some of your blood."

"No." No hesitation on his part. If he shared with anyone, it would be Ava. And only Ava. "And if I discover what I give to Mia for testing is used for something else, *on* someone else, I will kill everyone involved."

"And what if it doesn't kill the queen's disease, but just makes her stronger?" Noelle asked, inserting herself back into the conversation. On his side, no less.

Ava somehow broke the chains that bound their gazes and faced her friend. "Mia and I wondered the same thing, but we can try it out with Johnny tonight, when we escort McKell to AIR headquarters. If Mia says okay, that is. She's deliberating the pros and cons. I think she'll decide to go for it, though. It's not like we have many more options."

He loved that the agents had discussed him and his blood at such great length. And made decisions for him. Yeah. Loved. "Just so you know, I'd share my blood with the queen before I shared with Johnny." Which meant, never ever fucking never. And did no one take his threats seriously anymore?

Ava snatched up a gun and slammed the clip in place. "Maybe we can bargain."

He straightened, once again pulling away from the dog. This time, the beast growled at him. "You won't order me around," he snarled down at her. He had some bargaining to do, followed by some sealing of that bargain.

Hellina ducked her head and whimpered. McKell's shoulder's slumped as he reached out to pet her again. Stupid dog. "I'm listening," he said to Ava. "You mentioned a bargain."

"That's right."

What he knew: he'd only allow her to "convince" him to part with one drop of blood. For that drop, she had to kiss him. But he got to pick where that kiss would be located. "Begin."

"I'll start with my terms." She aimed the pyre-gun at him and fired before he could yell, move, or even stop time. "Oops. My bad. We'll have to finish this conversation later."

Blue, he realized with dread. Which meant she'd just stunned him. Again. Fury vapor-locked his lungs, and for several seconds, he couldn't breathe. When she closed the distance between them and pressed a swift kiss to his lips—not the kiss he'd wanted—his airway opened back up, allowing him to inhale deeply, sucking in that butterscotch scent. Savoring, hating.

"I'm sorry. I couldn't let you stop me, and I couldn't take you with me. Be a good boy," she said with an edge of repentance. "Stun will wear off in twenty-four hours, but I'll be done in . . ." She glanced at Noelle. "How long?"

"Six and a half hours until the meeting with Mia," the girl said, hurriedly shoving a few more blades in the holster around her waist.

"I'll be done in six hours and return for you. Noelle will help me—"

"The servants," Noelle interjected.

Ava rolled her eyes. "Noelle's *servants* will help me get you into the car and to AIR without a single burn. See, Ava has it all worked out." She patted his cheek.

He snarled.

"Don't you two go getting all sappy on me. My gag reflex is high today." Noelle pressed a series of buttons on the pad on the wall, and all the shelves of weapons began sliding back, disappearing behind another wall.

"Please don't be mad, and don't worry. We'll stun them before we ever have to fight them," Ava said before strolling off, Noelle on her heels.

Noelle called over her shoulder, "Guard him, Hell. No one enters the room. Not even Grandma."

Hellina growled, and McKell assumed it was the word *Grandma* that pissed her off, because she remained at his feet, rubbing against him.

He could have stopped Ava from leaving. Could have frozen her in place, and she had to know that. He'd done it before. But he didn't do it this time. He let her go, his jaw clenched tight, already aching. Not worry? When she was a walking arsenal?

There was another way to handle this.

He stopped time for everyone, excluding himself. So for him, the minutes stretched into hours, endless, wrenching. And every time he lost his mental hold on the clock, he rested for several minutes, then grabbed the reins again.

Before, he'd only done this during battle, stopping and starting repeatedly, but back then, he'd only needed a few minutes to pass for himself, enough time to destroy his enemy, not twenty-four hours of inactivity. Of waiting. But this *was* a battle, he supposed. And by the end, only a few hours had passed for everyone else, but the entire day had passed for him, stun gradually wearing off.

Only once did someone try to enter the room. His back was to the door, so he couldn't see who it was, but the scent was unfamiliar, so he assumed it was a servant. Hellina growled as if she meant to kill, and the person squeaked and ran, footsteps pattering.

Finally McKell could move. He worked his jaw, squeezed his fingers, arched his back, allowing his muscles to stretch. Every burn, every strain, tossed his fury to a higher level. He was fatigued, but that wasn't going to detour him.

"Come," he said to the dog, and she happily followed. As he'd suspected, the servants had returned, but no one tried to delay him. Not even when he stole a blanket from one of the bedrooms and draped himself with the material to protect his skin from the sun.

He compelled one of those servants into escorting him and Hellina to Ava's apartment. On the way inside the building, he saw a glittery expanse of air opening up, and he skidded to a halt. Again? Really? When would it learn?

Come. Please.

Why so persistent? "I don't have time for this," he muttered, trudging back into motion and side-stepping the stupid thing. Once ensconced in the apartment, unburned yet harried, he cut his wrist and let the blood drip into an empty bowl. Only a little, a few drops at most. Then he dug inside Ava's refrigerator and pulled out a tub of . . . yogurt. Did dogs like yogurt? He mixed the creamy concoction with his blood and set the bowl on the ground.

"Eat. It's experiment time," he said, and Hellina gobbled up every bite. Dogs liked.

He waited, watching her intently. She didn't change. Didn't suddenly grow fangs. Just kept staring up at him, wagging her tail, begging for more. So. Ava was wrong. Just as he'd supposed.

She'd find out she'd been wrong about other things, too.

"Stay here," he ordered, and then stalked to the bedroom to sift through his bag. He withdrew a clean set of clothing, showered, dressed, then pawed through Ava's weapon's closet. Theirs now, he decided, since he lived here. He confiscated a pyre-gun and three blades.

Ava clearly assumed she could assault him without any repercussions. She assumed she could leave him behind. She assumed she was in charge. It was past time he showed her the error of her ways.

He stalked out of the apartment with only one backward glance at Hellina, who had followed him to the door. Still no fangs. Didn't matter. "You're mine now," he told her. Payment for his mistreatment at Noelle's home.

She wagged her tail.

"Stay here, and stay quiet. I'll return shortly."

As he strode down the plain, gray hallway that led to the elevator, a man exited his own apartment. He spied McKell and the weapons strapped all over him, and rushed back inside. Probably to phone the police.

Wise of him. In McKell's current dark mood, anything could happen.

Outside, midday heat caused the air to ripple. And . . . the doorway appeared, of course, this time bribing him rather than pleading. If only he would enter, he would find shade, safe travels, a short cut, *blah, blah, blah*. He told the thing where to stuff itself and motored on.

He didn't have sunblock, as Ava had recommended, not that he thought so simple a solution would work, but he did have the blanket. Once again, he draped the material over his head and trudged through the thick crowd on the sidewalk. His body temperature rose unbearably, and sweat began to pour from him.

Ignoring the discomfort, the stickiness, he breathed deeply, searching for Ava's scent . . . the call of her blood . . . An hour passed with no results, and his frustration mounted. So did his irritability. Anyone who got in his way was shoved aside, hard.

Only one hour of the six remained, then Ava would return to Noelle's. But he wanted to find her *now*, proving she couldn't escape him. Ever. That trying to restrain him was useless.

A few times, he lost his grip on the blanket and felt blisters well up on his face. Not once did he consider giving up, though, and finally his determination paid off. He caught Ava's scent.

Grinning evilly, he followed.

Twenty-one

Vampire hunting was not as rewarding as she'd expected, Ava thought darkly.

One, they'd most likely killed the night before, the bastards, so they weren't thirsty while the sun dominated the sky. Meaning, no one stared at her pulse, no one sprouted fangs, and no one tried to mess with her mind.

Two, McKell was right; she couldn't scent them.

Three, after hours of walking around aimlessly, Ava and Noelle pricking fingers on the tips of their knives so that there was always a bead of blood on them, just kind of hoping a vampire would jump from the shadows and attack—something that hadn't happened in all the years of her life, so why she'd foolishly thought it would happen today of all days she didn't know—had produced no results.

It had just given her time to feel guilty about stunning McKell and leaving him behind. Even though it had been for his own good. He would have blistered and weakened, and she needed him in top fighting form for his meeting at AIR. If they tried to hurt him . . .

Her hands fisted. She couldn't do anything without jeopardizing her job, and she wouldn't jeopardize her job. She hoped. Where McKell was concerned, she sometimes acted without thought.

Either way, if they tried to hurt him, she prayed he kicked ass and escaped. He was a nuisance, but a sexy nuisance who was at once selfish and selfless, giving her pleasure without taking any for himself, and besides, his shit was at her place. She didn't want to have to store it indefinitely. There just wasn't room.

At least, that's the only reason she'd cop to for wanting him eternally safe.

He probably hated her. Would he *ever* return to her apartment, even if he escaped AIR? Even if AIR let him go freely, without restriction? Or would he avoid her forevermore?

She almost turned around and raced back to Noelle's house. She'd known he would eventually tire of her, but she wasn't ready to lose him yet.

"You listening to me?" Noelle's voice dragged her from the dark mire of her thoughts.

Concentrate. "No. Sorry. What'd you say?"

"I think we're gonna have to switch to Plan B."

"You're right," she said confidentially, though inside she groaned. The daylight vampires might not be thirsty, but would they be able to resist an open, gushing wound? There was only one way to find out . . . a way she'd hoped to avoid. "Let's do it."

They stopped in the next alleyway they came across. On this side of town, even the alleys were clean. No trash littered the walkway, and no graffiti marred the buildings. Ava leaned against a hot metal wall, upper body falling into the shadows, and held out her arm.

Noelle remained in the sunlight and withdrew a tiny knife from her cleavage. The bright rays showed hints of uncertainty in her features. "You sure about being the one to bleed?"

No. "Yeah." If this worked, no telling how many vamps would chase them—and no telling what kind of abilities those vamps would possess. She needed to be at top strength, but what good was being battle-ready if there was no one to fight? "Do it."

The tip of the blade inched closer . . . closer . . . Noelle's hand began to shake, and she paused just before contact. "Maybe I should be the one to take the slash."

"We discussed this earlier and decided it had to be me. Obviously, vampires like the smell of me. Case in point, McKell." *My McKell.* Still? "So it has to be me to drip all over the pavement."

"And I *am* the better fighter," Noelle replied in an effort to rally herself. "Therefore, I have to be the one to remain strong."

"I'd argue the term *better fighter*, but you're the one with the knife, so . . ."

They shared a smile, relaxing into their decided roles.

"McKell is going to kill me for hurting his property, but that just makes doing this a little bit fun, you know?" With a determined inhalation, Noelle slashed the blade from Ava's elbow to wrist.

Ava bit her tongue to keep from grunting. Or screaming. Whatever. Her skin and muscle split open, and crimson blood flowed. "Bitch, did you have to go so deep? Damn!"

"You big baby," Noelle muttered. "You wanted gushing, remember? 'Don't just scratch me,'" she said in a mocking parrot of Ava's earlier words. "Take that shit to the bone."

"You should know me well enough to know when I'm mouthing off." But this was another reason she'd stunned McKell. Noelle was right. He wouldn't have let her do this. He was too protective.

Although he might not be so protective anymore.

She couldn't hold back her grunt this time. Not of physical pain, but of mental.

"What?" Noelle asked, sheathing her blade. "I didn't touch you that time, I swear."

"Nothing's wrong." Ava held her arm against her middle, pressing the wound against her stomach. "Come on. We're wasting time."

They left the alley. There was a clinic two miles from here. They planned to walk to it, hopefully drawing vampires out in the open along the way. And if they didn't, if they failed, well, she'd kicked Noelle's ass for daring to agree to this shitty idea in the first place.

If she was going to lose McKell over this, she wanted something good to come of it. Not that any outcome would be good enough.

Maybe, if she apologized with a kiss, perhaps followed by some heavy petting, he'd be willing to listen to her side. Yeah, she'd jump on that grenade if necessary. Anything to keep him, just for a little longer.

What's gotten into you?

"Nothing so far," Noelle muttered.

People gaped as Ava walked by, but everyone jumped out of her way, as if she were an infected parasite. Bastards. Would a little compassion have been amiss? She could have been beaten by a boyfriend or have accidentally fallen into a window, for all they knew.

Worse, the more she and Noelle walked, the more brightly the sun shone, bouncing off glass and metal buildings and burning her skin. She wore her sunglasses, yet still her eyes watered. Why would the vampires want to walk around in this? She couldn't even remember why *she* did. Heat seemed to seep through her shirt and jeans, and little beads of sweat broke out over her skin, burning her wound. If *she* were a vampire, she would—

Oh, no. No, no, no. She wasn't going down that thought path. As she'd told McKell, she liked being human. Didn't she? And she still liked the sun. On every day but today.

"Anything?" she asked.

"Anything since sixty seconds ago, when I said nothing so far? Nope." Noelle was the lookout, searching for hungry gazes as they walked. "What if we're going about this the wrong way? What if vampires work at hospitals, where they have an endless supply of blood?"

"An endless supply of bagged blood and constant temptation from the injured? No. They'd give themselves away, and they're afraid of that." Well, afraid of being found by McKell and those like him.

"Good point."

"Of course. I said it."

"Remind me never to cut you again. You get grumpy."

They turned a corner and hit a crosswalk. They stood there, waiting for the streetlight to switch to red so they could cross. One minute, two, Ava's legs beginning to shake, but finally the signal flashed, allowing them to pass.

A car eased to a stop, honked at them, and the driver's side of the window lowered. A female head peeked out. "Hey, do you girls need a ride to the hospital?"

"No, thanks," Noelle called, and they continued onward.

Compassion at last. Still. "I'm starting to get pissed. And offended! Here I am, bleeding all over the place, yet no self-respecting vampire views me as appetizing."

"Maybe we should have used my blood. Clearly, I smell better than you."

"Then why didn't McKell call dibs on you?"

"Because he has no taste."

"Bitch."

"Stinker."

Laughing, they pushed through a throng of people

and rounded another corner. Ava tripped over her own boots, the shaking in her limbs more noticeable. Cold seeped into her fingers and toes, and despite the heat, she actually quaked.

"So you really like McKell, huh?" Noelle asked. "And don't try to deny it. He's lasted *days* without you kicking him out of your life for good."

She didn't want to talk about him. Not when she could only picture him frozen in place, cursing her very existence. "Maybe I just can't shake him loose," she said, hoping the subject would drop.

Stubborn Noelle never let *anything* drop. "Please. You could shake your teeth loose if you wanted. You like him. Just admit it before I remind you of how I found you when you pulled into my driveway. You know, on your back with your hand down his pants."

"Fine." She might not want to talk about him, but maybe she should. Worry about him and how he felt about her was eating her up inside. "I . . . like him." There. She'd admitted it. And lived. "He's just so . . . I don't know. Strong."

"Not strong enough. You've stabbed him and stunned him twice."

"I only got him that last time because he trusted me not to hurt him," she practically shouted. Why was she defending him so forcefully? Against Noelle, of all people?

Because she was weakened, she immediately rationalized. And because she didn't like the thought of anyone, even her best friend, viewing him in such a disparaging way. He was a good man. With faults, sure, but good all the same. And for whatever reason, he clearly did trust Ava. He'd slept at her house, had moved in, made out with her. Hadn't yelled at her for enjoying satisfaction, yet offering him no release after they were interrupted.

That was true strength.

"I wasn't badmouthing him. Much," Noelle added sheepishly. "But lookit. I know you better than anyone, and I know you have daddy issues."

"Do not." She raced through another crosswalk, but as she placed her foot on the concrete, her knee almost buckled, and black dots began spiderwebbing through her vision. She quickly righted herself and caught up with Noelle, who hadn't noticed her decreased speed.

"Ava. Your dad left when you were just a kid, and your drunk-ass mom dated a thousand assholes after that."

"Fine. I have daddy issues." So did a lot of other girls. And Ava was over hers. Really. She no longer cried herself to sleep because other kids had loving daddies to tuck them in at night. (She just didn't sleep at all.) She no longer watched kids being pushed on swings by their dads, clutching her chest to stop the sudden ache.

She didn't have a loving dad, and never had. So what. Her dad had walked away and never looked back. So what. Her mom had seemed to forget about her entirely the day she'd moved out of their trailer. Again, so what. She'd built a great life for herself.

"So. We've talked about this before, but you were drunk and not listening. So listen now. I'm glad you're giving someone a chance. Even someone who once belonged to me."

"He never belonged to you." Ava still didn't like the thought of McKell being owned by anyone but her. Even her best friend. And yeah, she'd realized that before, but now, weak as she was, she didn't have the strength to rationalize why. The statement was as much as part of her as her lungs or her heart. Just like McKell.

Her eyes widened. She liked him *that* much?

Noelle grinned, gray eyes sparkling with an undeniable I-told-you-so. "Alls I'm saying is that you have a fear of abandonment, so you leave before the guy can leave you."

True. She'd already realized that, too. Didn't mean she liked having it pointed out. "What are you, a doctor now?"

"Yes. Dr. Love. And Dr. Love is also very glad you stopped caring that McKell's a vampire and an enemy. I mean, Mia's willing to use him, so AIR doesn't view him as a bad guy. You shouldn't either."

She tripped again, over a rock this time, and her arm bounced. The subsequent sting had her wincing. A quick glance down showed that her shirt and the waist of her jeans were completely soaked through with blood—and she was still bleeding profusely. Great.

"Can we continue this conversation when I'm not

dying?" she asked. One more block, and they'd reach the clinic.

Noelle cast her a glance, and worry replaced the teasing sparkle in her eyes. Okay, no. They couldn't continue the conversation at another time. Noelle needed the distraction, and Ava now needed to ease her own sense of guilt.

"I'm not keeping him," Ava said. Not forever, at least. She wasn't *that* far gone.

Grateful, Noelle picked up where she'd left off. "See? You plan on leaving him before he can leave you, and you—" She gasped excitedly. "This is it! This is it! We've picked up a tail!"

"Who?" Ava barely restrained the urge to turn and look. Only the thought of tripping and kissing concrete stopped her. "Where?"

"Remember the car at the first crosswalk? The girl who wanted to help?"

"Yes." Human in appearance, young, sweet voice.

"She followed us. In fact, she just pulled over and is getting out of her car."

"How can you tell?"

"Duh. The reflections on the shop glass."

"Oh." Good thinking. "I, uh, just didn't think of that because of my tremendous amount of blood loss."

"Of course," Noelle said dryly.

"She could have just reached her office."

"Nope. Now she's following us on foot. And there's a guy with her. He got out of the car, too."

Excitement raced through Ava, which increased

the blood flow in her veins. Which increased the throb in her wound, and the rate at which she drained. The weakness grew more apparent, as did the trembling.

"We need cover." Noelle wrapped her fingers around Ava's forearm and tugged her into another alley, not stopping until they were in the center, at the edge of a Dumpster. "Pretend you're resting. I'll pretend I'm fixing your bandage." As she spoke, she slapped a pyre-gun in Ava's hand and palmed one for herself.

Ava kept the weapon at her side, hidden from the entrance to the alley. Sure enough, the pretty female from the car turned the corner and approached, along with an unfamiliar male.

Neither spoke. There was too much hunger in their eyes. Eyes narrowed on Ava's wound. The female licked her lips, revealing sharp fangs. Fangs. Even while the sun shone on both of them, their skin remaining unaffected.

Bingo. Daylight vampires.

"Can I help you?" Noelle asked them, unconcerned.

"Mine," the male slurred.

"Oh, really?" Noelle laughed. "Let's see about that."

Ava and Noelle flashed their guns at the same time and fired. Blue beams erupted, momentarily chasing away the shadows cast by the buildings on either side. Both beams hit their targets dead center. Only, the vampires didn't stop. Didn't even slow.

Ava blinked in surprise. "What the hell?"

The answer immediately slid into place. Along

with immunization to the sun, the vampires who drained humans to death also developed an immunity to stun rays. Shit! Why hadn't she thought of that?

Another answer didn't have time to form. The vampires launched at her, and there wasn't even a spare moment to dial her gun to its burn-and-kill setting. The gun was swiped out of her hand, and she was knocked to her ass.

Still at full strength, Noelle snapped into action, and stopped them from jumping on top of Ava. The three rolled on the hard concrete, arms and legs flailing. Teeth slashing. Noelle yelped, but she didn't let go. She punched and kicked, and somewhere along the way, she managed to withdraw two blades. She, too, slashed. Only, her weapons were sharper.

Blood squirted. From Noelle, from the vampires, but none of them slowed. The vamps continued to bite at her, and she continued to swipe at them. Just as Ava gathered the strength to insert herself into the fight, the female slipped past Noelle. Ava's hair was nearly ripped from her scalp as the vampire raced around her and jerked her backward, dragging . . . positioning.

Ava tore free and straightened. Breathing was a thing of the past, but she twisted, already swinging. Her fist connected with the woman's jaw, but weak as she was, the blow barely registered. And then the woman punched her back. *Her* jaw exploded with pain. She saw stars, was falling down . . . down . . .

Hell, no. She wasn't losing this fight. It was two

against two, and she liked those odds, even destabilized as she was. When she hit, she grabbed a handful of gravel and kicked the woman away from her, then again made her way to her feet. Without hesitation, she chucked the rocks in the vampire's face. A howl rent the air as her opponent staggered back and rubbed at her eyes.

Ava could see that Noelle was still struggling with the male. Bite marks marred her arms, and she was covered in blood. His, her own. Her friend was clearly tired, panting, sweating, her movements at last slower than usual.

Shit. Perhaps doing this without McKell hadn't been such a good idea. Perhaps? Ha! But there was no help for it now. She withdrew another gun, a taser, and aimed. Her arm shook, and her grip was feeble. She wasn't sure how long she could hold on.

"Noelle," she shouted. "Move!" Waited . . . waited . . . When Noelle had the opportunity, she jumped backward, out of the way. Ava fired at the male. Contact. He screeched, his entire body vibrating. Noelle then attacked, and now she had the advantage.

Another screech, this one female, and Ava knew she was about to feel pain. But she didn't have time to switch the direction of her aim. The gun was kicked out of her hand in less than a blink, the female on top of her, pushing her down. This time she hit, and her skull took the brunt of the fall.

Pain, oh, yes, pain. Black dots filled her vision as she tried to crawl away, creating distance while reach-

ing for a blade. Her fingers curled around the hilt
as something heavy slammed her back down. She
twisted, blade raised, but before she made contact,
sharp teeth sank into her neck. The pain exploded,
and she couldn't really pinpoint where one ache origi-
nated and another ended. She tried to slash. Her wrist
was knocked away and pinned like the rest of her.

She felt the suction, then the cold, then the fragil-
ity of her own body. No longer could she move, not
even to lift her arms.

She had lost. She had lost a fight. She was embarrassed, disappointed in herself, fading . . . This really
was it, she realized. The end. She wanted to laugh
bitterly, but the sound snagged in her ravaged throat.

One regret after another flooded her. She hadn't
made love with McKell. She hadn't told him good-
bye. She wouldn't see him again.

In the distance, she thought she heard Noelle curse.
A second later, the teeth were ripped out of her. She
expected Noelle to smooth the hair from her face, and
tell her everything was going to be okay now. Even
though they would both know it was a lie. Fading . . .
But it was a man's touch she next experienced, soft
and tender, and a man's voice that whispered in her
ear.

"Ava, darling. Can you hear me?"

McKell.

Pleasure overshadowed all other emotion. She
didn't know if McKell was really there or if she was
hallucinating, and she didn't care. If she was going to

die in an alley, she wanted him with her, one way or another.

He was strong, just as she'd told Noelle, and he treated her as if she were special, not the trash she'd always been called. Despite her human—and, according to him, inferior—origins. He teased her, *got* her. Didn't try to change her. Unless you counted changing her from human to vampire, but she didn't, because he'd promised not to feed her any of his blood.

"I'll make you better," he cooed, and she knew. He was real. Somehow he'd overcome stun, and found her. Her sweet, sweet protector.

And she trusted him, she realized. He wouldn't try to change her even now, injured as she was. Even pissed as he had to be. She knew it. She knew him. She'd told him no, and he wouldn't disregard that. Pride wouldn't let him.

Determined hands banded around her, lifted her, gentle and warm. He started forward. His gait was smooth, and she felt like she was floating.

Where was Noelle? Why wasn't her friend talking?

She began to struggle, wanting answers. McKell must have sensed the direction of her thoughts, because he said, "She's fine. Noelle is fine."

Ava relaxed.

"Now sleep," he said silkily, "and I'll take care of everything. Although, once I'm done, you'll probably wish I had stayed away."

Even then, she trusted him. She slept.

Twenty-two

McKell didn't know what else to do. He convinced a human to haul him and the injured females to Ava's apartment via removing the blanket hood and flashing his fangs while his skin sizzled. Oh, and issuing a threat of death. Along the way, he phoned Bride, who agreed to meet him there. In fact, by the time the driver had stopped in front of Ava's building, Bride was already there. With Devyn.

If that bastard turned the charm on Ava, as he'd done to Bride, McKell would butcher him. Although, to be fair, Ava was much smarter than Bride. He liked these thoughts. They spoke of a future.

"Open the door," he snapped at the human—who may or may not have peed himself.

"O—open." The passenger door split from the car frame.

Noelle was so rattled and weak, she hadn't said a word the entire drive.

McKell kicked his way outside with Ava cradled in his arms. She moaned. His blanket slipped and his skin burned, but he didn't care. He wasn't going to rush inside. He wouldn't risk jarring her.

Bride, who waited in the shade, protected, pushed Devyn forward, a hint to help with the girls. McKell instantly pivoted, moving out of reach.

"Uh, McKell," Bride said. "Let Devyn take her. You're nearly deep fried."

He ignored her, expecting her to cover herself and follow as he headed toward the building. As he strode past Devyn, he said, "The other one's yours. They left two dead vampires in an alley a few blocks away. You might want to call AIR for pickup."

"You sure they're dead?" Devyn called.

"Very." He'd removed their heads. Savagely. First his teeth had ripped out their tracheas, then his claws had finished the job. He hadn't been able to stop himself. Hadn't wanted to stop himself.

He'd followed Ava's scent, dying inside when he spotted her trail of blood. He'd run—and run and run, until finally spying her. And when he had . . . murderous instinct had taken over.

Once inside, he carried Ava past curious onlookers, allowing the blanket to fall the rest of the way, forgotten. Up the elevator and down the hall, until he stood at her door. He didn't set her down as he reached up and flattened one of his palms on the ID pad. A quick scan, and the door popped open.

He strode inside, finally allowing himself to glance at Ava. She was pale, the blue veins under her skin evident. There were shadows under her eyes, and cuts all over her neck and arms. The scent of her blood wafted to his nose, and he—

Sharp teeth sank into his ankle.

He stumbled, but didn't let go of his charge. Something growled as he looked down. And spied Hellina. She was drinking his blood greedily. Lapping up every drop she could, and then biting his ankle again for more. Trying, McKell thought, to get to Ava.

His eyes widened as realization struck. Hellina was a vampire. His blood had truly changed her. Impossible, he thought next.

"Where do you want Noelle?" Devyn asked from behind him. The warrior must have spied Hellina, because he laughed. "Your girlfriend's dog hates you. Priceless."

Realizing there was another person to snack on, Hellina switched her focus, launching at Devyn's ankles and biting.

Devyn howled. "What the hell?" He kicked out his leg, trying to shake the hungry dog loose but not succeeding.

"She's a new vampire," McKell said, "and she's hungry. Needs to feed." Even uttering the words was odd.

"I don't give a shit about Ava or Noelle being a vampire and hungry right now. I only feed Bride. Now get the dog—"

"The *dog* is the vampire. Hellina, stop." To his ever-increasing shock, the dog instantly obeyed, removing her teeth from Devyn's leg. She panted up at McKell, adoration in her big eyes, blood dripping from her mouth.

Did she have to obey him because of their blood connection?

He couldn't believe he was even contemplating the possibility. It never should have happened, shouldn't have been possible. Or did she simply love him and want to please him, as all females should? There would be time to sort that out later. After Ava was healed.

Ava. "Stay," he told Hellina as he carted Ava to her bedroom. "And put Noelle on the couch," he threw over his shoulder.

He eased Ava onto the bed, gently, softly, and she gave another of those pained moans. Perhaps he should have taken her to a hospital, but he'd known he could do more for her than anyone else.

And he *would* turn her if necessary. He hadn't known that was a possibility until seeing Hellina, but he'd meant to feed Ava his blood, anyway, mating them. Despite her absolute trust in him. He'd felt that trust as he'd lifted her from the ground, and it had sliced him like a fang. That wouldn't have stopped him, though. Nothing would have, not when it came to saving her.

He'd once worried about her shorter lifespan, and had later discarded the worry, uncaring that she would age as long as they were together while she lived. But seeing her so . . . broken, and feeling himself break in kind, he'd convinced himself that mating with her would twine them, their lifespans. She would live as long as he did, and he would live as long as she did.

Except, even with such a hope, he hesitated now. If he did this, she would hate him. He didn't want her to hate him. But he wouldn't be able to stop himself from acting much longer. She was covered in so much blood, so pale, so still, and he was . . . worried. Yes, that was the tightening in his chest, making a complete mockery of his anger. He should be screaming at this woman for placing herself in danger.

That's part of who she is. A danger seeker. Deal with it, or lose her forever.

He felt rather than heard Devyn and Bride approach. They stopped, one on each side of him, and peered down at Ava. If either one of them reached out, he would cut off their arms.

"So. How do you have a vampire dog?" Bride asked casually. To distract him? "Don't get me wrong, I can guess. I'm all-powerful, after all, but I'd really like to hear you say it."

Devyn shook his head. "All-powerful. Please. Mia told me what his blood can do, and I told you."

"That isn't important right now," McKell snarled. "How do I heal Ava without giving her my blood?" If there was a way, he'd take it. If not, he would just have to risk her wrath.

"I can give her *my* blood," Bride suggested.

"No," Devyn said with a firm shake of his head—*before* McKell could issue his own denial. "I'm tired of everyone getting a piece of you. The humans infected by the Schön, AIR agents, your friends. There has to be a line, and you've already given some today."

"No," McKell finally got to say aloud. If Ava had anyone's blood, it would be his. Still. There had to be another way.

"My blood won't turn her into a vampire," Bride said. "As Devyn said, a lot of people have sampled it, and none of them have turned."

Ava moaned, and he suddenly found himself wavering, possessiveness giving way to protectiveness. Damn it. She trusted him to keep her human, and that was a stronger deterrent than he'd realized. "What if you're wrong?"

"Devyn has a sip everyday, and look at him. Pure arrogance and sex appeal, but no fangs. And there's no danger that she'll ever have a chance to feed me *her* blood, binding us for life."

"Because you're already bonded for life," Devyn said, his voice stern. "And don't you dare try to get out of it again."

Bride rolled her eyes. "I only tried to leave you, what? Four times? Cut me some slack. Anyway," she said to McKell. "She'll heal quickly, and her pain will ease. I promise."

The thought of Ava healed . . . "She has to agree."

"Then wake her up and ask her already. Although waking her up will only cause her to thrash, and the thrashing could injure her worse. And if she's injured worse, the healing will take a lot longer. But it's your call." Bride reached out, as if to smooth Ava's hair from her brow.

McKell hissed at her, and she held her hands up,

all innocence. How had he ever thought himself in love with this woman? She was annoying. "Give your blood to Noelle first. I want to see how she reacts."

"Two patients now?" Devyn gave another shake of his head, dark hair falling over his brow and hiding the natural sheen of glitter in his skin. "No. That's where I draw the line, Bride. You were stumbling around earlier, so you need every drop you've got for yourself."

She patted his cheek. "I'll just be a few minutes." She strode from the room, leaving McKell alone with a sputtering Devyn.

"You owe me for this," the Targon muttered. "She's going to be weak when she's done, and that will seriously ruin my plans for later."

The man had the nerve to complain while Ava lay a few feet away, not really dying but cutting it close? At least, that's what he told himself. Otherwise, he would have been clawing at the walls.

"Make yourself useful," McKell snapped at him. "Her cupboards and refrigerator are nearly bare. Fill them."

Devyn's amber eyes widened. They were lighter than Ava's, but close enough in color that McKell decided the bastard could live. "You want *me* to shop?"

"Yes. And she loves butterscotch. Buy her as much butterscotch as you can find. She'll want a treat when she wakes up." Because he planned to yell at her, maybe make her cry, and the food would comfort her when he was done, his concern and anger appeased.

"You're serious?"

"Why would I lie about butterscotch?"

"Dear God, you're clueless. I meant, you're serious about expecting me to shop for *your* woman's treats? Won't she like them better if *you* buy them?"

"No. They'll still taste the same, and besides that, I don't have any money. In fact, I'm going to need you to open me an account." One of Ava's requirements for a man had been "rich." "I want enough money to last an eternity making this woman happy."

Devyn scrubbed a hand down his face. "So I'm your sugar daddy now?"

"You took my woman," he reminded the man. Yet the words tasted . . . wrong. He didn't like referring to Bride as his woman anymore. She wasn't. Never had been. Not really.

"She was never yours," Devyn growled in his first real show of anger.

"I know. And I'm glad. I like the one I have. Now help me keep her."

That drained the anger right out of the Targon. "Fine. I'll make a few calls and have shit delivered, but I am *not* leaving you alone with Bride. And I'll also open you an account, but that's the last favor I'm doing for you."

"Until I think of something else for you to do. Like buying me clothing." He nodded, realizing he did indeed need new clothes. "I like what you're wearing, though I'll probably need a bigger size." His gaze dropped to Devyn's waist. "A lot bigger. And make sure to get me something for every day of the week."

"Good Lord." Devyn was shaking his head as he withdrew his phone and started making those calls. He stated his demands simply, expecting absolute compliance from everyone he spoke to. He probably got it, too. McKell admired his authoritative superiority.

McKell sat beside Ava, careful not to disturb her. He failed. She groaned and rolled toward him, as if she'd been waiting for him. He twined their fingers, not liking how cold her skin was, how slow her pulse.

Finally Bride returned to the bedroom, Noelle at her side. Noelle was still pale, a little shaky, but she was on her feet and still human. Relief flooded him. Ava wouldn't be able to find fault with his choice for her. He hoped.

"Is she—" Noelle began.

"She'll be fine," he snapped. "What were you thinking, fighting vampires without me? Do you have any idea—"

"Lecture her later. I have business to attend to now." Bride strode forward, shaky herself, and eased on Ava's other side.

McKell held her arms down, just in case she awoke during the transfusion and tried to push Bride away. "Do it," he gritted out. "Feed her."

Bride unsheathed a knife from her side and slashed her wrist over a still-healing scab. Grimacing, she held the now dripping wrist over Ava's pretty mouth. *Closed* pretty mouth. Bride dropped the knife and used her freed fingers to pry those lips apart.

He tensed a little more with every drop that slid home. *Don't blame me for this. Don't you dare blame me.* If she did, he'd . . . what? He didn't know.

"We never would have worked out, you know," Bride said. "You're too bossy and, well, selfish."

"And you're not Ava."

"Yes, there is that."

An eternity passed while the vampire's blood continued to drip, but soon Ava began to swallow on her own. Still another eternity passed while Bride straightened, withdrew her arm, and they waited. And waited.

Finally, Ava's eyelashes fluttered open, and those dark eyes scanned the room, confusion in their depths. Several more minutes passed while she oriented herself. He waited, stiff.

"McKell," she croaked out.

Hearing her voice, he knew beyond any doubt that she would be okay, that her throat was healing. "Leave," he said.

Her brow furrowed. "But this is my house. Isn't it?"

"Not you. Everyone else, leave." He didn't look away from her. "Now." He wanted to explain what had been done to her without an audience. Meaning, he wanted to subdue her when she attacked him without an audience. She was going to blame him; there was no denying that now.

Footsteps sounded. A dog barked. From the living room, he heard Noelle say, "What's Hellina doing here? Come on, baby." Pause. "Come on." Another pause. "Why's she ignoring me? And why is she staring at the pulse in my neck?"

Bride and Devyn must have dragged her out, because the door finally snickered closed.

Ava watched him the entire time, rubbing her now scabbed-over neck.

"The vampires injured you," he began, bracing himself. "Bride Targon gave you her blood to repair the damage."

He waited for the explosion of temper.

"Oh, okay," Ava said, gingerly sitting up and resting her weight on her elbows. The cut on her arm had yet to fully close, and she winced.

"That's all you have to say to me?"

"Well, yeah."

Perhaps she didn't understand what had happened. "I fed you another vampire's blood. In your mouth, down your throat. You drank it."

"Yeah, and her blood has been given to many AIR agents already, so I know I can handle it."

All his worry, and *that* was her reaction? He jackknifed to his feet and paced in front of the bed. "Since you can handle so much, let's begin with your apology. But before you do, allow me to instruct you on everything you need to apologize for. You stunned me, left me in unfamiliar surroundings with unfamiliar people who could have tried to kill me."

"Now listen—"

"I wasn't done! *Then* you fought vampires. Even though you knew how dangerous they could be!" He was screaming now and couldn't temper his voice. "You almost died. How dare you almost die, Ava! You did not have permission to do that."

She blinked at him. "I need permission to die?"

"Silence!" Every time she spoke, his anger only intensified. "Your arm was mangled, and I thought you'd never be able to use it again. Your neck was savaged, and I thought you'd . . . I thought you'd . . . " He couldn't even say the words.

"You did not," was her only reply.

Anger . . . intensifying . . . He wanted her screaming back at him, concerned, worried, *something*. "The arm was almost a deal breaker, but I decided you could still please me with the other one."

Her eyes narrowed, and he thought he had her, but all she said was, "The injury wasn't that bad."

So. Much. Anger. His hands fisted. Without a word, he stalked to the bed, hefted her over his shoulder, and carted her to the shower stall. He dumped her inside and left her there, slamming the door behind him.

"Don't come out until you're ready to apologize for everything!"

He waited for a response. He didn't get one.

Fuming, he stomped into the living room, flopped onto the couch, and petted Hellina. She couldn't speak, so she didn't anger him. She even managed to calm him somewhat as she licked him, that adoration like a living thing in her gaze. If everyone he turned acted this way, he would turn Ava before the sun set. She'd love him too much to be pissed.

At some point, he heard her trudge out of the bathroom, putter around the bedroom, and dress, but she never came to find him. That was for the best. Devyn's deliveries began arriving, and McKell compelled the deliverers to stand still and allow Hellina to drink her fill. After the fourth feeding, the dog fell asleep on the floor.

McKell decided he was calm enough to deal with Ava now. Well, as calm as he could get without spanking her. Spanking. Yes. That was acceptable. He grabbed the whip he'd brought with him during his first visit—someone had placed it on the coffee table—and stormed into the bedroom with every intention of tying her up before throwing her over his knees. She sat at the edge of the bed, her siren's body wrapped only in a fluffy white towel. Rather than grabbing her, he studied her.

Her shoulders were hunched, her hair was brushed to a coiled shine, and all of her cuts and bruises were nearly gone. Her skin was once again a perfect sun-kissed peach, her pulse drumming wildly, strong. She smelled a little like Bride, flowers and mint, but underneath those new scents he still caught a hint of orchids and butterscotch.

His mouth instantly watered. All thoughts of spanking vanished, and though he wanted to jump on her, finally have her, take her, own her, her upset held him immobile. "What's wrong?"

"I—I lost a fight," she said, and there was a slight quiver to her voice.

That hesitation . . . he doubted she'd meant to mention the fight, but she had, so they would deal with that first. "You lost because you were stupid about it."

The quiver moved to her chin. "Spare my feelings, why don't you."

"You know you were." Was she about to . . . cry? This woman who often snarled, had stabbed him twice, tasered him once, and kissed him so intently he could have been lost forever, all without backing down?

She shrugged those dainty shoulders and looked away, to someplace he couldn't see. "Maybe."

"So what else is bothering you?" he asked gently.

"I just . . ." She swallowed. "You're mad at me."

And that pushed her to the brink of tears? "Yes." Even though he despised the thought of making her cry, he wouldn't back down in this. Her safety came before her feelings.

"So now you're going to whip me and leave." She stood in one fluid motion and finally, *finally*, he was faced with the fury he'd craved. Darks waves of it pulsed from her, wrapped around him, and squeezed tightly. He embraced every gossamer strand. "Well, guess what? That's fine. Do it! Go! I didn't want you here, anyway."

Mixed with the anger, he now heard fear, and *that* he couldn't welcome. Especially when the words that came with the emotion were like a knife in the heart. "I'm going to assume Bride's blood is talking, not you. Because you know I would never mar your skin. You also know I'm here to stay."

Just like that, the fire drained right out of her, and she gazed at him through the thick shield of her lashes, hopeful. "You're staying?"

That sting in his heart drained, too. He'd take the hope over the anger any day. "Yes. Why would I leave? I live here now."

"But I keep hurting you and nearly got myself killed. After you warned me about the dangers."

"Which you will not do again. Promise me." It was a command he wouldn't allow her to ignore.

"I promise, and I'm sorry," she whispered, delighting him. "But why do you care so—you need my blood." There at the end, her voice had picked up volume and flattened. "I get it now. You're not staying because you like me, you're staying because you need me. Why else would you have moved in with a lowly human? Not that you're officially moved in. I haven't said yes to anything permanent."

That he'd once thought the same thing—lowly human—now settled heavily on his shoulders, but he didn't let it weigh him down and send him fleeing. The outcome of this was too important.

"You aren't a lowly human, Ava. You're *my* human. And I'm here for your blood, yes." He wouldn't lie about that. Couldn't. "But I'm also here for you. Your kisses . . . your body . . ." He stalked toward her, intent in every step. "And now I'm going to have them, once and for all."

Twenty-three

So many thoughts whirled through Ava's mind as McKell closed the distance between them, and somehow she was able to reflect on each one in a heartbeat of time. She'd fainted during a fight. Which meant she had lost that fight. McKell had saved her as if she were a damsel in distress. Embarrassing. He had also arranged for her healing. Sweet. She'd trusted him not to turn her into a vampire, and he hadn't. Confusing.

Why had she trusted him while she'd been at her most vulnerable? Why had he helped her when he could have struck? She'd left him behind, almost helpless. "Almost," because McKell always found a way to save himself. And why, when she'd woken up in bed, McKell hovering over her, had she known everything was going to be okay? As if they were together irrevocably and would stay that way. As if he belonged in her life. As if he was exactly where he needed to be.

Then he'd stormed out of her room, pissed and seething. She'd taken a shower and wondered if he was packing his stuff. And she'd cried. Cried like a goddamn baby! She didn't need him, she'd told herself. She didn't need anyone, and never had. That's the way it had always been, and would always be. She could even live without Noelle, if necessary, though she didn't want to. But McKell . . .

Flayed her alive, left her reeling, panicked but eager. Desperate. Needy. He —

Was right in front of her now, she realized, and she was blinking up at him.

His face had healed, all hint of his burns gone. His nostrils were flared as he sucked in a torrent of air. His color was high, his usually violet eyes flecked with so much emerald they were like flashing "go" signs that reached her soul.

She didn't want him to stay just because he needed her blood. She wanted him to want her. Because he liked *her*. Her smile, her laugh, her sense of humor. Her crudeness, coarseness, *everything*. All the good, plus the bad. And yeah, she knew what a tall order that was. An order no man could probably meet.

She wasn't easy to be around at the best of times, and during the worst, well, she sucked flaming balls of mean. Look at the way she'd snapped at him, demanding he leave. Still, she wanted his eternal admiration.

But her most important wish? She wanted him to like her as a human. Not as a potential vampire. She wanted him to consider her good enough, just the way she was. And maybe he was on that road already.

You're my *human*, he'd said, and every feminine instinct she possessed had sung a choirs of hallelujah, reminding her that he did sometimes make her feel special. But as always, doubt intruded. How long would he feel that way? Eventually everyone found fault with who she really was.

"Ava," McKell rasped.

She licked her lips. He was here, and he was lusting after her. For the moment, that was enough. Because she couldn't send him away again. She just didn't have the strength.

"I'm going to have you, woman. If you resist, I'll tie you up. I swear I will." He lifted the whip threateningly.

"No need to tie me up."

His pupils expanded, but he didn't yet move in for the kill. "For us to be together, and be able to tell everyone about it, I must aid AIR?" His warm breath trekked over her skin, teasing her.

Why wasn't he touching her? Just then, she didn't care if the entire world knew. Just then, he was hers. Tomorrow—today? In her sick, weak haze, she'd lost track of time—she would take him to AIR headquarters, head held high. People could think what they wanted, and for once, the thought of her peers calling her trash didn't bother her.

"Ava," he prompted again. He bound one of her wrists in a loop he'd created in the leather. A warning. Then he traced a knuckle over her cheekbone, gentle, tender, and she quivered.

Finally. Touching. "McKell. I—I don't care if you aid AIR. That has no bearing on *this*." Shocking, even to her. "Only thing I ask is that you don't turn me."

He gave a tug, and the leather tightened on her. "Why?"

"Because I have to be good enough, just as I am."

"You are."

Fear once more reared its head. For how long? She had to make him understand what his claims of superiority did to her. "How would you like it if I insisted you become human?"

He blanched. "I wouldn't."

Just as she'd thought. "It hurts to be considered inferior."

"I never want to hurt you." His voice was a blade jerked from its sheath. "I'm sorry that I did. But I *am* going to have you, Ava. You're not going to push me away. Not this time."

She released a breath she hadn't known she'd been holding. "Well, okay. I'm glad that's still on the table."

His gaze flicked to the bed behind her, then moved back to her face. Heat pulsed from him. "A table? Yes, I can take you on a table."

Darling man. "No. I mean, I do want to have sex with you."

A dark brow arched. "Is the table an option or not?"

Part of her wanted to laugh, but all of her trembled with anticipation. "Does it matter?"

He crowded her, easing her back until her knees hit the edge of the mattress. He claimed her other wrist, wrapped the leather around it, too, forcing her to arch her back, her breasts rubbing his chest. Took all of her strength, but she managed to remain upright. Leaning, but upright.

"I'll take you however I can get you," he whispered roughly.

The words, his voice, the need in his eyes, like electrical currents raging through her. "Then let me go and I'll get rid of the towel."

Like a rubber band being snapped, he yanked his body into a straight line, increasing the murmur of air between them. He unwound the whip and tossed the coiled length to the floor.

With shaky hands, she tugged at the towel. The material fell in a pool at her feet.

A bead of sweat formed on his brow. But he reacted to her nakedness in no other way.

"Mc—McKell?" Uncertainty intruded.

He kept his gaze on her face, a muscle ticking in his jaw. "Before we begin, and if I look down, I'll begin, let's be clear on what I want to do, as sex and fucking aren't apt descriptions. I'm going to have you, every inch of you. With my mouth, my hands, my cock. I'm going to drink from you, straight from your neck, perhaps even your thigh. When I'm done, there'll be no part of you I haven't touched."

A cool breeze enveloped her, but she suddenly didn't care. She liked the goose bumps that formed. They were like a road map to every location she wanted his tongue. In other words, everywhere.

"Ava. Your response. Now."

"Promises, promises," she said, and wrapped her arms around his neck. She jerked him down for a kiss.

He didn't hesitate. Their lips met, and their tongues instantly tangled together. His body aligned with hers, rigid determination against melting softness, and her entire world spun out of control. She held McKell tighter, her only anchor in that sensual storm.

He tasted like butterscotch and wicked sex, filling her mouth, sliding down her throat. Overwhelming her, branding her. It was as if she hadn't been sad and depressed a short while ago. As if she'd been sensitized and hungry for days, years, and had only now found sustenance.

Her legs shook uncontrollably, and she barely stopped herself from climbing him. The orgasm he'd given her earlier should have left her sated, but as McKell continued to feed her kiss after drugging kiss, fire spread through her, increasing the hunger pains, heating her up, demanding another.

She might never get enough of this man.

And that thought should have scared her enough to send her running and screaming from the room. But one of his hands snaked around her waist and forced her deeper into the hard line of his body, that wall of strength and fire, and the thought of running was massacred. Brutally. Wonderfully. The thought of screaming, however . . .

More. She needed more. All. All that he'd promised. His other hand kneaded her breast frantically, rolling her nipple, pinching, and she gasped, strong tendrils of pleasure shooting through her.

"Clothes," she rasped, tugging at the hem of his shirt. Skin-to-skin. Now.

"Yes," he replied, biting at her lip. "I have them."

"Take them off."

Both of his hands settled on her waist. A second later, she was soaring through the air. There was no time to react, no time to wonder what was happening. The next time she blinked, she was lying on top of the mattress, and he was at the foot of the bed, stripping.

The separation allowed her to catch her breath. Catching her breath allowed the fever in her veins to simmer.

She watched as he ripped his shirt over his head, revealing rope after rope of muscle, the bone necklace clinking as it settled on his chest. The scar she'd admired the night they met, the one bracketed between his pecs, had her mouth watering.

"How'd you get the scar?" she asked, certain he picked up on her desire to lick it.

"Training with my father. I was young, not yet able to heal without lingering effects, and he cut me open from neck to navel to teach me a lesson." His motions never slowed.

"You learned that lesson?"

"I thought I had. Never trust an opponent. Even one you love."

He unfastened his pants, and down they were

pushed. No underwear. She caught sight of his erection and nearly wept with wonder. Maybe, since vampires seemed to live forever, he'd been on earth during the human/alien war some eighty years ago and had come into contact with some kind of nuclear . . . something. Because damn. He was *huge*. Bigger than any man she'd ever seen.

Long, thick, hard, with a plump head that would stroke her just right. His sac was drawn up tight, beautiful. He had no body hair that she could see, and anyone else she would have assumed waxed. But he wasn't the type to care what anyone else thought. He liked himself just fine. Maybe too fine, but still, that kind of confidence was attractive. Heady. And in his case, warranted.

One knee, two, he climbed atop the bed. His gaze never left hers, even when he stopped at her waist, his legs cradling hers. Rather than fall on her and devour as she hoped, he stayed where he was, just breathing her in.

"Now I get to look at you," he rasped.

His gaze tracked her, every inch of her, lingering on her beaded nipples, her quivering navel, between her legs. Soon she was panting, on fire again, utterly desperate because those eyes *caressed*.

"Your nipples are like berries," he said. "Your stomach is a naughty little tease leading to . . ." He traced a fingertip to the small thatch of curls, so soft, so gentle. "This little treasure."

Oh, God. She needed a stronger touch, a deeper touch. Now.

"McKell," she said. Begged. "Victor. Please."

He leaned back on his haunches, grabbed her legs and spread them wider, as wide they would go. But again, he didn't fall on her. His gaze returned to her core, and his fangs extended.

He licked his lips, flicked his tongue over those sharp incisors. "You're so pretty there. So wet. So mine."

He wasn't going to touch her yet, she realized. He was simply going to torture her.

"Can I touch what's yours? Please." She reached down and thrummed her clitoris. At that first needed contact, her hips arched off the bed, and she moaned. *Yes.*

"Ava," he growled.

She stilled, the mattress quaking with the force such a cessation required. "Yes?" Would he tell her to stop?

"Do that again," he said, a hoarse entreaty.

One she didn't mind obeying. Over and over she circled her clit, her hips pumping with the movement. All the while he watched, stroking himself, fangs sharp and gleaming, and that ramped up her arousal.

"Make yourself come."

Again, she didn't mind obeying. She pressed harder, circled more intently, the pleasure building, breaking, slamming through her. She cried out, muscles clenching on bone, stars winking behind her eyes.

As she came down from the high, she refocused

on him and realized he was still stroking his shaft, up and down, the motions smooth, even though his hand trembled. Her needy body once again lit up in flames, craving a taste of the sensual man in front of her.

"That was beautiful," he croaked out. "I've never seen a woman take care of herself before."

Just watching him, that plump head hidden by his hand, then revealed, then hidden again, caused her excitement to veer toward the edge of another climax. *He* was the beautiful one. Pure masculinity, utter warrior.

"More," she said.

"For you, yes." He stilled.

She moaned, reached out. "For you, too."

"I almost lost you," he whispered, taking her hand, kissing her knuckles. "Promise you'll never leave me behind like that again." When she hesitated, he added, "You've already promised not to purposefully endanger yourself. This vow asks no more of you than that one."

This wasn't an ultimatum on his part, she knew. He wouldn't leave her unsated if she refused. He was concerned, that was all, and even that was a stimulant. "I promise," she said, and she meant it.

"My good girl." *Finally* he fell on her. He sucked on her nipples, hard, his fangs nearly breaking skin. She loved it, loved every sensation. For every swipe of his tongue, every nibble of his teeth, drove her need higher . . . higher . . . just the way she'd wanted, until she was writhing, clawing at his back, tugging at his hair.

He was going to make her come again, just by lavishing attention on her breasts. No, no, no, she thought. That would make three for her and zero for him. Even in her lust-fog, she knew she wanted him receiving an equal amount of pleasure.

Ava flattened her hands on his chest and pushed. He fell to his back, and she rose over him, honey curls forming a curtain around their faces. His hips arched up, rubbing his shaft against her moist folds, but not penetrating, and they both groaned. At last she got to lick his scar, tracing the edges with her tongue, and clearly, he liked. He gripped the sheets, ripping them to shreds.

"I'm going to suck you," she said, "but I won't let you come. Not yet."

"Why not? Do you think you'll dislike the taste of my seed?" How disappointed he sounded.

"Oh, I know I'll like the taste." Truth. There was nothing she disliked about this man. "But I want you to come inside me." Or rather, in a condom, while thrusting hard and deep. Oh, yes. Soon. Please.

"I'm not like those puny—those humans." He reached up and smoothed the hair from her face. "I can come in your mouth, *please let me come in your mouth*, and then immediately come inside you."

The disappointment had given way to desperation. "Immediately, hmm? So you don't think you can last once you get inside me?"

"That's not—I won't—I can last!"

She tried not to grin. So easy to tease, this one.

"Well, lucky for you I'm going to make you prove both claims."

"Just prepare to be awed."

The grin grew, unstoppable. Ava inched down his body and when that beautiful cock was poised at the entrance of her mouth, she sucked him inside without hesitation. His width stretched her jaw, made it burn, but wow, a burn she welcomed, taking him all the way to the back of her throat and humming.

His hands fisted in her hair. Over and over he chanted her name, but soon he was incoherent. She cupped his balls, squeezed, tugged. Everything she did seemed to fuel his need, and that made her proud, made her want to work him harder. So she did. As she pushed down, she rubbed her tongue over the shaft. As she lifted, she lightly scraped with her teeth.

"Ava," he groaned, and that was the only warning she had before he jetted white-hot inside her mouth.

She swallowed every drop, loving that she had brought him to this point, astonished that her own need was stronger than ever. That her skin was heated, molten, her muscles aching, and her bones shaking. She couldn't bring herself to release him, especially when, true to his word, he immediately grew hard. Harder, actually.

As she began eating him up yet again, he latched onto her arms and jerked her upright, at the same time rolling her over. Still no penetration. Not yet. She pleaded with her gaze. *Please. Need. Now.*

Understanding or not, he cupped her jaw and peered deep into her eyes, perhaps seeing into her soul. His violet eyes were bright, his lips swollen, red, his fangs elongated, sharp.

She wrapped her legs around his waist, and locked her ankles against his lower back. Hint, hint, but still he didn't sink inside. Maybe his come was an aphrodisiac, because she burned. She craved. She had to have him, would die soon, surely. Was lost, falling, spinning, riding a wave of pure sensation, more and more of those stars winking.

"You're mine," he growled. "You know this, yes?"

Yes. Oh, yes. Forever. But with the strange thought—forever?—common sense intruded for a brief moment. "C-condom," she said.

He frowned. "What's that?"

"A . . . wrapper for your cock . . . to prevent pregnancy . . . and disease . . . and if you don't fuck me soon, I'm going to *kill* you."

His hips pressed, teasing. "I don't get diseases."

"Well, do you want to make a baby with me?" She'd never wanted a child. Thought she never would. But this conversation reminded her of the little McKell she'd imagined running around her apartment, and how she hadn't been completely repulsed, and had maybe even been a little intrigued, and . . .

Stop, she screamed at her mind. Enough thoughts of forever and kids.

"No," he replied, "no children." Like her, he didn't sound convinced. "But I think I told you that vampires don't produce children very often, and never with humans."

"You're sure?"

"Yes."

So they couldn't have kids. That was a good thing. Really. She could have McKell all to herself . . . "Then why aren't you inside me? Make me yours, McKell."

The last word left her, and he reacted instantly. He shoved inside her at last, roaring, hitting her deep, all the way to her core. *Sweet merciful heaven.* She arched up, sending him even deeper, and shouted his name.

Her nails drove into his ass, urging him to slam in and out of her. Which he did. With so much force her brain rattled against her skull. But God, she couldn't stop him. Didn't want to stop him. Just wanted more, more, more.

True to his word—again—he lasted. Every thrust increased her need, her pleasure. She bit at him, wanting so badly to break his skin, to taste his blood. A want she couldn't tamp down. She wanted to stay joined with him forever.

Forever. There was that word again. Just thinking it was almost enough to send her flying over the edge. Almost. There was something else she needed . . . something just out of reach . . .

"McKell," she gasped, not knowing what it was, what she had to have.

But he knew, he understood. He sank his fangs straight into her neck, so deep he hit a tendon. God, even that was ecstasy. She climaxed immediately, tightening around his shaft, screaming, begging, lost again, so lost.

He drank and drank and drank, his gulps in rhythm with his thrusts, and then he, too, was coming, shooting inside her, shouting her name. And maybe his seed really was a drug, an aphrodisiac like she'd assumed, because knowing they were skin to skin, that there was nothing between them, that he was filling her up, the first man to truly touch her this way, had her coming again. Coming so hard she couldn't breathe, could no longer speak.

A long while later, she collapsed against the mattress, McKell still on top of her, still inside her. He collapsed, too, his weight smashing her. She didn't care. She loved that weight.

He'd said she belonged to him, had called her his, and just then, she believed him. And she liked it. Maybe that was the afterglow talking, but she'd figure everything out later. Right now, there were better things to do.

For once she didn't hop from the bed and leave her lover behind. She closed her eyes and slept. Content. She was content.

Twenty-four

*H*is woman had let him love her and drink from her, McKell thought, satisfaction slamming through him. He tightened his hold on the still sleeping Ava, and a breathy sigh escaped her. That sound . . . like a match being lit . . .

Only an hour had passed since she'd slipped into this unconscious state, yet he suddenly wanted her again. Wanted her with a desperation that frightened him. Craving a human this much, a nonmated human, was unwise.

When the bond was complete, if she would ever allow him to complete it, he would want her even more. Which meant he would be even more obsessed, more under her spell, more hers than his own. Not that he cared. He just wanted to turn her. *So* badly.

That wasn't going to happen anytime soon, though. He'd bruised her pride, made her feel like humans were inferior—and they weren't. How could they be when Ava was one? But Ava was better than humans *and* vampires. Now she wouldn't even consider the possibility of turning.

His fault, he knew. *How would you feel if I insisted*

you become human? she'd said. He would have hated it, felt inferior. As he'd made *her* feel.

If he would have kept his big mouth shut, rather than making her feel like she wasn't good enough, just as she was, she might have entertained the notion one day. So that they could be together. Forever.

Forever, exactly what he wanted with her.

Perhaps he could fix things, he thought. She had mentioned reversing time before. Perhaps he could. Perhaps his past failure stemmed from the fact that he just hadn't had the proper motivation. And as Ava had said, since he could manipulate time in one direction, why not all directions?

If he could reverse time, to the first day he met her, keeping the memories he had, he could change the way he'd acted, the way he'd treated her. He could make her feel special from the very beginning, so that she would be happy to become vampire, protecting herself for eternity.

He liked that idea. A lot. Only problem was, he didn't like the thought of her not knowing him. Of waiting to kiss her and touch her until she got to know him again. Of living somewhere other than this home. *Their* home. And what if, by starting over, *he* lost his memory of *her*? He would do nothing different. Or would he? Would he even end up in the same place?

Hmm. Were the possible rewards worth the mounting risks?

He didn't know. Whatever happened, he just wanted to be with her.

How he laughed at his earlier foolishness, thinking he would one day kill her to make room for someone else. There would be no killing her. Ever. He didn't want to be set free. Didn't want to find anyone else. Someone more suitable. He snorted. How could he ever have thought such a thing? There was no one more suitable.

She was wonderfully lusty, uninhibited, brave—perhaps too brave—determined, stubborn—perhaps too stubborn—and witty. There was no one more beautiful, both an angel and a devil. No one who could calm him from a temper with only a smile. No one who could capture his notice so thoroughly, the rest of the world fading away. No one who tasted as sweet or strengthened him so completely.

She was the other half of him, the better half, and something he hadn't known he'd been missing until now. But . . . how did she feel about him? Not for one moment did he presume to think sex had changed everything and now she would want him unconditionally. That wasn't her style. Not this woman who made him work for every scrap of affection. Work he didn't mind. Actually enjoyed, challenged in a way he'd never been before.

If anything, she would have *more* demands for him. More rules—for him to break, he added with a twinge of anticipation.

He wouldn't worry about the problems just yet, he thought. He had too much to look forward to. Namely, having her again.

McKell grinned as he, too, fell asleep.

* * *

"Wake up." Ava shook McKell's shoulders. Big, strong, hot shoulders. Bare, lickable. She'd squeezed and kneaded those shoulders. Scratched and pounded on them. With those thoughts, an ache only he could assuage bloomed.

Her teeth ground together. No more thinking about him that way. At least while there was work to be done. Later, though . . .

She shook him again, harder than she'd intended. Nothing. No reaction.

"McKell."

Again, nothing.

He hadn't moved when her cell had erupted, signaling a text from Mia. He hadn't sighed as she'd scrambled from the bed, shocked that she'd slept so long. Or at all. How many years had passed since she'd snoozed more than an hour at a time? And never that deeply.

On some soul-searing level she didn't yet understand, she must have felt safe with him here. Knowledge that thrilled her even as it scared her. The longer they were together, the more she'd come to depend on him.

Thoughts derailing. Again. Anyway. He hadn't made a noise while she'd showered, dug through her dressers, and found something to wear. He hadn't peeked while she'd grunted and groaned, shimmying into the clothing. She knew because she'd been staring at his beautiful face the whole time.

Okay, his penis. She'd been staring at his penis. The covers had fallen off the bed, revealing every inch of his delectable body, but that penis hadn't even twitched. And she'd so hoped . . . *Not gonna think about him that way*. Anyway. No twitching meant no peeking.

Had she left him in a sexual coma of bliss?

Mama liked the idea. A lot. And she liked seeing him in her bed, knowing he was surrounded by her scent. That kind of made him hers, in an undeniable, almost tangible way. Like he wore a "Property of Ava" stamp. At least for now. Until they parted. Which *would* happen, despite the fact that she wanted him more than she'd ever wanted anyone else, because they couldn't meet each others' needs. Not all the way. She couldn't forget that fact; it was one of the reasons she had to stop thinking of him in such sexually explicit terms.

Sex equaled addiction when you placed it before duty and addiction equaled a need for more. Mmm, more . . .

Argh! "McKell." Not knowing what else to do, she slapped him.

Finally. A reaction.

He blinked open his eyes and stretched his arms over his head, his muscles rippling. "What?" His voice was rough with sleep, utterly inviting.

How easy it would be to accept that invitation, crawl beside him, and curl into him. Damn, damn, damn. "Time to go to work."

"After my nap."

"Now. Mia sent a car for us. And why is Hellina here?"

"She's ours now."

Ours? Like a freaking kid they'd adopted? Together? Butterflies took flight in her stomach.

"Oh, and she's a vampire. Don't get too close to her." Lids closing, he rolled to his belly. Wouldn't you know it, his ass was perfect, even with claw marks.

And what did he mean, Hellina was a vampire? "McKell!"

"Nap. Then sex. Then work."

First thought: *Excellent plan.* Second: *Resist.* "If you insist on staying in bed, I'll stun you and cart your carcass to AIR myself."

"Good. That'll give me twenty-four hours of napping."

Speaking of stunning and twenty-four hours, how had he come out of it so soon last time? He still hadn't answered that question. "Napping? Ha! Think again, you lazy bum," she said, hoping to shame him into rising. "There's too much to do."

He shaped the pillow over his head so he wouldn't have to listen to her.

Ava pressed her tongue into the roof of her mouth, then left the room in a huff. In the kitchen, she discovered her refrigerator had been stocked, and was nearly bursting with food and drinks. Her cabinets, too. And on the counter was a bowel of butterscotch candy. Real candy, not the fake stuff she could afford.

McKell's doing, she was sure. Forget lazy. He was diabolically genius. Rather than fill a glass with ice water to dump on him, she sucked on a candy—like sex in her mouth, man—and filled a glass with water, minus the ice.

She'd already chewed and swallowed the candy by the time she reached the bedroom, glass in hand. A girl couldn't teach her man a lesson under those circumstances. So, before she did any dumping, she returned to the kitchen, unwrapped a second morsel, chewed, swallowed, unwrapped another, then finally skipped back to McKell, humming under her breath.

He still lay on his belly, that pillow over his head, the rest of him completely bare. Impervious to cold? She'd soon find out. She emptied the glass directly over his shoulders, and he jumped up sputtering.

No goose bumps, but definite anger. "What was that for?" he demanded. Droplets splashed onto his stomach.

She arched a brow, praying she appeared stern rather than sated from her candy—and awed by the sheer beauty of him. "Oh, good. You're up. We can go to work now."

He crossed his arms over his chest, his nostrils flaring with his every inhalation. Then his pupils expanded, and he grinned slowly. "You discovered the butterscotch."

Mmm, butterscotch. Would it ruin her waistline if she had one—fifty—more?

"Nap time is over, yes," he said with a husky edge,

"but I believe the next item on my list was sex. And after all, you made me wet, so now it's my turn to return the favor."

A tempting proposal wrapped in such a wicked package. One thing she knew: where he was concerned, she was *always* wet. Not that she'd admit it. Until later. "We're leaving in five minutes whether you're dressed or not. The car's been waiting for a while already."

"The car or the driver?"

"The car. There's no driver."

That kept him quiet for a minute, then he shook his head. "The car won't mind. Besides, I can love you and dress in four."

She had to turn away from him to hide her smile—and her sudden surge of panic. *Love.* The word beat through her brain, both a paradise and a churning storm. "I'll, uh, be waiting in the living room." With that, she stomped out of the bedroom and jabbed the wall console to close the door. So she wouldn't coax herself into returning. Or peeking.

Resisting, though, became harder and harder with every minute that passed. Didn't help that Hellina stared at her the entire time, fangs protruding past her bottom lip, sharp, glistening. McKell really had turned her. Un-freaking-believable.

When he finally deigned to join her, he was clean and smelled divine. Like he'd slathered himself in the butterscotch bodywash. Maybe he had. Her mouth watered for another taste of him. He also wore clothing she'd never seen him don before. Clothing that hadn't been in his bag. A real cotton T-shirt, too expensive for someone who made a pittance like her. Soft-looking black slacks that fit him perfectly, as if tailored exclusively for his magnificent body. Leather boots.

Holy Lord, he took her breath away.

"Did you rob a bank?" At the moment, they didn't look like they belonged together. They were opposites. Her, the poor good girl. Him, the rich bad boy. To his credit, he didn't seem to notice the difference. He eyed her as if she had never looked lovelier, as if she was already naked and he was already pumping inside her.

"A bank? No. I robbed Devyn Targon." As he spoke, he petted Hellina behind the ears, the adoring dog licking his free hand. A domestic sight, one that had Ava's chest clenching. "Perhaps *robbed* is the wrong word. He owed me."

"And you didn't make him buy *me* clothes like yours?" she demanded, hands on her hips. Had he *wanted* the scale to be off?

"No. That's my job. Which I can now do." He could have been banging his chest, so proud did he sound. "He gave me money, too."

Wait. Backtracking. "So *you'll* be buying me stuff with *his* money?"

"Yes."

"But *he* wasn't allowed to buy me anything?"

"Right." Fury suddenly detonated in his expression, and he stiffened, as if ready to attack. "Do you *want* him to buy you something?"

Men. "No. I just don't want to look like your poor girlfriend." Who was using him.

The fury faded, the danger passed. "Haven't you realized yet? No one will ever look good enough *for you*." A sultry promise, seductively delivered. "How can they? You're so far above the rest of us, we can never hope to compare."

The clenching in her chest migrated to her lungs, building so much pressure that tears actually beaded in her eyes. Freaking tears. No one had ever complimented her like that before. She spun away from him, not wanting him to see. "We'll, uh, discuss this later. Right now, we need to leave."

"All right. Later. But we *will* discuss it." He paused. "Hellina, stay," he said, then strode to the door, bypassing Ava and thankfully not looking back. He pressed the correct code, and the entrance opened. "So what would you have bought yourself?"

She wiped her face and squared her shoulders, under control by the time she passed him. "A kilt for you."

"I don't understand," he said as they trekked out of the building and into the car. "I thought you wanted something for yourself."

"That's something else for us to discuss later." The sun had disappeared, the moon taking its place, but unlike all the other nights of their association, this one was not cool and dry. Rain pounded. Dirty rain, probably acid, and enough to sting the skin.

During the drive, he told her the *True Story of Hellina Tremain-McKell, How I Became a Real Vampire*, and she could only shake her head in wonder. At herself! She should have known he would experiment. He wasn't the kind of man who took things at face value. He had to see for himself.

"So how do you feel?" she asked. "About being able to change, well, anything and anyone?"

He stared up at the roof, at the panel revealing the constant sledgehammer of rain. "Relieved, tortured, confused. Why am I able to do so, yet no one else can?"

"I don't know. Mia mentioned something being off about your blood, but she wasn't sure what it was."

"Off?"

"Yeah, like it was *more* than vampire."

"That's impossible. As I told you, vampires can't procreate with other species."

"Just like your turning Hellina was impossible?"

He glowered at her, dark emotion pouring off him and as toxic as the rain. "My parents were vampires. There's no . . . question of that." He frowned.

That hesitation . . . "What is it? You can tell me, McKell." She reached over, squeezed his hand. "You can trust me."

He accepted the touch as if it were his right. "Vampires came to this planet a millennium ago, living in secret until recently, as you know. There weren't many, but they came here because their planet was dying. There were hundreds of doorways to other planets, and so the people divided, some going one way, others another, and so on. Once they crossed, the doorway closed. Until . . ."

"Until—," she prompted with another squeeze.

"My mother. She and my father had been wed for years with no offspring. But one day, suddenly, she disappeared. She returned a few months later, and a few months after that, she gave birth to me. For most of my childhood, I was teased, other children claiming my mother had cuckolded my father."

That kind of explained his superiority complex. He'd *needed* to view himself as better than everyone else. Otherwise, he would have had to view himself as inferior, as everyone else had, and that was a weakness a warrior wouldn't allow.

They were more alike than she'd realized.

"So, the rumors died—"

"When I began hurting those who spoke them."

That's my McKell. "Could your mother manipulate time? Could anyone? You might have told me, but I'm drawing a blank."

His chest puffed up. "No. I'm the only one who has ever been able to do so."

So, that might not be a trait of the vampires, but of another race. Could he be more than vampire? If so, how? "Your mother never spoke of another lover?"

"No. Nor did my father."

From the corner of her eye, she caught of glimpse of the structure looming in front of them. "We'll have to continue this, along with everything else, later."

He nodded as the car eased to a stop at the AIR gate.

She flashed her badge, as always, but the guards wouldn't let her through. They had to wait for Mia herself to arrive—in the company of three other agents—and then follow her to the back of the building.

Ava's nervous system kicked into gear as the car eased forward. "Let's come up with a code word or something, in case you need my help." Maybe she shouldn't have brought him here. Maybe she should have told him to run.

He lifted her hand and licked the wild pulse in her wrist. "If I need aid, I'll say, 'Ava, I need you.' " His mouth curled up at the corners. "How's that for a code?"

"Unbreakable," she replied drily, trying not to squirm in her seat as she savored the soft press of his lips.

"Well, I promise I won't need your help."

Her desire suddenly chilled. "Because you now think I'm weak?"

"You always think the worst of me first," he said on a sigh. "No. I don't think you're weak. I know just how strong you really are, but I don't want you in trouble with your coworkers. Not for my sake. I'll behave."

How . . . sweet. "I'll—I'll do better. About not thinking the worst."

"Thank you."

Still. The nervousness returned, welcoming another round of doubts. What had she gotten him into? How would this end? "Just answer Mia's questions, give her some more of your blood, and then we'll get out of here. Okay?"

"For you," he said, giving her hand another kiss, "anything."

This new, tender side of him *destroyed* her.

The car stopped in the underground parking lot. After sharing a long, long look, they emerged, Mia already waiting for them and tapping her foot impatiently. The other agents were still with her, pyreguns now palmed.

"He's not going to cause any trouble," Ava said, stepping in front of him.

He grabbed her by the waist and shoved her behind him. Having none of that, she pulled free and returned to her favorite spot. In front, acting as his shield. A low growl left him, and he once again jerked her backward. This time, he didn't let go of her, no matter how hard she pulled.

"I know that," Mia replied, "but it pays to be careful. Now, come on. Let's get this done." She turned to lead the way, paused, then glanced at McKell over her shoulder. "Oh, and thank you for the vampires you sent me, injured or not. They're recovering nicely and are currently in lockup, awaiting testing and sentencing."

He inclined his head in acknowledgment.

Mia guided them through a part of the building Ava had never been inside before. There were no other agents here, the walls and even the hallways padded, with ID scans at every turn.

"Mia," she said, hating the tremble in her voice.

McKell still hadn't released her, so she quickened her step and twisted her wrist, twining her fingers with his rather than attempting to sever contact, hoping to offer comfort but knowing she was taking it instead. She had brought him here. Had *rushed* him here. If her boss meant to lock him up like she'd done the others, Ava would—what? Tear down the entire building? Kill every AIR agent? "He's here of his own volition. In peace. To help. Careful or not, please tell the guards to lose the guns."

"Sorry," was the reply. "Not gonna happen."

She popped her jaw. "Keep in mind, he's the only one who can help you track the Schön queen. You don't want to accidentally hurt him."

The threat had no effect. "Actually, Dallas can track her. Not to mention all my Rakans."

"And none of them have done any good," she reminded her boss.

"Anyway," Mia continued with only the barest pause, "he hasn't been helping us, has he?"

"He called you when he found her, didn't he? And he's been looking for ways to go out in the daylight so that he can do more." A stretching of the truth, but she didn't care. And why the hell wasn't McKell speaking up in his own defense?

She peeked up at him, blinking when she saw his smile. A genuine smile of pearly whites and amusement. He wasn't afraid. Not even a little. No, he was enjoying himself. Why?

"McKell," she said, exasperated.

"Yes?"

"Stop time," she whispered for his ears alone.

He did, without question. Everyone around them stilled completely. Ava stared up at him, her heart thundering in her chest. "What's going on? Do you want to run or something?" Though she knew, deep down, running would do no good. Not now.

"Run?" He laughed, the sound like a rich soothing balm. "Why would I run? You're trying to protect me. No one has ever tried to protect me before, and I . . . like it."

That explained the smile. And warmed her from the inside out. Still. "Don't you realize you're in danger? I can't open the doors we've passed. We're stuck here. What if Mia—"

He reached up with his free hand and rasped his knuckles over her cheek. "I don't think she's leading me to my death. I smell disease here. I think she means to test my blood."

Ava's stomach curdled. "Disease?"

He nodded, and time kicked back into gear, Mia and the guards continuing on as if they'd never stopped. Ava remained quiet the rest of the way. Disease. Testing. What she'd wanted, but she couldn't lose the sick feeling cramping her insides.

Finally, they reached a hallway that ended in a half circle, locked doors all around, darkened windows showcasing five different rooms.

Mia pointed, and Ava followed the line of her finger. Johnny. Shit. She'd forgotten about Johnny.

Now he rested on a cot in one of the rooms, probably dying, his skin gray, peeling, his cheeks sunken, his hair clumped around him, sores open and oozing all over him.

"He doesn't have much time left," Mia said, grim.

"What can we do?" Ava croaked.

"We're going to give him McKell's blood, as we discussed."

McKell lifted his chin, nose in the air. An emperor. "Ava mentioned the idea to me, and I said no. I still say no."

"Once that's done," Mia went on as if he hadn't spoken, "you have some questions to answer, McKell."

"Questions, fine. Blood, no."

He'd seemed happy with the whole thing only a few minutes before, willingly following Mia. Why the refusal now? "Please," Ava said, staring up at him.

He must have stopped time, because suddenly the rasp of Mia's breathing stopped, the guards ceased shifting from one foot to the other.

McKell gripped her shoulders and shook her. "You beg here the way you beg in bed? For this man?"

"Yes."

His eyes narrowed to tiny slits, though that didn't hide the danger that lurked there. "Why?"

"Are you jealous? Because I thought we'd gotten past that."

"Jealous, no. You're mine, and no one and nothing will change that. But he once taunted you, embarrassed you in front of your friends. Remember? The bar? I haven't forgiven him for that."

He'd loved when she protected him, and she realized she loved when he defended her. He knew what others thought of her, but he didn't care. Wasn't going to change his mind about her. And that . . . affected her.

"Thank you," she said, fighting those stupid tears again. "Even though I understand where you're coming from, I'm still asking you to heal him. Not because he deserves it, but because it's the right thing to do. And because, if he gets better, we can take turns kicking him in his man junk without any feelings of guilt."

There was a long pause, McKell studying her face every second of it. Then he nodded stiffly, and time once again propelled into motion. "I'll do it," he said to Mia, releasing Ava.

Mia's smile was cold, hard, and determined. "I never doubted you. So, let's break out the needles, dig into your vein, and then send Ava into the cell with the vial."

Ava stiffened, suddenly speechless. The last time she'd been with Johnny, he'd eyed her like a slab of meat. He'd threatened McKell. Well, the queen had threatened McKell through him, but a threat was a threat. Yet he'd been restrained. Now he was free to prowl that cell. To attack.

McKell spoke for her. Snarled, really. "Ava is *not* going in there."

"Yeah, what?" she demanded, finding her voice.

Mia anchored her hands on her hips. "Someone needs to inject Johnny or get him to drink the blood, but he attacks every doctor and agent we send in. I can't risk anyone else becoming infected."

"Which is why Ava is not going in there." Another snarl from McKell.

"Johnny won't attack Ava," Mia said, confident.

McKell shook his head. "Don't care."

"Then let's get you a cell of your own," Mia snapped, "because having Ava feed Johnny that blood is your only ticket out of here."

O-kay, then. "I'll do it," Ava said before he could reply. One, she needed no more convincing, and two, as she'd told McKell, it was the right thing to do. She didn't want to risk anyone else, either.

He huffed and puffed for half an hour, stopping time, pleading with her, pacing, yelling denials and demands, before finally nodding again, because she refused to back down. "I'll stop time and she may enter. *If* he isn't immune to my ability—I've listened and eavesdropped and I know the Schön adapt—and if I'm at her side. That's the only way I'll allow this to happen."

"Thanks for your permission," Mia said dryly.

"But if anything happens to her, I will destroy you and all of AIR."

Bless his heart. "Shut up, McKell," she said through both a smile and a grimace. "You're going to get yourself killed. And remember our plans for later?" *Our bedtime plans,* she silently added. "I kind of need you alive."

He kissed her, hard and fast. "You belong to me, and you *will* take care of what's mine. As will I."

"Promise?" she asked, wishing she could grab on to him and never let go.

"Promise."

"And don't worry," Mia said. "I won't lock you away for threatening me and all those under my care. Threats don't faze me. Maybe because I'm married to an alpha myself." She beckoned one of the guards, who lifted a walkie-talkie and summoned a doctor on staff to come and take that sample of McKell's blood.

She could handle this, Ava told herself. Anything to win McKell his get-out-of-jail-free card. And that's what this was. If she got hurt, that was a small price to pay.

With that thought, realization sunk deep. She wasn't just in this relationship for the short term. She more than liked the man, the vampire. And oh, shit, that stung. Panicked her all over again. Because with the knowledge, she knew she had a lot of decisions to make. Life-and-death decisions.

And the outcome might not end in her favor.

Twenty-five

T o Ava's surprise, injecting Johnny with a vial of
McKell's blood proved uneventful, almost an-
ticlimactic. Especially after all that fuss. Her one-
time-only former flame hadn't moved as she rushed
in and out, hadn't even breathed, until the door closed
behind her and McKell released him from the time-
stop. Then his eyelids had popped open and he'd
flung himself against the window, screaming in pain.
Screaming Ava's name, too, as if he could scent her,
see her, and wanted to eat her alive. But Mia hadn't
allowed them to stick around and watch what happened next.

And to further the surprise, Mia escorted them
to the part of the building Ava was very familiar
with, the interrogation wing, as promised. Without
any *added* fuss. She waved them to their seats, then
settled across from them and fired off three questions. Three. That was it, which was yet another
surprise.

"Will you help us hunt and kill the Schön queen?
Off the record and without pay, of course, because
you're, you know, a fugitive."

A quick "yes" on McKell's part.

Ava began to relax.

"Good. And if you succeed, will you stick around and work for us on the record and with pay? Because, as my employee, your crimes will be expunged."

"If that's what Ava wishes."

Mia arched a brow at her. "Ava?"

Work with McKell? "Yes." The thought gave her a small thrill, as well as another dose of that panic. Together . . . always . . . Wonderful, exciting. Addicting, doomed.

Mia nodded with satisfaction, crossed her arms, then unleashed the final question. "McKell. You know I'll murder you dead if you harm another AIR agent, right?"

"Yes," McKell replied, as unconcerned about that as he'd been about everything else.

"Good." Mia grinned, a rare, genuinely amused grin. "Then we're done here."

Just like that, he'd been given a second chance. A *real* second chance, something that was as rare as Mia's smile. Ava didn't know whether to laugh, cry from sheer relief, or (accidentally) force McKell's face to interact with her fist. All that worry, suddenly wiped clean. Thank God the need for his services had superseded the need for his punishment, otherwise this would have ended a lot differently.

Finally she decided. She laughed, a hysterical sound.

Mia and McKell shot her a strange look before Mia stood and motioned to the door. "Oh, and Ava," she said before leaving. "You and Noelle are now officially on my team. Don't disappoint me."

Wait. What? Ava barely made it to her feet. "On your . . . team?" Maybe Mia had said "seam." Or "beam." Or even "cream." Seemed too presumptuous to assume Ava had heard correctly.

McKell stood, as well, and wound an arm around her waist to hold her up.

"Yeah," Mia said. "You passed your trainee test, so you're hired. Now go. Get out of here. You two have a queen to find." She paused. "Word of warning, though, Agent Sans. You're in charge of McKell. Which means if he messes up, hurts a civilian, you'll take the brunt of the blame. Cool?"

McKell stiffened, but the reaction didn't really register.

Agent Sans. Freaking Agent Sans. "C-cool." She could only gape as Mia walked away, her mind still whirling. She was an agent. A real agent. No longer in training. This was a dream come true. Because she'd done it; she'd proven herself worthy.

"I have to tell Noelle," she squeaked, turning in McKell's arms to face him. She was trembling uncontrollably.

"Congratulations." At first, she thought he meant to kiss her. Then he canted his head to the side, his expression becoming pensive, his gaze faraway. "Apparently Mia called her earlier. Noelle's even waiting for us outside, a few of the trainees with her. They're supposed to help us hunt the queen."

Still in shock, head now buzzing, feeling as if she were floating, Ava fisted his shirt. "How do you know?"

"I just heard Mia inform the guards."

"In the hallway?" Ava listened and heard . . . only that annoying buzz in her head, she realized. When would it stop? When would her feet settle back on the ground?

"Yes."

"Nice trick." She'd just have to remember to watch her mouth whenever he was nearby. No way she wanted him to overhear her telling Noelle how sexy he was. Or anything else she might wax poetic about him.

He leaned down and nuzzled her cheek. "Well, your blood makes me strong."

The reminder sobered her, and the buzzing faded. Her feet hit cold concrete. She suddenly wished they hadn't.

One of her dreams had just come true; she'd just realized how much she liked this man, maybe even wanted some kind of future with him; and yet, she still wasn't complete. With just a few words, he'd put her back in her place. Blood donor. He might like her, defend her, protect her, even enjoy her, but in the end, that was the string that held them together.

Not true. You're just looking for reasons to dump him now that you know he means more to you than anyone else ever has. You're trying to find a way out of those decisions you need to make. Like turning from human to vampire. Like trusting him with her eternity. Like sharing all that she was, all that she would be. Like letting go of her fears, trusting him with not just her eternity but her heart and her concerns, believing that he felt the same and would never leave if, say, her blood no longer sustained him.

A lump grew in her throat. Maybe she *was* looking for reasons to dump him. Maybe not. Now wasn't the time to ponder. "Let's get this hunt started, then." Suddenly cold despite the heat he radiated, she pulled from him. "We have a lot to do."

He frowned. "What's wrong, sweetheart?"

Sweetheart. He'd never called her sweetheart before, and she fell a little harder for him. *What's wrong?* he'd asked. The truth wouldn't appeal, but neither would a lie suffice. "Come on. We'll talk later."

"Our later is already overpacked."

Very true. Still. She followed the same path Mia had taken, silent. McKell quickly caught up, silent himself, and took her hand. They strode through the building like that, like a couple. Every agent she encountered knew of her promotion and slapped her on the back, cheered, and congratulated her—even the ones who had once whispered behind her back, calling her trash.

They might have been pretending to be happy for her now, though. A wee bit of jealousy radiated from some of the girls, and a tad bit of resentment wafted from some of the men. In their minds, a slutty trainee had simply seduced a target to bring him in, and she had no true skill.

She ignored them all, still floundering and raw on the inside, and held her head high for her first true victory walk. No matter what they thought, she'd done the impossible, as Mia had said. Won the vampire—and kept all her fingers.

Noelle was waiting in the parking lot, just as Mc-Kell had claimed. "Congratulations," she said, grinning and throwing her arms around Ava.

The hug forced her hand from McKell's. "You, too." Her tone was just as raw as her emotions.

"Can you believe it? Official badasses, you and me." Noelle pulled back, her smile fading. "What's wrong? Why aren't you happier? I've got trainees in the van. *Our* trainees! We're in charge of them now."

"I'm happy. I swear."

Noelle eyed her suspiciously. "Why don't I—"

"Add this discussion to our list for later." McKell pulled Ava away from her friend and smashed her into the hard line of his body. His arms were as strong as always, and this time, she didn't feel so numbed against their heat. She curled into him, even though he was at the center of her turmoil. To be honest, though, he was also the center of her calm. "I have an idea to begin our hunt for the queen."

"I'm listening," Noelle said.

"The queen approached Dallas at his home. Therefore, we will go there, and I'll follow her scent. Wherever it leads."

Simple. Easy.

"All right. I like it." Noelle nodded. "You can follow me and the trainees—*our* trainees," she added, grinning again.

"Can do." Their vehicles were side by side, so Ava didn't have too far to walk. She climbed in, McKell beside her. A few minutes later, they were on the road and headed into . . . danger?

The moon was still high, but muted, and the rain had stopped, allowing the streetlamps to illuminate his perfect features. She didn't like the thought of him in danger.

"What about daylight vampires?" she asked him. This she could do. Chat about something uncomplicated, be with him . . . lust for him. Beautiful man. It was familiar. "Are we giving up the search?"

There was a pause, as if he debated venturing down this path. "Just for now," he finally said. "They aren't the biggest threat. However, if we happen to run across one or twenty, we won't walk away. And you won't engage them without me," he added in a rush.

"Fine." She'd learned her lesson well. "You'll get no argument from me, promise."

He paused again, but this one was far more tense. "Ava."

Oh, no. Was he preparing to ask what was wrong with her again? She—

"Tell me about yourself," he said gently. "I've tasted you, yet I know so little about your past, and I desperately want to know."

Gold star for McKell. He'd just made a direct hit to her deepest, most secret longings. Maybe she *was* more to him. Maybe she didn't have to fear. "Why don't we trade information? I'm curious about you, too." Just as desperately.

"Like for like?" he asked, and there was an edge of satisfaction in his voice.

She nodded.

"A sound plan." His violet eyes swirled. "You may begin."

"What would you like to know?"

Now that violet gaze roved over her, leaving heat, so much heat, in its wake. But when he next faced her, it was yearning she saw, causing her heart to skitter. "What were you like as a child?"

"A troublemaker, I guess."

"So not much has changed." He chuckled affectionately.

She punched his shoulder, but she couldn't stop the grin lifting the corners of her lips. That grin didn't last long. She wasn't going to lie to him and dress her childhood up. He already thought humans were inferior; what would he do when he learned that she was the lowest of the low? Or rather, had been.

Finally leave her? Well, good riddance! View her as trash? Bastard! He'd already heard Noelle's mother refer to her as trash, already heard Johnny refer to her as a slut, so why not confirm it for him?

That's not how McKell is with you, and you know it. You're letting your fears take over again. Stop. Now. She wasn't going to think the worst of him.

"Ava," he said, clearly confused. "I can hear the

blood rushing through your veins. Something's wrong again. Do you wish to discuss something else, then?"

How accommodating he was. Part of her wished he'd just grab her and jerk her onto his lap again, then kiss the breath—and the words—right out of her. The other part of her, the part that had resisted him from the first, finally wanted him to know everything.

"I grew up in a trailer park in Whore's Corner," she said flatly. "You know, the poorest part of town. My mother was a drunk, and my dad was a convicted felon who liked to steal and use Onadyn. You've heard of that, right? Aliens who can't breathe our air have to take it. Humans and aliens who *can* breathe our air use it to get wasted, even though it's illegal. My mom's many boyfriends came and went throughout the years, and they were just as vile as my dad. Users, thieves, unconcerned about those around them."

"Did any of them hurt you?" he asked, his voice as flat as hers.

That comforted her, helped her continue on. "Not for lack of trying. I learned to sneak out, to stay awake. To fight. Then I met Noelle and started spending a lot of time at her place. And getting drunk. And fighting. And stealing, just like my dad. I was arrested a lot. And when I wasn't in jail, I dated boys I shouldn't have. Bad boys who didn't really care about me, yet managed to make me feel wanted, if only for a little while."

His fingertips traced the veins in her hand, soft, tender. "I'm glad you weren't hurt. I would have had to tear this world apart, finding each and every one of the men who had done so, and letting you cheer me on as I ripped them to shreds."

"Just so you know, so there are no misunderstandings, I—I was considered a beggar. Dirty. T-trashy."

Now he stiffened, his eyes slitting dangerously. "By who?"

"Everyone."

"Looks like I'll be tearing this world apart, after all. The citizens are amazingly foolish. What you grew up with, around, doesn't define who you are. And you are the best person, human or vampire, that I've ever met."

Tears. Those stupid, stupid tears were forming again, burning.

"My turn," he said, as if he hadn't just destroyed her so exquisitely. "I was a beautiful child, and most everyone loved me." He peered over at her, as if waiting for a reply. What did he want her to say? She'd tell him anything. Finally, though, he gave up, shoulders sagging a little, and continued. "My father was commander of the king's army, and my mother cousin to the queen. I—"

"Wait. So you're royalty?"

"Yes." He said it simply. As if the confirmation didn't make her want to puke.

"Yeah, but *royalty*?"

"Yes. Isn't that wonderful?"

No! "Go on," she croaked out.

"Well, it was clear early on that I was destined for greatness." Again he paused, waited. Again she remained silent, unsure of what he wanted to hear from her. His shoulders sagged a little more. "At a very young age, I could defeat even my father. So, I was recruited into the army. I climbed the ranks quickly, until a few years later, I was second in command."

Back to an image she could handle. McKell, kicking ass. "What kind of battles do vampires fight in those tunnels?"

"We are a monarchy, and rebels sometimes sprout up. They must be extinguished. Also, twice a year we must leave the underground and hunt humans up here, bringing them below to be our food-slaves. I've told you that before, haven't I?"

Food-slaves, yes, but she hadn't realized they were hunted and incarcerated. After the Schön were taken care of, she and McKell might be taking a trip to those caves and freeing the "food."

"Anyway," he added, and his eagerness intensified her confusion. He liked sharing about himself? Well, of course, she thought next. With his past, why would he want to hide it? "My father died while fighting a *nefreti*."

"A what?"

"A vampire too powerful to live. Like Bride. Remember, they possess every gift you can imagine. Mind reading, teleporting, invisibility. The *nefreti*

killed the former king and my cousin the queen, and
Manus, their oldest son, took over."

Backtracking. McKell had been engaged to Bride.
She'd known that. The all-powerful, wonderful Bride.
She'd known that, too. As Ava had told McKell earlier, she thought they were over their jealousy issues.
Apparently she wasn't. Hearing him even say Bride's
name made her want to sharpen her nails into dag-
ger-points.

"As you can imagine, *nefreti* are difficult to kill.
When my father fell, I assumed control of the army,
and I've been leading them ever since. Until recently,
of course. Anyway, that was centuries ago."

Her eyes almost bugged out of her head. "Centuries. You've been alive centuries?" Yeah, they'd talked
vampire lifespans before, but she must not have connected the dots. He was *old*. Experienced.

"Yes." He watched her intently, gauging. "Don't
you see? I'm strong enough to fight this queen and
her disease. You have nothing to fear. I will defeat
her, and all will be well with your work, your . . .
life."

He'd sensed her anxiety, she realized. No wonder
he'd been so eager to talk about himself. He'd wanted
to prove to her that she could rely on him. *He* was the
sweetheart. "Thank you."

"Welcome."

He was soothing her, all of her. Gentling her. Oh,
yes, she had a decision to make. To turn or not to
turn being the most glaring. Though, after watching

Johnny hit that window, she wasn't sure that was a viable option. Yet that was the only way they could connect. Truly connect.

Forever.

Still such a scary word, but not as scary as the thought of losing him. Maybe she could do this. Maybe she could try. "So why were you kicked out of the underground?" she asked, picking up their conversation.

"For allowing Bride to live. For lying to the king about who she was. For bringing her back with the intension of wedding her."

Bride again. Ugh. "You once said lying was for people who feared consequences."

"Yes, and I feared being without her."

Stomach . . . twisting . . . *Old fear alert, old fear alert*, her brain screamed. She couldn't stop it, though. Bride had been his first choice. He'd lied for her, given up everything for her. So what did that make Ava? Second choice? Oh, God, oh, God, oh, God. Yes, old fears. They'd never really left her, she realized. They'd merely waited for their chance to pounce.

She was tired of them. So tired. Which meant she had to fight them.

She squared her shoulders. "Do you ever think about going back underground?"

He began tracing the veins in her hand again. "At first, yes. I think some of the army would follow me, did I ask, and attack the royal house. Which would need to happen for my successful return."

"And now? Do you want to go back?"

"Now I know too many lives would be lost. Besides, I have no desire to rule the vampire world. Palace life . . ." He shuddered. "The balls, the deciding of *everything* for *everyone*. People constantly invading my space, touching my things. No. Unless . . ." He frowned. "Would you like to be a queen?"

"No." Hell, no.

"You're sure?"

A queen of vampires, each one with a special gift and lethal fangs? Her, just herself. "Completely sure."

He pushed out a relieved breath. "Good."

Had he been considering fighting his people? For *her*? "Are you sure the king won't send that army of his to hunt you? The ones who wouldn't follow you if you returned?"

"Not completely, but he knows I could destroy them all, and I doubt he'll risk it. He hasn't yet. Now tell me a secret," he urged, leaning closer to her. "Something you haven't told anyone. Even Noelle."

The car stopped, and she peered out the window. Dallas's building came into view, and disappointment sliced through her. "Yet another thing for us to do later," she replied, and commanded the door to open. Not that she knew what to tell him.

"Very well," he grumbled.

She emerged from the driver's side and walked to the sidewalk, where Noelle and the others already waited. McKell exited, unfolding his big, strong body, and towering over everyone. Even Jeremy Deschanel, who was pale and tense. From worry about his brother? Had he even been allowed to see him?

Ava approached Jeremy and patted his shoulder in what she hoped was a comforting gesture. "He was given vampire blood," she said, and Jeremy's eyes widened. No, he hadn't been allowed to visit, and he hadn't been given an update. "There's a chance he'll heal."

"So he's alive?"

"Yes."

"Thank you." His eyes squeezed shut. "Thank you so much. He's an asshole, but I love him."

Hard hands settled on her shoulders, tugging her away from Jeremy and into—McKell. His breath was leaving him in an angry rush and lifting strands of her hair. That pleased her. She'd just reacted to Bride; helped that he'd reacted to Jeremy.

"Everyone will remain outside," McKell said in his calm, you'll-do-it-or-die voice. "I don't need your scents mingling with the ones already there."

"Wait." Ava circled her fingers around his wrist, holding him to her. "Noelle and I are in charge of tonight's activities, so *we'll* tell them what to do." Her narrowed gaze swept over the trainees, and some of them glared at her resentfully. She'd made it, after all, and they hadn't. "I've decided. You'll all stay out here.'"

"I'll keep them in line," Noelle said with relish. "Oh, and here." She handed Ava a digital info-pad as she faced him. "You'll need this."

"Give her any trouble," McKell said, "and I will personally remove your fingers." He pulled his necklace from under his shirt, the bones clinking together as they fell back to his chest.

"Now, then. I'm going with you," Ava told him, grip tightening on the pad as she faced him.

He arched a dark brow, looking sardonic and amused at the same time. "One day you'll have to learn to obey me."

"Sorry, but that day isn't today." She urged him forward. Behind her, someone muttered, "He really is an ass, isn't he?"

Ava stilled. Oxygen suddenly burned her throat, her muscles clenching in fury, red dots dancing through her line of vision. She whipped around, a knife in her hand, though she didn't recall withdrawing it.

"Who said that?" she demanded through gritted teeth.

Noelle pointed to the male trainee standing beside Jeremy. "Little boy, you're in trouble now," her friend sang.

Following those red dots, which formed a path straight to her target, Ava stalked forward. Until McKell's hard hands once again settled on her shoulders, stopping her.

She fought for release. *I will murder you.*

"No need, sweetheart," McKell said, and he sounded happier than she'd ever heard him. "I'm not offended by the comment."

Why was he happy? Not that his happiness would

have prevented her from attacking. No, it was the "sweetheart" that calmed her. She'd never liked endearments before. They encouraged affection she rarely entertained. Yet . . . when he did it . . . rainbows and gumdrop trees always seemed to sprout in her mind.

"He needs to suffer," she huffed.

"Later." McKell spun her around and anchored his arm on her waist, forcing her into the building. Along the way, he maneuvered her to the left, into grass, and ushered her around—nothing. She was confused, but didn't question him.

Dallas lived on the fourteenth floor, and Noelle's digital pad gave them the pass-code to enter his apartment. Which was dirty as hell. Had gossip not warned her about the mess, she would have thought someone had broken in and trashed the place.

McKell grimaced. "The bitch has been all over this apartment. It reeks of her disease."

"Did you smell her outside?"

"No. Nor did I smell her in the hallway. Which means she's teleporting rather than using invisibility."

Fabulous. "Can you follow someone who teleports?"

"No."

Extra fabulous. "This was a waste of time, then."

"Not necessarily." He hustled her outside. Without a word, he helped her back into the car.

Noelle sputtered for answers as she shepherded the trainees back into their van. Answers McKell didn't give. Not even when Ava demanded them. The car once again sped along the roads, and this time, Noelle followed them. They didn't stop until they reached the bar where the queen had first appeared to Dallas.

Again McKell emerged, and again he tugged Ava along silently. Noelle and the trainees trekked a safe distance behind, acting as bodyguards rather than detectives. A few more blocks, another snaked corner, several instances of him frowning, pushing her away from what seemed to be a perfectly fine patch of air, and he stopped, looked around.

"This is where she approached Johnny."

He kicked back into motion, sniffing all the while. Another block, three corners, four more pushes out of the way, constant mumbling about "stupid doorways," and they reached another apartment building. Johnny's. Ava knew because she'd been there. Which had her ducking her head and praying McKell's sniffing ability wasn't *that* keen.

Without any prompting, he led her to Johnny's apartment and shouldered past the door. Clean, sparse, with not many personal effects. As if he wanted to be able to pick up and move at any time.

McKell walked through every inch, then returned to the bedroom. Ava wanted to do more than duck, but all he said was, "The queen teleported out of here, too, but her guards didn't."

She frowned. Johnny hadn't mentioned guards, but then, maybe Johnny hadn't seen them. "So these guards weren't at Dallas's place?"

Twenty-six

*D*allas sprawled in his hospital bed, healed enough to go home, yet not quite ready to leave. He'd had nothing to do but watch time tick away, then listen to the monitors beeping in tune to his heart; and when those started to bore him—like, within minutes—he'd only been able to think about his beautiful Schön queen.

His? He immediately chided himself. Never his. Bitch was a stone-cold killer. And while he usually admired that quality in a woman—he'd been known to date porn stars, emotionally bankrupt heiresses, and the coldest of ice princesses—he wasn't a fan of rampant disease.

Here's what he knew. Trinity was a woman who took what she wanted, damn the consequences. Proof: she infected men, kept the ones she liked, and discarded the rest, letting them fend for themselves and infect others. Proof: she ruined one planet and then quickly moved on to another one. Proof: she claimed to like Dallas, to desire him, yet she'd allowed him to be shot rather than take the rays herself.

So, if she was so selfish and self-indulged, that begged the question of why she hadn't just infected him, since that's what she so badly wanted to do. Only one answer made sense. She couldn't. Physically, emotionally, whatever the reason, she needed his cooperation to act. Through seduction or manipulation, she needed him to say yes. *Had* to have that yes.

It was so clear now. Trinity was woman, disease—and followers. Three, as he'd suspected, but without that yes, she was stuck. Unable to harm him. Which meant he finally had what he'd been searching for: a weakness.

How could he exploit it, though?

If she would appear before him, solidify again, he could wear one of AIR's Night-Night rings. The rings looked innocent, but when you moved the stone in the center, there was a tiny needle that—*needle*. The word chilled his blood.

Injecting her, even with so tiny a needle, could have devastating results. For him, for all of AIR. The rings weren't like the darts, and didn't cauterize the wound. If one little bead of her blood spilled—and it would, because the Schön disease always knew when an escape hatch, for lack of a better term, appeared, always knew when a new host was nearby . . .

Some of AIR's finest had been infected that way while first testing the Schön.

A thought suddenly crimped his newest theory about Trinity needing a yes before doing her dirty work. The doctors hadn't willingly agreed to be infected, yet they had succumbed.

Or maybe they *had* welcomed the virus. Unintentionally, of course. The virus was alien, alive, and could have whispered to them, tricked them.

"Up and at 'em, I see."

Dallas pulled himself from his contemplations to eye the speaker. Mia. She stood beside his bed, grinning, all her pearly whites showing. She was a walking contradiction, and years ago he'd thought himself in love with her. He'd promised himself he would never think about those dark years, when he'd watched her, wanted her, but she'd kept him firmly in the friend zone, and he'd never gone back on his word. Until now. He blamed the painkillers pumping through his system.

Noelle Tremain was a lot like her, he thought. Pretty, yet tough as fucking nails. Maybe that's why he'd eventually sleep with Noelle and end his friendship with Hector. Maybe he'd be pretending she was Mia.

Thought you were going to stay away from Noelle from now on.

I bet she gives amazing TLC.

Even in his sad condition, his body reacted to that thought.

Don't throw a love triangle into the cluster-fuck of your life right now. You've got too much to worry about. Hector had stopped by to see him multiple times, and Dallas had almost broken down and asked the guy what he thought of the new agent. He'd kept his mouth shut, though. They *all* had too much to worry about.

"Ignoring me?" Mia asked, fake grin fading. Yeah, he'd known it was fake. What he didn't know was why. "Or has your abused brain finally given up and withered away completely?"

"Hey," he said in greeting. "And the brain's just fine, thank you."

"Let's see that chest." Without waiting for his permission, she removed the bandage covering his wound. She whistled under her teeth. "That's gonna leave the cutest little scar."

If by "cutest little scar" she meant "mountainous crater," then, yeah. It was.

A knock sounded at the door, and Dallas shifted his gaze. As if his earlier thoughts had summoned him, Hector entered.

"I brought you a cupcake from the bakery downstairs." Hector extended his untattooed hand as he approached the bed. The one that couldn't dematerialize and punch through *anything*.

Dallas had been living off of soup and eagerly took the—empty wrapper. He frowned. "Where's the fucking cupcake?"

Hector shrugged his big shoulders. "I ate it on the way up. Sorry."

Dallas flipped him off, then tossed the wrapper at him. "So what's going on?" And something was definitely going on. Despite the smiles and the "gifts," both radiated a tension they couldn't hide.

"Well," Mia began, putting his bandage back in place.

"Hello, hello. I brought my handsome boy some flowers," Devyn said from the doorway, seizing center stage.

A reunion. Great. "Don't they have a limit on the number of people I can have in my room?"

"They sure do," Devyn said with a nod. "Give me a minute to get rid of everyone for you."

He'd do it, too. Force everyone to leave by controlling their bodies. Devyn never cared who he pissed off, and Dallas had always loved that about him. "They can stay. You can stay. Will someone just tell me what the hell is going on?"

"In a minute," his best friend said. "When your attitude has improved."

Please. Like he could improve. "So where are the flowers?" he asked, noticing Devyn's hands were empty.

"Oh. I gave them to a nurse."

Dallas rolled his eyes.

"What?" Devyn said, all innocence. "She looked sad."

"Mia?" Dallas focused on her. "You were saying?"

She turned and kicked the door shut, then jammed the crash cart in front of it, ensuring no one else would enter. When she straightened, she rubbed her hands in a job well done.

"Okay, so," she began again.

"Wait. I need to get comfortable." Devyn grabbed the only chair in the room, moved it to Dallas's other side, and plopped down. He waved his hand, a king before his court. "Continue."

Mia popped her jaw. To Dallas's surprise, she didn't give the Targon shit, just started up again. "We gave Johnny some of McKell's blood. We hoped it would kill the Schön disease, and maybe it did. After a terrible first reaction, Johnny seems to be better. Looks one hundred percent better. Except . . ."

Again, she shifted from one foot to the other, and looked over at Hector.

He nodded and picked up where she'd left off. "Except he's now obsessed with Ava."

"Obsessed, how?" Dallas asked.

"He screams for her. Constantly. He wants to drink from her. He bangs at the window in his room to get to her, and has managed to crack the supposedly uncrackable shield armor."

"What about starving him?" Devyn asked. "That'll weaken him, right?"

He knew a thing or two about vampires, Dallas supposed.

Mia tugged at the short length of her ponytail. "When we noticed he was healing, and by that I mean looking human again, we threw bags of blood in his room, and at first he digested them just fine, but then he started vomiting the blood."

What did that—

"Which means he's encountered his mate," Devyn said with a nod. "Ava. Which is why he calls for her. He won't be able to keep anyone's blood down but hers. He'll weaken whether you feed him or not."

Hello, complication. "That's gonna piss McKell

off." Dallas had only been around the pair the once, but that had been enough. The connection between them was fierce and almost frightening. The vampire would allow no one to get between him and his woman.

"We knew Johnny had a crush on Ava," Mia said, and there was guilt in her tone because she'd encouraged that crush for results, "but that wouldn't explain his intense desire for her. We think it's because McKell's blood changed him. We think McKell's desire for her transferred to him."

"Well, someone has to warn McKell," Dallas said.

"Not it," Mia said, and Hector and Devyn quickly followed with refusals of their own.

What were they, five-year-olds? "Fine. The cripple will do it." Dallas offered each of them his darkest frown.

That earned him an "Awesome," from Devyn, and a huge smile of thanks from Mia and Hector.

"But in the meantime," he went on, thinking they all needed a good slap on the head, "we have to find out if Johnny's still infected or not."

"I agree, but we're afraid to test him," Mia admitted. "He's wild, strong."

McKell could stop time. Stop Johnny. Kill him, just in case, so they wouldn't have to worry about testing him, but that wouldn't give them any answers.

Dallas fell back on his bed, moving away from thoughts of Johnny's death and concentrating on Trinity's. McKell could probably stop time for Trinity. And if McKell could stop her, just for a few seconds, Dallas could—what? He would have to kill her without cutting her. Maybe he could snap her neck. Would she heal?

Hector could atomize his right arm and reach inside her body. Maybe good ole Hec could reach inside Trinity's chest and stop her heart. Would that put him in contact with her blood, though? Willingly? Probably. So maybe Dallas could—the scent of roses filled his nose.

Cursing, he forced his mind to blank. He'd suspected Trinity could read minds; she'd even told him she could. And he knew damn good and well she could enter a room without anyone the wiser. She might have just popped in, might be reading him even then. Invisible, planning. He'd have to be careful.

"Guys," he said. "I need you all to leave now. Don't talk about any of this with anyone. Don't even think about it. The queen, Trinity, can pop in, listen, and even read minds." *Understand what I'm saying.*

Grim silence followed his announcement.

"Anything we do from here on out needs to be spontaneous. Feel me?"

"Shit," Mia said, fingering her ponytail again. A cute, nervous habit.

"My mind only ever goes to Bride, anyway," Devyn said with a shrug, "so that won't be a problem for me."

Spontaneous *was* going to be a problem for everyone else, though. How could they work together, how could they help each other, if they didn't know what the other agents were doing?

"Well, shit," Mia repeated. "This is gonna be a whole lot of fun." She patted him on the shoulder before dragging Hector out of the room. "Come on. We got stuff to do. Or not."

"Want me to stay and read you a bedtime story?" Devyn asked. "Or I can share the painkillers I took from that nurse. You know, the one who has your flowers." He reached in his pocket and withdrew a handful of white pills.

"I thought you gave her the flowers because she looked sad."

"She did look sad. After she realized someone had stolen all her drugs."

Despite the harsh reality they faced, Dallas found himself laughing. "Get out of here, you bastard. Dally needs to not think about what to do next."

Devyn stood, then leaned down as if to kiss him. On the mouth. Dallas blinked, unsure how to handle the situation. Just before contact, Devyn grinned and straightened, saying, "You wish."

"Jackass."

"What would you have called me if I'd actually done it? Sweetheart? Well, you'll just have to get better without having me kiss your boo-boos." He was laughing as he exited the room.

Alone again. Dallas should have been able to relax. Only, he could suddenly *feel* the queen's eyes on him. They bored into him, deep into his soul, and caused every muscle in his body, even the still-injured ones, to tense.

She really was here.

How long had she been there? What had she heard?

His gaze flew through the room, searching, before he said, "You can come out now."

She appeared in the chair Devyn had just vacated, a vision of loveliness in a cobalt-colored robe that revealed one delicate shoulder. Her hair was red today, and piled high on her head, ringlets falling down to frame her temples.

There was something else different about her this visit. She was as beautiful as ever, and yet he could somehow see past that beauty, to sickeningly gray skin, oozing sores, and concave cheeks.

Was her own disease destroying her? Was infecting others no longer saving her?

"You're not playing fair," she said with an angry twinge.

Fair? *He* wasn't playing fair? "How?" *Mind blank.*

"Planning to shield your thoughts, to act against me randomly."

His hands clenched on the bars at the side of his bed. "We're just trying to survive. Surely you can understand that."

"Of course I can. That doesn't mean I have to like it." She leaned forward and traced a finger along his bandaged sternum. "Have you thought about my offer?"

Mind blank. No reaction. "Yes."

Her lashes lifted, and her gaze met his, hard, determined. "And?"

"And I won't let you infect me. I won't talk to Mia for you."

He expected her to erupt, to strike at him, *something*, but all she did was fall back into her chair, severing contact. She drummed her fingers against the arms.

"I've never encountered this much resistance before, and I admit I'm at a loss."

"We're in what's called a Mexican standoff, baby, so one of us has to cave. On something. And it's not going to be me. So tell me what you want with Mia, and we can go from there."

That sunken gaze hardened a little more. "I could just kill more agents of yours as I planned." Cold, so cold. "I believe I promised to visit the vampire next."

Mind fucking blank. "But you won't because you realize that will only cause me to resist you more intently."

Trinity sighed. "Very well. I will tell you . . . something I want . . . and that is . . . Mia's body." She watched him, waiting.

He couldn't mask his surprise. "I don't understand."

Trinity licked her lips. "I want to possess it."

Sexually? "Still don't understand."

She tensed. He thought she meant to leave, but she surprised him by saying, "Every time I go to a new planet, I need a new body. One already adjusted to the temperature, the atmosphere, the . . . *everything*. My . . . essence leaves the old one and enters the new."

Now they were getting somewhere. "What would happen to her?"

"Her essence would enter the body I left behind."

Not good. Not good at all. "So how does the disease follow you? I mean, there would be no blood exchange in essence-switching, right?" God, he couldn't believe he was discussing essence-switching, whatever the hell that was, as easily as if they were discussing switching T-shirts.

She flashed her teeth. White, sharp, almost shark-like. "My essence *is* the disease."

"So, what? You'd take over her body and no one would know Mia was actually you?"

"Exactly."

"And they'd follow you," he said, finally understanding. With understanding came a sick, cramping stomach. "They'd do whatever you said, thinking you were their beloved leader."

"Yes. That's the way it always goes. And by the time they realize something's different, wrong, they're already infected and serving me."

"Cold," he said.

"Necessary," she countered.

"Selfish." By telling him now, she'd ruined the element of surprise.

Gray cheeks pinkened with fury. "No different

from anyone else. We all do what we must to survive. Didn't you just say that?"

Before he could reply, a sharp pain exploded through his temple, and he grimaced. Damn it. He knew what that pain meant. A vision of the future wanted to open up in his mind. He fought it, held it back, because he didn't want Trinity seeing it, whatever it was.

"We'll find a way to stop you," he gritted out.

She sighed, a little sad. A trick, surely. "No, you won't. I'll have this planet as I've had so many others. I will stop AIR before they can hinder me in any way."

"Is that what you want more than anything?"

"No. I want . . . I want a cure." One confession making way for another?

Another trick. She enjoyed what she did, the power she wielded. "And if the only cure is death?"

The sadness melted away, revealing her true emotion. Calculation. "I wanted to rule this planet with you," she said, refusing to answer. "I like you, but again, you've given me no choice. I will find someone other than Mia. Someone who will willingly trade bodies with me."

So. She'd sensed his long-ago desire for Mia and had thought to use it against him. "There's no one who would do anything so stupid."

She laughed, the calculation giving away to another wave of sadness. He simply couldn't keep up with her mood changes. "Someone is always willing."

"Not here. Not on Earth."

"Love is all the motivation people need. I threaten one of their loved ones, and they give me whatever I want."

The sickness intensified, but like the vision, he beat it back. "Then why didn't you threaten Kyrin, the man Mia loves?" He knew he wasn't planting ideas into Trinity's head. He knew she'd considered all the angles, all the players. "Why did you threaten *me?*"

Slowly she eased to her feet, peering down at him. "I told you. Because I like you. And because Kyrin is a man so deeply in love he would kill himself before allowing himself to become a weapon used against his woman. If he died, Mia would never agree to anything I asked."

Or maybe Trinity simply couldn't infect Kyrin.

A muscle twitched under her eye. Had she read that thought? "There are other couples within AIR that might be willing to bargain."

Mind blank. No reaction. "Like?"

"Like time will tell, sweet Dallas." She didn't wait for his reply. She disappeared.

Fuck. Dallas leapt from the bed, but before he'd taken a single step, his vision busted past his mental block and slammed into vivid focus. Ava and Noelle, fighting the Schön. Ava, falling. Blood spilling. Her body, motionless. Her . . . death.

Unchangeable.

Fuck, fuck, *fuck*! He was panting as he came back to the present. He couldn't tell her, he thought. He couldn't risk being the one to drive her to that point. That had happened to him before. He'd had a vision, done everything in his power to stop it, but *because* of his actions, the vision had come true.

So, while there was nothing he could do for Ava— damn it!—there was something he could do about Trinity's threat. Dallas raced from the room, uncaring that his hospital gown was split in back and revealed every inch of his bare ass. He was going to contact every fucking AIR agent who was dating, married, or in love and warn them. Which meant he had to contact every AIR agent working for Mia. Even Ava. Before it was too late for the rest of them.

Twenty-seven

McKell found himself standing in front of the most exclusive apartment building in New Chicago, a towering monstrosity of gold-veined marble and rising columns. Mia and Kyrin lived in the penthouse—and that's where the Schön queen's men had visited after leaving Johnny's.

Had Mia and Kyrin known? McKell wondered. He didn't think so, or hardass Mia would have thrown a fit all the city would have heard about.

Those men hadn't lingered for long, though, and had next visited . . . Devyn and Bride's city house a few miles away. McKell positioned himself outside the closed gates with Ava tucked safely beside him, the rest of the gang remaining about a yard behind. Silent, he stared at the mansion on the hill, certain the otherworlder and vampire hadn't known about their visitors, either.

The Schön bitch had certainly made the rounds. How many agents had she watched?

Thankfully, the stink of rot that followed her and her men created a very clear path. A path he had to walk, just as they had, that glimmering doorway popping up every ten minutes. *So. Annoying.* Ava kept up beautifully, though she called him all kinds of bad names for dragging her, walking too swiftly, and stopping too abruptly.

He loved when she called him names. Meant she cared for him with the same intensity she cared for Noelle. That she was comfortable with him, that she trusted him. At least, that's what he told himself. And as he was most often right . . .

He didn't even mind the other agents tagging along. Even Jeremy. Every time McKell released Ava to study something, that boy would close in on her. To shield her—and as selfish and unwilling to share as McKell was, he found that he didn't mind that someone coveted something of his because Ava's protection came first.

Of course, the fact that Ava was in danger at all had his nails elongating and his teeth sharpening. He wanted this case over, done. Didn't help that the doorway was appearing more frequently now, harriedly breathing his name. So far, he'd managed to keep Ava away from it. What did it want? What was its purpose?

"Whatever pissed you off," Ava said, "dial it down a notch, 'em kay? You've already taken the fun out of *my* hunt. The way you're cutting my palm with your nails is going to take the fun out of *your* morning. You know, when we get home. After our talk, and before our nap."

Home, she'd said. Theirs. He immediately loosened his grip. "Just one more stop, then, and if the queen isn't there, we'll pick up where we left off tomorrow night." The sun would rise soon, anyway, and McKell would have to move indoors.

"Sounds good."

Only a block later, Ava said, "Wait." She pulled from his grip and withdrew her phone. She frowned as she read the screen. "Just got a text from Dallas. The Schön queen plans to target a couple. She'll threaten one so the other will do whatever she wants. He says she can read minds, so we aren't to think about what we would do to her if that happens."

A mind reader. Wonderful. Exactly what they'd needed to add to the equation.

"She already threatened you. I wonder if this means she changed her mind." Ava pocketed her phone, and they picked up speed. Soon they were back in the heart of the city, people strolling along the sidewalks, shop lights flashing, but two corners later, he tensed, tendrils of rage nearly choking him.

He recognized this neighborhood.

"Decide to call it a night already?" Ava asked, recognizing it as well. She should, since she lived here.

If the scent led to her door, he would . . . do anything, he realized. Anything to stop the queen. Drain humans to remain in the sunlight. Yes. No matter how much of a hypocrite that made him. He wouldn't sleep until the queen was dead.

"McKell?" Ava prompted.

Another yard, and they would be standing in front of their apartment building. Dread filled him, mixed with rage, and he slowed his steps. Little by little, his feet ate up that yard until—a low growl rose from deep within. No, the queen hadn't changed her mind about him.

He hadn't smelled her disgusting scent in Ava's building before. That meant the first visit had been *today*. Did that also mean he and Ava were the targeted couple Dallas had mentioned?

"McKell?" Ava insisted. "We done?"

"She was here," he gritted out. "She came to our home."

Silence. Now Ava tightened her grip on him, *her* nails cutting *his* skin.

"What do you want to do?" Noelle asked, coming up behind them. "I was eavesdropping and heard what you said to each other, so no need to explain. Plus, I got Dallas's text, too." The trainees were close on her heels.

What did he want to do? He wanted to keep searching, that's what. Things were personal now. This was war. Resting wasn't an option.

"Count me in on the eavesdropping, too," Jeremy said. "If she's been here, I don't think Ava should stay here. Not that my vote matters."

"When you agree with me, it counts. Now. Not another word out loud," McKell snapped. "Don't even think about what we should next do."

"Remember, the queen can read minds," Ava said with a tremor. She leaned her head on his shoulder. "But the thing is, we can't leave Hellina in there alone. We have to get her."

"I'll get her," he said, then kissed the top of her head.

"No," she rushed out. "She, the queen—" She pressed her lips together, flicked him a glance, looked away. "I can't say it. Can't think about it. Sorry. Just, let me do it. I'll get the dog. Okay?"

McKell inhaled deeply, trying not to think or plan or panic. Along with the sweet scent of butterscotch from Ava, he discovered an increase of rot. He stiffened. Were the queen and her men here, even now?

And, damn it. Wouldn't you know it. The doorway opened, air churning wildly.

"What you just said, about not thinking, not talking." He forced her to look up at him, noses almost touching. "Take the others to AIR headquarters. Now. I'll grab Hellina and follow."

Truth or lie, he didn't know. He only knew that he had to keep his mind clear, not plan, just act on instinct. Hopefully Ava would do the same, obey him or not, without thinking about it.

Ava opened her mouth—to argue?—but closed it with a snap. Wariness clouded her lovely dark eyes. So did worry. But darling that she was, she nodded. Trusting him. "Be careful," she said.

"You, too. Do nothing to put yourself in harm's way."

"The van is just around the corner. I had one of the guys follow us," Noelle said, and the group marched off. She had to tug Ava along, though.

Ava's gaze remained on McKell until the last possible second. He stayed where he was, sniffing, ensuring that the queen—or her men, *whoever*—didn't leave with the others. The scent of rot never lessened, so he knew the queen had stayed with him.

"You might as well come out of hiding," he said, scanning the darkness. The command agitated the doorway, the churning now so frantic a hard breeze hit him.

A laugh echoed a split second before a woman appeared out of nowhere, leaning against the cracked brick of Ava's building. Red curls hung down her back, and she wore another robe, this one blue and streaked with dirt. In fact, there was dirt on her face and arms, too.

Not a single guard appeared. Did that mean they were still hiding, or that they weren't even here?

McKell. Come. Never had the doorway sounded more desperate.

No, he projected. *Never.*

"I like you, McKell," the queen said, seemingly oblivious.

Like everyone else, she probably was. "I can't say the same about you."

McKell. Please.

I hear nothing. Know nothing. "I don't like that you came here. I don't like that you stalked my woman. And do you know what I do to people I don't like?"

"You hurt them," she replied with a smile.

Please! Now.

Silence, ignornace. "Yes." He lifted the necklace he

wore, the human bones clinking together. "Your fingers would look nice resting beside the others."

"You cannot hurt me," she said confidently. "You can't make me bleed without severe consequences."

"There are other ways," he said. *Don't consider them,* he reminded himself. "And I guess it's up to me to save the day. I'd prefer you left this planet, but if I have to kill you and everyone who serves you to do it, that'll just be a bonus."

McKell. The danger . . . too great . . .

Another feminine laugh chimed from her. "Others have tried to scare me away, too. Ask me if they succeeded."

Such smugness. He should choke the life from her. In fact, nothing was stopping him from doing so. He closed the distance between them, and if she knew what he planned, she didn't react. Not even when he reached out and wrapped his big hands around her small throat. "Leave, or you *will* die."

McKell!

Wind danced the strands of his hair together.

Unaffected, she said, "You think you'll be the one to finally fell me? You think there'll be no consequences for doing so? You think my men won't want revenge? You think I'm not the only reason Ava's alive, right. This. Second?"

Her threats . . . He tightened his grip, relaxed his grip.

Danger, so much danger.

"The moment I'm dead, they'll attack your girlfriend first," she continued, voice strong, as if his lethal intention meant nothing. The wind kicked up. "There's so many of them, you won't be able to stop them all. Won't be able to get to her fast enough. Not even with your ability. We adapt to abilities such as yours, after all. We learn to override them. Do you really want to risk that? What if we've *already* adapted?"

Intimidation. He'd used that tactic himself. When it came to Ava's well being, however, he had no defenses.

"Go ahead and freeze time," the queen said, taunting now. "See if I lie. Only, know that the moment you do so, I will consider this little truce over."

Truce? She called this a truce? "What do you want from me, female?" God, the wind. If the queen didn't kill him, the mind just might.

"I'm surprised Dallas didn't tell you, didn't try to help you figure out how to deal with me." The grin returned. "Maybe he wants you to fail."

If you won't come with me, leave the area.

Can't leave Ava with such a threat hanging over her head. McKell's eyes narrowed. Damn it. No more communicating with the door.

"So . . . how much do you love your Ava?" she asked silkily.

The sun was slowly rising, warming the restless air, heating his skin. Beads of sweat formed on his brow, and he could feel blisters already trying to form on the back of his neck. Not by word or deed did he act as if he was bothered, though. "I don't. Love her, that is." True or not, he didn't know, but he wouldn't think about his feelings for her right now. He couldn't. Too much was at stake.

"What would you be willing to do to save her?"

"That, you will never know, because you won't touch her." His hands fell to his sides, fisted. Just like that, the wind died.

"Maybe I already have."

That. Was. It. The need to act exploded through him. She claimed her men would attack Ava the moment McKell killed her. She claimed he wouldn't be able to reach Ava in time. Could be lies. Could be truth. Either way, he couldn't allow this woman to walk away.

Ava was in danger either way. If the queen died, she had a chance. If the queen lived, she didn't, and that was where this Schön had made her biggest mistake. Anything else, and he might have walked away.

With only a thought, McKell froze time. Froze the queen, as well. And she was frozen, he was sure of it. She didn't move as he once again wrapped his hands around her neck, as he squeezed hard enough to smash her trachea.

Oh, McKell. No, the doorway said.

Except, before he could snap her neck, she broke free of his hold. Both physically and time-wise, throwing herself backward, gasping for air. Her skin was pallid, revealing the thick gray of her veins. Clearly, no mask. The sores he'd only glimpsed before popped up all over her, and he could see where patches of her hair had fallen out.

The doorway wavered, cried with a pain of its own, then vanished.

He froze time again, but she pulled herself out once again, faster this time, before he even reached her. Desperation flooded him, and still he approached. She hissed at him, baring her teeth, sharper and longer than his, and backed away.

When he reached her, his steps quicker than hers, she snapped at him, trying to bite. He jerked backward, avoiding contact—but just barely.

"Mistake, vampire. Big mistake. You'll . . . pay . . . for . . . that," she gasped out, and a second later, she disappeared.

The scent of rot didn't fade, though. Which meant her men were still here. Why hadn't they helped her—

They appeared out of nowhere, just as she had done, and they were scowling at him. Only three in total, but each held a pyre-gun.

He stopped time, intending to choke the ones in front of him as he'd tried to do to the queen, then race to Ava, wherever she was. He couldn't believe this was happening, that he'd failed, but just before he reached the guards, just as they too jerked themselves out of his time-hold, blue stun beams erupted, dozens of them. Not at him, but at the guards.

His attention whipped to the side, and he saw that Ava was kneeling, aiming her own pyre-gun. *That's my girl.* Pride filled him. Noelle and the trainees were there, too, aiming guns of their own.

The civilians on the sidewalks cried out, scampering out of the way, and soon the area was deserted.

"You okay?" Ava called.

"I'm fine. Let's get you out of here, though. I'm not sure how long stun will last, and—"

A new group of warriors appeared behind Ava and the others. Before McKell could stop time—before he could do *anything*—fists were pummeling at his woman. And then, as he raced forward, his ability not helping in any way, a sharp pain tore through his back, and he fell face-first into the pavement.

Twenty-eight

*T*aken unaware, Ava thought as stars obscured her vision. Someone had punched her in the head from behind. She'd been feeling all smug and superior, getting the group of trainees to Noelle's van, then making them haul ass back to her apartment building without thinking ahead or announcing her plans.

She'd wanted to pat herself on the back when she'd stunned the men about to attack McKell. She'd wanted to preen when McKell had looked over and realized she had helped, his expression hot and sweet and proud.

Then she'd felt breath on the back of her neck, had seen horror fill McKell's violet eyes. A hard, meaty club had slammed into her temple, knocking her sideways. But when she turned, no one was behind her.

"Let's kill 'em!" Noelle shouted.

"Without drawing blood!" Ava added, pulling herself to her knees. An odd statement, coming from her. Usually when she fought someone, she wanted blood to pour. "Now let's get these bastards!"

As if her cry was the starting bell, the trainees burst into action. Fists battered, legs kicked. A few were cut by the otherworlders, several were knocked down, and one was even tossed into the street and run over by a car, its sensors not, well, sensing him in time.

Where was McKell? She couldn't see him. *He can take care of himself.*

The aliens moved quickly, strongly, assuredly, doing their damage before spinning and inflicting more. Too bad for them, she'd fought men who were quicker, stronger, and far more assured. She ducked when she needed to duck, punched in the throat, chest, stomach, and groin when given the opportunity, and jumped out of the way when all else failed.

They could have bitten her, that would have infected her, but they didn't. Didn't even try. And it was strange. The fight would have been over then. Instead, they punched and kicked her. The others weren't so lucky. They were knifed.

Jeremy's arms looked like tattered ribbons, and the rest of the gang like discarded rags. Noelle faired better than any of them, even the aliens. She'd confiscated three blades already, and slammed the hilts into their owners' temples. All three fell to the pavement, unconscious. Ava thought she spied blood on one—a cracked lip. There wasn't time to check it out. Or worry.

The moment they hit, they disappeared. They weren't just invisible, they were gone. Ava tried to kick one as he fell, not realizing what would happen, and encountered only air, falling flat on her ass. Oxygen abandoned her in one massive heave; stars winked over her eyes.

Through those stars, she could see a bulky black form flying her way, silver blade flashing in the sunlight. She barely had enough breath to shout, "Tag team!"

Noelle understood instantly. With a whirl, her friend was in front of her, absorbing the impact. She knew where Ava was, and managed to send the male away from her. He hit the pavement, hard, his skull cracking. Every muscle in his body relaxed, his head lolling to the side, and like the others, he disappeared. Only, he left a puddle of blood behind. No maybe about it.

"Shit!" Ava shouted, scrambling back and dragging Noelle with her. "Schön blood!"

Probably looking for a host . . .

With the thought, her stomach cramped, and she moved in front of Noelle, as if she could block her friend from contamination. She would rather endure infection herself then risk Noelle. Or McKell. Hell, she'd willingly accept the disease if it meant saving them.

A second later, a wave of dizziness hit her. Before she had time to panic, that wave dissipated.

The trainees caught on quick and scampered onto the street, willing to risk any oncoming traffic over the disease. Several Schön warriors were still standing, still geared up for—and clearly wanting—a fight.

They approached . . . Stun rays hit them; they didn't stop.

Ava geared up, too, waiting. "Anyone touch it?" she demanded.

A chorus of "no"s rang out, but none of them sounded sure. No, they sounded scared.

Once again she glanced over to where McKell had been standing. This time, she saw him. Her eyes widened, her stomach clenching. He was down, an ax handle sticking out of his back, but he was pulling himself to his hands and knees, shaking his head to clear his mind, irises glazed but expression determined, furious. His exposed skin was bright red and blistered, steam rising from him and curling around him.

Fury of her own filled her, so much fury, as bright as the sun currently was. Worry and dread, too, but they couldn't compete with the fury. No one but Ava was allowed to hurt him. She forgot about the spilled blood, forgot about the consequences. Only thoughts of saving McKell had any bearing.

She launched forward—or would have, if Noelle hadn't grabbed her by the shoulders, tossed her to the ground, and pinned her.

"No," her friend shouted. "Stay."

"They hurt McKell," she screeched, struggling for all she was worth.

Noelle held tight. "He'll live."

"You don't know that!" Damn it, how was her friend so strong? "He needs my help."

"I can't let you risk it."

"You don't have a choice." Ava managed to twist

free and was on her feet a second later, stalking toward her prey.

Two steps in, she saw past the red haze surrounding her and realized that McKell, injured though he was, had things under control. He had snapped the necks of all but one warrior, who was flailing in his grip. Stilling. Dropping. Disappearing.

And just like that, the fight was over. The physical part, at least.

"Call Mia," Ava threw over her shoulder. "This area needs to be quarantined."

Her heart pounded in her chest as she rushed toward McKell. His gaze burned her, and he met her halfway, his arms immediately wrapping around her. Those same arms had just murdered four men, but they were tender with her.

"Tell me you're okay," he commanded.

"I'm okay, but you, you were stabbed in the back." She held him as tight as she could, praying she never had to let go. Then she remembered his skin—now she could actually *hear* the sizzle—and tugged him into the shadows between two buildings.

She removed her shirt, uncaring who saw her bra, and tried to pull the material over his head, protecting him where the shadows couldn't reach. He flinched, grabbed her wrists, and stopped her.

"What are you doing?"

"Helping you." She tried again.

Again he stopped her. "Your shirt will cover your beautiful breasts or nothing at all." He practically wrestled the fabric out of her hands and jerked it back over her head. All the while, his gaze swept the agents behind them. He hissed at anyone who looked her way.

Ava thought she heard Noelle laugh as she hugged him, ready to restart that holding-on-forever thing. How close had she come to losing him?

"Uh, Ava, sweetheart? You're running your fingers through the very wound you mentioned," he gritted out.

That's right, and she didn't stop. "We almost died, and here I am, alive and affectionate. Yet you're standing there complaining about a little wound?"

"Yes! That hurts. And it's massive."

She grinned as she loosened her grip, rocked back on her heels, and stared up at him, reassured, happy, thankful. "You're such a baby."

"You're a vixen." His fingers tangled in her hair, angling her chin higher. "You'll never allow yourself to be taken unaware again. Vow it."

"I vow it. But you, too, Ax. You've got to be more attentive to your surroundings."

His lips twitched with humor. "I vow it."

They both knew they couldn't keep those vows, but Ava didn't care about that either. She felt better, knowing they would *try* to be more careful.

"Mia says she'll be here in five," Noelle called.

Ava tensed, reminded that the real danger hadn't passed yet. "One or all of us could be infected," she whispered. "There was blood on the ground. Infected blood."

"I know," he replied gravely. "I don't fear for myself, but for you. And if you're infected, I'm going to turn you." He latched onto her forearms and shook her. "Do you understand?"

Turned, she'd have a chance with him. To make things work, despite her hang-ups and fears. And having almost lost him, she was suddenly on board with that plan. Before, she'd hated the thought of never being able to go out in the sun again. But what did the daylight matter if she couldn't be with McKell?

"I—okay," she said. "Okay. I don't like being forced to do it before I'm ready, but okay."

"Thank God." He jerked her into his body, kissed her, tongue thrusting deep.

She took, she gave, she conquered. Ultimately, she submitted. They made love with their mouths, savoring, slow one moment, lightning fast and grasping at each other the next. It was a desperate kiss, one born of fear and determination. Of passion and more of that fear.

He might be selfish, possessive, and straight-up mean, but he left her reeling, falling, and reaching for an anchor. For him. *He* was her anchor. Had been since the day she'd met him.

He didn't run when a fight got rough. He made the fight rougher. He didn't turn away when she threw attitude in his face. He got right up in *her* face. He didn't back down, he didn't cry, he didn't bend to her will.

Actually, he bent to no one's will.

A relationship with him would never be easy, but it would be fun. And yeah, if things ever fell apart, she would be destroyed. She doubted she could be with him and not give him everything. He wouldn't settle for anything but full measure. Men like him never did. Not that there was anyone like him. So decision made. She was in it for the long haul, no matter the reason he wanted her. Human, vampire, trash, royalty. Good enough, not good enough. She would give him everything—and demand equal measure.

In the distance, she heard sirens.

Fear of infection hit her again, and she ended the kiss. She'd told McKell someone "might be" infected, but she knew the truth. Someone *was* infected. No question. When Schön blood left its host, it always found another. She and Noelle had been closest.

McKell licked his lips as though savoring her taste as he smoothed the hair from her brow. His hand was shaking. "I won't allow them to separate us."

"Good," she said with a nod. She had a feeling she would need him in the coming hours.

Tires squealed as vehicles parked. Finally, she looked away from McKell—one of the hardest things she'd ever done—and faced the coming agents. They wore protective gear from the top of their heads to the soles of their feet, not an inch of skin visible. They knew it wouldn't help, but it probably made them feel better.

First thing they did was find the blood splattered over the concrete and spray some kind of chemical over it. They had to know the disease had already found a new host, that the blood was no longer contaminated.

How long until the newly infected sickened? She gulped.

The new agents hustled her, the once-again-sizzling McKell, Noelle, and the trainees into a metal van. Without a word. The door locked, sealing them inside. There was a bench on each side, hard, no cushions. Everyone, including McKell, sat. She'd expected him to balk at such treatment, but he never did. And when she tried to sit between him and Noelle, he tugged her into his lap.

She snuggled close, her gaze finding and staying on her friend. The fear Ava felt was mirrored in Noelle's pretty gray eyes. Ava reached out. Noelle did the same. They twined fingers, squeezed. Their earlier fight was forgotten.

"Now isn't the time to make out, girls," McKell said. Was that, dare she think it, amusement in his voice? "Well, all right. If you insist. You can kiss, but make it quick."

"Wow. McKell sharing something he considers his." Noelle smacked her lips in mock astonishment. "Will wonders never cease?"

"When you've had something precious taken away from you," he said, "you learn to guard everything else. Especially that which means the most to you." His warm breath trekked over her temple. "Are you comfortable, sweetheart?"

Something hot bloomed in Ava's chest. Sweetheart, again. "Oh, yes."

The vehicle jostled to a start, soon winding along the roads. The windows were darkened, so she couldn't see outside. Only the overhead light allowed her to see the men and women trapped with her.

Where they headed to AIR? To be locked up as Johnny was?

"Your jaw's swollen," McKell said, brushing his knuckles gently over the wound in question.

Even so slight a touch sent a sharp pain shooting through her, and she flinched. She hadn't realized she'd been punched there. "Now that you mention it, it *does* hurt like a son of a bitch."

"So," he said on a sigh, "you won't be able to do certain . . . things for a while. That's almost a deal breaker."

Things like suck that beautiful cock? She laughed, then flinched again. "Jaw wounds take the *longest* time to heal." His teasing was distracting her, lightening her mood. Maybe hers would do the same for him.

"How long?"

"Months."

His shoulders sagged. "I was playing at first. But months, you say?"

"Oh, yes." She burrowed her head in the hollow of his neck, hiding her grin. "And God forbid if I have to have surgery. I mean, the bones feel out of joint. Healing could take years."

"Years?" he squeaked.

"You, Ava Sans, are evil," Noelle said with a laugh of her own.

Ava slapped her shoulder. "Stop listening to our conversation."

"Then stop *having* a conversation for me to listen to. You know I can't help myself."

They didn't have to stop. The car did, and everyone in the van sobered instantly. Ava tensed. McKell crushed her to his chest as footsteps sounded. Then the doors opened, and Ava caught sight of multiple agents and an unfamiliar—and very intimidating—building. A warehouse, deserted, dark, nothing around it.

"Let's go," one of the agents said, motioning them out.

Twenty-nine

*T*hey were given a room—or, more aptly, a cell—of their own. Maybe because McKell threatened to rip their escorts' throats out if they pushed him and Ava into the same room as all the others. They believed him. Which did, in fact, save their lives.

His parting words to them? "Watch us through the window, and I'll know. I'll feel your eyes, hear your heartbeats. And nothing will prevent me from reaching through it and, what? Slicing your goddamn throats."

The door closed with a click, enclosing him in a four-by-four with his darling Ava. They had a cot, padded walls, and a toilet, but he paid those things no heed. He stood in front of a door without any discernible seams, listening beyond. Footsteps pounded, voices murmured, and the rush of blood faded. Again the guards had heeded his advice and saved their own lives.

That done, McKell switched his full attention to Ava. She sat on the cot, elbows resting on her knees. Once again there was fear in her lovely eyes, and he didn't like it. Distraction, that's what she needed. Had worked before, in the van.

Touch, that's what *he* needed. He had to reaffirm that she lived.

When he'd seen those warriors appear behind her, hit her, when he'd tried to race to her, only to be stabbed in the back before he could get to her, he'd experienced utter despair and instant rage. He couldn't abide the thought of her being hurt. He couldn't abide the thought of failing her.

She was everything to him.

And she would let him turn her. He'd never thought he would have that option, but thankfully, fate had planned otherwise, and he knew his true gift, or vampire ability, was his blood. He was finally on the right path. Being together. Forever. Only thing he didn't like was the fact that she wasn't actually ready for the change. Deep down, he didn't want to turn her before she was ready.

The Schön queen had asked him if he loved her. He hadn't known then, but he knew now. He did. He loved her. He couldn't live without her, and it had nothing to do with needing her blood. He needed *her*. Ava. Her smile, her laugh, her scent, her hands, her breath, her stubbornness, her fury, her wit. Everything. Every part of her.

"Ava," he said, needing to tell her all of that. He didn't wait for her reply. He approached her and knelt in front of her, clasping her hands and feeling her heat, her pulse. Yes, touch—connection—was exactly what he'd needed.

"McKell." His name was a plea, a benediction.

She'd wanted to be touched as much as he'd wanted to touch her.

In an instant, holding hands wasn't enough. He gathered her in his arms, pivoted, and sat on the cot. He settled her in his lap while petting her hair, her nape, her arm. "I have to tell you something," he began. There was no better time for a confession.

She was just a little stiff when she said, "That sounds serious."

"It is. I . . . love you." How would she react? He'd never declared his feeling to another. Ever. "I love you more than anything and anyone."

The stiffness drained from her. "Really?"

"Really." Part of him had expected a denial, he realized as a relieved breath fanned from him. "You delight me, Ava, in so many ways."

"Tell me those ways."

Anyone else would have laved him with kisses; Ava demanded proof. He smothered a laugh he knew she wouldn't understand. "I'm free to be myself with you. I have fun with you, even when circumstances are dire. You didn't have the easiest life, yet you never let that hinder you. You grew into a strong, stunning woman. *My* woman." He didn't want to pressure her into saying the words back to him. In this, he would *not* rush her. He stated his case and quickly changed the subject. "Now. Tell me a secret about yourself. You promised to tell me 'later,' and now is later."

At first, she gave no response. Then she was sniffling and shaking, grinning and crying. Mostly crying.

"What thoughts are dancing through your head, love?" Of all the reactions he'd thought she would give him, that wasn't even on the list.

She cried a little harder. Then, "I—I—all right," she said, ignoring his question. "I'll tell you a secret."

He kissed her temple. "Let's hear it." He wanted to know everything about her, even at the expense of his need to soothe her. He wanted to pamper her for the rest of eternity.

"Well." She wiped her eyes with the back of her wrist. "I adore old kung fu movies. That's where I picked up my mad ass-beating skills."

Again, he tried not to laugh. "That's a wee bit surprising. I've seen a few of them, and know kung fu is all about fighting with—and don't take this the wrong way, love. Fighting with honor."

"Are you saying I'm not honorable?" She straightened and glared at him.

"Ava, love. You tasered me. Stabbed me. Stunned me twice. You lack honor, and I'm glad. Honor won't win a battle."

"True." With a sigh, she relaxed back against him. "Now tell me a secret about you."

He thought about what to tell her, and before he knew it, five minutes had passed in silence. She waited patiently. "I don't think children are too terrible of monsters," he finally said. An easy fact based in truth; one she might like.

She knew him well enough to understand what he was saying. "You want a family?"

"One day, yes."

"With . . . me?"

"*Only* with you." And when she turned vampire, children would most likely be possible. If not, well, he wouldn't be too disappointed because he would have Ava all to himself.

She pressed a soft kiss into his nape, lingered . . . licked. "I don't think kids are too terrible of monsters, either."

His blood heated, rushing through his veins to meet her lips. Though he wanted to toss her down on the cot, strip her, have her, he didn't move. The conversation was too important.

"McKell?"

"Yes." He hadn't meant to growl. That heat . . .

"I—I love you."

Thank God. He hadn't wanted to rush her, but damn! He'd needed to hear those three words so badly. "You don't have to say it back if you—"

"I love you. I've never said that to anyone before, but I do. I love you. You're stubborn, possessive, and passionate. You make me laugh, and ache, and dream. And sometimes, like now, you make me feel so special. I like that."

"You *are* special and I want to make you feel that way always." His arms tightened around her, probably breaking her sweet little bones. But he had two choices, and he knew it. Either hold her like this, or throw her down as he still craved. "When did you realize your feelings for me?"

"When you were bleeding to death."

He barked out a laugh, unable to stop himself this time. "That's all it took, hmm? Almost dying?"

"Mm-hm." Her fingers traced the scar on his chest, and he leaned into the gentle touch.

Can't throw her down, can't throw her down. "Had I known, I would've allowed someone to stab me much sooner. But you do realize now that I was never close to death, yes? I'm too strong to die." And he had too much to live for.

The wicked tip of her tongue emerged, giving his pulse another caress. "Speaking of dying, what are we going to do about our little problem?"

"Little problem. So you don't mean the big problem you're creating in his pants?"

For the first time since he'd met her, she giggled. He adored the sound.

"You're talking about the queen?" he asked. "Our imprisonment?"

"Yes. I think . . . I think we're gonna have to escape this compound. No one knows how to defeat her, and you're the best chance AIR has of winning."

"She defeated me before."

"Yeah, but now you know what to expect."

True. He didn't mention how easily the queen adapted to *everything,* even his tricks.

"So you're going to do it? Escape? Fight her?"

"Of course. I want you safe, love. By fair means or

foul, I'll see it done." And he would. Whatever he had to do.

Ava's teeth came out to play, nibbling where she'd licked. "Well, then, you'll need to be properly nourished."

In seconds, his need racketed close to I-can't-control-myself territory. Biting her, drinking her, holding her, hands roving . . . He might not be strong enough to turn her down. "What are you saying, love?" Maybe he had misunderstood.

"That I want you to bite me," she said, confirming his thoughts. "You need the blood, and I need to feed you. *Want* to feed you." She traced a heart on his chest. "Let me do this."

He captured her hand and kissed the fluttering pulse at her wrist. He was shaking, mouth watering with the force of his desires. "Are you sure?" No, he wasn't strong enough.

She lifted her head and peered at him, a tigress determined to get her way. "I'm sure. So let me do this for you, McKell. Victor. *My* Victor. For me. I tortured you for days, not giving you more than a few sips. Let me give you everything."

Like that, he *did* reach the point where he lost control. More than his mouth filling with moisture, his tongue was swelling. His teeth were aching. His heart was threatening to explode. "You're sure you're not too weakened from the fight?" he asked again, because he would rather die than hurt her further.

Slowly she grinned. "Believe me, I wouldn't lie about something like that."

He tumbled her to the cot so that he loomed above her, and she immediately turned her head, offering an unobstructed view of her neck. Her lovely neck. Her pulse fluttered there, too, and he could hear the rush of her decadent blood.

Mine.

First he licked her, softening her skin. She moaned. Then he sucked, drawing the blood up and causing it to pool, readying for him. She groaned. Then, sweet heaven, *then* he bit. Sucked. Swallowed.

And reared back in horror.

The hot flow of her blood trickled from his mouth, but he didn't lick it up. He wiped it away with his hand, trying not to cringe or shout.

"Ava," he said shakily.

Frowning, she sat up. Suddenly there were dark circles under her eyes. "What's wrong?"

No, he thought, nearing hysteria in a heartbeat of time. *No, no, no.* He knew he could turn her, had planned for it. Would. But he was suddenly so damn afraid. What if that didn't work? What if she died anyway? What if *he* killed her?

"McKell! What is it? What's wrong? You're scaring me."

He swallowed the lump forming in his throat. "You're . . . you're the one infected, love. You have the Schön disease."

* * *

At first, Ava denied McKell's claim. As the hours ticked away, her warrior pacing in front of her, trying to decide what to do, how best to save her, she could feel herself weakening, denial no longer possible. She could even hear a voice inside her head. A female voice. Not her own, either. This voice grew stronger with every minute that passed, and the stronger it became, the more it seemed to take over. As if Ava's will was no longer her own.

"Turn me," she said to McKell—as she had the thousand other times since he'd said those damning words. *You're the one infected.*

"We don't know what happened to Johnny," he replied. Again. And just like before, he banged on the glass panel in their cell. "Tell us about Johnny, damn it!" But he'd warned the agents away, so no one responded.

She'd never seen McKell so panicked. And that he was for her, well, if she'd still harbored any doubts about his feelings for her, she no longer did. He wanted to change her, not because he viewed vampires as superior, but because he loved *her* and feared losing her.

A sudden pain tore through her chest, and she groaned.

McKell rushed back to her side, cupping her jaw and forcing her to look up at him. Black dots were winking in front of her, weaving together, forming a solid wall.

"Ava."

"Turn me. You're the one who insisted."

"I know. But . . . I'm so afraid. I would rather you infect a thousand others and live than risk poisoning you with my blood."

"You won't kill—"

"You don't know that. Not for sure. We have no idea how Johnny responded after the initial exposure, and I think we both remember the way he screamed."

Yeah. Johnny's pain-filled scream still haunted her. "I love you, and I'm willing to risk *anything* to be with you," she said, and she meant it. Maybe it had taken nearly losing him to realize the truth, but she did. She loved him.

"No. Besides everything else, you're not ready. You said so yourself before we got here." His grip tightened on her. "There has to be another way to save you. There just has to."

A terrible thought hit her. What if she'd exposed *him* to the disease? They'd kissed, and he'd drunk from her. "Oh, God, McKell. What if you're sick?"

His hard expression didn't change. "I've been watching for a symptom. Nothing so far."

She'd lied to him, she realized. She wouldn't risk "anything." She wouldn't risk *him*. She would rather die. And she just might. Because there was no way in hell she would sleep with anyone else. Even to save herself.

Tears burned her eyes, eyes that now felt like they'd been rubbed raw with sandpaper. Another symptom for her? What did it matter? she thought next, nearing hysteria. Finally she'd committed to someone, and she was going to lose him.

"Ava, damn it!" McKell punched the cot, right beside her temple, and she bounced up at the force he used. "I love you more than I love myself. Do you hear me? I wasn't exaggerating earlier. I love you so damn much, I hurt. There has to be a way to fix this. To save you and keep you human."

Another pain tore through her, and she squeezed her lids shut. That didn't help, even a little. Only managed to hurt her more. To hold her cries inside, she bit her lip until she tasted blood. Rotten blood. She gagged, and McKell patted her back, leaning closer to her. Gradually she became aware of a gnawing, gut-wrenching hunger . . . of McKell's divine scent . . .

A taste, one taste, she thought. Of his skin, his blood, his organs. That would ease the pain. Surely.

"Ava?"

Her eyes widened when she realized the direction of her thoughts. Oh, God. She wanted to eat him.

Gasping in horror, she flattened her palms on his chest and pushed him. "Go! Please! Go!" The tears rained in streaks of acid, scalding her checks. "You have to go."

"I'm not leaving you."

"Go to the queen. Kill her. Because if you stay here, I'll try and kill *you*. And I would hate myself, McKell. *Please*." The last left her on a choking sob.

If he replied, she would never know. The voice . . . consuming her, becoming all that she knew.

You stupid bitch! You weren't supposed to become infected. Now I can't use your body.

Ava found herself wanting to apologize. She loved that voice. It was the calm in the storm, her anchor. She frowned. No, McKell was her anchor. She hated that voice and she—was edging toward McKell, teeth sharpening, she realized. Gasping again, she reared back.

"I'll fix this, sweetheart," McKell said flatly. "I'll fix this, I swear. I have no life without you."

Thirty

McKell kept an eye on Ave as he paced through their cell. She hadn't leapt at him and attacked, but she was poised to do so at any moment. He could have busted out and probably should have. He'd drunk from her, he was strong enough, wasn't sickening, but he couldn't force himself to leave her.

Soon she would die.

No! Ava loved him. She'd offered everything he'd ever wanted. The love, of course, plus acceptance, challenge, and understanding. And then, a heartbeat later, that had all been taken away. She truly was dying, slowly wasting away. Soon she would kill. There was hunger in her eyes. Hunger for human flesh. He would give all that he was, even that, to save her.

Sexual intercourse and the exchange of blood, and possibly saliva, were the only ways to pass the disease. He could now be infected himself, as she'd guessed, but he honestly didn't think he was. Hours had passed, a wretched infinity, but he was fine. Still strong. Like Bride's, his blood must hold the cure. Except, the disease always adapted quickly. Because *he'd* been exposed, because *he* was well, he could drain himself into Ava and still not save her.

He could actually do more harm than good. Johnny's scream . . .

There was only one thing left for McKell to do. He had to reverse time, and he had to do it *now*. Whatever was necessary, he had to stop Ava from becoming infected. That was the only way.

If he did manage to reverse time, though, she would no longer love him. She wouldn't see him stabbed, wouldn't realize her heart belonged to him, and might try to kick him out of her life. If he didn't, she would die. So really, there was no contest. He simply *had* to reverse time.

Stopping time was easy. He simply thought, *Halt*, and it obeyed. Stopping the people around him, so that they didn't realize time was passing, was easy, too. He simply thought, *Freeze*, and they obeyed. Making time whizz by faster, he could do that, too. But for the last hour, he'd been thinking, *Reverse* and *Rewind* and *Backward*, yet nothing had happened. He was running out of words to say, things to try.

You can do this. "Time bends to my will," he gritted out. As Ava would say, "Time is my bitch." Nothing. No reaction.

Ava watched him, licked her lips.

Concentrate. He had to try something else. He thought back to when he was a young child. Way, *way* back. He'd had no control of his gift, freezing time and people when he'd had no desire to do so, unable to freeze them when he did want to, but his parents hadn't seemed concerned.

Let your worries fade, his mother had said in her gentle voice. She'd had long black hair and vivid violet eyes, her face so perfect it could have been sculpted by an angel. *They merely block your passion for this task.*

Besides his few conversations with Ava, McKell hadn't thought of his mother in so long, his chest ached. How he wished she could have met Ava. Granted, she would have been horrified at first, because there'd been no one more timid than Carina, and no one more determined to ensure propriety was adhered to in the home, but with time, the two would have fallen in love.

He pictured his father, standing behind his mother, hands resting on the woman's delicate shoulders. Now there was a man who hadn't cared about propriety in any way. He'd loved his woman, though, and had striven to make her happy, despite the whisper about her infidelity.

Who is stronger? his father had asked. The complete opposite of his wife, Dante had looked as rough-and-tumble as a man could. Scars all over his face and arms, lips always thinned as if stuck in a perpetual scowl. *You or time?*

Me, he'd thought then. *Me,* he thought now. He squared his shoulders, closed his eyes. He blanked his mind. *I'm in control. Time bends to my will.*

Over and over he repeated the claim. About the hundredth time, he stared to believe. Yes, he could do this. He was strong. Stronger. He managed to release his worry, his cares, and pictured the threads of time as he'd had to do as a child. Those threads were woven together, a road leading forward, backward, side to side. Millions of tiny little lights traveled that road, all heading in the same direction. Only a few veered off course and moved along the curving side paths.

"McKell," Ava said.

For her own good, he ignored her. *I'm in control. Time bends to my will.* As a child, he'd needed to touch the threads. To trail his fingertips in the direction he wanted to go. He reached out.

"McKell!" Such a hungry, hungry growl. She would jump him. Any moment now, and she would jump him.

McKell latched on to the threads, experienced a jolt of electricity, almost dropped them but managed to stop time as a warm current of breath wafted over his neck. Shit. He hadn't heard Ava move, but she had closed the distance between them. Had almost bitten into him.

Concentrate. All the lights stopped winking, just sort of waiting for his next move. *I can do this.* He tugged, as hard as he could, his shoulders nearly pulling from their sockets. Nothing. The threads remained in place. Just like the other times he'd tried this. He didn't give up, didn't lose confidence.

He tugged again and again, his palms stinging, his entire body still vibrating with the electricity. When he stilled, he barely had any energy left. Damn it! There had to be a way to move these threads.

Okay. So. He took stock. Tugging obviously wouldn't

work, but he couldn't let go because time would kick back up the moment he did, and Ava would start munching on him.

Ava. His precious Ava. He *would* return her to the way she'd been, so pink and fresh and vital . . . An image of her consumed his mind—and as easily as if he'd been pulling a feather on a string, the lights moved backward.

At first, he could only stand there, disbelieving and incoherent. How had . . . what had . . . But even those thoughts tapered off when he realized he was peering over at *himself*. He and Ava were still inside the cell, but she was on his lap, and they were talking and hugging.

Had he done it? Had he truly reversed time?

Emboldened, he tugged the threads again. They remained in place. What the hell? He nearly shouted in frustration. What had changed? What had he done differently? He thought back. He'd decided tugging didn't work, and had then visualized Ava.

He pictured her again. Cheeks pink, skin fresh, body vital. The threads glided backward another inch, and he watched himself lift Ava off his lap and place her on the cot. Watched himself stride away from her—backward.

Relief and joy both flooded him, consuming him, overshadowing the painful jolts still working through him. Yes. Yes! He truly had done it.

He knew now he couldn't manipulate time with force. Not when going in reverse. He had to manipulate time with pictures. Pictures of . . . who he wanted to see, when he wanted to see them?

He pictured Ava as she'd been in the van, and once more the threads glided back until he was viewing exactly what he'd imagined. He began sweating, shaking, the threads fighting for release, burning his palms. *Come on. Just a little further.* He pictured Ava on the street, walking beside him, at the same time tugging those threads so forcefully his bones rattled.

Seconds later, he saw himself, Ava, and the street. At that point in their lives, they hadn't yet come into contact with the Schön queen and her men. Here, Ava was healthy, whole. This was it, then, the time frame he needed.

He almost let go. Almost. What would happen next? Would the man he was now disappear, along with his memories? No, he thought with determination. No. That couldn't—wouldn't—happen. He always remembered when he manipulated time in the other direction. Why not this way, too?

Only way one to find out . . .

Remember, remember, please remember. Deep breath in, hold . . . hold, release. He opened his fingers as the breath expelled from him. The threads jumped as far away from him as they could, bouncing together as they realigned.

The electricity abandoned him in a rush, leaving McKell burning, scalding, blistering like he did when he ventured into the daylight, and just when he was about to roar from the pain, he blinked, the pain faded, and he realized he was standing alongside Ava, not just watching but actually walking down that sidewalk with her.

"Wait," Ava suddenly said, and he knew—*knew*— what was about to happen.

He had remembered.

He wanted to whoop as she stopped and withdrew her cell phone. Wanted to hug her as she frowned. Somehow he managed to stay where he was,

"Just got a text from Dallas. The Schön queen plans to target a couple. She'll threaten one so the other will do whatever she wants. He says she can read minds, so we aren't to think about what we would do to her if that happens."

"He's right," McKell said, heart slamming against his ribs. This was it. He couldn't mess this up. Had to keep Ava safe.

Her frown deepened. "How do you know?" Clearly, she didn't remember.

Still. The question pleased him. Already he was changing the future. "Just do. Come on."

She pocketed her phone, and he pulled her into motion. Faster, faster, his determination to save her so intense his shaking renewed. He led her away from her apartment building and to a nice coffee shop. Inside, he forced her into a chair and motioned distractedly for Noelle and the trainees, who had followed them, to find their own.

"Buy her the biggest butterscotch latte they have,"

he commanded Noelle. "And do not let her leave. Do you understand? Her life is at stake."

Confusion fell like a curtain over Noelle's features. "O-kay. How, may I ask, is her life at stake if she doesn't get a latte?"

He ignored her, his gaze locking on Ava. Such pretty pink skin, such healthy blood flowing underneath. That wasn't going to change. Not this time. "Stay here," he said, willing to beg. "There's an army of Schön warriors stationed around your apartment. If you go there, they'll kill you. Do you understand? I've seen it. And for God's sake, whatever happens, remember that I love you."

Her jaw dropped. "You—*what*?"

In this new reality, he hadn't yet told her that, had he? "I love you. I love you for who you are, what you are, though we'll discuss turning you into a vampire at a later date. Perhaps after I allow someone to almost kill me. But until then, stay safe, damn it."

"Almost kill you?" All the color abandoned her face. "Stay safe? McKell, what are you talking —"

He kissed her, hard, silencing her. He allowed himself to enjoy, because he couldn't help himself. He'd come so close to losing her, was so relieved by this second chance. When he raised his head, her eyes were glazed, her lips red and swollen.

"I love you," he repeated, then turned away. A bell chimed as he left the shop.

Part of him expected Ava to follow, but he didn't pick up her scent as he headed toward her apartment.

Last time, he'd tried to freeze the queen and had failed. He'd tried to choke her and had failed. There was only one other thing he could think to do. And it meant . . .

Shit! It most likely meant losing Ava, he realized, bile churning in his stomach. Even after reversing time, he still might not be able to keep her. He almost backtracked, almost returned to her, gathered her up, and ran away with her.

But he had to do this. He couldn't allow that bitch of a queen to walk freely, so powerful, so assured, threatening his woman and those she loved. He would rather die keeping Ava safe than live while she remained in danger.

The bile mixed with another round of determination. His plan might still fail, but he would have tried. He would have done all that he could to protect his woman. That's what mattered.

Enough pondering, worrying, obsessing, he thought. Wouldn't do to warn the queen of the fate that now awaited her.

The moment he spied Ava's building, he slowed his steps, waiting . . . waiting . . . A doorway opened, just as before, glittering so prettily in the moonlight. McKell gulped back the lump forming in his throat, stopped time before he could change his mind, and sprinted forward. The queen hadn't been able to fight him right away last time, which meant she wouldn't be able to do so this time either.

He only had a minute, maybe two, to do his damage.

She was there, he knew she was, for he could once again smell her rot. Rage overtook him as he remembered where she'd stood. *You're going to pay, female.* He beelined for her, stretching out his arms.

Behind him, he heard Ava shout his name. "McKell! What are you doing? McKell!"

Damn her! Of course she hadn't remained behind. He'd been a fool to think she would. That wasn't in her nature, was one of the many reasons he loved her.

He couldn't allow her near the queen or the queen's men, so he increased his speed. *Boom!* He slammed into the bodies, four that he could tell, continuing to surge forward. He heard a feminine gasp, several male grunts, and drove them all straight into the waiting doorway.

Ava screamed, "*Nooo!* No! McKell! Where are you—"

As before, the suction began the moment he approached, pulling him faster and faster. Soon he lost the foundation under his feet. His world began to spin, the air darkening, thickening. The queen and her men shrieked, a horrified choir, and he lost his grip on them, too. Down, down he fell, still spinning, faster and faster.

Was this the eternity that awaited them all? To spin and spin and spin? Fine. He could accept that. For Ava, he'd suffer anything.

"McKell. Finally." A man's contented purr drifted into his ears.

McKell's momentum slowed, the spinning ceased,

and he was eased to his feet by gentle hands he couldn't see. His surroundings blinked into focus. A black sky was dotted by the very flickers of light he'd seen on the threads of time, an endless maze of midnight, both perfect and horrific because there was no beginning or end.

"Welcome home, my son."

Home? Son? He shook his head in denial, anger rising. "Who are you? Where are you?" *Come out and fight me, you bastard.* "Where are the ones I brought with me?"

"I'll tell you about them. In time." A second later, a man stepped from the darkness. He was tall, taller than McKell, with ankle-length black hair and eyes that glowed bright green. He looked human, for the most part, with a long forehead, a slashing nose, and a wide chin. His limbs stretched more than normal, and his body was a little thinner than average. He wore some kind of bodysuit that molded to his pale, pale skin.

McKell didn't rush him. Not yet. Information first. Killing second. "Are you the one who's been calling me?"

"Yes." Like the purr, the deep voice whispered straight into his head—but the man's lips never moved.

What kind of powers did this being wield? "Why?"

"I don't think you're ready to hear the answer." Still no movement from those lips.

"Tell me!"

"Give me time, and I will—"

"Tell me, damn it!"

The pause that followed his second demand extended uncomfortably. He thought he would be thrown back into that endless spin. Instead, the man sighed. "You're not ready for the truth, but I can see now that you will not calm down until you have answers. I wish I could fault you for your impatience, yet you are your father's son. And I—I am that father. *Your* father."

Even after the "my son" comment, the announcement still managed to shock him. "No," he automatically insisted. "No. My father is dead."

"I assure you. He is very much alive."

"No."

"Your mother once came to me as you have done. Did you know that? Did she tell you?"

"I heard rumors," he gritted out, hating to admit even that. To do so lent credit to the man's claim. "And sometimes I heard her crying at night when she thought no one listened."

The man, being, whatever, seemed to wilt at that. "She missed me as much as I missed her. I didn't want that for her."

"No." His hands fisted, the anger suddenly a living force inside him. He could handle anything but a false declaration of concern for his mother's well-being. At last he attempted to close the distance between them, to lash out, but he found that his feet were somehow rooted in place. "What have you done to me?"

His denial and question were ignored. "I saw her, wanted her, and talked to her as I talked to you. She, too, eventually joined me and we spent many months together. She grew to love me as I loved her, but always the husband stood in our way. She needed his blood, and mine would not sustain her."

As the man spoke—still straight into his mind— images colored the midnight canvas around them. Images of McKell's mother, here, dancing, dark hair flying. He heard her, too; her laughter stroked his ears, flinging him back to his childhood, to days in the caves, his bruises tended by loving hands, violet eyes watching him with concern.

"I—I am not your son," he croaked. "I can't be." He knew his father. Loved his father. Had mourned his father.

"Before you deny my claims, hear the rest. Please."

A moment passed. He nodded stiffly. What else could he do? He was still rooted in place, helpless. Still needed to know what had happened to the queen and her men. Antagonizing wouldn't help.

"She convinced me to let her go, to let the child I had given her go. She couldn't survive with him, nor could she tolerate the thought of leaving you behind. She said she would have no life without you, only one of despair and loneliness. And so I finally agreed, even though I feared you would be different from your kind. Set apart, perhaps loathed. Still. I swore I would not return to the caves, and I never did. I thought you would be lost to me forever, but you came to the surface. And now you have come to me."

Again, images formed around them. His mother tearfully clutching the man's cheeks as she begged him to understand. The man crying, too, hugging her fiercely, his heart already breaking.

"I sensed your trepidation, each time I approached you, but I also promised your mother I would not force you to come here, that I would not tell you who I was unless you did, that I would not interfere. So thank you. Thank you for offering me this opportunity to at last meet my son." He truly did sound grateful.

McKell fought for breath. He wanted to continue denying what the man was telling him, but tendrils of doubt were working through him. He could manipulate time, yet no other vampire could. Not even the *nefreti*. His mother had been barren with his father, yet months along in a pregnancy between one day and the next.

This was surreal, a total upheaval in everything he'd ever believed.

"How can you be my..." His jaw ached, he clenched the bones so tightly. He couldn't yet say the word *father*. Not in conjunction with this stranger. "Vampires can't procreate with anyone but their spouse."

Those green eyes softened. "I am . . . different. As are all my people. We live in this plane, able to open doorways into any world, any time. And so, during our months together, I returned your mother to her unmated days, though still my blood was not what she needed. And when we parted, I returned her as close to the day I took her as possible, without affecting her memory."

Unbelievable. Impossible. And yet . . . true. Suddenly he knew the truth deep in his soul. There was no reason to lie to him, nothing the man could gain. And he could actually scent the affection and joy wafting around him. Scents he'd learned because of Ava.

And really, everything made sense now. Who he was, what he was, what he could do, what he couldn't. His mother's sadness. She had loved this man, probably would have died here, unwilling to drink from anyone else, but had left him. Had lived. For McKell.

His anger drained, the fight leaving him. "What do you want with me?" he asked, realizing his feet had been freed. He could move unrestrained now. He did, approaching the man. He reached out, shaking, and touched that pale white skin. It was smooth, cool. "What's your name?"

Lips nearly as pale as his skin quirked at the corners. "I am called Viktor."

So they shared a name. That, more than anything, proved his mother's love for this man. "What do you want with me?" he asked again, adding, "Viktor."

The glow in those green eyes brightened. "Time. I want time, a chance to learn about each other. I can show you all the worlds in existence. I can show you people and riches you could not even imagine. I can take you to the sunless vampire world when it bloomed like a night flower, the petals rich and silky."

Time, yes. A little, he could give. A chance to know each other, he suddenly wanted that, too. "I have a woman." His eyes widened as he realized he might be able to return to her. That he might not be stuck here. His . . . father had returned his mother to her world. He could do the same for McKell.

Some of the glow dimmed. "I have seen her, this Ava Sans. She is very lovely, but she is not bonded to you as your mate."

"I want her to be." His arm fell to his side. "I want to be with her. Always. I *have* to be with her. Not only for blood, but for . . . life. I'm nothing without her."

Viktor's head tilted to the side, and sadness claimed his long features. "She followed you from the café. She saw you disappear and broke down. The warriors who remained on the street appeared and attacked, because they, too, saw you take their queen. Ava was infected. She will die, and you will no longer need her blood."

No. *No!* His knees almost buckled as panic infused his every cell. He hadn't risked everything, his life, his happiness, his future, for his woman to die out there, alone, afraid. "Take me back to her. Now. If you won't, I'll reverse time again and I won't come here." A threat he *would* see through.

When his father next replied, McKell understood exactly where he'd gotten his ruthless streak. "Give me what I ask for. Time, a chance, and I will return the Schön to their world before they have a chance to infect your Ava. That will not keep them away from

Earth forever, but as barren as their planet is, they will be too weak to return quickly."

Ava would be safe, then. Ava would be healthy. Would live. "Before I agree, tell me something. What did you do with the ones I brought with me?" He could still hear them screaming.

"They are between portals at the moment, but again, I can't hold them like that forever. I need to send them somewhere. Agree, and I'll send them to their home planet with the others."

"Ava—"

"I won't keep you from her forever, McKell. Just give me time. Please. Agree, and you *will* see her again."

"When?"

"Soon."

"Soon" wasn't soon enough, he wanted her *now*. "I'll give you a week."

"And we'll learn nothing about each other. A year."

Everything inside him rebelled. "A month."

"Six months, and that's as little as I'll accept." That purring voice had firmed.

"She will be healthy? Remain healthy?"

"Yes."

McKell knew Viktor wouldn't budge on this. Their determination was obviously equaled. "I . . . agree." Damn, damn, damn! Six months without Ava. He wasn't sure he would survive. Physically, yes, he probably could. He could sip from others. Still. He'd be weak and emaciated when he finally reached her and he would have to be careful not to accidentally drain her at his first true feeding, but he wasn't going to allow her to be purged from his system. Ever. "Go one day over the allotted six months, and I'll tear this world apart—and you with it. I don't care who you are."

"Agreed."

Thirty-one

*T*hree days after McKell had told her how much he loved her, that he wanted her safe, Ava realized he'd abandoned her. She'd expected the abandonment from the first, but had maybe kinda sorta convinced herself it wouldn't happen.

What made it worse was that she knew he hadn't wanted to leave her. There hadn't been a good-bye in his last kiss. Merely relief and joy. He wouldn't have felt those things if he'd been planning on leaving her. Because he loved her. He fucking loved her. But he was missing, and there wasn't a goddamn thing she could do about it.

She knew he would come back to her if he could. Which meant he *couldn't* come back.

Oh, God. A new round of sobbing started up.

The last few minutes together kept replaying in her mind. He'd plopped her in that seat at the coffee shop and taken off as if his feet were on fire. She'd sat there a moment, staring at Noelle, confused, overjoyed that her live-in had just admitted to deeper feelings, real feelings, when she'd realized he had also told her that Schön warriors were at her apartment. In a snap, she'd known he meant to battle them on his own.

Like she could allow that to happen.

She'd gathered her group and taken off after him. Only to watch him disappear. She hadn't known what had happened to him, where he'd gone, *how* he'd gone. But she'd waited. For hours. A day, then two. Never moving from the sidewalk. On this third morning, she'd been weak, shaky, crying, nearing hysteria because he could be hurt or worse, and Noelle had managed to overpower her and whisk her home.

Along the way, her friend had told her that Johnny and every other Schön-infected person locked in AIR headquarters had disappeared the same morning McKell had. Just boom, there one moment, gone the next.

Where? How? she wondered. Where they with McKell? Was he infected now?

And then, yesterday, Johnny had been returned to AIR. Again, just boom, pop, he was there when he hadn't been a moment before. He'd been confused, yet healthy. And thirsty. So thirsty. Thanks to McKell's blood, he was a vampire now. And he wanted Ava.

He called all the time. Only once had she answered, and that had been to ask him where he'd gone, how he'd gotten back, if he'd seen McKell. He hadn't known, so she didn't care to talk to him.

Another round of sobs started, and she rolled to her side. She lay on the bed she'd shared with McKell for one glorious sexcapade, his scent all over the sheets. She might never leave.

Noelle was in the process of packing McKell's things, trying to clear any memory of him from Ava's mind. A good plan. Except for the fact that he was burned into her memory no matter what was around her.

Ava squeezed her eyes shut, holding the rest of the tears in place.

The mattress eased down on one side. "You look terrible," Noelle said gently.

"Don't care."

"Hellina's doing well. She's sleeping on the couch with a nice warm bellyful of my blood."

"Good."

"Okay, how about this." The bed dipped again as Noelle stretched out beside her, turned, and draped an arm over her waist. "I'm gonna do you a solid and let you out of your promise to go to my mom's cock-tail party."

"Thanks," she offered, and it was the most she could do. She hadn't felt this lonely, this abandoned— didn't matter if McKell had left willingly or not— even when her father had taken off.

While she'd stood propped against that building, feet aching unbearably, heart aching worse, she'd called Mia, asked if there was a way to track McKell or any of the others. The answer had been an un-equivocal no. They'd disappeared as if they'd never been.

She hadn't cared, though, because the disease they'd all feared had been seemingly eradicated in one swoop. AIR had broken down and tested Johnny upon his return and discovered McKell's blood *had* healed him.

When he realized he couldn't get her by phone, Johnny had tried to visit her a few times, but Noelle had barred him from the apartment. McKell would have beaten him into pulp for daring to try to steal what was his. If he'd been here.

Great. More sobs.

"McKell's crazy about you," Noelle continued in that gentle tone. "He'll come back. One day."

"I don't want to talk about him. I can't talk about him."

"Okay, okay. I'll take mercy on you and change the subject." Soft fingers stroked her hair. "So get this. I was at AIR headquarters this morning, and Dallas and Hector Dean were both there. Both of them were watching me like I was a turkey and it was Thanksgiving."

"You should be used to that." The words were thick, her nose stuffed. "All men look at you that way."

"Yeah, but they also looked ready to kill me. As if I was a Thanksgiving turkey that hadn't yet had my neck snapped and feathers plucked."

She sniffed. "Why would they want to kill you? You're one of them now."

"That's what's so crazy about the whole situation."

"Maybe you misread them. Maybe they were looking at you but thinking of something else."

A pause. Then, "Maybe. So let's backtrack to

McKell." Noelle's mercy hadn't lasted long. "He can't exist without your blood, Ava. Like I said, he'll be back."

"Bride told me that vampires can drink a potion that removes the need for their . . . mate's blood. That once they ingest it, they can drink from anyone they want again. And that they can never . . . they can't ever . . . they can't see their former mate ever again."

Part of her feared that had happened. That McKell had taken the potion. Part of her hoped that he had. Because three days had already passed, and he would soon weaken. Wherever he was, whoever he was with, he would need strength to stay safe. And she'd rather be without him, knowing he was alive, strong, than delight in the knowledge that he would never be able to drink from anyone else.

"I'm sorry, Noelle, but I'm terrible company right now. Could you maybe go?"

Another pause. A sigh. "Of course, baby doll, but I'll be back."

Footsteps sounded, followed by the slide of her front door. All the sobbing had worn her out, and Ava drifted into a fitful sleep, letting the darkness wrap around her and offer what little comfort it could. Without McKell by her side, she tossed and turned, unable to truly rest despite her fatigue. A few hours passed, and she dazedly thought she should be hungry, but no. Her stomach hated the idea of food.

Hellina barked from the living room, growled, then whimpered happily. Ava didn't rouse from the bed.

"Ava!"

She must be daydreaming, depression and heart-ache shooting her straight into a land of insanity. What did she care, though? She liked this daydream. That had been McKell's voice, as hard and uncompromising as she remembered and loved.

"Ava! Where are you?"

Would her mind actually supply her with an image of him? "McKell," she called weakly. "I'm here."

"Ava!"

Boots thudded against her floor, and then her vampire was stalking into her bedroom. He flipped on the light, spied her on the bed, and his expression darkened with concern. "What's wrong with you?"

This couldn't be a daydream, she thought then, common sense finally sparking to life. He was panting, pale, unsure, and she could smell the unique scent of him. He looked just as he had the first night she'd met him. Shirtless, that necklace of bone hanging from his neck.

"Are you real?" she asked hesitantly, too afraid to hope.

"Yes. I met my father." The words poured from him in a frantic rush as he moved to the bed and crawled on top of her, as if he couldn't wait a second more to touch her. "My real father. He removed the Schön from this world, so you're safe for the moment, and then asked me to stay with him. I didn't want to, but I agreed. For you. For your life. You were going to be infected. Did you know that?"

He was truly here, she realized. He was real. He

was alive. His weight pinned her, his heat enveloped her, and his minty breath caressed her.

Oh, God.

"McKell!" She threw her arms around his neck, and held on tight. His heartbeat hammered in time with hers. "I missed you so much. I worried. I—I—" She was sobbing again, but this time with were tears of joy.

Gently he brushed those tears away. "I saw the past, the future. Reversed and forwarded. And the outcome was always the same, until my father intervened. But he could only endure my company for two weeks before my whining about being away from you irritated him beyond his never-before-encountered tolerance level. His phrasing, not mine."

Some of his words finally penetrated her happy fog. "Your father is alive? And you've been gone two weeks, according to your timetable, but three days according to mine?"

"Yes."

Confusing, she thought, but what did time matter? He was here! "I'm just so glad you're home. I love you. I love you so much."

He squeezed her so tightly she lost her breath. "I love you, too. So, so much, that I'm dead without you." He pulled back to press little kisses all over her face, even as he kicked the covers away from her. "I'm going to have you now."

"Yes."

"Good girl, agreeing quickly." He licked her neck.

"Did I ever tell you that with you, there is no deal breaker?"

She tugged at the waist of his pants. "You mean it?"

"I mean it. Now let me prove it."

Without another word, McKell lifted Ava's shirt over her head and tossed the material aside. Her amber curls tumbled down her shoulders and arms. Leaning in, he inhaled deeply. Oh, that butterscotch. He would never get enough.

When she cupped her breasts, lifting them for his waiting mouth, his thoughts realigned. Oh, those breasts. He would never get enough. He tongued her nipples through her bra.

Those nipples beaded for him, which lit a fire in his blood. He almost laughed. When he was around Ava, there was always a fire in his blood. But in his exuberance, his fangs ripped through the fabric and scraped her skin. Not enough to break it, but just enough to cause her to shiver into goosebumps.

Her hands tangled in his hair, nails scouring, and she scooted her hips toward him. The core of her brushed his erection, and he moaned.

"Ava," he rasped. Just her name, but the plea was evident.

Shaky fingers finally popped off the button on his pants, and then those wonderful fingers were clutching his length, squeezing. So good. So damn good.

"Mine," she said.

"Yes. Yours. Always."

She must have liked his reply because she squeezed even tighter, dragging the first drop of pre-come from his cock. After that, he lost control. Not that he'd ever had control with her.

His hands moved all over her, kneading her breasts, caressing her belly, tearing at her soft shorts and panties. Finally she was naked. All that sun-kissed skin . . . those lithe thighs . . . the sweet, glistening spot between her legs . . . His.

"Spread your legs for me, as wide as they can go," he commanded, even as he stood. She obeyed, and he quickly disposed of his shoes and the rest of his clothing.

She watched unabashedly, pinching her nipples before delving her fingers between those mouthwateringly beautiful folds. Her hips arched up. Her teeth nibbled her lower lip, those amber curls splayed around her delicate face. The most erotic sight he'd ever beheld.

He was pretty sure he'd thought that about her before, about something else she'd done, but each new thing she did revealed a new pleasure to his eyes. Therefore, he was confident he would change his mind again, think the *next* thing she did was the most erotic.

"Want to join me?" she asked huskily. "I need you. Missed you."

He fell back on top of her. She gasped, and he thought he might be crushing her so he flipped them over, allowing her to take the lead. She did. Eagerly.

Up she sat, placing his cock at her sex. Down she slid, unwilling to wait a moment more. He filled her, had to grip her hips to still her before she could begin moving. The exquisite pleasure . . . He was ready to come from that alone. She surrounded him, enclosed him, held him tight.

She flattened her palms on his chest, gaze meeting his. "I love you like this," she whispered. "Mine for the taking."

Oh, the words she used. *Love. Mine.* "More?"

"Always."

Up and down she moved, and he was lost, wild, needy, hers, desperate, arching up, thrusting deep. Her head fell back, hair tickling his thighs. Little hisses were escaping him, his claws so long they were probably cutting her, but he couldn't stop, couldn't even slow.

She didn't seem to mind. No, she seemed to love everything he did. Hips swirling, meeting him, taking him, demanding more. *Have to taste, have to taste.* McKell jerked upright, and as she sank deeper, he claimed her mouth with his own. Their tongues tangled, rolling together, dueling for supremacy.

Soon she was moaning every few seconds, gasping; he swallowed the sounds, loving how they hummed through his body, connecting them on yet another level. He was feverish, and she was both the fuel and the cure.

He reached between them and strummed her clitoris with his thumb. She bucked wildly, then, wrapping her arms around him, nearly choking him, shuddered her release. Screamed.

Her orgasm made way for his, and he jetted inside her.

"Ava!" he shouted, muscles clenching painfully.

When the last drop left him, he fell backward on the bed, those muscles finally loosening their grip. Ava tumbled with him, remaining on top of him, utterly relaxed and, he liked to think, completely sated. He petted her hair.

"You didn't drink from me," she said with a pout.

"I'm saving that for round two."

McKell did bite her during round two. And round three. But their connection wouldn't be complete until *she* bit him. Ava knew that.

She lay utterly exhausted on the mattress, her man perched above her, staring down at her. They'd been too busy relearning each other's bodies to talk, but now that she'd been reintroduced to every inch of him, it was time.

"Those three days without you were miserable, you know," she said softly. "I want you now, later, for more days and years than a human life can give me."

"Oh, sweetheart. There's no happier man than me in this world or any other. Believe me." Love shone in his eyes. So much love. And in that moment she knew beyond any doubt. He would never leave her, no matter how cranky she was. He would always want to be with her. Human, vampire, she was his.

A girl couldn't ask for more than that.

"But I'm not going to turn you yet," he said firmly. "Not until you're ready."

Was it any wonder she loved him? "Thank you. And I will be. Ready, I mean. Soon. First, I need to work some things out with my job."

"Good. Just as long as you never realize you're far too good for me, as a human or a vampire, I'll be happy."

"You keep saying things like that, and I'll quickly become your slave."

His lip quirked at the corners. "Impossible. There can only be one slave in a relationship, and I'm already *yours*."

"There you go again." Grinning, she caressed the curve of his cheek. "I won't wait too long to vamp it up, I swear. Believe me, I'm not going to become an old hag while you walk around so gorgeous."

Suddenly serious, he rubbed two fingers over his chin. "So you think I'm gorgeous, huh?"

She playfully punched his shoulder. "Just hush that beautiful mouth. You know I do. I've been hot for you from the first moment I saw you."

"Prove it."

"If only I had the energy, you lech."

"A vampire would have the energy," he teased. She'd never seen him in so playful a mood, and she loved it.

That was why she spent the next half hour proving exactly what a human could do. And then, after round four, she was *really* exhausted.

Now, back in their previous position, a sigh slipped from her. "So what do we do now?"

"Round five?" He sounded as exhausted as she felt.

"You wish."

He thought for a moment. "Now we love each other, prepare AIR for the return of their greatest enemy, and then love each other some more."

"I like that plan."

"I hoped you would, sweetheart. If you hadn't, I would have had to switch to Plan B."

"And what was that?"

"Tying you up with my whip, loving you, warning AIR, spanking you, and then loving you again. By the way, where *is* my whip?"

"I think Noelle stole it." She laughed, so happy she could have burst. "Who would have thought I'd end up with such a master strategist?"

"Me. Obviously I'm the smart one of this pair. I fell in love with you, didn't I?"

"Yes, but that's because you're also the pretty one."

"And you *did* want a cute husband. You're so lucky," he told her with a grin.

"I know," she said, sobering. "I really do know."

"Sweetheart," he replied, leaning down to kiss her. "*I'm* the lucky one, and I'll prove it." And just like that, they spiraled straight into round five.